Joker in the Pack

Elise Noble

Published by Undercover Publishing Limited

v8

ISBN: 978-1-910954-53-9

Edited by Nikki Mentges at NAM Editorial

Cover design by Abigail Sins

www.undercover-publishing.com

www.elise-noble.com

the joker in the pack
phrase
A person or factor likely to have an unpredictable effect
on events.

CHAPTER 1

"WOULD YOU HURRY up?"

I gripped the ladder with sweaty hands as Maddie balanced on top. We'd been best friends since primary school, an unbreakable bond that had formed the day Robbie Stevens called me a nasty name and she crawled under the table to tie his shoelaces together in revenge.

"Why are you whispering, Liv? He's not here."

She leaned to the side, and the ladder wobbled. I clung on tighter as my grip on sanity loosened.

"But he'll be back any minute!"

"Almost done. Just pass me the pink, would you?"

I handed over one final tube of glitter and tapped my foot as she carefully sprinkled the contents along the fourth blade of my ex-boyfriend's ceiling fan. His professionally decorated cream-and-grey lounge would look wonderful covered in a hail of rainbow sparkles.

I glanced at my watch—almost seven o'clock. Please, say Edward hadn't left work early today. We should have had time to spare, but we'd got delayed taking down the curtain poles to put the hard-boiled eggs inside. Some of the screws were really sticky. Not only that, mixing his hideously expensive conditioner with hair removal cream and squishing it all back into both the bottle in the shower and the spare in the cupboard had taken longer than anticipated.

But we'd managed in the end, and now I was torn between shrieking with glee or backpedalling and putting everything back how it was.

I wasn't normally vindictive like that, you understand, but buoyed as I was by the glass of wine I'd drunk with lunch and the vivid memory of Edward boinking his personal assistant over his dining room table, it hadn't taken much for Maddie to persuade me. I'd chosen that dining table with him, for goodness' sake. When he'd asked the assistant in John Lewis how sturdy it was, I'd had no idea what he had in mind. How stupid did I feel?

Maddie clambered down the ladder, grinning. "Grab that screwdriver, would you? We don't want to give the game away by leaving evidence behind."

No, we didn't. I stuck it in my pocket and grabbed one end of the ladder, which we carried back to Edward's garage. Inside, I took one last look at his new Mercedes. We'd chosen the colour together, and he'd even ordered the heated seats because I didn't like getting cold. Six weeks he'd owned it, and we'd only taken a handful of trips before that awful day.

"Ready to go?" Maddie asked, hovering by the door.

"Yes. Yes, I am." Out of my old life and into the new.

We giggled like schoolgirls as we ran towards the Tube station, but it wasn't until we were sitting on the train that the guilt really hit. What had we done?

"Do you think the hair remover was a bit much?"

"No, I bloody don't. She was wearing *your* Jimmy Choos when you caught them, remember?"

I did, but I didn't want to.

"And look on the bright side, his little slut might borrow some of it for her own tresses."

There was that, but still... "He's going to know it was me."

Maddie didn't hold back with her filthy laugh. "No, he's going to know it was *me*. When's he coming over to your place to pick up the rest of his stuff?"

"Tomorrow evening." I knew that from the claws that squeezed my guts harder with every passing second. "Perhaps we should have waited."

"Nah. Carpe diem, remember? Seize the day. Do you want me to be there tomorrow?"

"Isn't Tuesday your date night with Dave?"

Maddie and Dave had been seeing each other for two years, and although he'd never surprised her with a trip to Antigua like Edward did for me one day, Dave also didn't cancel date night at the last minute because a "meeting" came up. *Meeting*. I knew better now.

"Yes, but Dave and I go out every week. If you want me there, I'll come."

I'd have loved the moral support, but with Maddie working shifts as a nurse and Dave's overtime as an electrician, I understood how much they valued their evenings out.

"Honestly, I'll be fine. I know Edward hasn't been very nice to me since...since the...*incident*, but I can cope with being in the same room as him for a couple more hours."

Okay, that wasn't entirely true. Last time we'd spoken, I'd gone through an entire box of tissues, a tub of chocolate ice cream, and a bottle of wine afterwards. I couldn't cope with being in the same building as him, let alone the same room. Every time he got within touching distance, I couldn't decide whether to stick pins in him or cry.

"If you're sure..."

"I'm sure." I plastered on a grin I absolutely didn't feel. "Everything'll be fine."

The door rattled in its frame as Edward slammed it behind him.

"Pig!" I shouted.

The nosy old lady upstairs banged on the ceiling as I stumbled over to the freezer for another pint of Ben & Jerry's finest. I carefully placed the tub of Chunky Monkey next to my economy-sized glass of white and alternated spoonfuls with cutting Edward's face out of every photo ever taken of the two of us.

Snip, snip, slurp.

Snip, snip, slurp.

Snip, snip, slurp.

I'd just got through the album of our first year together when Maddie called.

"How did it go?"

"Oh, it was just super. Perfect. Couldn't have been better."

"And how did it really go?"

I threw the scissors down on the coffee table, and lots of little Edward-faces scattered everywhere.

"He insisted on taking the chafing dish. I was the only one who ever used it. He can't even turn it on, for goodness' sake! He's...he's just...an asshole!"

"Well, we already knew that."

"And he took the set of glass bowls we brought back

from Venice. I picked those out, and he knew how much I loved the colours. But he said he paid for them, so he was having them."

"He's just being spiteful because you wouldn't let him have his cake and eat it. It makes me glad I rubbed cut chilli on his toilet paper."

"You did *what*?"

"While you were trying to get the curtain pole down. Habaneros. I bought them specially."

I didn't know whether to laugh or cry, so I ended up snorting instead. Mother would have been furious at how unladylike I'd become. My eyes began watering again, although I wasn't sure whether it was from the grief of finalising my break-up with Edward or the thought of what two-hundred-thousand Scoville units would do to the delicate skin of his backside. Maddie hung on, patient as always, as I blew my nose.

"Will the peppers leave any permanent damage?"

"I don't think so, but I'll be keeping my fingers crossed."

"I don't know whether to kiss you or curse you."

"I'll settle for a hug next time we see each other. You really are better off without him—you know that, right?"

I carefully avoided answering her question. "You're the best friend a girl could have. Did I ever tell you that?"

"Maybe once or twice."

I smiled to myself. Maddie sure was one in a million. "Get back to your date."

Maddie had told me a hundred times that I was better off without Edward, and while my head could accept that, it was taking longer for my heart to comprehend. A month ago, it had been filled with affection for the man I'd hoped to marry, and now there was a yawning hole in my chest. Empty. I was empty.

Four weeks, two days, and three hours had passed since I walked in on Edward doing the dirty on me, and after two weeks of numbness where I'd ignored every call, the wounds were still raw. Little things got to me, like fetching one mug of tea instead of two in the mornings and the absence of his low-fat soya milk in the fridge. My solitary toothbrush in the holder in the bathroom. The excess of space in the hall closet.

Then there were the intangibles. The cold stillness of the flat late in the evening. The times I turned around to pass comment on some triviality, only to remember I was alone. Those things were the worst, but of course, I couldn't escape the practicalities either. I'd never had to worry about budgeting before, and now the bills were mounting up.

Although I'd dropped plenty of hints about us moving in together, Edward had clung on to his bachelor pad. Hardly surprising now I knew what he'd been doing there. But despite that, he'd warmed my bed at least five nights out of every seven.

"I love coming home to your cooking, Olivia," he said to me at least twice a week.

The last meal I'd made for him had been salmon en croûte with a chocolate roulade for dessert, and it had taken me most of the afternoon. All that time I'd spent pandering to Edward's needs and neglecting my own. After the ten o'clock news finished and he'd had a nightcap, he'd always snuggled up to me, whispering sweet words and telling me how much I meant to him.

Lies. All lies.

Looking back, I realised how stupid I'd been. Blinded by love and, if I was honest with myself, a little by money as well. The one area where I couldn't fault Edward was his generosity when it came to my living expenses. While I'd paid the rent, he'd covered the utilities and groceries.

Seven hundred pounds a month wasn't a lot for him, seeing as he earned thousands as an investment banker. He carried that much around in his wallet. When we'd gone out for dinner, he'd favoured lobster and steak with a hundred-pound bottle of wine, whereas my income ran to Marks & Spencer on a good month. And there hadn't been many of those lately.

As a self-employed website designer, I could theoretically increase my hours and make more cash, but the market had become saturated since I first started my little business. Finding new clients wouldn't be easy.

But I had to try. I gazed around my tiny flat, the space I'd once been so proud of. Yes, I needed to work because otherwise, I'd be homeless.

CHAPTER 2

I TOOK ANOTHER sip, okay, gulp of wine as I rued the choices I'd made over the last two years. Of course, dating Edward was my biggest mistake, but that had led to a whole host of smaller problems. I'd become too reliant on him.

"Let's go out for supper with Ferdinand and Petronella," he'd said all too often. Other days, it was a trip to the opera or drinks in Chelsea, and he'd always expected me to be available at the drop of a hat to accompany him.

I'd secretly loved that. I enjoyed going to the opera too. Well, apart from the singing. And sitting still for two hours. Fine, I liked having ice cream in the interval and being seen out with Edward, who nobody could deny was heart-stoppingly handsome.

So, when work contracts came to an end, I hadn't worried about replacing those clients with new ones. Parties with friends had won out, and despite that, I hadn't heard a word from Petronella and co. since three days post-*incident*. I groaned at the mere thought of that encounter.

Edward had still been insisting that his little indiscretion had all been his PA's fault. She'd come on to him, he claimed. She was only supposed to be in his townhouse to work on a profit-and-loss analysis. And

I'd been racked with self-doubt—perhaps he'd strayed because I'd put on a few pounds or hadn't put enough effort into cooking lately? Which was why I'd gone to the gym that Friday afternoon. As if twisting my ankle on the treadmill hadn't been bad enough, I'd been changing in the farthest corner of the locker room when Petronella and an acquaintance walked in. And they were talking about *me*.

"Apparently Olivia finally found out about Edward and Becki," Petronella said.

"I heard. When I spoke to Becki after yoga, she said Olivia looked totally shocked."

"Really? I'm only surprised it took so long. After all, she didn't notice when he was messing around with the waitress from Norton's every Thursday night."

What? Edward had told me Thursdays were team night at work. A bunch of guys getting together to discuss deals and compare their golf handicaps.

"Or his tennis coach. How long did that affair last? Five months? Six?"

"And don't forget that thing Edward had with that Thai masseuse."

"Pai?"

"Yes, her."

"I always thought she was a man."

"Whatever. She's great at working the kinks out of my shoulders."

I sagged back onto a bench as their voices faded away. How could he? I must have been the laughing stock for months. And worse, if the seminar on web coding I'd been due to attend one fateful Tuesday hadn't been cancelled, and if I hadn't decided to surprise Edward with a nice bottle of burgundy and a selection of Marks & Spencer's finest, I'd still be in the dark.

Only one of our joint friends had phoned me since the split. Beth, my sometimes doubles partner at badminton, a petite brunette married to the CEO of a bathroom design firm. But once I'd finished optimising her lifestyle website for search engines, she'd stopped returning my calls, and when I bumped into her outside the wholefood store a week later, she'd studiously looked the other way.

After that, I'd avoided the gym and the wholefood store—in fact, going out at all. Waitrose delivered the essentials, and apart from my foray back into Edward's apartment with Maddie, I hadn't left the house.

But darn it! That meant Edward had won, and the very thought made me sick.

I couldn't even cook properly. Normally, I loved baking, and barely a day passed without me turning the oven on and making a cake or a quiche or a batch of cookies. But I'd spent the last month living on junk food.

Well, no more. Tomorrow, I'd begin getting my life back. I'd make soup for lunch, advertise for new clients, and go out in the evening.

Tomorrow, Olivia mark two would be born.

"Are you sure this is a good idea?" Maddie asked the following afternoon.

I'd put my phone on speaker while I got ready, and I paused, mascara wand in mid-air.

"I can't let Edward overshadow the rest of my life."

"But if you wait until the weekend, I can come with you."

Four days? No, I had to get this over with.

"Maybe we can do something on Saturday evening too, but I need to go out tonight."

I poked myself in the eye, dammit, and it started watering. Not tears. No, not at all.

"Well, okay." Maddie sounded doubtful. "As long as you're sure."

"I'll be fine."

Fine. Fine in the same way as I told Edward I was fine when he cancelled our holiday to Switzerland because of a client meeting. Fine in the same way as I told my mother I was fine when she insisted I forgo Maddie's thirteenth birthday party to attend a ballet lesson because all little girls should learn grace and poise. If I recalled correctly, I'd tripped over my own feet that day and spent the evening getting six stitches in my eyebrow. You could still see the scar in the right light.

I pushed thoughts of them out of my mind as I curled my hair. If I had the money, I'd get it highlighted again. The colour had darkened over the years, more of an ash blonde now than the platinum I'd been born with. At least my aquamarine shift dress matched my eyes perfectly.

By the time I slipped my feet into a pair of heels and headed for the door, my toes were feeling decidedly chilly. But I pushed on because *Edward would not win*.

I didn't feel brave enough to venture far, but I'd been to the Wild Orchid in Clerkenwell a few times with Edward and our friends, and I wouldn't look completely out of place on my own. Even better, I could walk there and save a cab fare.

Music played softly in the background as I shuffled in, and a group of men glanced up. One smiled. I smiled back, but inwardly I was cheering. Maybe I still had it after all? Then a skinny brunette pushed past me and kissed him on both cheeks. Darn it.

I slunk off to the bar and perched on a stool next to a man in a suit. Not a particularly well-fitting one, either.

"Can I buy you a drink?" he asked.

"A glass of white wine, please."

At least he was polite. Or so I thought until he tried to put his hand up my skirt. Who did he think he was? A presidential candidate? I shoved him away and inched closer to the middle-aged lady on the other side of me as he staggered off, muttering about "frigid sluts." Didn't he realise that was an oxymoron?

"Bad luck, honey," the lady said. "That one was a politician. Lord something or other. Loaded."

Really? For a second I wondered if I'd— *No, Olivia!* Having money didn't give him the right to do that.

"I wasn't interested."

"Waiting for your young man, are you?"

On second glance, the lady might have been slightly past middle age. Her face was wrinkle free, but there was a tautness that spoke of the surgeon's knife. Even her hands were smooth as she clutched her dirty martini like a lifeline. Judging by her lack of focus, it wasn't her first drink of the evening.

"No, I'm not meeting anyone in particular."

Her gaze dropped to my lap, where my skirt had been hiked upwards by Lord Pervert, and when she met my eyes again, her disgusted look said it all.

"Oh, one of those, are you? You won't find much business here."

What? Eww!

"No, I'm not a prostitute! If you must know, I just split up with my boyfriend." I tugged my skirt down and wished I'd worn something longer. Like a nun's habit or a burka.

"What was it? An affair? Or are you just hoping to trade him in for a better model?"

"That's not really any of your business."

She nodded, and I thought she tried for a sympathetic smile, but nothing much moved. "Affair, then."

Was it really that obvious? My sigh confirmed her suspicions.

"You know, sometimes it's better to forgive a few little transgressions when they're holding the credit cards."

Maybe she wasn't so different from me. After all, I'd considered doing just that, hadn't I?

But I couldn't. My mother may have tried to stop me believing in Cinderella, but I still wanted the fairy tale. A man who came home to me, and only me. I didn't want to be the girl waiting in his thousand-thread-count sheets while he was out entertaining his latest plaything.

No, I'd rather be single, no matter how much I might have been hurting.

"So, how did it go?"

Maddie phoned at eight in the morning, and my head still hurt from the four martinis Botox-lady had poured into me last night.

"Not so well. I got groped, and then Jackie Collins's long-lost sister corrupted me."

After Maddie finished laughing, she had a hiccupping fit.

"It's not funny. All I wanted was a quiet night out, and the only man I managed to attract was more like an octopus."

"Oh, it is a little bit funny. Look on the plus side—if your mother were alive, she'd march you right back to the bar and insist you get his phone number."

Maddie meant it as a joke, but the shame of it was she was exactly right. Before my mother's passing, she'd attempted to impart many pearls of wisdom, and one of her favourites related to my choice of future husband.

"Olivia," she'd said. "You need to put a price on your heart, and don't you dare sell yourself cheap. Set your sights high. Find a doctor, a lawyer, or a banker—preferably one with a family seat and a title."

Well, last night's pervert had the title, while Edward had certainly fulfilled her career specification, and now look at me. At the moment, my net worth was more akin to a bottle of Lambrini and a box of Milk Tray than the champagne and caviar she'd dreamed of. My mother would turn in her grave if she saw the state of me, sprawled on the sofa wearing week-old pyjamas and the pair of Bugs Bunny slippers Maddie gave me last Christmas.

"Mother only wanted the best for me."

"She read you DeBrett's etiquette guide at bedtime,

Liv. Most little girls got Rapunzel or Cinderella."

"I'll concede she wasn't very fond of Cinderella."

Okay, so she'd hated Cinderella and her lack of effort to make a better life for herself. I'd once asked for a pair of glass slippers, but Mother had only scoffed.

"Fancy leaving something like that to fate," she'd said. "If you want to find your Prince Charming, you'll need to go out and hunt for him."

"Where?" At fourteen years old, I couldn't exactly go far.

"You can start by joining the debating society as I suggested, young lady. Every girl should strive to raise her profile."

The debating society. One hour after school every Wednesday. Better than walking around with a book on my head or practising which cutlery to use, which was what Mother would have made me do otherwise. I'd signed up and spent the whole year sitting at the back and saying as little as possible. Maddie had joined too, for moral support, although she'd been far more vocal than me.

Now was no different.

"Liv, I know she was your mum, but she made you live the life she wanted rather than the one you wanted. I mean, she'd have loved Edward, wouldn't she?"

"Yes, but I did too, once."

"Don't defend what he did. It was inexcusable."

"I know... It's just I hate being alone."

"You're not alone. We'll go out at the weekend, just you and me, and we'll have some proper fun. You'll see."

"Promise you won't get arrested again."

"That was all a big misunderstanding."

"Just a quiet dinner."

"I'll organise something fabulous. You won't regret it. Promise."

A long, drawn-out groan escaped the instant Maddie hung up the phone. Perhaps I could feign illness at the weekend? After all, the symptoms of flu and a hangover weren't totally dissimilar. Or maybe Maddie would take pity on me and bring pizza and a DVD instead. With three days to go until the weekend, I tried to block the idea of partying out of my mind. Sleep was calling.

CHAPTER 3

BY SATURDAY, ALL I wanted to do was crawl under my duvet and turn into the McDonald's breakfast I'd just eaten. Normally, I didn't touch fried food, but today I felt I deserved bonus points just for leaving the house.

The rest of the week hadn't gone well. I'd finished one project, but I hadn't picked up any new jobs to fill the gap in my finances despite hustling online. And I'd barely slept last night because one of my nine remaining clients was an inconsiderate pig. Derek Braithwaite, CEO of DB's Sportswear, figured that in the digital age I should work twenty-four hours a day, so he'd sent over a change request at eleven in the evening. Most likely while he was in the pub, but he'd still expected me to implement it by opening hours the next morning, weekend or not.

And I couldn't afford to lose him, no matter how unpalatable sucking up to him was.

I'd spent Thursday cancelling all the non-essentials —my health club membership, Netflix, those little organic snacks I got delivered every week. Even my fortnightly manicure. Mother had always drummed the importance of having perfect nails into me, but the stress had made me start biting them again.

But the biggest problem was my rent. In London,

where a converted broom closet once sold for six figures, even the smallest flat cost four figures a month. And I was tied into my contract for the best part of a year.

Yesterday, I'd raked through my wardrobe and piled anything I could sell onto the couch. The designer dresses Edward bought me to wear to his corporate events could go to a consignment store, but the rest? I'd opened an eBay account and used the app on my phone to list fifty-seven lots.

But selling my excess clothes was a one-off. Once they were gone, they were gone. I still needed to conjure up another two hundred pounds a month from somewhere.

Looking at my beautiful clothes and knowing they wouldn't be there much longer made my chest tighten, and that was followed by the telltale prickle of tears I'd experienced all too often lately. And that feeling was made even worse when I poured myself a glass of wine and decided to stalk Edward on Facebook.

"You did what?" Maddie asked an hour later after I'd sobbed down the phone at her.

"I know, I know. It was stupid."

"No, Liv. Stupid was when Jenny Henderson called you fat in year nine, and we borrowed that frog from the biology lab to put in her locker."

"We?"

"I only did it to help you out. How was I supposed to know the thing would escape from my bag in English and Miss Foster had a phobia of amphibians?"

"But he's changed his status. He's in a relationship with Becki Harris. A relationship! I thought it was a new thing, but from her photos, they've been shagging for over a year."

"Think positive. He cheated on *her* with the tennis bitch and the masseuse too."

Becki's profile showed a fondness for micro skirts, her eyebrows were habitually drawn on with a felt-tip, and if she didn't have breast implants, someone had certainly got creative with Photoshop. And I already knew she had cellulite from the way Edward's crystal chandelier had glinted off her backside when she legged it out of his dining room.

"I just can't understand what he saw in her. He always said he preferred the natural look."

"He lied about everything else. Why not that?"

Becki listed her occupations as executive assistant and model/actress, but a quick internet search showed her recent projects and they certainly didn't involve Shakespeare.

"But seriously, Maddie—she starred in a film called *Wenches vs. Werewolves*."

"I don't think Edward and his friends hire their secretaries for their brains."

Speaking of brains, I'd clearly misplaced mine. How could I have been so stupid?

Never again.

Never again would I trust a man.

The pain they brought simply wasn't worth it.

When I didn't answer Maddie's calls on Saturday afternoon, she used her key and found me slumped on the sofa, surrounded by empty wine bottles and the remains of a family-sized tin of Quality Street.

"Come on—we're going out."

"I haven't got any money."

"My treat."

"I have to work."

She leaned forward and sniffed my breath. "When you've been drinking?"

The last time I'd tried that, I'd got Longacres Garden Centre mixed up with Hair by Camilla and accidentally uploaded a banner reminding Camilla's clients it was time to get their bushes trimmed. That little mistake had taken a lot of apologising.

"Maybe not."

Maddie pulled me to my feet and shoved me in the direction of the shower. "Chop-chop. I'm not taking no for an answer."

She wouldn't give up; I knew that. Her tenacity in the face of my mother's disapproval had kept her by my side since childhood.

While my mother had been a firm advocate of "keeping up with the Joneses," she'd made an exception for Madonna Jones and her family. Maddie had worn hand-me-down clothes and lived in a council house, and my mother had never managed to see past that to the person underneath.

"Who on earth calls a child Madonna?" she'd asked one day. "It's bordering on child abuse."

I kept my mouth shut because my opinion wouldn't have mattered, anyway. But no matter what my mother thought, Maddie and I had been inseparable.

When my father went through his midlife crisis, announced he was marrying a woman ten years his junior, and moved to Spain, it was Maddie who'd brought around the darts for us both to throw at the wedding photo he'd thoughtfully sent me.

After that, my mother had suffered her own breakdown, and we moved from our nice four-bedroom detached in Notting Hill to a pokey terraced shoebox. The doctors said Mother made a full recovery, but I knew better. Appearances meant everything to her, and giving up her life of luxury meant taking a huge hit to her social standing. I'd often wondered whether that was why she'd piled so much pressure onto me.

I'd been shunned by the popular set too, and I spent most of my GCSE year cowering behind the bike sheds to avoid their name-calling. Of course, then I'd failed my exams and hidden at Maddie's for two days straight before I plucked up the courage to go home.

"You're grounded, madam. Do you hear me?" Mother screeched when she found the results slip in my bag. "How could you do this to me?"

To her. Always to her. My feelings didn't matter, and I couldn't do anything right.

When I turned eighteen, Maddie was the one by my side when Mother lost her battle against lung cancer, blaming my father's smoking habit to the end. And even as she slipped away, her remaining hair had been neatly curled, her lipstick perfect.

Now Maddie was here for me again. The least I could do was go out with her for the evening, and now she wandered into the bedroom while I finished getting dressed, a glass of wine in her right hand and a digestive biscuit in her left.

"You can't go out wearing that. You look as if you're in mourning."

I glanced down at my black pencil skirt and matching blouse. "I am. My relationship died."

"Stop thinking like that. I can tell I still have work to do."

She rummaged through my closet, coming up with something sparkly that had somehow missed the eBay pile.

"Here, put this on."

I unfolded the garment. Did I even buy that? "I'll need some trousers to go with it."

"Don't you bloody dare!"

I put the offending item on, and it didn't even come to mid-thigh.

"I can't go out like this. It's positively indecent."

"Nonsense. You can and you are."

The look of determination in her eyes said I wasn't going to win this one.

"Fine. Just don't make me pause on any street corners, because I'll probably get arrested."

She rolled her eyes. "Stop being so melodramatic."

"You're not the one who's going to be flashing her underwear if there's even the slightest breeze. Where are we going, anyway?"

"Oh, just a club."

"A club? I thought we said dinner. I'm not sure I'm up to visiting somewhere rowdy."

"Well, it's more of a cabaret. And there's a buffet."

"Why don't we get a takeaway instead?"

"Come on, where's your sense of adventure?"

Adventure? Adventure? DeBrett's girls didn't need a sense of adventure. I had a sense of class, and I had a sense of decorum. That was all I needed.

Right?

Two hours later, I blinked under overly bright lights as I slid around on a black plastic chair. It had got a little slippery when I missed the stripper's body with the baby oil and squirted it all over myself instead. No way would this dress be going on eBay. Once I'd peeled it off, it'd be heading straight for the bin.

With a dozen disturbingly named cocktails in me, I chanted along with the rest of the hen-night crowd in the audience.

"Strip! Strip! Strip!"

The muscle-bound hunk gyrating in front of me duly obliged and whipped off his leopard-print thong. He flashed the crowd then turned back to me, his sausage and meatballs swinging hypnotically just inches from my face. I couldn't tear my gaze away.

This was great! Why hadn't I thought of coming to a cabaret before?

The music was funky. The flashy lights were so pretty. And the men were really, really shiny. This was my new favourite thing!

As the music wound down, my new friend, Taurus, offered me his arm to help me back to my best friend in the whole wide world. I could see her waving at me from the front row. Both of her.

I waved back.

"Hiiiiiii, uh..."

What was her name again?

M-something? Mary? I was just puzzling over that when my feet shot out from under me. The crowd gasped as I grabbed at Taurus, but he was covered in so much oil he slid right out of my grasp.

What's-her-name disappeared from view in slow motion, replaced by hot-pink spotlights and a wide-eyed hunk staring down at me. The last things I saw before it all went black were his muscled thighs overhead, meat and two veg looking so deliciously edible between them.

Oops.

CHAPTER 4

THE SOUND OF beeping woke me up. Strange. Usually, I set my phone to play Pharrell's "Happy" at seven every morning in a vain attempt to convince myself that I actually was.

It failed every time.

I reached out to shut off the noise, but something tugged at the back of my hand. Ouch! That stung.

"Easy, easy."

Why was Maddie in my bedroom? My eyelids felt heavy, but I forced them open. Why was everything white? My best friend swam into view, concern etched over her face.

"What's wrong?" It came out as, "Wash ron?"

"You had a teeny, tiny accident. You're in hospital."

Well, that would explain the bland colour scheme. "Wa kinda assident?"

"You slipped over and knocked yourself out for a little while."

Really? How on earth had I managed that? I'd been intending to do some tidying, but...

"How'd it happen?"

"Uh, we were in a club, and you slipped in a pool of, uh..." Her voice dropped a few decibels. "...baby oil."

My voice, on the other hand, got louder as it recovered. "Baby oil? I don't even have any baby oil."

"Well, it was kind of provided at the club."

"What kind of club provides baby oil?"

My memory came back in fits and starts. The lights, the music, the chanting, the steroid-riddled guy standing naked in front of me.

"You took me to a strip club!" I screeched.

"Shh, keep your voice down. There are other patients around."

Much as it pained me, she was right about that. "Fine. I certainly don't want anyone else finding out."

Her cheeks coloured as she shuffled backwards. "It might be a bit late for that."

"What are you talking about?"

"Er... Perhaps you should get some rest."

"Maddie, what are you talking about?"

"Okay, okay. Do you remember Mandy Clark? We went to school with her."

"That perky blonde whose life's ambition was to bag herself a Premier League footballer?"

She'd even learned what the offside rule was. We'd had a bust-up in year six when she'd said my accent was so posh it was stupid and I'd grabbed her Barbie doll and put its arm in the electric pencil sharpener, and she'd never forgiven me.

"Well, she's getting married. To a footie player, surprise, surprise. But she's had to slum it. He's only in League Two."

"Terrific. And?"

"Well, she might have been at the cabaret last night. And she might have brought her camera. And one or two of those pictures may have found their way onto Facebook."

Oh, bloody hell. "Get her to take them down.

Please!"

"I tried, but it was too late. They'd already got over seven hundred likes and made it onto Twitter."

I closed my eyes. This couldn't be happening.

"I didn't know Mandy even had seven hundred friends."

"She doesn't. She tagged you, so some of them are yours. Then the photos went a little bit viral. People have been commenting from as far away as Ecuador. The one where you were stroking the dude's wotsit was particularly popular."

Bang went my plan of running away to South America. All that training, all that effort my mother had put in to turn me into a lady, and I'd just ruined it. I couldn't even behave properly at a strip club.

Still, on the bright side, the embarrassment I'd felt about Edward's affair paled into insignificance beside this latest debacle.

I was never going to another club. Never.

On second thoughts, I wouldn't even be able to set foot outside my front door again. I'd lock myself in my flat forever. Waitrose delivered, so I'd be fine. In sixty years, someone would find my corpse surrounded by empty chocolate boxes, mummified after it had lain undiscovered for six months.

My obituary would be short.

Olivia Porter, daughter of the late Frank and Victoria. Known for her lewd behaviour and her complete inability to attract a man. Survived by her seventeen cats.

I dropped my voice to a whisper. "Maddie, I'm going to

kill you. You know that, right?"

"Gosh, would you look at the time? My shift's just about to start. Gotta run."

Coward.

An hour later, a doctor examined me, poking and prodding and shining a torch in my eyes.

"You have a slight concussion, and we need to keep you in overnight for observation. If nothing worsens, you can go home tomorrow."

Was I supposed to be grateful for that? I guess so, but I didn't fancy being alone in my flat, either. What was there for me? An underwhelming amount of work, a half-empty wardrobe, and a gaping hole in my life. So much to look forward to.

"Leaving so soon? Are you sure that's safe?"

He shrugged one shoulder. "We need the bed for patients who don't inflict injuries on themselves."

His pursed lips told me the doctors hadn't found Maddie's tale of a strip night gone wrong very funny.

The nurses did, though. By the time I was discharged, at least ten of them had asked about it, and they gave me a leaving gift of furry handcuffs and a bottle of baby oil.

I tried to smile, but my sense of humour had all but deserted me. Every day, I became more like my mother. The only positive thing about the constant jibes was that when Maddie waved a white tissue taped to a pencil around the edge of the door in surrender, I was pretty much desensitised to the whole mess.

"Are you still planning to kill me?" she asked.

"No." A sigh escaped. "I can see you were only trying to help, and besides, I'm not sure how I'd go about hiding the body."

Plus, I couldn't drive, and she was my lift home.

When we got back to my flat, she insisted on coming in and making me toast and a cup of tea before she returned to Dave.

"That way I'll know you've eaten something other than junk food. I bought you fresh milk and a few groceries."

At least somebody cared. "Thank you."

"It'll all blow over, you'll see. A celebrity'll fall out of a club or something, and nobody'll be interested in your video anymore."

"I hope you're right. And I really do appreciate the food."

"We'll do a takeaway next week. Deal?"

"Deal."

After Maddie left, I shuffled to bed. My head still hurt, and I craved sleep as though I hadn't spent part of this week unconscious.

Two days passed before I felt well enough to turn on the computer, and even then, a dull ache pulsed behind my eyeballs. The pain only got worse when I read my emails.

Olivia,

Several of my clients have shown me the video of your shenanigans on Facebook, and I can't express how disappointed I am at your lack of professionalism. First the "bushes" faux pas and now this. Regrettably, I'll be taking my business elsewhere.

Camilla

And it got worse as I scrolled down.

Olivia,
  I need you to discount all tracksuit prices by ten percent immediately.
  Derek

Then when I didn't reply straight away...

Olivia,
  I see you haven't made the changes. Is there a problem?
  Derek

Twelve hours later...

Olivia,
  Are you ignoring me?
  Derek

And the final message, timed at eight o'clock this morning.

Olivia,
  As you're non-responsive, I've found another web designer. He's cheaper too. Send your final invoice to my secretary when you eventually get around to reading your emails.
  Derek

That...that...asshole! Without their recurring fees, my situation had become even more dire. I opened up my spreadsheet and recalculated everything. If I ate nothing but oatmeal and didn't use the heating, ever, plus picked up one more decent client, I could just about afford to live. As long as nothing else went wrong, that was.

But what else could go wrong? My life disappeared down the toilet when Edward did the dirty on me. Taurus had only pressed the flush.

For so many years, I'd worn a mask, working to give the impression that I was of the same social standing as Edward and my friends, but with one drunken mistake, that illusion had been shattered. I'd been revealed for who I truly was. Common little Olivia Porter.

I'd been outed as an impostor.

How could things possibly get any worse?

CHAPTER 5

A MONTH LATER, I stood in the kitchen, surveying the horrific mess that only a burst pipe could cause. My tears had only added to the puddles shimmering under the single light bulb, now bare because I'd sold the shade.

I'd been out job-hunting when it happened. A day of futile sales pitches to small businesses in the local area had turned into a nightmare when I'd walked in to find Niagara Falls coming through a gaping hole in the ceiling and a furious downstairs neighbour hammering on my door.

How the heck did I turn off the water? Shouldn't there be a master tap somewhere? I panicked and called Maddie, who put me on to Dave, who told me about the stopcock in my airing cupboard. The neighbour was still yelling as I paddled through and finally stopped the torrent.

Then the neighbour called the landlord, and he came around and shouted at me too.

"Look what you've done."

I squelched across the carpet behind him as he examined the damage, cringing when I realised I'd left my underwear out on the bedroom windowsill to dry.

"But how did it happen?" I asked. "How can a pipe just burst like that?"

The plumber he'd brought with him tutted. "It probably froze overnight. It's like the bloody Arctic in here. Is the heating broken?"

The landlord obviously knew I hadn't reported any faulty radiators, and he turned to glare at me.

"I, uh, turned it off. I can't afford the utility bills right now."

"So you decided to cause thousands of pounds worth of damage to my property instead?"

"It was barely freezing."

"One degree below would have been enough. Bloody women!"

Thousands of pounds? His words echoed in my head, and I felt physically sick as I sagged against the counter.

"I can't afford to pay for all the repairs at the moment. Maybe I could pay a bit back each month? As long as I get some more work, that is."

"I've got insurance to cover the building damage. Some of us aren't entirely stupid. Your security deposit will pay the excess, but I'm not taking any chances on something like this happening again. I want you out by the end of the month."

"But it's almost Christmas. How am I supposed to find a new place over the holidays? Nobody'll want to move then."

"Not my problem," the landlord said over his shoulder as he stomped out.

My heart hammered as I stared after him. Obviously, the place was a mess, but surely he had to understand it was an accident? In the three years I'd lived in the flat, I'd always paid the rent on time and never asked him to fix anything, not even when a pigeon flew into the lounge window and broke it.

Worry settled in my stomach like one of the bad Chinese takeaways I used to eat with Maddie before I met Edward. Homeless as well as penniless? Just when I thought things couldn't get any worse, fate drop-kicked me into a lower level of hell. Now I needed to add finding a new place to live to my list of seemingly impossible tasks.

I looked around the little flat I'd loved so much. From agonising over the colour schemes to selecting just the right vase for the sideboard, I'd put my heart and soul into it. Mother always said a tidy home meant a tidy mind, and mine both lay in tatters. Every time someone bid for one of my items on eBay, it felt as if my soul were under the hammer as well.

"But I still don't understand why you turned the heating off," Maddie said as she helped me to sponge the living room carpet dry.

Murky splodges covered every inch of the once-pristine cream pile.

"You know how Edward liked the place tropical? Well, the electric bill came last week, and it ran to four figures."

"Over a grand?"

I nodded. "Almost two. So I panicked and turned everything off."

"You should have said something, you daft mare. I've got a few hundred quid saved up."

Tired of life, I went to sit down, then remembered I'd sold my table and chairs. "I can't take your money, not with it coming up to Christmas."

"You can't freeze, either. What are you doing at night?"

"Wearing lots of layers, and I've got two duvets on the bed."

At least I still had a bed. Apart from that and my desk and chair, the flat lay empty. The last thing to go had been the three-piece suite. My beautiful maroon leather sofa with its two matching armchairs. The guy who bought it had the cheek to try and haggle me down further when he'd come to pick it up. I'd stood my ground, but the whole experience left me drained.

"Look at it this way," Maddie said. "At least now you can leave this place and find somewhere cheaper."

"I won't have a security deposit."

"We'll sort something out. I've got tomorrow off, so let's have a look at some adverts this evening. We'll find you a new flat in no time."

"You really think so?"

"Of course. Things'll be fine, you'll see."

Based on my newly revised budget, we found four places with the potential to be suitable. One flat, a tiny house, and two house shares. The house especially surprised me because I hadn't thought we'd find anything that nice with my meagre finances.

As I went to sleep that night, I felt the faintest glimmer of optimism for the first time in weeks. Perhaps Maddie was right and every black cloud had a silver lining after all?

First thing in the morning, Maddie showed up with cappuccino and croissants, and we carried them with us on the bus as we travelled to viewing number one.

For the past few years, I'd lived in Clerkenwell, and

before that, Notting Hill, prioritising a good area over size when it came to choosing my abode. Now I couldn't afford either.

The closer the bus chugged to our destination, the more boarded-up properties I saw. Three in a row on one street alone.

"I'm not sure about this," I said to Maddie.

"The listing said this area was up and coming."

"On what? The crime-rate tables?"

Her grimace said it all.

"Be careful, ladies," the bus driver said as we went to get out. "You don't want to be out after dark around here."

I clutched my handbag across the front of my body as we hurried along the road. Garden landscaping consisted of barbed wire and broken household appliances, with graffiti adding the odd splash of colour. Maddie stopped in front of me as I stepped over a pile of doggy poop, and I walked into her back.

"This is it," she said. "Number forty-three."

"It's a chicken restaurant," I hissed. Neon-yellow letters spelled out "Clive's Chicken Coop," and the red eye of an orange rooster blinked demonically as I tried to decide whether to laugh or cry.

Maddie's gaze went higher. "I think the flat's on the first floor."

Sure enough, a flicker of light shone through one of the dingy windows above the garish facade.

"How do we get in?"

"Those stairs at the side?"

"Do you think they're safe to stand on?"

The rusted metal creaked ominously as I put weight onto the first rung, and visions of the whole lot giving way and landing on top of me made me pause.

"Let's go one at a time, shall we?"

At the top, Maddie knocked on the door and wrinkled her nose at the dirt on her knuckles. It swung open to reveal a man in a grease-stained "Chicken Coop" apron, and from the way his belly strained at the ties, he was a big fan of his own products.

"You ladies here to look at the flat?"

Why on earth would we be there otherwise? It wasn't a neighbourhood one visited by choice.

Maddie answered for me. "Yes, that's us."

"Come in, come in." He threw the door open. "It could do with a bit of a clean."

No, it could have done with being napalmed. Black mould grew up the walls, and the grimy carpet was a jigsaw of dark footprints. A film of dust coated the mismatched furniture, and the couch only had one cushion, not that I'd have wanted to sit on it, anyway.

"Did you just see something move over there?" Maddie whispered.

"Where?"

"Under the pile of fast-food containers in the corner."

Even if I scrubbed for a month, I doubted I'd make a dent in the filth, and that wasn't the worst part. I'd held my breath in horror as we walked in, but when it came to the point where I had to inhale or faint, I almost choked. The stench of chicken fried in rancid fat permeated everything.

"It'll be snapped up in no time," the guy told us. "Last time it went on the market, someone rented it the same day."

Really? Did that person have an olfactory problem?

Chicken Man grinned, revealing a row of brown teeth. "Just for you, I'll throw in a ten percent discount downstairs."

Vomit rose in my throat as I ran from the room and down the dodgy stairs. Air. I needed air. Maddie followed more sedately and met me on the pavement.

"I told him you ate some bad sushi last night. That was a no, I take it?"

"More than a no. An *absolutely no way*. How could you stay in there a second longer?"

"Oh, I've smelled far worse things than that at the hospital. One time this guy with a bowel problem came in, and—"

I held up a hand. "Please. Just don't. Can we get out of here?"

"It's like that Arnie movie—*The Running Man*. You've seen that, right? Where people have to escape from the game zone without dying."

"You're not helping."

"Sorry. Let's find a bus. And look on the bright side —the next place can't be any worse."

CHAPTER 6

A QUICK BUS ride took us to our second destination—one of the house shares. "Modern accommodation within easy walking distance of public transport and local shops," according to the blurb. Thank goodness there were no fast-food outlets within sniffing distance, and the outside of the property looked just as it did in the advert, if not a little close to a road junction.

At Maddie's knock, a guy with dreadlocks opened the door and greeted us with a toothy grin. Light glinted off his gold incisor.

"You here about the room?"

"Yes, we are," I said.

He swung the door open wider to allow us in. "I'll show you around. Do you like music?"

"I enjoy Beethoven. And nothing beats Mozart being played by a full orchestra."

His eyebrow ring tilted to the side as he frowned. "How about rock?"

We stopped short in the lounge. Or what had once been a lounge, but now seemed to be...a recording studio?

"Um, I've never been a big fan of rock, no."

Not that I'd really listened to that type of music. Mother never allowed it, and Edward had looked at me like I was crazy when I played a Coldplay CD. Rock, especially the heavy stuff? Way, way outside of his comfort zone.

Dreadlock Guy waved at the array of speakers. "Don't worry. We rarely play all night. Usually, we quit at two or three in the morning. The last guy who rented the room reckoned he could barely hear us with his earplugs in."

Maddie caught my eye and gave her head a shake. Yep, I was with her on that one.

"Uh, I've got a problem with my ear canals. I can't wear earplugs."

"Aw, bummer."

"Yes, isn't it? Well, thanks for your time."

I smiled and waved as we backed out, and the guy seemed genuinely disappointed. Hard Rock House was better than Chicken Castle, but only marginally.

"I couldn't cope with that noise," I said to Maddie. "Not when I work from home."

"I was more concerned about the stink of marijuana."

That strange, smoky smell? "I just assumed someone had burned dinner."

Maddie giggled. "You honestly didn't realise?"

"No! I've never touched drugs."

Truly, this was impossible. Two places left to see, and I didn't hold out much hope for either one after the morning.

Third on our list was the house. We stopped off at the agent's on the way there to pick up the key, and a man with coffee stains on his tie put his hand over the phone receiver and handed us a map scrawled on the back of a window cleaner's flyer.

"Would you mind showing yourselves around? I'm

rushed off my feet today. Phone hasn't stopped ringing."

I had my suspicions about that, unless he called all his customers "Mum," but it suited us fine. At least we wouldn't be getting the hard sell from him.

The SatNav app on Maddie's phone led us to a quiet backstreet. Number fifteen turned out to be a narrow terrace with a bright blue front door and polished letterbox.

"This is really nice," I said to Maddie after we'd taken a quick walk around.

"Isn't it? Look, it's even got a built-in microwave."

Although the rooms were smaller than those in my flat, the tiny lounge and fitted kitchen were pristine, and the double bedroom and well-appointed bathroom would suit me perfectly.

"It's exactly what I'm looking for."

The faint smell of fresh paint permeated throughout, and bits of fluff on the carpets suggested they'd only just been laid. The house even came with a tiny outdoor space, complete with wooden decking and a couple of potted plants. I opened the glass doors and stepped outside. Birdsong was audible over the faint hum of traffic, and we'd already checked the place wasn't near any busy roads or railway lines.

So peaceful. I could almost imagine being alone in the world out there.

"Cooee."

A voice came over the fence, but I couldn't see anyone.

"Hello?"

"Over here."

I hopped onto an upturned flower pot and peered

into the next garden. A tiny grey-haired lady looked up at me, adjusting her glasses as I came into view.

"Are you going to be moving in?" she asked.

"I'm thinking about it." Although the answer was almost certainly going to be yes.

"Oh, that'll be nice. The house has been empty for far too long, and I've been lonely. You can come round for tea and a nice chat."

"Really? How long has it been empty?"

"Going on three months now."

Three months? But it was such a sweet little house. Why hadn't it been snapped up? Had I misread the price and missed off a zero? Or was it haunted?

"I don't suppose you know why it's been vacant so long?"

"Of course I do, dearie. I may be almost eighty, but not much gets past me. It's because of the shootings."

The what? I goggled at her. "Shootings?"

As in, plural?

"Yes, dearie, the drive-bys. They happen every so often. This is Acacia Road, and people keep getting it confused with Acacia Avenue." She dropped her voice to a whisper, even though there was no one else about. "Number fifteen Acacia Avenue has gang members living in it, or so I've heard."

"Someone shot at this house?" My voice came out as a squeak.

"Only four times. They did try a fifth, but the police came and there was a standoff. Like an episode of *The Bill*, it was, blue lights and one of those megaphones. But I looked in through the windows last week and the landlord's done an excellent job of patching up the bullet holes. You'd never even know they were there."

No, you wouldn't, would you? How nice of the agent to mention that the house was inadvertently in the middle of a gang war.

"Well, it was lovely to meet you." I glanced at my watch. "Ooh, is that the time? We're late for our next viewing."

I practically ran through the house, collecting Maddie on my way out the front door.

"It's a no."

"What? Why? Did you see the light-up mirror in the bathroom?"

"I don't care if it's a magical mirror that makes me look like a supermodel."

Once I'd explained the story, her mouth dropped open.

"I'm going to castrate that bloody agent. No wonder he didn't want to come to the viewing."

"Please don't. You know I hate the sight of blood, and I can't afford to bail you out."

"He deserves it."

"I'm just glad I found out before I moved in."

Back at the agency, Maddie threw the keys at the man who'd sent us into the danger zone. Hard.

"What the—"

He didn't have time to finish the sentence before she marched out again, and I wasn't about to stay and enlighten him either.

"One place left," Maddie said once we'd made it safely out to the pavement. "Keep your fingers crossed."

Another house share, and although I spotted a few weeds growing through the cracks in the front path, the maisonette itself looked tidy.

"I'm still not sure about living with a stranger," I

muttered to Maddie.

"You never know, you might meet the man of your dreams."

The door swung open as I raised my hand to knock, and when I saw the person behind it, I almost fainted.

Holy cannoli! He could have been Mr. January. No, scratch that. He could have had his own calendar and been all the months.

"Ladies." His wide grin made my underwear melt. "Do you want to come in?"

Maddie's face bore the same glazed expression as it had two years ago when she won a thousand pounds on a lottery scratch card, so I took her hand and pulled her inside after me.

"Sven."

The hunk held out his hand, and mine sizzled in his firm grip. That *zing*—I'd never felt anything like it before.

"I'm Olivia, and this is Maddie."

Who was still gawping, mouth slightly open.

"Which of you is looking for the room?"

Maddie started to raise her hand, but I slapped it down. "Me. I'm looking for the room."

"We could share," Maddie hissed in my ear.

"The room or the man?" I whispered as Sven turned and headed along the hallway. "You've got a boyfriend."

"I know, but... Oh my gosh! Would you look at that?"

Look at it? I couldn't tear my eyes away. Sven's butt cheeks could have cracked walnuts. Edward had gone to the gym regularly, but Sven... Sven should have been a spokesmodel for StairMaster.

"So, Olivia, this is the room that's up for rent."

Up until then, I'd never found a Scandinavian accent sexy, but he could have spoken Klingon and made my heart skip.

"The carpet's new," he continued. "And with the double glazing, you can barely hear the road."

A bed. That was pretty much all I noticed, at least about the room. Believe me, I noticed plenty about the man standing in it. His twinkling blue eyes, his chiselled jaw, the way his blond hair fell over his tanned forehead.

"What do you think?" he asked.

"I'm interested."

"Shall I show you the rest of the place?"

"Yes, please."

In reality, I only wanted to see one other room: his. I know I'd sworn off men, but when I made that decision, I hadn't envisaged Sven and his buns of sculpted marble. Perhaps I'd been a little hasty.

"This is the bathroom. Shared, but I promise not to leave my toenail clippings in the sink."

The sink? Who clipped their toenails in the sink? Maybe it was a Nordic thing? Ah well, at least he bothered with good foot hygiene. I lagged behind again to enjoy the view, smiling as he led us into... What was this? A jungle?

"Uh, you sure have a lot of plants."

"They're for my babies. I like them to feel right at home."

His babies?

Movement caught my eye as a snake slowly descended from the branch next to me, its beady yellow eyes locking on mine as I stood frozen to the spot.

"What the..."

"*Opheodrys aestivus*, the rough green snake. She's called Belinda."

Sven stepped forward and Belinda wound her way up his arm, pausing halfway to poke her tongue out at me. Next to me, Maddie let out a whimper, and I followed her gaze.

"I-i-is that a tarantula?" I asked.

The spider was sitting on the back of an armchair, and as I watched, it lifted one leg as if it were waving hello.

"Yes—Margot's a Mexican red-knee. She's very friendly."

"But aren't tarantulas deadly?"

"A myth. Margot's bite is no worse than a wasp sting. No, it's the black widows you need to watch out for, but I keep those in a tank."

I heard a muffled *thump* as Maddie fell to the floor beside me. She never had been too keen on spiders.

"Maddie, wake up!" I crouched beside her and fanned her face as she blinked a few times.

"What's wrong with her?" Sven asked.

Seriously? How could the man think it was normal to have a venomous menagerie in his lounge?

"Haven't you ever seen *Arachnophobia*?"

Sven's eyes grew moist. "Those poor spiders. Murdered. All of them."

Maddie swayed as I pulled her upright. "Is it gone?"

I glanced to the side where Margot was still advancing along the arm of the chair.

"No, but it will be. Run!"

With Maddie still unsteady on her feet, I half dragged her as we stumbled from the house of horrors into the street. Man of my dreams? Nightmares, more like.

"Tell me I just imagined that," Maddie said.

"If only."

With our last prospect a bust, we trudged back to the bus stop. Maddie had an early shift the next day, and if her yawn was anything to go by, house-hunting had left her as exhausted as me.

"This isn't as straightforward as I thought," Maddie confessed.

"Next time, we need to ask better questions. Like 'Do you keep any deadly pets?'"

"And 'Have there been any attempted murders recently?'"

Maddie giggled first, but I wasn't far behind. We earned several odd glances as we stood laughing by the side of the road, and one woman gave us a dirty look as she led her toddler to the opposite pavement, well out of the way of the two lunatics. I kept laughing anyway. It was either that or sit and rock.

"Shall we take a break tomorrow?" I asked.

Maddie nodded. "Good idea. We can regroup and try again the day after. There's got to be one habitable flat out there that isn't filled with weirdos."

The following afternoon, I swallowed a paracetamol as I updated Longacres' website. "Make it colourful," the owner had told me, and the bright flowers were entirely too cheery for my mood.

A knock at the door made me stiffen.

Please, let it be someone from the insurance company and not my downstairs neighbour. He'd already left me a snotty note yesterday, and a visit from him in person was just what I didn't need. I totally appreciated how much I'd inconvenienced him, but shouting at me wouldn't get things fixed any quicker.

Deep breaths, Olivia. I cracked open the door and peered through the gap. Phew. Not the man from downstairs, but a stranger, shifting from foot to foot as he looked up at me.

"Olivia Porter?" he asked.

"Are you from the insurance company?"

He looked like an insurance person—brown suit, clip-on tie, the shifty demeanour of a man whose clients hated him.

"Insurance? No, I'm not selling insurance."

"That's not what I meant. I had a small problem with a pipe, and... Actually, never mind. What do you want?"

He straightened an inch, meeting my eyes for a second before he looked away again. Nervous. Why was he nervous?

"I was wondering... Do you know Eleanor Rigby?"

CHAPTER 7

"ELEANOR RIGBY? IS this some sort of joke?"

Why on earth had a stranger showed up on my doorstep asking if I knew an old Beatles song?

The man gave a little cough. "No, I'm not joking, I assure you. Do you know her?"

"What do you mean, her?"

"Eleanor Rigby."

"The song?"

"No, the person."

"I'm ever so sorry, but I have no idea what you're talking about."

Why me? Was this karma's idea of a joke? I'd left a few little gifts for Edward in his house, and in return, I was destined to meet every weirdo in East London?

"You're not the daughter of Frank and Victoria Porter, then?"

My eyes widened. How did he know that? Okay, this was getting a little creepy. Not quite as creepy as Margot, the tarantula, but close.

"Yes, I am, but who are you?"

"Mickey Scudamore." He held out a hand, and I shook it out of habit. "I work for a company called Heir Today, Gone Tomorrow."

"What's that got to do with me? Or my parents?"

"My research suggested you might have an aunt

called Eleanor Rigby."

Eleanor Rigby... Eleanor... Ellie... Aunt Ellie? Dim memories of a childhood birthday party surfaced. A plump lady handing me a bowl of jelly and ice cream before she sat back down next to my mother. I'd seen her a handful of times before that day, and every time she visited, Mother had worn a scowl.

"I do have an Aunt Ellie, but I never knew her surname."

"Do you know where she is?"

"I haven't seen her since I was seven years old. Maybe eight. Look, what's this all about? I'm busy with work."

Well, busyish. Choosing the perfect shade of pink for Longacres' homepage background was a very important job.

"My company looks for unclaimed estates and tries to reunite them with their rightful beneficiaries. I'm sorry to tell you this, but I think your aunt died a couple of months ago."

But he didn't seem particularly sorry. More... hopeful.

His words slowly sank in. Aunt Ellie was dead? By rights, I should have felt sad at the news, but I'd barely known her.

And when I scratched around in the recesses of my mind, I vaguely remembered shouting. A row. Mother rarely shouted, but that day, she'd yelled long and loud at Aunt Ellie while I hid in my bedroom with my father.

"Why's Mum cross with Aunt Ellie?" I'd asked him.

He'd shrugged. "Those two have never got on. Like chalk and cheese."

"What do you mean, chalk and cheese?"

"Never mind, Livvie. Why don't we read a story?"

At that age, I had more important things to worry about than Aunt Ellie and her absence. Ballet lessons and frilly dresses, if I recalled correctly. Mother had begun teaching me to act like a lady as soon as I learned to walk.

Indeed, I'd barely thought about Ellie at all until Mickey turned up at my door. And now she was dead?

"I'm sorry to hear about her passing," was the best I could come up with. "Should I send flowers?"

"The funeral's already happened. I spoke to the priest, Father McKenzie, and he said nobody came."

Now, that made me sad. Imagine going through your whole life and meaning so little to anybody that all you were worth was an empty church and a sermon nobody heard.

Mind you, who would come to my funeral? Probably only Maddie and Dave.

"I'd have gone if I'd known."

She'd been family, after all.

"I understand she was a bit of a loner."

That left one big question. Well, two. "So, how did you know Aunt Ellie? And why are you here?"

"Each day, my company reviews the Bona Vacantia list, and—"

"Wait a second. What's the Bona Vacantia list?"

"It's a list of unclaimed estates published by the government."

"Like when people die without a will?"

"Exactly that. Anyway, we review it and try to track down the deceased's missing relatives to inherit what's left."

I narrowed my eyes at him. "And what do you get

out of that?"

The whole arrangement sounded suspiciously like a scam to me. I may have been poor, but I wanted to believe I wasn't entirely dumb.

"We help potential heirs with the paperwork in exchange for a small fee." He gave me a sheepish smile. "But between you and me, I just love the research. Genealogy's always fascinated me, and being able to make a living from studying it is a dream come true."

"So you think, what? That I may somehow be Aunt Ellie's heir?"

"I can't find that she has any other family left."

I opened the door wider, hoping that he wasn't a serial killer. He stood an inch shorter than me, so kind of small for a man, and a year older at a guess. I didn't feel any threatening vibes. But then again, my character judgement had been a little off lately, hadn't it? While he stepped over the threshold and looked around, I inched closer to the ugly lamp sitting on the floor in the lounge. A gift from Edward's aunt last Christmas, nobody wanted it, not even the good folks who shopped on eBay.

"Where's all your furniture? Have you just moved in?" Mickey asked.

"No, I'm in the process of moving out."

"Good thing I caught you, then. It could have taken me months to track you down at your new place. Are you going far?"

We'd made it to the kitchen by then, and I leaned against the counter and sighed. "I don't know yet. I haven't been able to find anywhere suitable nearby. Every place I've looked at has been awful in one way or another."

Mickey bobbed his head. "That happened to me too. It took weeks to find my current flat, and even then, I ended up with a bedroom the size of a matchbox."

Tears pricked at the corners of my eyes, and I gave an involuntary sniff. My search was hopeless, wasn't it?

"Uh, don't cry." Mickey glanced towards the door as if he wanted to run out of it. "What about Eleanor's house? If we get the paperwork done quickly, you could live there until you find somewhere better."

I gripped the edge of the counter as my knees threatened to give way. "Did you just say 'house'?"

"Well, it's more of a cottage from what I understand."

When he referred to Eleanor's estate, I'd imagined some rickety furniture and a few china ornaments sitting in a storage unit somewhere. A house? I gave up trying to stay upright and slid down the kitchen unit until my bottom hit the floor. "But a whole building?"

"Are you all right?" Mickey asked. "Shall I make a cup of tea?"

I nodded.

"Which is that? Yes, you're all right, or yes, you want tea?"

"Both, I think. I can't quite believe this."

He chuckled. "It's not the first time I've seen that reaction. I'll put the kettle on."

Mickey bustled around while I stared at a smudge of dirt on the wall opposite, numb, half expecting a camera crew to pop out of thin air and announce this was all a joke. Try as I might, I couldn't remember much about Aunt Ellie. She'd never paid me much attention. Apart from my birthday party and the argument, the only solid recollection I had was a visit to the Natural History Museum one rainy Saturday, when she'd tagged along with Mother and me and spent most of the time yawning.

"Where's the milk?" Mickey asked.

"Sorry, there isn't any. Cutbacks."

"Black it is, then."

He sat opposite me, cross-legged, and I took a sip from the mug he handed over. He may not have put any milk in, but he'd certainly found the sugar.

"So, what now? You mentioned a fee, but I don't have any money. The website design business hasn't been too lucrative lately."

"You're a web designer?" He scratched his chin, looking thoughtful. "Maybe we could come to an agreement?"

Two hours later, we'd got through several gallons of tea and a packet of chocolate digestives Mickey found hidden behind the baked beans—slightly elderly but still edible—and he'd become my second-best friend.

Not only was Mickey a researcher extraordinaire, he part-owned Heir Today, Gone Tomorrow with a friend he'd met at university. While they shared a love of history and family trees, neither was particularly proficient with computers. The company had only been going for a few weeks and was in dire need of a decent website.

"I'm not so great at the business side of things," Mickey confessed. "My partner was doing that part, but his wife's just had a baby and the lack of sleep's getting to him."

"Well, I can build you a website, design you a logo, organise flyers—anything you like—if you'll help me with my forms."

"Deal."

A handshake sealed the arrangement, and that was how, two weeks later on the thirty-first of December, Maddie, Mickey, and I found ourselves standing outside a rather shabby-looking cottage in the quaint little village of Upper Foxford.

CHAPTER 8

"ARE YOU SURE this is the right place?" I asked Maddie. "It's bigger than I thought."

And a whole lot uglier.

Mickey held out the piece of paper with the address on it, and Maddie compared it to the map she'd printed out from the internet.

"Yep. Lilac Cottage. This is it."

The bottom of the rickety wooden gate scraped over the path as Maddie pushed it open, and we followed her towards the house. And when I say followed, I mean we shoved our way through overgrown bushes and stepped over the tendrils of ivy that criss-crossed the path like mutant spaghetti.

"Imagine what a mess this'll be in the summer," Maddie muttered.

"I don't think I want to."

Mickey reached out and rubbed the fragrant leaves of a rosemary bush between his fingers. "You enjoy cooking, right?"

"Yes."

"At least you've got garnish."

To me, rosemary came in a plastic bag from Waitrose rather than in tree format. Living in London my whole life, I'd never had more than a cluster of decorative pots and a barbecue area outside, even when

I lived with my parents, and I couldn't deny my feeling of panic as I gazed around the jungle I was about to call home.

"Where do I start?" I spotted two beady eyes glaring at me from next to a tree. "Is that a fox?"

Maddie took my arm and led me towards the cottage. "One step at a time, Liv. Tackle the house first." She looked towards the roofline and back to the ground floor. "That might take a while."

"Why is the door made from plywood?"

The cottage may have seen better days, but plywood and a padlock rather than a proper front door? Even in my worst nightmares, I hadn't imagined that.

Mickey grimaced. "I didn't want to say anything..."

"What? What is it?"

"The ambulance crew had to break into the house to help Eleanor."

"She took ill in there?" I'd been so busy worrying about packing, and my landlord, and the endless paperwork, that I'd barely thought about how she died. A heart attack, according to her death certificate, but I'd assumed she'd passed peacefully in hospital. "Poor, poor Ellie."

Flowers. I should take flowers to her grave. Presumably, she'd been buried in the local churchyard, and in a village the size of Upper Foxford, that shouldn't be too difficult to find.

It would have to be a small bunch of flowers, though, at least for now. Without the need to pay rent, I could afford to live now, but things promised to be tight. Lilac Cottage would cost more to heat than my old flat, and I'd learned my lesson over the burst pipe.

Mickey held out the key. "Do you want to do the

honours?"

As I took it, a flutter of excitement stirred in my belly. Would the inside be nicer? Until the paperwork was finalised yesterday afternoon, I'd barely allowed myself to think about the house, too afraid that the place would be snatched away from me by some administrative glitch at the eleventh hour.

But my luck had finally changed.

As we'd driven up from London, the three of us squashed into Maddie's Ford Fiesta, we'd tried to guess what Lilac Cottage would be like. Lilac... Even the name sounded pretty.

"My money's on seventies wallpaper," Maddie had said. "You know, with the big flowers."

Mickey grinned at us in the rear-view mirror. "That's making a comeback at the moment. My sister just used it in her lounge. But I reckon it'll have an avocado bathroom suite, dodgy carpet, and one of those old CRT televisions."

"And it'll be all musty and stink of mothballs. I stood next to a guy on the Tube yesterday who smelled of mothballs." Maddie wrinkled her nose. "I didn't even realise people still used them."

"Me neither," Mickey said. "Let's hope it doesn't have damp. That can play havoc with your furniture."

Good thing I'd sold most of mine then, wasn't it?

"Guys, it's bad enough that I'm moving to the middle of nowhere, without the thought of having to live in a time warp."

Maddie patted me on the hand. "Only trying to be realistic. It's hardly going to be a palace, is it?"

I laid my head against the car window and groaned. Yes, she was right. But at least it came at the right price.

When Mickey said "cottage," my imagination had run wild, thinking of one of those chocolate-box affairs with white walls and a cute thatched roof. A couple of overstuffed armchairs in the lounge, some chintzy curtains, and a bedroom where you had to duck under a quaint wooden beam to go inside. I could visualise myself living somewhere like that, even if it was clinging to the edge of civilisation by the ivy twisted artfully over its front porch.

But I could already see from the outside that my daydreams had been wide of the mark. In the next county, most likely.

Brown. That was the overriding theme of Lilac Cottage. Drab brick walls, paint peeling from once-beige window frames, the makeshift front door. The only hint of colour on the cottage itself was the green moss growing all over the roof.

Mickey winced as he poked at the window frame nearest the front door. "These need replacing. Painted at least."

The whole cottage needed replacing. Preferably with a tidy apartment near shops and a Tube station. Butterflies battered my stomach with heavy wings as I reached for the padlock. How bad would the inside be?

Judging by the creak, nobody had oiled the hinges in years, and as I stepped over the threshold into the dim hallway, I found Maddie had been right about the mustiness. Ick. I reached out for the light switch and clicked it.

"Why is nothing happening?" I hissed.

"The electricity's probably been cut off," Mickey said. "Eleanor wasn't around to pay the bill, was she?"

Another job for tomorrow, or rather, the day after, what with the first of January being a bank holiday. Good thing I'd brought a torch.

Mickey peered down at a set of shelves next to the front door, the only furniture in the otherwise empty hallway.

"What are you looking for?" I asked.

"Her face."

"Huh?"

"Eleanor's face. You know, like in the Beatles' song, where the old lady kept her face by the door in a jar. Always thought that sounded like a horror film."

"I'm pretty sure Paul McCartney didn't mean a real face."

"I guess."

But that didn't stop Mickey from singing a few off-key lines as I picked up the chunky phone sitting on the top shelf. No dial tone. It was as dead as its owner. Next to it, Aunt Ellie had started a shopping list she'd never complete.

Microwave chips.

Pizza.

Dairy Milk chocolate.

Lottery scratch card.

Hmm... Looked as if she hadn't been much of a chef.

A flight of stairs ran up the wall to my right and disappeared into the gloom above. On the ground floor, four doors led off the hallway, three at the far end and one next to me. I pushed it open and immediately regretted that decision.

"Eeuch! Who does that?" I screwed my eyes shut, wishing it would go away.

"What? What's wrong?" Maddie asked.

I shuffled to the side so she could look into the downstairs toilet. The orange downstairs toilet. And not a muted shade of peach or a subtle tint. No, bright, in-your-face tangerine, the love child of a can of Tango and a bottle of Tropicana.

"Ouch. Did your Aunt Ellie have impaired vision?"

"I don't think so. Just incredibly bad taste."

"At least it's not avocado," Mickey said.

"No, that's probably upstairs."

I pulled the toilet door shut, wishing I hadn't sold my Gucci sunglasses on eBay. I'd need them every time I got the urge to pee.

"Wonder what's behind door number two?" Maddie muttered as I followed her along the hallway.

Mickey had been spot on about the carpet. Grimy and threadbare underfoot, I'd certainly never walk on it without slippers.

"Do you want me to open it?" Mickey asked, his hand hovering above the door handle.

"Yes, go on."

Light coming in through the grimy window of the lounge revealed an oversized velvet sofa, the antithesis of the bathroom with its drab brown swirls. It sat opposite the biggest plasma TV I'd ever seen.

Mickey let out a low whistle. "Well, I guess we know where her pension went."

We sure did. Edward had spent a fortune on his fifty-inch flat screen, but Aunt Ellie's looked bigger.

"I guess she must have really enjoyed her soaps."

The TV was the focal point of the room, but clutter dominated the rest of the space. A cheap-looking veneered shelving unit spanned one wall, full to bursting with nicknacks. China figurines, decorative plates, candles, teacups and matching saucers. How on earth did she dust? I ran a finger across one ornamental jug and studied the grey layer on my finger. Guess I'd answered that question.

Out in the hallway again, I hoped it would be third time lucky. Maddie opened the door this time, revealing a kitchen with stained Formica countertops and a lingering odour of cigarette smoke. The ceiling was stained yellow from old tobacco, made worse by the clash with the beige walls. I couldn't help shuddering.

"It needs a bit of modernising," Maddie said.

"Congratulations. You just won the prize for understatement of the year."

A newish microwave sat in one corner, but the kettle, the stove, and everything else could have come from the Ark. In fact, I wasn't sure I'd dare to turn the cooker on. The only thing worse than having to live in Lilac Cottage would be burning it down.

"Guys! You have to look at this." Mickey's voice drifted through the open door.

"Look at what?" I asked.

"The... Oh, you've got to come in here."

I tried to push door number four open, but it got stuck halfway. Even a shove didn't help. I squeezed through the gap, and my jaw dropped open.

"What the hell is all of this stuff?"

Maddie leaned in behind me, and judging by her sharp intake of breath, she couldn't believe her eyes either.

"Your aunt seems to have bought everything QVC has ever sold."

"Or else she was acting as a satellite warehouse for The Shopping Channel," Mickey said.

No kidding.

The boxes were stacked from floor to ceiling, everything from a steam mop to slimming underwear in extra-large. A halogen oven jostled for space with a replica lightsabre, and I spotted four different hair-removal gadgets. Good grief—was that... Yes. A life-size cutout of Cliff Richard grinned at us from beside the window.

"Bloody hell," Maddie said. "I've always wondered who bought all this crap. Now I know."

My first instinct was to run and never look back. In fact, I'd got halfway out the door before Maddie grabbed my arm and hauled me back into my own personal hell. Even as a child, I'd arranged my books in alphabetical order and put my toys into their box at the end of each day. But this... Lilac Cottage was so far removed from my love of neatness and order that I felt the beginnings of a migraine just looking at the mess.

Old Olivia longed to climb into Maddie's car and go straight back to London, but new Olivia didn't have the luxury of being fussy anymore. At least it was cheap. Those words became my new mantra.

At least it's cheap. At least it's cheap. At least it's cheap.

"How are you going to cope with this lot?" Maddie asked. "You know, with your OCD?"

"I do not have OCD," I snapped.

The expression on Maddie's face told me she thought otherwise.

Okay, maybe I did, just a little. "I'll manage. I have to."

She poked at a box containing a steam iron. "There could be anything buried under this lot."

"A World War Two bomb, a dead body, a portal to a parallel universe," Mickey added.

I forced a laugh. It was either that or cry. "I'm going to have a field day on eBay."

"Flipping heck, you will, won't you? And now Christmas is over, you could borrow some of Santa's elves to help you with all the packing."

If I'd thought the ground floor was bad, the situation only got worse as we climbed the creaking staircase.

"I was right," Mickey said as he pushed open the first door to the left. "Avocado. And it could do with a clean."

Marvellous. Still, if I was lucky, there'd be a white bathroom suite stacked in the mess downstairs. To the right, Eleanor's bedroom had the same tired air as the lounge, from the faded velour headboard on the sagging double bed, to the tatty wardrobe, to the dressing table covered in half-empty bottles of lotions and potions.

But the other two bedrooms?

If only I could unsee the horrors. Jigsaw holders, TV dinner trays, garden kneelers, and ugly kaftans. Fancy toilet roll holders, foot files, garish scarves, and a machine that looked like a torture device but claimed it would give you a "Hollywood butt lift."

And an idea began to form in my mind...

CHAPTER 9

"THERE'S A LOT of stuff here from The Jewellery Channel," Maddie said, picking up a couple of boxes. "Simulated diamond, garnet... What's kunzite?"

"No idea, but I hope somebody does because I'm going to sell it. Everything."

"Like, on eBay?"

"Exactly that. Sell it and get a bathroom that won't make me go blind."

Mickey's grin matched my own. "Might I suggest a new kitchen as well?"

"Good idea." I wasn't sure I could bring myself to touch any of the appliances downstairs. "But who knows how much this lot'll raise?"

Maddie picked up a paint-by-numbers picture of a boy and dog. "Someone'll buy it. It's all new. I mean, I know someone who sold an old carrier bag on eBay for one pound fifty."

"I can only hope."

Unbeknownst to her, Aunt Ellie had given me a second chance at life, and I intended to seize it with both hands. The eBay app on my phone was about to become my new best friend. But first I needed to get through the next few days.

"Has anyone seen a packet of sheets or a duvet? I need to work out where I'm going to sleep tonight."

"In Eleanor's bed?" Maddie suggested.

"That's a bit weird, don't you think?"

"It's only for a night. Dave can bring your bed over tomorrow."

My bedstead and mattress, the only furniture I had left, were sitting in the back of Dave's van. He'd planned to come with us today, but an emergency at work meant he'd had to change someone's fuse box instead.

"I think I'll just sleep on the sofa. It's big enough."

Maddie wrinkled her nose. "It's kind of grubby."

I agreed, although it was difficult to tell with its hideous pattern. "Then let's find something to cover it up."

The light was fading fast as we rummaged through the cupboards. Maddie hit the jackpot downstairs with a set of blue-and-orange polka-dot bed linen, while Mickey found a box of matches in the kitchen drawer and lit a few of the candles from Aunt Ellie's nicknack shelf.

The usable rooms were soon bathed in a flickering light, and we gathered in the lounge. I sagged against the wall next to the door while Mickey thumped Maddie on the back as she had a coughing fit.

"Must be all that dust. Drinks. We need drinks."

That meant venturing back to the kitchen. "I'll go and look for something."

One cupboard held a jar of Nescafé, while I found three chipped mugs in another. The rack next to the sink yielded a new packet of scouring pads, and I made the most of them.

Coffee. I needed coffee. The kettle seemed safe enough, but just as I was about to turn it on, I remembered the lack of electricity. Heat and light were things I'd always taken for granted, and now that I was stuck in Lilac Cottage, I developed a new appreciation for the basics in life. It would have to be cold water all around.

"What are you doing for dinner?" Maddie asked.

"I haven't thought that far ahead. Do you think there's a supermarket anywhere near?"

"In this place? I doubt it." She made a face. Maddie was as much of a city girl as me.

"How about going to the pub?" Mickey suggested. "We drove past one on the way into the village."

"Great idea. My treat," Maddie said.

I tried to protest, but she wouldn't listen.

"Liv, you've got enough on your plate without starving as well."

Mickey blew out the candles, and when we got outside, I put the padlock on the front door.

"You don't need to worry about that," Maddie said. "I can't see anyone breaking in to steal an LED disco ball."

"I left my laptop in the lounge, remember?"

"Oh, yeah. Perhaps next time, you could hide it under the neoprene waist-trimming belt or that blanket thing with the feet."

The three of us piled back into Maddie's car for the short drive to The Cock and Bull. The twee country pub was a far cry from the sleek wine bars I'd been accustomed to visiting in the city, and the flashing sign outside still wished us a merry Christmas. Inside, someone had tried to go upmarket with a polished metal bar, understated lighting, and sleek glass tables, but then they'd spoiled it with leopard-print bar stools and a life-size reindeer complete with freaky red eyes.

"Cock and Bull?" Mickey muttered as Maddie tried to get the barmaid's attention. "What kind of name is that?"

"Used to be called The Elusive Count," the old man propping up the bar next to us said. "But the local kids kept crossing out the O."

"The Elusive C... Oh dear." Maddie screwed up her face. "Maybe the change was for the best."

The man shook his head. "Wrecked this place, young Barry has. Ever since he took over from his father, it's been new this, new that. Used to be a nice place for a quiet pint, and now look at it." He gestured at the cactus on the corner of the bar. "The place is full of shite."

"Now, now, Bernie," the barmaid said, pushing a bowl of crisps in his direction. "Don't you be scaring off the newcomers." She smiled at us. "Haven't seen you around here before."

"I've just moved here. Into Eleanor Rigby's house."

"The old lady who died?"

I nodded. "She was my aunt, but I hadn't seen her in a long while."

"Sorry to hear that. If it helps, nobody in the village saw much of her either. Kept herself to herself. I've worked here for almost ten years, and not once did she come in for a drink."

"I'll try to be more sociable." Otherwise my life in Upper Foxford promised to be a lonely one. "I'm Olivia."

"Jean. I live down by the old railway station."

"Those were the days," Bernie said. "My father used to work on the railways, and his dad before him. Got any more nuts, Jeanie?"

"Only the wasabi peanuts, and you don't like those."

Bernie gave a long sigh. "Bloody Barry and his newfangled ideas. What's wrong with dry roasted?" He fixed his gaze on me. "You don't eat that rubbish, do you?"

Actually, I was quite fond of wasabi. "Uh..."

"Ignore him." A voice came from over my shoulder. "Bernie's not happy unless he's complaining about something. Right, Bernie?"

"Easy to do here."

I turned to look at the stranger and found a sandy-haired guy three inches taller than me, wearing an easy smile.

"So, you're new to the village?" he asked.

"I moved into Lilac Cottage about six hours ago."

"I'm surprised old Eleanor's place has even got the electricity connected up."

"It hasn't."

His eyes widened. "Then how can you live there?"

"Oh, I've got candles. It'll be like camping." Far better to brush off the situation than admit the truth; that I couldn't afford to live anywhere else.

Maddie helped me out too. "We used to love camping when we were kids."

We did, if you counted the blanket fort in Maddie's bedroom. My mother refused to stoop lower than a five-star hotel, and as our budget wouldn't stretch to that after my father left, we stayed at home while Maddie's family made their annual trip to Butlins.

The stranger's expression suggested he didn't believe my story, so I tried to change the subject. "I should probably introduce myself. I'm Olivia, and this is Maddie and Mickey."

He held out a hand for us to shake. "Warren Hannigan. Artist and taxi driver extraordinaire."

"An artist? What do you paint?"

"Landscapes, mainly. There's plenty of inspiration in the countryside around here."

"Have you lived in the village long?"

"My parents moved here when I was fifteen."

And I guessed his age at twenty-five now, so he'd been there a while.

As we chatted, I could feel eyes on me from all around the pub, and being honest, it creeped me out a little. In London, people kept themselves to themselves, and this attention felt unnerving. Anyone making eye contact in the city was immediately branded a pervert or a nutter.

I risked a glance behind, and the couple at the nearest table studiously averted their gaze.

"Everyone gets curious about strangers," Warren said, following my line of sight. "It's not often an outsider moves in."

An outsider. The interloper. The new girl at school. Still, at least Warren was talking to me, and in time, hopefully the rest of the crowd would too. I had to think positive. The other option was to move back to London and live on Maddie's sofa.

Mickey's stomach grumbled, and that reminded me why we'd come to The Cock and Bull in the first place. Food. And we needed to eat soon because Maddie and Mickey had to drive back to London this evening.

I mustered up a smile for Warren. "Well, I hope I'm not an outsider for long. Do you know where we can find a menu in here?"

He reached behind the bar and came back with a handful. "Here you go."

"Is the food good?" Maddie asked.

There was a long pause before he answered. "It's… different."

"Different in a good way?"

"Uh, you'll see."

We did indeed see. It was as if Heston Blumenthal had visited the local supermarket with his eyes closed, then taken LSD before he started cooking.

"What's oat risotto?" Mickey asked.

I peered over his shoulder. Oat risotto with celery. Oat risotto? Porridge. "Celery porridge."

"Who puts celery in porridge?"

"The same person who pickles octopus," Maddie muttered. "Where are the chips?"

I quickly scanned the rest of the page. "Fillet steak with mushroom ketchup and sweet potato fries?"

"I guess that'll have to do."

Warren tapped me on the shoulder as I headed for a table with Mickey and Maddie.

"Just a tip—come here on Wednesdays. Wednesday is curry night. Barry tried to do away with it, but there was a mutiny, so it's here to stay."

"Thanks. I'll do that."

Despite the strange dishes, I drew out dinner for as long as possible, picking at my salmon with crispy beans and quinoa. The thought of going back to Lilac Cottage in the dark didn't exactly fill me with joy. I even ate dessert—creme brûlée with what looked like Weetabix sprinkled over the top—but it was only putting off the inevitable.

"You'll be okay," Maddie said when she dropped me

back. "The pub wasn't so bad, apart from the food. I mean, Jean was nice, and I think Warren likes you."

"Really?"

After the Edward debacle, I'd been off men. But did I truly want to spend the rest of my life alone?

"Oh yes. I caught him looking at you a couple of times."

"I'm not sure he's my type."

"And who is your type?"

"Well... Edward, I guess."

When we'd started dating two years ago, he'd seemed perfect. Even our initial meeting had been the modern version of one of the fairy tales I loved so much.

I'd been waiting on a crowded Tube platform at Barbican one hot summer's day when delays were long and tempers were frayed. A woman laden with shopping bags had sent me flying, and I would have fallen onto the tracks if Edward hadn't caught me. My heart had been racing as I looked into his hazel eyes for the first time, and not just from my near miss. My white knight had arrived.

With no sign of a train, he'd wrapped an arm around my shoulders and led me to a boutique wine bar near St. Paul's. I could still remember the warmth that spread through me at his closeness.

"Champagne?" he'd asked. "You're the kind of girl I should celebrate meeting."

"Really?"

"You're quite a catch."

Mother always told me I would be, but I didn't think she meant literally. Edward had ordered a bottle of Veuve Clicquot and a platter of light snacks, conversation flowed along with the alcohol, and when we shared a cab home, we'd bypassed my flat altogether.

Back at Edward's place, we'd spent half the night discussing the literary greats over glasses of crisp Sauvignon Blanc. He'd charmed me, although not out of my knickers, I hasten to add. Not that night, anyway. It turned out we shared many of the same interests— long walks on a Sunday afternoon, visiting the many art galleries London had to offer, and the spectacular architecture of England's stately homes.

When a stunning bouquet arrived at my flat the day after, complete with a gift card for a year's joint membership to the National Trust, I realised Edward had stolen my heart. Life changed. I was no longer Olivia Porter, single girl in the city, but one half of Edward and Olivia.

If Mother had been alive, she'd have been thrilled. Edward ticked all her boxes, and mine too, or so I'd thought. Somehow, I'd missed the "cheating bastard" option hidden away in the small print.

He'd broken my heart, torn it right out, and do you know what the worst part was? I still missed him.

"Forget Edward," Maddie said. "Edward was an arsehole."

"I guess."

"Livvie, don't do this to yourself. You're making a fresh start, and look at you—you're a property owner now."

"You know, the camping idea looks more attractive at the moment."

She leaned forward to give me a hug. "Keep your chin up. I'll come back tomorrow with chocolate, and we can make a start on the tidying."

"Thanks for everything, Mads."

"This'll work out fine, you'll see. A couple of months down the line, this place'll be a proper home and you'll be breaking the hearts of all the men in the village." She gave a little squeal as she straightened. "This is so exciting!"

At least one of us was happy. As I waved her and Mickey off, then closed the front door, I couldn't dismiss the feeling of foreboding that overcame me.

Would my move to the country be the fresh start I needed or the biggest mistake of my life?

CHAPTER 10

AUNT ELLIE MAY have spent half of her life on the sofa, but it wasn't as comfortable as it looked. No matter which way I turned, a broken spring stuck into my back, and the seat sagged at one end.

Even so, I couldn't blame my lack of sleep entirely on it. My mind hadn't stopped churning all night, creating nightmares about the stacks of junk and the state of the kitchen. Although if the oven did blow up and burn the house down, it wouldn't be the end of the world. The flood at my old flat had taught me one important lesson: buy insurance. I'd spent the last of my savings on a policy, and for a moment I considered "accidentally" knocking one of the candles over myself. At least that would solve the tidying problem.

The sheer volume of junk in the house made me cringe. I hated clutter. Hated it! It'd take me months to clear this lot. Years, maybe. Even if I managed to sell everything on eBay, I'd still have to package it up and take it to the post office—no mean feat without a car. Oh, and in between that, I needed to carry on with my web design clients because I couldn't rely on online auctions for my bread and butter. Did Lilac Cottage even have a broadband connection?

If not, I'd be spending an awful lot of time nursing a coffee in the local branch of Starbucks. If there was a

Starbucks. Here in the sticks, I'd probably end up with Bernie in The Cock and Bull, which at least had free Wi-Fi even if it didn't have edible food.

Despite being exhausted, I forced myself to get up as soon as the sun rose. Without electricity, I couldn't afford to waste any of the precious daylight hours at this time of year.

Okay, start small, Olivia.

That meant tackling the third bedroom first. Most of the jewellery seemed to be in there, and hopefully that would bring in enough cash to pay for the basic repairs the house was crying out for. I'd already discovered the upstairs toilet didn't flush properly. What other surprises were lurking beneath the mess?

I spent the first few hours of the day carrying items down to the kitchen, where I'd set up a makeshift photo studio in front of the window with a white sheet draped over the open door. By the time Maddie and Dave arrived just before noon, I had thirty-two items catalogued and up for sale on eBay, and aching thighs from all the stairs. Who needed that weird exercise machine?

Maddie bounded in through the open door. I couldn't lock it from the inside, but last night, I'd dragged the shelves next to it across so if anyone tried to get in, Aunt Ellie's collection of junk would spill all over the place and wake me up.

"We've brought your bed," Maddie called.

Oh, thank goodness. I greeted her with a hug. "You're a star. I was dreading another night on that sofa."

Dave kissed me on the cheek and looked around. "Maddie said it was bad, but not this bad. Bloody hell, look at the size of that spider."

I sprinted outside after Maddie, who leapt into Dave's van and locked the doors.

"You didn't tell me there were spiders," she screeched through the glass.

"I didn't know. Honestly. Look on the bright side— at least it wasn't Margot."

Dave leaned out of the doorway. "It's okay. I've flushed it down the loo."

A little coaxing got Maddie into the house again, and between the three of us, we wrestled Eleanor's ugly old bed downstairs. No doubt I'd have a hernia by the time the cottage was habitable.

"Now what?" I asked. "We can't leave it there."

Dave had propped the mattress up against the front wall, and it created an eyesore.

"We'll have to take it to the tip," he said. "Any idea where that is?"

"I don't even know how to get back to the main road."

"Tell you what—me and Maddie'll get rid of the bed while you sort out lunch."

Maddie made a face. "Liv, are you sure you don't need a hand with the food?"

"No!" Dave and I both said, a tad too quickly. Maddie may have been my best friend, but there was a reason I did all the cooking. She made the chef at The Cock and Bull look like a genius, and Dave had to change the batteries in their smoke detector at least once a month.

"I'll need you to lift the other end of the bed," Dave told her.

While they putt-putted off down the lane with

Dave's van sounding in desperate need of a service, I went inside to fetch my purse. There must be shops in the village, right?

I knew there was nothing but fields and the odd cottage between Aunt Ellie's and the pub, so I set off in the other direction on foot, searching for signs of civilisation. Oh, what I'd have given to find a branch of Waitrose or even a Sainsbury's.

No such luck. Ten minutes later, I stumbled across a handful of storefronts in what passed for Upper Foxford's high street. A betting shop, a tiny café sharing space with a hair salon, and opposite them, an Indian takeaway and a newsagent.

As I headed past a pet shop with rabbit hutches and a few struggling potted plants outside, I was pleased to see the newsagent doubled up as a post office, so at least I had somewhere convenient to take my eBay shipments. Anything that didn't sell could go to the Age Concern charity shop next door but one, on the other side of a tiny pharmacy. The line-up was completed by Floyd's supermarket, and that was where I headed.

Floyd himself sat behind the cash register, wearing a name badge with a smiley face on, completely at odds with his own expression. He reminded me of a basset hound—sort of droopy with doleful eyes. Both he and the two other customers tracked me as I picked up a basket and perused the shelves, hunting for snacks that didn't require cooking.

Cheese, ham, bread, and butter, with a bit of salad thrown in to give the illusion of healthiness. Once, I'd been religious about getting my five-a-day, but lately, I'd started counting the bottles of wine Maddie kept bringing around as fruit. On the way to pay, I walked past the household products shelf, and my OCD got the better of me as I added bleach, limescale remover, antibacterial spray, cloths, oven cleaner, and more scouring pads to my basket. Floyd's eyes widened as I struggled to the checkout, dragging a mop and bucket with my spare hand.

"Planning on doing some cleaning?" he asked.

No, I planned to make special sauce down at The Cock and Bull. "Just a little."

"Haven't seen you round here before."

Was I going to get questioned at every establishment I visited? "I only moved to the village yesterday. I'm living in Eleanor Rigby's old house."

"Really? I didn't see that one go on the market."

"No, I inherited it. I'm her niece."

His semblance of a smile faded entirely. "Well, I hope you'll be a better customer than she was. Always went into town, she did, on the bus every morning. People like her kill small villages like this."

I could get a bus into town? That was great news! Hopefully, I'd find a proper shopping centre there. But at the same time, I couldn't afford to upset my new neighbours.

"I promise to shop here more often than Aunt Ellie." That shouldn't be difficult. "I'd like to support local shopkeepers now I'm living here."

Floyd cheered up at that, hardly surprising when one considered his prices. They made London look cheap. No wonder Aunt Ellie had gone elsewhere—my wallet shed a tear each time he took an item out of my basket.

"Did you bring a bag?" he asked.

"No, sorry."

He tsk-tsked under his breath. "Folk round here tend to bring their own bags. Good for the environment, it is."

And better for his profit margin too, no doubt.

He packed my purchases into plastic carrier bags, six of them, and I began to regret my penchant for cleaning. How was I supposed to get that lot home, plus the mop and bucket? I didn't fancy making two trips. One dose of Floyd was quite enough for today, thank you.

If only Aunt Ellie had left me a car. Not that I could afford driving lessons at that moment, but walking everywhere would get old really fast, especially when it rained. I made a mental note to check the bus timetable and pined for London. I already missed the hustle and bustle of the city, and Pawel, who'd run the corner shop near my old flat, had certainly been more cheerful than Floyd.

The *honk* of a horn behind me made me drop the bucket, and I was about to glare at whoever was driving the blue Ford Galaxy when the window rolled down and Warren leaned out.

"Sorry about that. Didn't mean to make you jump. I just thought you might want a lift with that lot."

Ah, yes. He'd mentioned being a taxi driver. How did I politely decline without revealing quite how little money I had?

He must have read my mind. "Don't worry—I won't charge you. I'm driving past Lilac Cottage, anyway."

"If you're sure?"

He climbed out, and the brush of his hand against mine as he helped me stack my bags in the back made me stiffen. But when I looked at him, he smiled.

"You okay?"

"Absolutely fine," I lied. The contact had felt...nice, but was I ready to contemplate spending time with another man? "I really do appreciate your help."

"It's no problem. Any time you need a ride, just give me a shout. It can't be easy moving to a new place on your own."

"It's even harder than I thought."

"I know the feeling. Took weeks for the other kids to speak to me when I arrived. Every night, I begged my parents to move back to London."

"You're from London as well?"

"Grew up in Hammersmith."

"We must have been practically neighbours—I lived in Notting Hill until I turned eighteen. Do you still miss the city?"

"Some parts of it, but this place has grown on me. The slower pace of life, actually speaking to your neighbours. People look out for their own. It just takes a while to be accepted."

"But how do I get accepted?"

"Best just to talk to people. Hang out in the pub and the café, maybe join the Women's Institute or the horticultural society?"

As if I didn't have enough on my plate. "How do I join those?"

"I could find a few phone numbers for you if you like?"

"I'd be very grateful."

We pulled into Aunt Ellie's driveway, and my heart soared at the sight of Dave's van parked outside. Two more friendly faces in addition to Warren's would help me to get through the afternoon.

"Thanks so much for the ride."

"Do you need a hand with your bags?"

I spied Maddie and Dave heading towards us and shook my head. "I've already got help."

The instant we got inside, Maddie started with the interrogation, after first reminding me that she was always right.

"I told you Warren liked you."

"He only gave me a lift because he was passing."

"And I saw him staring at your arse as you walked into the house."

"Really?" Was that denial in my voice? Or hope?

"Really. So, do you like him too?"

"I've only met the man twice."

"That was enough for me and Dave. Have you waxed lately? I think I saw a kit in one of the spare bedrooms."

"Maddie, please. I'm only just getting over Edward."

"You know what they say about falling off a horse."

I thought about it for a second. "I'm not getting back on Edward."

"Okay, so maybe that analogy isn't quite right. But you could always ride a different man."

"I'm going to make lunch now."

Despite Maddie helping in the kitchen, we soon had a plate of sandwiches with crisps on the side, and Dave grabbed a handful before taking a seat at the kitchen table.

"What's the plan for this afternoon, boss?" he asked.

I only had them for today, and then I'd be on my own until next weekend, five long days away. "Could you help to carry my bed upstairs? I can't manage it on my own."

"Sure thing. And when you've got the electricity turned back on, I'll check over your wiring."

Dammit, why couldn't I meet a Dave? Edward may have been well off, but Dave had stayed loyal to Maddie from the moment they met, and he'd never been anything but kind to me as well.

But all too soon, he'd gone, driving Maddie back to London ready for another Monday morning. That left me alone, perched on the good end of the sofa as Aunt Ellie's collection of china figurines glinted eerily in the flickering candlelight.

A sigh escaped. A new year, a new start, but I still wished I could back up 365 days. This time last January, I'd been bursting with joy as Edward and I headed for a minibreak in Barcelona.

But I was stuck at Lilac Cottage, and I needed to make the best of it.

Woohoo! I checked my emails as I made myself a cheese sandwich for breakfast and found I'd sold four items on eBay. A window squeegee, two necklaces, and the blanket with feet. I spent the morning packing them up as well as listing more junk while I waited on hold for the accounts department at the electricity company. Maddie had lent me her super-duper recharging battery, but my phone was almost dead.

By lunchtime, I had a promise of reconnection that afternoon, and I couldn't help smiling as I carried the first lot of Aunt Ellie's tat out of the house. One small step for Lilac Cottage, one giant leap for Olivia.

In the post office, a grey-haired lady adjusted her glasses and craned her neck up to look at me. At five feet three, I'd never felt tall, but I towered a clear head above her.

"You're the new girl. You've moved into Eleanor Rigby's old house."

News sure travelled fast. "That's right."

"Living with a man, are you?"

Living in sin, she meant. Her disdain when she said the word "man" was all too obvious.

"No, I'm on my own."

She narrowed her eyes. "I heard you bought an awful lot of food yesterday."

So, old Floyd enjoyed a bit of gossip, did he? It was tempting to fan the flames, but then I thought back to what Warren said about being accepted.

"Some friends came to help me move furniture and, er, things."

"Things? You mean all that rubbish Mrs. Rigby kept buying?"

"You know about that?"

"Could hardly miss it, could I? The postman used to moan about her packages doing his back in every morning, and all because the woman was incapable of passing up a bargain."

I thought back to the junk I'd been cataloguing that morning. How much of a bargain were an extendable backscratcher and a roll-up jigsaw mat?

"There is rather a lot of stuff in the house."

"You'll be needing a skip, you mean?"

"Actually, I'm hoping to sell most of it on eBay."

The woman cackled so hard her false teeth came

loose. She shoved them back in with one hand and held out the other to me.

"I'm Betty. I should introduce myself seeing as you're going to be my new best customer." Her grip was surprisingly strong.

"Olivia Porter. Did you know Mrs. Rigby well?"

"I don't think anybody around here did. She and that no-good son of hers kept to themselves."

A chill ran through me. A son? Aunt Ellie had a son? How had Mickey missed that? Could this son have me evicted from the house?

"Does he live around here? Her son?" The quake in my voice was all too evident.

"In a manner of speaking. He's buried in the churchyard not too far from his mother. Good riddance, I say."

Dead? Relief washed through me, quickly followed by guilt. "Oh. That's, er..."

"You didn't know him, then?"

"I barely knew Aunt Ellie. Inheriting her house was a complete surprise."

Betty cackled again. "At least the woman finally did something good for somebody."

First my mother, then Floyd, now Betty. Aunt Ellie hadn't been popular, had she? What did she do to upset so many people?

A cheery "hello" came from behind me, and Betty's attention turned to her next customer. No matter—I'd be back there soon enough.

I returned to Lilac Cottage four parcels lighter but with a weight on my mind. Would people's feelings towards Aunt Ellie reflect on me? I needed to fit in here or life had the potential to be difficult. And speaking of difficult, I needed to get a phone line installed so I could work, then draw up a proper budget.

Over lunch, I formalised the to-do list floating around in my head on the back of a flyer for over-sixties yoga that someone had shoved under my makeshift front door. It started with "clean everything" and ended with "explore the jungle." I'd taken a quick look around the garden behind the cottage, but the twisted tree limbs and thick mass of brambles suggested it had been untouched for years.

Reading through the list made me want to crawl into my bed, pull the duvet over me, and hide from the world, but I had to make a start. Blinking back tears, I picked up a bottle of bleach and headed for the downstairs toilet.

Chapter 11

THE NEXT TWO weeks passed in a blur of brown paper, string, and bubble wrap. I must have posted out a hundred parcels, but I'd still made no visible dent in what I'd taken to calling the "piles of peril" and Maddie had termed the "rooms of doom."

On the bright side, I'd paid off the arrears on Eleanor's utility bills, and now I had gas, electricity, and internet.

From the state of the cottage, I'd assumed Eleanor was technologically backwards, but when I'd spoken to the telecoms company, I'd found she'd had not one, but two broadband connections. Why two? Even I didn't need two, and I relied on the internet for my job.

The two lines undoubtedly went with the two computers I'd found in the bottom cupboard of the monstrous shelving unit. A state-of-the-art laptop and a MacBook Pro, both new, both expensive. I'd tried turning them on, but I didn't have her passwords, so I'd shoved them back where they lived until I decided what to do with them. Could I use one of them to replace my creaking Toshiba? Or should I try selling them? Trouble was, I had no clue what was on the hard drives, and I didn't want to risk flogging any confidential data to the highest bidder.

Maddie had mentioned a computer programmer on

a couple of occasions—a brother of one of her colleagues, or maybe a cousin. Would he take a look? I jotted a reminder on my calendar app to ask Maddie what she thought. She'd been due to visit last weekend, but last-minute work problems had meant I got a phone call instead.

"You know that promotion I got?"

Maddie had been made ward sister six months ago, and Edward had been miffed because I went out to celebrate with her instead of accompanying him to one of his work get-togethers.

"I'm not likely to forget. You got me drunk on cocktails right after you found out."

She giggled. "That was an awesome night. But the honeymoon period is officially over. Do you remember that other girl who wanted the job?"

"The one who calls in sick whenever she's got a hangover?"

"That's her. Anyway, she's got it in for me now. Her friend in the admin department does the rotas, and they keep putting me on horrible shifts."

"Can't you say something? Who's in charge?"

"Wish I could, but I need to keep my head down at the moment." She went silent for a few seconds. "I got reported for filling in a patient's chart wrongly last week. I know I made a mistake, but I was so tired I just couldn't see straight. Three guesses who reported me?"

"What a mean cow. Is there anything I can do to help?"

After the help Maddie gave me with Edward, I felt I should offer to unpick the seams on the woman's clothes or stuff a mackerel in her sofa cushions.

"I'll manage, but I might need to let off steam over

the phone every so often."

"Any time."

Aw, it was almost disappointing. I'd quite enjoyed the guilty buzz I got from my revenge on Edward.

"I'll visit you soon, I promise."

"You'd better. I think we both need a hug."

Even though Maddie couldn't make it, Dave came on his own and poked around for a morning.

"I've changed the fuse box and rewired the light in your bedroom, but apart from that, it's in surprisingly good nick."

"How about the oven?"

"Old, but usable."

Hurrah! At least I could cook properly now. At times like this, a girl needed cake.

I spent three solid afternoons cleaning the kitchen from top to bottom, and gradually, the years of grime receded to reveal a serviceable work area, at least until I could afford something better. The ceiling still had a yellow hue to it, but until I repainted, it would have to stay.

And painting came somewhere near the bottom of my list. There was still too much junk around for me to get at most of the walls, and I couldn't afford paint, anyway.

No, I needed to get my priorities straight. With the sale proceeds from one of the three hedge trimmers I'd found, none of which had been anywhere near the overgrown garden, I bought enough ingredients to make several batches of cupcakes. A morning spent baking made the house feel more like a home, especially once the delicious aromas began drifting around downstairs.

And while I couldn't deny I was looking forward to sampling the spoils, I did have an ulterior motive as I piped on frosting and added a few white chocolate curls. Once I'd packaged up the cakes neatly on paper plates, half a dozen to each, and added gift bows, I took them around to the neighbours.

Lilac Cottage lay second from the end in a row of five, although the large gardens meant they were widely spaced. Nobody answered the door at the house to the right, so I left the cakes inside the porch with a note and carried on to the other three.

At Woodbine Cottage, directly to Lilac's left, a lady in her sixties opened the door while I was admiring the outside of her home. Built in the same style as Aunt Ellie's place, nobody had skimped on the maintenance, and the neat exterior showed what was possible with a bit of effort. In short, it gave me something to aspire to.

"Come in, dearie. I've been wondering when we'd meet our new neighbour."

"I've brought you some cakes."

"Such a treasure. Why don't you join me for a cup of tea and we can share them?"

So far, so good. Inside, Woodbine Cottage had a real country vibe going with bouquets of fresh flowers and little touches like the antique boot scraper near the front door.

The lady led me through to a rustic kitchen, complete with copper pans hanging from a rack over the central island. She certainly had all the good taste Aunt Ellie had been lacking.

"I'm Olivia, by the way," I told her.

"And I'm Yvonne."

Over a calming cup of camomile, she told me more

about Upper Foxford. The village sounded as if it was in limbo, stuck between a time warp of retired people and the commuters gradually replacing them as they died off.

"So I'm an anomaly, then? Seeing as I plan to spend my days here rather than trekking back into the city?" Although when I thought about it, the lure of London formed an attractive option.

"Well, yes, but there's plenty here for everyone. The Women's Institute is having a fundraiser tonight for the local hospice. I don't suppose I can convince you to come and bring a plate of those lovely cakes for the raffle?"

Hmm, my desire for acceptance battled against the prospect of an interrogation from every lady in the village. Was I ready for that level of scrutiny?

No. Not yet. I just couldn't do it.

"I can certainly donate a selection of cakes, but I'm afraid I already have plans for this evening."

Her raised eyebrow said she didn't quite believe me.

"Uh, a conference call with a client," I garbled. "In the United States. It's been arranged for a while."

And now I'd have to pretend to be on the phone for an hour just in case she sent someone around to check.

"In that case, you really must come to our next event."

"Absolutely. I'd love to." Did she realise I had my fingers crossed behind my back? "Oh dear, look at the time. I'd better get going—I've got cakes to deliver to our other neighbours as well."

"I can save you some time there—Dennis and June at the far end are on one of those around-the-world cruises, and Samantha and Julian in between are commuters. They never get back until late on weekdays, and they're out most of the weekend. Honestly, they'd be better off living in town."

Apart from the insane property prices, obviously.

I ate the leftover cakes myself while catching up on web design work, and by the end of my first fortnight in Upper Foxford, that side of my life was up to date. I'd also begun making more money from eBay as more auctions ended, and four rooms in the cottage were pretty much habitable. Life began to get a little easier, apart from one small issue: loneliness.

I'd always imagined that if I moved out of my London flat, it would be to shack up with Edward. Despite the rawness I felt from his fling, I still missed him, or at least his company. I longed for somebody to talk to as I pottered around the house, a soulmate to curl up next to on the sofa while I read a book on chilly evenings.

Night-times were worst, when I had a cold double bed to myself. Would I ever meet another man? One who could love me even with those photos of my Taurus escapade plastered all over the internet? I was still getting messages every day about that, including one this morning from a Middle Eastern prince who wanted to marry me if I'd only help him to launder six million dollars through my bank account.

I was still moping alone on Friday evening when I heard a quiet scratching coming from the back door. The hairs on the back of my neck stood up as I grabbed the poker from its spot beside the fireplace and tiptoed through to the kitchen.

"Who's there?"

More scratching, followed by a plaintive miaow.

A cat?

I opened the door and a skinny tabby slunk between my legs, heading for a spot by the fridge and sniffing around. I recalled the tins of cat food I'd found in one of the kitchen cupboards. Could he be Aunt Ellie's?

"Do you live here, little one?"

He wove in and out of my legs, and I could feel his ribs against my ankles.

"Are you hungry? Let me find you something to eat."

He wolfed down a bowlful of Whiskas and a saucer of milk then stared up at me, eyes big.

"Do you want more?"

I opened another tin, and he ate that too.

"You're kind of cute. Do you have a name?"

I reached down to scritch his head, and he purred softly. He'd been surviving on mice all this time, no doubt. There were plenty of them running around in the garden, which was something else that gave me the creeps, and I could hear their little paws pitter-pattering around inside the roof too. The sounds had given me several sleepless nights before I'd worked out what the noise must be.

I'd never had a pet before, but there was a first time for everything, and a mouse-hunter certainly had appeal.

"Let's call you Twiglet, shall we?"

He mewed in response.

"I'll take that as a yes."

Apart from the mice, I'd had to get used to the ominous creaks and groans as the house settled for the night. In London, I'd tuned out the slamming of car doors, the shouts of drunken revellers, and my upstairs neighbour clomping around, and now the relative silence kept me awake. Apart from the occasional hoot of an owl or the terrifying screams as a fox caught its prey, nights in Upper Foxford were as quiet as the grave.

Twiglet did his best, but by the time another weekend drew to a close, I was craving human company. I couldn't keep running to Maddie every time I felt lonely. She had enough on her plate at the hospital.

So, on Monday morning, I pulled on my brave pants and ventured into Daisy's café on the high street, gingerly scanning the menu on the table nearest to the door. Oh, thank goodness—no celery porridge in sight. In fact, the light lunches looked delicious, and they served afternoon tea as well. I'd always loved afternoon tea with Edward, usually at the Four Seasons or the Savoy, but those places were well out of my price range now. Daisy's served a selection of crustless sandwiches with a scone and mini cakes for six pounds fifty.

And Daisy herself turned out to be only a year older than me, living out my dream of running a bakery with a few tables for patrons to enjoy her delights. She loved to stop for a natter too, which allowed me to find out more about the local area as well as getting out for lunch each day.

"I grew up in Lower Foxford," she told me a week later over quiche. "It's the next village but one, the other side of Middleton Foxford. You've got to give medieval people ten out of ten for originality with those names, huh?"

"Are the villages that old?"

"Lower Foxford appeared in the Doomsday book. If you take a walk around, there are some beautiful old Tudor cottages."

"I'll do that one day, but for the moment, I'm using every spare second to sort out the mess in Aunt Ellie's house."

"I heard she was addicted to online shopping. Is that true?"

I gave a hollow laugh. "Is it ever. She seemed to buy six of everything, whether she had a use for them or not."

"The postman used to complain she was giving him a hernia. It was him who found her—did you know that?"

"What do you mean, found her?"

"Dead. On the couch. It was a Monday, so she'd been there over the weekend. All swelled up, he said, just like a beached whale."

I clutched at my stomach as I ran for the restroom at the back of the café, and luckily, I made it to the toilet before I lost my lunch. Aunt Ellie had died on the sofa? The sofa I'd been sitting on? Hell, I'd even slept on it that first night. The mere thought of that had me heaving again.

"Are you okay?" Daisy passed me a handful of paper towels.

I wiped at my mouth, but it was a few minutes before I felt well enough to walk back out to my table. Even then, the sight of my half-eaten food nearly sent me running back.

"It's just the sofa..." I explained, and Daisy clapped a hand over her mouth.

"I'm so sorry. I didn't realise."

"How could you? I didn't even know she'd died in the house. Someone told me the ambulance crew broke down the door to get to her, so I assumed they took her to hospital and she died there."

"I think the ambulance was just a formality."

"I have to get that sofa out of my living room." The mere thought of it kept my stomach churning.

Daisy rose to her feet. "The lunchtime crowd are all gone now. How about I close up for half an hour and give you a hand?"

"Really? You'd do that?"

"It's the least I can do after the whole..." She gestured at the restroom. "You know."

Back at Lilac Cottage, we donned rubber gloves and stared at the evil brown monstrosity. I gave one arm a tentative tug, but it barely moved.

Daisy wrinkled her nose. "Even with two of us, this is going to be difficult."

"This sofa is leaving the house today, even if I have to hack it to pieces with nail scissors."

"Do you have two pairs?"

No, but I did have a brainwave. "I think Aunt Ellie had a saw in all the stuff she bought. I saw it a few days ago, if you'll excuse the pun."

I'd grown immune to the piles of peril, but Daisy's gasp as she followed me into the dining room reminded me just how bad they were.

"Holy crap! I mean, I imagined Mrs. Rigby had a lot of nicknacks, but this is unreal."

"It was worse than this when I first arrived. Hold on, I think the saw was somewhere near the window."

I clambered over a couple of boxes containing

George Foreman-esque grills, cursed under my breath as I stubbed my toe on a fancy plant stand, and emerged triumphant.

"Here it is."

"Isn't that a wood saw?"

I didn't know one type of saw from another. When we'd had to select our classes, I'd done home economics instead of woodwork.

"If it can cut through wood, surely it must be able to go through a sofa?"

"I guess."

Over the next hour, we sweated and swore as we sawed the disgusting thing in half, straight down the middle. Now that I knew that parts of the pattern most likely belonged to bodily fluids, I felt queasy the whole time.

Stuffing flew everywhere and one of my eyes nearly got taken out by a wayward spring, but finally, we got the whole thing into the back garden next to the tumbledown shed I'd discovered last week. I had no idea what to do with the sofa from there, but at least it was out of the house. I'd worry about the next step later. Over a glass of wine with Maddie, most likely.

Daisy glanced at her watch. "I really should get back to the café now."

"Thanks so much for your help, and I'm sorry it took so long."

She waved my apology away. "Nonsense. If I were in your position, I couldn't have had that thing in the house a moment longer either."

"But still... Thank you. I'll stop in tomorrow for lunch, okay?"

She gave me a quick hug. "I promise not to mention

dead people again."

I shuddered. "And I promise not to puke up your food."

"It's a deal."

I smiled as she hurried off up the road. With Warren and Daisy, at least I'd made some new friends in the village.

CHAPTER 12

THE NEXT DAY, someone bid six hundred pounds on Eleanor's TV and picked it up two hours later, leaving me with a handful of crisp twenty-pound notes. I celebrated by taking the bus into town and buying silicone sealant to fix the leaky edges around the bath. My life was just one big party.

A party with no food, because in the evening, I put my freshly made lasagne into the oven and it refused to turn on. Wonderful. Did anything else want to go wrong?

I shoved the lasagne dish into the freezer and pulled on my coat. With the money I'd made, I could just about afford to risk my taste buds at The Cock and Bull again and wash anything dodgy down with a glass of Prosecco.

I'd expected the place to be quiet like last time, but the car park was full and cars overflowed out onto the grass verge, and even outside, I could hear music and the low hum of voices. A chalk sign outside the door gave the game away—I'd forgotten it was Wednesday. I perked up a little. Hadn't Warren said the food was at its best during the weekly curry night?

"How does this work?" I asked a passing waitress who was balancing more plates than a circus performer.

"Pay a tenner at the bar, then grab a plate and help yourself to as much as you want."

"Where's the food?"

She jerked her head towards an archway on the far side of the room. "Through there."

The space looked packed, but I spotted an empty stool at the bar and decided to stop there for a drink first. I'd been on my feet most of the day.

"What can I get you?" Jean asked.

"Lime soda, please. I can't believe how busy it is tonight."

"People come from miles around. The chef used to work in Brick Lane, and his Indian dishes are to die for."

Brick Lane? How I missed London's premier destination for a curry. That explained the crowd, although I wasn't sure I wanted to follow in Aunt Ellie's footsteps and pop my clogs in Upper Foxford.

"Settling in, are you?" the man next to me asked, and I stifled a groan as I recognised Floyd from the supermarket.

At least I'd made the effort to use his shop so he couldn't moan, although on the last two occasions, I'd been served by a teenage girl more interested in her phone than the customers.

"I'm gradually getting the place sorted out, but it's slow going."

His animal-like chuckle would have scared small children. "Aye, I heard about the mess. Planning a bonfire, are you?"

"I wasn't, but now you mention it…"

"Thought that was why you had what's left of a couch dumped in your garden."

"I put it out there because I found out Aunt Ellie died on it."

"I heard that rumour too." He turned to bellow across the room. "Oi, Graham. Is that true?"

A red-faced man made his way over to us, clutching a pint like it was a life preserver in a turbulent sea. His gait rolled from side to side as if he were on board an invisible ship.

"What was that you said, Floyd?"

"Is it true old Eleanor Rigby died on her couch?" Before Graham could answer, Floyd explained, "Graham's our local policeman. Mrs. Rigby caused him no end of paperwork—isn't that right?"

"I'm not supposed to talk about that." Graham tapped the side of his nose. "Official police business."

"But this is Mrs. Rigby's niece, Olivia. It's only right that she should know what happened to her aunt."

Graham still didn't look convinced, so Floyd attempted what I assumed was supposed to be a smile. "Can I get you another pint?"

"Floyd Peterson offering to buy someone a drink? Wonders will never cease." Graham waved Jean over. "Another pint of bitter, young Jeanie, and put it on this gentleman's tab."

Floyd's plan worked. The alcohol soon loosened Graham's tongue, and once he started talking, he couldn't stop.

"Got the call at eleven on Monday morning when the postie spotted her through the front window, and that was a shock, let me tell you. Nothing much ever happens around here."

"Don't normally have much in the way of work to do, eh?"

Graham glared at Floyd. "I worked that day, all right. We had to break the door down to get in, and she was all swelled up in the lounge. Never seen anything like it. She wasn't small before, but I swear she was twice her normal size. Took six men to carry her out."

By then, a small crowd had gathered, and everyone grimaced at his words.

"But she was on the couch, though?" Floyd asked.

Graham's eyes struggled to focus. "She was. Propped up in front of her computers. The screen was frozen on one of them, and she played her last poker game just before midnight the previous Friday. She lost her gamble with God, didn't she?"

He laughed at his own joke while someone else muttered, "With the devil, more like."

Another voice piped up. "She'll be feeling the heat now alongside her husband and son. Bad apples, the lot of them."

Had Eleanor really been that awful? I considered asking what she'd done to upset so many people, but in the end, I decided against it. No point in reminding people that we were related, and besides, she was dead. You shouldn't speak ill of the dead.

No, a subject change was in order. "Well, it looks like the queue's gone down. About time I got some food. Can anyone recommend a dish?"

Twenty voices spoke at once, suggesting everything from a mild korma to a blow-your-head-off phall, and I made my escape into the next room to scoop aloo gobi and rice onto a plate. Finding a table presented my next challenge, but everyone seemed to be sharing, so I gingerly sat at the end of a large group who all seemed to know each other.

After a few mouthfuls, I understood why The Cock and Bull was packed. The delicate mix of spices burst across my palate, and I might even have moaned.

"That good, huh?" the guy next to me said. "Always good to hear a woman moan, although I'd rather she was underneath me while she did it."

Inappropriate much? The speaker was a man not much older than me, and an arrogant smirk tugged at his lips.

I shuffled my chair an inch or two farther away. "The food's tasty, yes."

"I can see something else that's tasty."

He ran his fingers up my arm, and I shuddered. He wasn't ugly, but his slug-like qualities weren't offset by the Ferrari key casually tossed next to his plate.

"Please, just let me eat."

"Oh, I will. I like a woman who knows what to do with her mouth."

I almost suggested he look for his type of woman on a street corner, but Mother would have turned in her grave. Instead, I tried another sideways shuffle and accidentally bumped into a brown-haired man standing next to me.

"So sorry. I didn't see you."

"Is he bothering you?" the newcomer asked, motioning at the sleaze.

"Uh..." *Don't offend the new neighbours, Olivia.* "Maybe just a little."

"Henry, leave the lady alone."

"She was enjoying it, weren't you, sweetheart?"

Delusional as well as slimy? "Not really."

My saviour took a step closer. "I'm not going to tell you twice. I'll have you thrown out if you keep harassing her."

Henry shoved his chair back and elbowed his way through the crowd, earning himself more dirty looks and a few muttered curses as I looked up at the man who'd come to my aid.

"Thank you."

"Don't mention it. Henry's got a nasty habit of behaving that way. You must be new around here—all the other girls in the village avoid him like the plague."

"I've been here for almost three weeks now."

"Well, it's nice to meet you. I'm Tate."

I forced myself to meet his eyes, and very nice eyes they were too. A pale blue, twinkling to match his smile. "Olivia."

"From Lilac Cottage?"

"How did you know?"

"News travels fast around here."

"I'm beginning to get that. So, you live in the village?"

"Not this one. I'm from Middleton Foxford."

"That's only a couple of miles away, isn't it?"

He nodded. "Just under two by road. If you cut across the fields, it's a little closer."

"Is it as big as Upper Foxford?"

"Slightly larger. Upper and Lower Foxford are about the same size, but because Middleton Foxford's in between them, more businesses have tended to gravitate there. So, we have the library, the doctor's surgery, and more restaurants."

"Perhaps I'll venture over there when the weather's warmer."

"Why wait?"

"I don't have a car at the moment." At the moment

—that sounded better than admitting I wouldn't be purchasing one for the foreseeable future.

"How about I pick you up one day? I can show you around both of the other villages, and we could stop for lunch on the way back."

Lunch? Was he asking me out on a date or just being friendly? I couldn't tell from his expression. Should I accept his invitation? It seemed like only yesterday that I was eating out with Edward, and I wasn't sure I was ready to step out with another man, platonic or not.

But then again, I felt terribly lonely...

Tate picked up on my indecision. "Relax, it's only lunch. There aren't many people our age around here, and we've got to stick together. The WI ladies hunt in packs."

A giggle bubbled out, unbidden. Apart from Warren and Daisy, most people I'd met were my parents' age at least, and Yvonne had already hinted I might like to join the committee of the WI to "bring in some new blood." Yes, I wanted to fit in, but I didn't have the time to organise the summer craft show and I was terrible at flower arranging.

And while I may not have planned on meeting a man in Upper Foxford, when an admittedly handsome one was standing right in front of me in a Ralph Lauren button-down shirt that showed a certain amount of taste, it seemed rude to turn down his offer. What did I have to lose? I certainly didn't want to spend the rest of my life alone, and at the very least, I could use another friend.

"In that case, I'd love to join you one day."

Tate tapped his number into my phone then called

his, and before he headed off with a group of friends, he promised to message me to arrange a time to suit both of us.

"Nice to meet you," I said as he turned to leave.

"The pleasure was all mine."

Okay, so that line was a little cheesy, but the smile that accompanied it was genuine. I left The Cock and Bull with a matching grin of my own, frantically cataloguing what was left of my wardrobe as I hurried home. I couldn't go out with Tate dressed in jeans and a faded jumper. Oh, if only I'd kept hold of a few of my nice dresses.

"Need a lift?"

I'd been so preoccupied I barely heard Warren approach in his taxi. Spots of rain dotting my decidedly non-waterproof jacket made the decision easy.

"Thanks so much. It's so dark without any street lights here."

"You should get a torch to carry in your handbag."

"I'm sure Aunt Ellie's left one in the cottage somewhere."

"Or just call me. If I'm not working, I'll give you a ride."

He'd already said that, but I'd feel guilty calling him out when I couldn't afford to pay. "It's kind of you to offer."

Lilac Cottage was dark when we pulled into the driveway, and I wished I'd been able to leave a light on, but the electricity bill would be painful enough already.

Warren drew to a smooth halt outside the front door. "Let me give you my number, just in case."

Just in case. That couldn't hurt, right? I handed my mobile over for the second time that evening and waited while Warren did his thing.

"You've met Tate, then?"

Oops. Warren must have seen the number in my messages. Was it me, or did his voice hold a hint of jealousy?

"Just now, in the pub. He helped me out when Henry was bothering me."

"Henry's an idiot. And Tate..."

"What about Tate?"

"Never mind." A long pause followed, but Warren still had my phone. "Look, I don't suppose you'd be interested in going out for dinner with me one evening?"

Now that... That definitely sounded more like a date-type question, and damned if I didn't consider it. Warren was the boy next door versus Tate's distinguished gentleman, and after Edward, a down-to-earth man did present an attractive option. But I still wasn't ready for that.

"Uh... The thing is, I just got out of a long-term relationship, and when I moved here, I decided I'd try the single life for a while."

"Can't blame a guy for trying, right?"

"No, I guess not."

"How about lunch someday? Just as friends. You can never have too many friends."

Another man, another lunch, and Warren had been so kind to me. Besides, the way he spoke, it didn't sound as if he meant tomorrow or even this week. "Lunch would be lovely, someday."

After I closed the door behind me that night, I leaned back against it and closed my eyes. So much for staying single—I'd gone from no men to two I quite liked, and that made me more nervous than anything else.

Boy, did I need to talk to Maddie.

CHAPTER 13

THE FOLLOWING MORNING brought an unexpected bonus. After a frenzied bidding war, a set of Aunt Ellie's sad-faced china dogs sold for four figures and the buyer paid right away. I stared at the balance for ages and even refreshed the page in case I was dreaming.

"Maddie, you'll never guess what just happened."

"What?"

"Someone bought those hideous dogs from the dresser, and I've finally got a chunk of money."

"Seriously? Did they have impaired vision?"

"I think they must have." After all, I'd have felt guilty offloading them on the charity shop.

"But that's it? For a moment, I thought you were going to tell me you'd met an eligible country gent with a Land Rover and room for a pony."

"Uh, that too. Well, I don't know if either of them has got room for a pony, and Warren drives a Ford Galaxy."

"Warren? The taxi driver? He asked you out?"

"Last night."

"Ooh, where's he taking you?"

"Nowhere. I said no to dinner."

"What? Why?"

"Uh, it was a bit awkward. I'd already agreed to go out with Tate, and I'm not sure Warren's my type. I mean, he's nothing like Edward."

"Wait a second. Back up. Tate? Who's Tate?"

"I met him in the pub last night, and he asked me out for lunch. Although it's not a date. I made that very clear."

"So what's this Tate got that Warren hasn't?"

How did I explain his charm and his twinkling eyes? I tried to think of the right words, but what came out was, "He was wearing Ralph Lauren."

Ouch. How shallow did I sound? I cringed inside and pictured Maddie as she smacked her palm off her head. The noise certainly echoed down the phone line.

"Olivia Porter, you've got to look beneath the superficial. The last thing you want is another Edward."

"I know. Really, I do. But Tate stepped in like a white knight when another man was bothering me, and the fact that he knows how to dress is just a bonus."

Maddie sighed, long and loud. "I suppose it's about time you met a nice guy. Tell me you didn't sell your Agent Provocateur lingerie?"

"Of course not! Who would want to buy used underwear? I certainly wouldn't, even if it was washed."

"Olivia, you're so sweet. Don't you have any idea how many men get off on that? And they don't want it washed."

"Are you serious? That's disgusting!"

"They pay top dollar, babe."

"I don't care if they pay in gold bullion. I'm not selling my dirty undies."

What would they do? Sniff them?

"At least that means you've still got something saucy to wear for Tate. Or even Warren. I still think you should consider him."

"Don't you ever give up?"

"Not often."

"It's only lunch with Tate. I won't be removing any of my clothes."

"What about his?"

"I'm not that sort of girl!"

"One word: Taurus."

I put my head in my hands. "Can we just not talk about that?"

She took pity on me. "Okay, okay. What are you going to wear? Do you want to borrow something of mine? Or shall we go shopping?"

"I don't have a lot of money to spare."

"That doesn't matter. Shopping on a budget is the story of my life."

Maddie had Saturday off, so early that morning, I printed off the bus timetable and braved rural public transport with my handbag and a "deluxe faux-leather multiway laptop case" with Aunt Ellie's computers in it as well as my own. That way, I could work on the bus. I'd forgotten to ask Maddie about her techy friend, but I figured I'd take them just in case.

Curry night at The Cock and Bull might have a buzz about it, but it didn't compare to an evening out in the West End. I couldn't wait to visit some of my old haunts and experience the delights of Oxford Street again. Even the two-hour journey couldn't dampen my mood. Not only was I going to see my best friend, but on Monday, Tate would be introducing me to what he claimed was the best spaghetti outside London at

Middleton Foxford's Italian restaurant. He'd originally suggested going today, but I'd had to give my apologies and ask him to reschedule.

"No problem. I'm free next Monday or the following Saturday," he'd said.

Not a grumble—such a far cry from Edward, who'd sulked for days if I asked him to rearrange a meal out.

Maddie was already dressed for a day of bargain hunting when I arrived, complete with sensible shoes and a handy umbrella.

"Good to go?" she asked. "Or do you want a cup of tea first?"

"I'd love a cuppa. And I don't suppose that computer guy you know might be around today?"

Maddie wrinkled her nose. "Vitaly? He went to visit his family for an extended Christmas break."

I quickly explained the situation. "I just want to know whether they can be made to work properly, either to sell or use myself."

"Vitaly'll definitely take a look. He loves challenges like that, but he's not due back until the end of the month."

A few weeks? It was a setback, but a minor one, and I had plenty of bric-a-brac to flog in the meantime.

"Can I leave them with you? I don't fancy lugging the extra bag back on the bus with me." My slim Toshiba would fit in my handbag.

"What, that classy pleather contraption? How many pockets does it have?"

"Enough that if I put my phone in there, I'd never find it again."

Shortly after our second cup of tea, we headed for Oxford Street, where under Maddie's critical eye, I picked up a floaty top and a pair of smart trousers in the sales.

"There you go," she said. "That's classy enough for your posh bloke."

"He's not *my* posh bloke. And I'm not even sure he's that posh. I only spoke to him for a couple of minutes."

After all, Mother had trained me to speak the Queen's English, and I certainly hadn't been born with a silver spoon in my mouth.

"You could also wear that outfit to go out with Warren. Just saying."

"Maddie, enough."

Mission accomplished, Maddie agreed to indulge my love of Japanese food by eating at a sushi place. I wasn't likely to find maki rolls or salmon sashimi within a ten-mile radius of Upper Foxford, so I had to make the most of London's restaurants while I could.

I was smiling as I climbed onto the last bus of the night back to the countryside. An evening out with Maddie always cheered me up, and even though I missed the city, life could be worse. After all, I had three new friends, a house of my own, and an adequate though unpredictable income. Oh, and a date-and-possibly-more with a hot guy. I'd deliberately downplayed the heat factor there so Maddie didn't get too excited.

And maybe, just maybe, the memories of Edward and Becki would eventually fade.

That positive vibe lasted the whole trip home, a long bus ride and the short walk from the bus stop to Lilac Cottage.

It lasted while I stumbled down the uneven path

and pushed past the rosemary bushes.

It lasted until I saw my open front door.

CHAPTER 14

I'D CLOSED THAT door.

I knew I'd closed that door.

Maddie may have made fun of my OCD tendencies, but they meant I always checked the house was firmly locked at least twice every time I left.

My heart hammered as I crept closer and squinted in the dim moonlight. Was it my imagination, or... Yes, the door frame was splintered around the lock.

A bead of sweat trickled down my forehead as I froze, peering into the dark hallway. Could the burglar still be inside? What should I do?

My brain screamed at me to run, and eventually, my feet got the message. I narrowly avoided face-planting as I tripped over a tree root on my sprint next door. Breathless, I jabbed my finger at Yvonne's doorbell.

The tinny sound of "Auld Lang Syne" rang out into the night, the best part of a month too late, and I uncurled my clenched fists as footsteps sounded in the hallway.

"Who are you?"

The man who answered the door didn't look thrilled to see me, and understandably so. I must have looked a fright.

"I'm so sorry for disturbing you. I live next door,

and I think I've been burgled."

His glower didn't shift, but he swung the door open wide enough for me to squeeze past him. "Well, you'd better come in."

I followed him through to the kitchen, where Yvonne was elbow-deep in the washing up. Her eyes widened as she took in my appearance.

"She's been burgled," her husband said.

Yvonne dried her hands and rushed over. "Oh, you poor dear. Did they take much?"

"I don't know yet. The door...open... I'm too scared to go inside." I clutched at the back of a chair as I began shaking. "What if someone's still in there?"

"Have you called the police?"

I shook my head. "I just ran here."

"Bob, don't just stand there! Call Graham."

Bob moved slowly into action, reaching for the phone on the wall by the door while tutting about missing his fishing programme.

"I'm so sorry I came here. I didn't know where else to go."

Yvonne glared at Bob. "Don't mind him. He always falls asleep in the middle of that show, anyway."

Graham's enthusiasm rivalled Bob's when he ambled in with a colleague the best part of an hour later.

"There's nobody there."

"But somebody was inside, right? I mean, the door was open."

The other policeman grimaced. "Not sure you'll want to see inside, love."

"Why? How bad is it?"

"Your visitor's left a bit of a mess."

My *visitor*? Good grief, he made it sound as if I'd invited the burglar in. "How much of a mess?"

Yvonne put an arm around my shoulders. "Why don't we all go and take a look?"

The tears came a few seconds after I stepped through what was left of my front door. A hurricane had rampaged through downstairs, leaving a trail of crumpled boxes and broken ornaments, knee-deep in places. Why had somebody done this? I'd tried so hard to fit into the village, and now my new start in life had been pushed under a bus.

Yvonne gave me a squeeze. "I'm so sorry, Olivia. Why don't you stay at ours for the rest of the night? We can come back here in the morning."

"But the house... I can't even lock it."

"I'm not sure there's much more damage they could do. Besides, Graham'll be wanting to fingerprint first thing in the morning, so we shouldn't disturb anything. Isn't that right?"

From the look on Graham's face, he hadn't thought that far ahead. "Right. Of course. Fingerprinting, yes."

I couldn't get the mess out of my mind as Yvonne led me back up the path. "I can't believe this."

"It's a bit of a shock, isn't it? But I'm sure the police will find whoever did it."

"Really? Graham didn't seem too confident." Or competent.

"He's not used to all this drama. Until Eleanor died, the worst thing to happen in years was a spate of missing cats. Although there was a touch of vandalism last year, and someone broke into an empty house and held a party, but everyone thought that was kids."

Yvonne's spare bedroom could have come straight

from the pages of *Country Life* magazine, with its comfy, overstuffed armchair and artfully distressed wardrobe. But as I huddled under the floral quilt, I found myself longing for my ugly room next door. Funny how you missed things when they were gone, wasn't it?

I barely slept, and I wasn't hungry either, but out of politeness, I forced down a few mouthfuls of the porridge Yvonne made me in the morning. My stomach rebelled with every swallow, and in the end, I put my spoon down and apologised.

"Thank you for everything, but I really should get back home."

Home. It didn't feel like much of a home as I scrubbed the remains of a bottle of ketchup off the kitchen floor. And the counters, and even the window. The burglar's artistic streak had come out, and he'd covered my kitchen with a variety of condiments then smashed every jar in the cupboard.

I said burglar, but I couldn't see that anything had been stolen. There was nothing worth much in the house anyway, but I found the watch Edward gave me for our first anniversary safely in its box at the back of my underwear drawer, and Mother's gold earrings were on the floor under the bed.

Could it have been kids? Anger welled up inside me. How dare someone come into my home and wreck it? Whoever broke in had been out to create as much mess as possible.

All my crockery lay in smithereens on the kitchen floor, and I found the contents of my wardrobe at the bottom of the stairs. In the piles of peril, random boxes had been opened and the contents broken and strewn around. My temporary livelihood, ruined. Thank goodness I'd posted those ugly dogs on my way to visit Maddie yesterday.

And all I could do was start clearing. My first thought had been to call Maddie, and she'd definitely have come, but she'd also have called in sick to do so. With her already in trouble at work, I didn't want to add to her problems.

I threw the remains of a plate into the bin, wishing I was aiming at the vandal's head instead. Although a shard of china in the eye would be too good for that scum. If I ever got my hands on them, I'd... I'd... Well, I didn't exactly know, but it wouldn't be pretty.

My phone rang as I mopped up a bottle of shampoo in the bathroom, and although I wiped my hands on a towel as quickly as I could, it stopped before I grabbed it. Tate. Dammit, lunch with him tomorrow had been the last thing on my mind, but I needed to cancel or at least postpone it. How could I get ready to go out when I didn't even have a mirror left intact?

I called back, even though I didn't want to speak to anyone. Mother's manners were blueprinted on my soul.

"Did you call?"

"Olivia. So kind of you to phone me back. If it's not too much difficulty, I was hoping to pick you up at one tomorrow rather than half past twelve. One of my colleagues has arranged a conference call with Japan, and it's not easy to get out of it."

"About lunch... I actually need to postpone it, I'm afraid."

"Oh?"

"I've been burgled, you see, and I've got rather a lot

of mess to clear up."

"Burgled? But this is the Foxfords. Nobody's been broken into around here for years."

"Well, I guess I'm just lucky." I struggled to keep the sarcasm out of my voice.

"So sorry—I didn't mean to sound unsympathetic. It's just I can't remember the last time we had a burglary around here."

Judging by Graham's reaction, he couldn't either. At least the forensics team had seemed competent when they dusted for prints this morning. They'd certainly used enough fingerprint powder.

"I understand, and I'm sorry for cancelling at such short notice, but the place is a mess and I'm at my wit's end cleaning it up."

"I'll come and give you a hand."

"No, really, there's no need for you to do that."

"It's the least I can do. I don't want you getting the wrong impression of the area. I'll be there in half an hour."

Tate surprised me by knocking on what remained of the door twenty-five minutes later. Surprised me because I'd been used to Edward's timekeeping, and when he said half an hour, I was lucky if he turned up in double that. Emails and phone calls always took precedence.

Tate's eyes widened as he stepped inside. "I know you said it was a mess, but this... I wasn't expecting this. It's outrageous."

I'd held it together up until then, but when he voiced the indignation I felt, I began shaking. Visions of a black-clad figure prowling through my home took root in my mind, and a tear leaked out and rolled down my cheek. *Hold it together, Olivia.* I didn't want to lose it in front of Tate, of all people.

But his expression softened as he picked his way through the debris. "You look like you could use a hug."

Despair trumped awkwardness as I nodded, and as I stepped forward, I tripped over a stray box and landed right in his open arms.

He held me while I sobbed, and when his jumper became damp from my tears, he handed me a monogrammed handkerchief: *TP.*

This was ridiculous, crying all over a man when I didn't even know his surname. I made an effort to pull myself together and levered myself backwards out of his grip, swaying slightly on unsteady feet as I tried to regain my composure.

Tate took me by the elbow. "You need to sit down."

"I don't have anything left to sit on." Both of my kitchen chairs had been left splintered.

"Have you eaten?"

I shook my head.

"In that case, I'm taking you out for a late lunch before we do anything else."

I tried to protest, but he pressed a finger against my lips.

"You can't tackle this..." He waved an arm at the hallway. "If your body's running on empty. You might not feel like eating, but even a little food will help."

My head knew he was right, even if my body tried to rule it with strong feelings of nausea. Tate half carried me across the hallway then set me on my feet next to the door. Only when I caught a glimpse of myself in the jagged shards of the hall mirror did I come to my senses.

"I can't go out like this! Look at the state of me."

His sweet smile would have given me butterflies if my stomach hadn't been replaced by a cement mixer.

"You look beautiful."

My cheeks heated. "I don't want everyone to start gossiping."

"We'll go to Middleton Foxford. Nobody knows you there. To them, you'll just be the pretty girl eating lunch with Fenton Palmer's son."

He certainly was charming. "All right. But I can't stay out for long. I need to sort out the bedroom so I can sleep in it tonight."

"We'll have something light, and the service is excellent in Basilico. You do like Italian food?"

"I love it." I went to pull the door closed and the handle, which had been hanging on by a single screw, fell off in my hand. The tears threatened again. "But I can't even lock the door. What if someone comes back while we're out?"

"I'll call a locksmith. He can fix things up while we have lunch."

Visions of twenty-pound notes floated before my eyes at the thought of Sunday call-out charges. "I can wait until tomorrow. I'll drag something up against it tonight."

"And I wouldn't sleep tonight from worrying. Our gardener's son's in the trade, and he'll come today as a favour to me. It's no bother."

I didn't want to be in Tate's debt, but at the same time, I hated the prospect of sleeping in a house where the only barrier between me and a possible psychopath was Aunt Eleanor's nicknack shelves. Last night, I'd destroyed half of the nails I'd managed to grow since I left London as my fingers found their way to my mouth in a reflex action, and I didn't want to chew off the rest of them.

"I'll pay you back as soon as I can afford it." He opened his mouth, to protest, no doubt, and I held up a hand. "Please. I have to for my own peace of mind."

I didn't want to be treated like a charity case.

"As long as you let me treat you to lunch."

That I could deal with, and I smiled for the first time since I found my home wrecked. "That's very kind of you."

I followed him out to a shiny blue Mercedes S-Class, identical to the one Edward drove except for the colour. Edward's had been silver. Tate opened the door for me, and I sank into the soft leather seat and breathed in the new-car smell. I'd missed that.

My appetite had returned by the time we pulled up outside the Italian restaurant, fuelled by Tate's charm and the feeling of safety that came from being away from Lilac Cottage.

"So, what made you move to Upper Foxford?" he asked me as the antipasti arrived.

"My aunt died, and I inherited the cottage."

"I didn't realise you were related to Eleanor—were you close?"

"I hadn't seen her since I was a little girl. When I found out about the house, I didn't even know where it was."

Tate tilted his head to one side. "Then why did you move here? Why not sell the cottage or even rent it out?"

I'd hoped to avoid that question. "The lease was up on my flat in London, and I couldn't find much within my price range what with Christmas coming up. Moving to Upper Foxford seemed like the perfect solution, at least until now."

If his clenched fists were anything to go by, some of my anger had rubbed off on Tate. "I can't believe the mess those scoundrels have made. If I hadn't seen it with my own eyes..."

"It must have taken them most of the day. Back in London, one of the neighbours might at least have noticed the noise and called the police."

"One of my colleagues lives in London, and a thief convinced the doorman of his apartment building that he was an interior designer there to renovate. The doorman actually helped to carry all the furniture out." Tate paused. "Sorry. That probably wasn't what you wanted to hear."

"Not really." I decided to change the subject. "So, what do you do at work?"

"I'm a lawyer, for my sins. I passed the bar exam last year."

"That sounds exciting."

"Not as much as John Grisham likes to make out. I'm in the corporate division. In reality, most of my cases settle before they get to court. Nobody wants their name dragged publicly through the mud."

Something I understood very well, and so, unfortunately, did Mandy Clark when she plastered shots of me with my dress around my waist all over Facebook.

"Are you at a local firm?"

He shook his head. "I join the happy throng travelling into London each day."

"Have you always lived around here?" I asked.

"My family's owned the Prestwold Manor for generations."

"You still live there?"

"Yes and no. My father lives in the main house, I have one of the cottages, my uncle converted the tithe barn, and my cousin has the old stables."

Wow—that sounded like some place. Posh. For once, I was glad my mother made me recite DeBrett's before each meal instead of grace. And I liked that Tate was still close to his family.

I smoothed my napkin over my lap and made sure to keep my elbows off the table as the food arrived. Tate had chosen the restaurant well; I had to give him that. My tagliatelle with white truffle shavings was the tastiest meal I'd eaten in the post-Edward era. Tate may have been forking his food down, but I forced myself to chew slowly, my mother's voice echoing in the back of my head.

"You'll never catch yourself a suitable gentleman unless your manners are impeccable, Olivia." She'd repeated those words over and over.

And while my head tried to tell me I wasn't interested in Tate, that it was too soon after Edward and I needed to settle into my new life before adding any more complications, my subconscious, the part of me that had been trained from birth to hunt for the perfect man, perked up her ugly head.

No! If I ever dated again, it would be for love alone, not because of a potential suitor's social standing.

But with Tate, maybe I could have both.

"Be quiet!"

Tate looked up from his stone-baked pizza. "I didn't say anything."

"Sorry. I'm sorry. I was just talking to myself."

He raised an eyebrow, and I gave a helpless shrug. Great. Now he thought I was crazy.

Mind you, he probably wasn't far wrong.

CHAPTER 15

A KNOCK AT my newly patched-up front door woke me early the next morning. At least, it felt early because I'd barely got any sleep, but when I checked the clock, it had gone eight.

"Warren? What are you doing here?" I pulled my dressing gown tightly around me as the chilly morning air drifted inside.

"I heard you'd had a break-in, and I wanted to check you were okay."

He did? But I hadn't told anyone except Yvonne, Tate, and the police. "Where did you find that out?"

"One of my passengers mentioned it. She said the burglar smashed everything up."

"Which passenger?"

"Edna Curry."

"But I don't even know her."

"Doesn't matter in a place like this. Gossip spreads faster than a winter cold. If one of the ladies in the village knows, they all know."

Marvellous. With the number of committees Yvonne was on, she must have told someone about my bad luck. Mental note: watch my words around the neighbours. Otherwise, I'd have no secrets.

"Well, the person who broke in made a huge mess, but I'm getting it cleared up."

"I wish I could stay and lend a hand, but Tuesdays are always busy with pre-booked rides. Do you want me to pick anything up for you in town?"

"I'm still working out what's usable and what isn't. Maybe tomorrow?"

"No problem. You've got my number—just call me if you think of anything."

Not ten minutes after Warren pulled out of the driveway, Tate turned up with a horsebox.

"Do you have the wrong place? I haven't sat on a pony in years."

Not since Mother made me take riding lessons as a child because all young ladies should know their fetlock from their forelock.

Tate gave me that handsome smile of his. "I thought we could use it to take the unsalvageable items to the rubbish dump. Better than making a dozen trips in my car."

"Don't you have to work today?"

"Sometimes, there are more important things in life than work."

Did he mean me? My skin tingled as he met my gaze.

"Besides," he continued, "my godfather's a senior partner at the firm, and when he heard what happened to you, he told me to take the day off and help."

"Is there anybody left in southern England who doesn't know about the break-in?"

Tate's smile turned sheepish. "Probably not. The Women's Institute holds its weekly meeting on a Sunday afternoon, so you can guarantee that the only people in the three villages who didn't know by Monday morning are either too young to speak or dead."

My every move being common knowledge made me squirm a little inside. I'd lived in my London flat for over three years, and I'd only known the name of one of my neighbours. And that was only because the postman kept getting number one confused with number seven and delivering me his post by accident.

But the close-knit community did have its good points. As Tate and I carted broken things out to the horsebox and put anything left intact back into its rightful place, people I'd never even met before stopped by to offer condolences or home-baked snacks. By the time the lorry was packed, I'd eaten so many cakes and quiches and sausage rolls I could barely move.

One lady had insisted on cleaning the kitchen, and another had done the windows. I felt particularly guilty over the latter because their filthy state was nothing to do with the burglary. Eleanor couldn't have touched them for years, and I'd barely been able to see out of the dining room in particular. Eleanor had worried as little about natural light as she had about salmonella.

By the time Tate drove the horsebox back to the cottage, it looked better than I'd ever dreamed it could, and we'd salvaged a lot of the stuff for me to sell. A stranger had even donated a pair of wooden chairs to replace the broken ones in the kitchen, and I sank gratefully onto one while Tate took the other. Through the now-sparkling window, the sun set in a blaze of pink and orange, signifying the end of one of the strangest days of my life.

And while I couldn't say I'd enjoyed the last forty-eight hours, they'd certainly turned out to be less unpleasant than I'd anticipated.

"Let me make you dinner," I said to Tate. "It's the

least I can do."

"I'm not sure I could eat another thing. I got through at least six of those blueberry muffins alone."

Same for me. Good thing I'd worn trousers with an elasticated waist. "They were rather good, weren't they? There are some spares left if you want to take them home."

"That's kind of you." He nodded slowly and pushed his chair back a couple of inches. "Well, I'd better be going."

"Stay for coffee," I blurted, then felt my cheeks turn red. "Oh, gosh. That sounded a bit dirty, didn't it?" A nervous giggle bubbled up my throat. Everyone knew what the coffee euphemism meant.

Tate grinned. "You're too sweet to think like that, but I'll take a cup of coffee. For now," he added under his breath.

I replayed those words over and over as I lay in bed that night. Or rather, what was left of it. My unwelcome visitor had slashed the mattress, but we'd flipped it over so it was still usable.

Had Tate meant what I thought he meant? And if he had, what should I do about it? After Edward rode roughshod over my emotions, I'd thought it would be years before I felt ready to spend time with another man, but Tate was so incredibly sweet. Edward would never have dropped everything and stepped in like that. Hired someone to help, maybe, but not got his own hands dirty.

And Warren? He'd been nothing but kind too. What if Maddie was right and I should consider spending time with a man more on my level?

The last thing I wanted was to get hurt again.

Red sky at night, shepherd's delight, red sky in the morning, shepherd's warning, or so the old saying went. It had certainly held true today. Last night's sunset heralded a clear dawn, the birds were singing in the old apple tree outside the kitchen window, and I had a whole bundle of things we'd saved to list on eBay.

I'd barely got any work done on the bus to Maddie's last Saturday because I kept getting distracted by the scenery, and when I got to London, I'd cursed about having the extra laptop to carry, but it had turned out to be a blessing in disguise. At least I didn't need to spend my meagre savings on replacing it.

With that in mind, I decided it was important to celebrate the small victories in life and headed to The Cock and Bull. Would their lunch menu be as strange as dinner? I could get to know the locals better and take advantage of their free Wi-Fi while I waited for my food to arrive, killing two birds with one stone.

At least, that was my plan. I spotted a quiet table in the corner and waved at Jean as I headed towards it, but she didn't return the gesture. In fact, she scowled.

I checked behind me, but there was nobody else there. That expression had definitely been aimed in my direction. And when I went to the bar to order fish and chips, she didn't say a word, just took my debit card and swiped it through the machine.

"Could you ask the chef to leave out the pea and chilli purée?"

"As you wish."

What had I done wrong?

My meal turned up twenty minutes later, slammed onto the table in front of me without a word. No cutlery. I had to borrow that from the next table, along with a bottle of ketchup. It seemed the kitchen had run out of plates too, because the fish came on a tiny surfboard and the chips were served in a miniature plastic bucket.

The story continued in the post office. Betty had been chatty for the last few weeks, but today she weighed my parcels without a word.

"Seventeen pounds fifty." She held her hand out for the money.

Why so grumpy?

I tried to put their attitudes out of my mind as I recoded a client's online shop in the afternoon, but when I caught myself typing "Betty" instead of "Checkout," I realised it was a hopeless task. At least Tate was still talking to me. He'd messaged me this afternoon and suggested we have dinner together tomorrow.

Just dinner, but my subconscious was trying on wedding dresses, my head was adamant we'd only ever be friends, and over both of them, I could hear Maddie's voice telling me to, "Get in there."

Until she met Dave, she'd gone through a man every month, and I'd secretly envied her ability to have a good time while keeping her heart intact. Would I ever be capable of doing the same? I very much doubted it.

CHAPTER 16

"ARE WE GOING to the Italian place again?" I asked Tate as I settled into the passenger seat of his Mercedes.

"I thought we'd head to my house, actually."

"Your house?" My pulse ratcheted up a notch.

The two of us, alone?

"My housekeeper's prepared us something for supper. Although if you prefer, I can take you to a restaurant. I suspect we'd get interrupted a lot with questions about the burglary, though."

He did make a good point, and I had to admit I was curious to see where he lived.

"No, your place is fine."

It was almost dark as we drove through an imposing pair of iron gates that hid a winding driveway from view. In the fading light, swathes of grass stretched out on either side, dotted with trees and the occasional statue. This wasn't so much a garden as a park.

Ahead, the outline of the manor house came into view, silhouetted against a full moon. The whole setup made me think of werewolves for some reason, and I gave an involuntary shiver.

"Cold?" Tate asked, and without waiting for my answer, he reached over and turned up the heater.

"Just a little." Better to feign a chill than admit to my wild imagination.

Tate drove past the main house and pulled up in front of a sweet little cottage around the back. Thanks to some artfully placed spotlights, I could see it was everything I'd hoped Lilac Cottage would be. Wisteria wound its way over the front door, wooden beams added to the period look, and a cherub balanced over a fountain in the middle of the lawn.

Tate hopped out and opened my door, then took my elbow to lead me inside.

"It's a touch on the basic side, but it suits my needs until I inherit the manor."

"Wow," I breathed as I stepped over the threshold.

He thought this was basic? It made Aunt Ellie's home look like a shack.

The interior was traditional with a modern twist, obviously decorated without care for the budget. In the hallway, a velvet sofa and cast-iron boot stand glowed under recessed lighting, and in the kitchen, heat radiated out from a proper Aga. Sad though it sounded, I dreamed of owning a range like that. They were the heart of a home. I could just imagine my children rushing in after school and pulling off their wellington boots before they stopped to warm their hands in front of it.

Stop! What was I thinking? What happened to not rushing into anything after Edward?

Tate pulled out one of six padded leather chairs surrounding the long oak table and gestured for me to sit.

"Would you like something to drink?"

"Just a glass of water for the moment, thank you."

As I took in every wonderful detail, from the old-fashioned copper saucepans hanging from their rack to the matching silver kettle and toaster, Tate set about getting dinner ready.

"I hope you like lasagne," he said.

My mouth watered from the delicious smell that escaped as soon as he opened the oven door.

"I love it. Can I do anything to help?"

"No, I'm doing all the work tonight. You need to relax after the last few days."

So, relax I did. Tate opened a good bottle of red, and seeing as he had to drive me back, I drank most of it.

"I feel guilty drinking three glasses full," I told him as we curled up on the sofa later. "Especially when you haven't touched a drop."

"We've got plenty more in the wine cellar." He paused for a long moment, reaching over to tuck a lock of hair behind my ear. "Or you could just stay the night," he added softly.

Even through my alcohol-induced haze, I could tell from his heated eyes that he didn't mean in the spare room. And I was tempted. The rush of heat between my legs as the words left his mouth told me that.

But it was too soon. After Edward, I was determined not to fall for the wrong man again.

"I'd rather take things slowly."

"Anything you want, darling."

He nuzzled my neck, his lips fluttering along my jawline until they met mine. His sweet kiss left me craving more. I pulled him towards me, and he gently parted the seam of my lips with his tongue, exploring. The sizzle in my veins tempted me to reverse my earlier decision, but the part of my heart that still ached after Edward's betrayal stopped me.

Tate held my hand the whole way back to Lilac Cottage, and at every junction, I bit back the words on the tip of my tongue: *turn around and take me back*. Good Olivia battled with my inner harlot over how desperately I needed an orgasm.

In the driveway, Tate left me breathless with another kiss before hopping out to open my door.

"I'll walk you inside."

Such a gentleman. If I'd had a decent bed, I might well have invited him into it, except as he dipped his head to press his lips against mine once more, something registered in my peripheral vision.

"What the..."

I pushed away from Tate, my mouth dropping open in horror as I took in the jagged hole where my front window had been.

Tate followed my gaze. "Good heavens. How did that happen?"

"I don't know. But it sure as hell wasn't like that when I left earlier."

No, ladies shouldn't swear, but under the circumstances, I forgave myself for being a potty mouth. My hands were shaking too much to fit the key in the lock, so Tate opened the door for me. It didn't take long to spot the muddy brick sitting in the middle of my living room carpet.

Tate drew me close and wrapped me up in his arms. "Shh, it's okay."

"Why me? What have I done?" I mumbled into his chest.

"It's probably just kids."

"People keep saying that, but where are they? I haven't seen any teenagers hanging around since I got here."

"They could have come over from one of the other villages. Stonystead had a problem with somebody keying cars a few months back."

I knew he was trying to make me feel better, but as we cleared up yet more mess, I couldn't shake the feeling of paranoia. First the burglary and now this.

What if it wasn't kids? After the way Betty and Jean treated me today, I imagined the worst—a vendetta to make me leave the village.

"Are you sure you don't want to spend the night at the manor?" Tate asked. "Even in one of the guest rooms?"

Tempting. So tempting. But you know that old saying about an Englishman's home being his castle? Turned out it applied to Englishwomen as well. Lilac Cottage was my home now, and I needed to keep it safe.

Even if it meant I was drunk with exhaustion the next day.

After lying awake for most of the night, jumping at every creak and groan from the house, I didn't even have the energy to make lunch. I stared at the kitchen counter for five minutes before giving up and traipsing out to the café instead. Putting one foot in front of the other seemed a safer option than operating a saucepan or a can opener.

Except when I sat down at my usual table, I knew straight away that something was wrong. Daisy's normally easy smile seemed forced, and it didn't reach her eyes.

"What can I get you?"

"Quiche Lorraine with salad, please."

"Coming right up."

She disappeared into the kitchen and didn't return until she put my plate down in front of me. On past form, she'd have stayed with me for a while and chatted, but she practically sprinted back to the counter.

"Sorry, terribly busy today," she muttered over her shoulder.

Really? There was only one other customer in there, and he was reading the newspaper. Was there something in the water? Why did everybody dislike me all of a sudden?

When the other patron left, I decided I'd had enough of being kept in the dark.

"Daisy, what's wrong?"

She let out a peal of false laughter. "Nothing! Why on earth would you think something was wrong?"

"I'm not stupid. Since yesterday, everyone's been treating me like a leper."

She approached gingerly and perched on the edge of a nearby chair, ready to run at any moment. Her posture reminded me of an antelope watching a lion.

"There might be a few stories going around."

Dread settled in my stomach like a dodgy curry. "What kind of stories?"

"About your life back in London."

Oh hell, it was the stripper thing, wasn't it? How many people had seen the pictures? Had the WI handed out copies at their latest meeting?

"I should have guessed. I suppose nothing on Facebook can ever remain a secret."

A flicker of confusion crossed Daisy's face. "Facebook? What's on Facebook?"

She didn't know about the photos? Then what stories had she heard?

"Never mind. What are people saying about my life back in London?"

"That you go after rich men and take them for everything you can."

"Seriously?"

"You've only been here for five minutes, and you've already got your claws into Tate Palmer."

They thought I was a gold-digger? I couldn't deny Mother had encouraged me to marry well, but our ideas of what constituted "well" had certainly differed. For me, it wasn't all about the money. There had to be love too. That was why it had hit me so hard when Edward cheated.

"But I didn't go after Tate. He approached me."

"People are also saying you faked your burglary to get sympathy."

"That's crazy."

She shrugged. "It's what they think."

"Look, I can see how people might think I only date rich men, but that couldn't be further from the truth. Yes, my ex-boyfriend was a banker, but that wasn't why I loved him."

"And Tate? Women around here have been chasing him for years. You've been here five minutes, and you're already going to the manor for dinner."

How did she even know that? Barely half a day had passed since I left his cottage! I couldn't even fart in this place without somebody sending out a news bulletin. Not that I would fart, obviously. That would be unladylike.

"He invited me, and since he's been nothing but a gentleman, I accepted."

"Tate deserves better than you."

Oh, the green-eyed monster was out in full force now.

"Like you, you mean?"

"At least I'd be interested in more than the size of his wallet."

"Well, unlike you, I know about the size of other things as well, so I'm one step ahead, aren't I?"

I shouldn't have stooped so low, but the words just popped out. And I wasn't totally lying, either. I'd felt it digging into my hip last night.

"I think you should leave."

Fine. I shoved my chair back from the table. "I've lost my appetite, anyway."

I felt sick as I half ran back home, and it wasn't just from Daisy's cooking. Did everyone else share her views? Did they all think I saw Tate as an ATM?

If so, how could I convince them I wasn't that girl? Yes, I could stop seeing Tate, but I liked him, and I didn't want to throw away a possible future with what might be the perfect man.

I'd come to Upper Foxford hoping for a happy, peaceful life, and instead, I'd been cast as a vampire after Tate's blood.

How could I fix this?

CHAPTER 17

THE NEXT DAY, the alarm on my phone rang at seven, and I shut it off and burrowed under the duvet. I didn't want to face the outside world that day. Or, in fact, ever.

A message from Tate at eight woke me up again. Apparently, he'd arranged a glazier, and Tate must have had some clout because the guy hammered on the door twenty minutes later. I threw on a dressing gown and ran downstairs, where I thanked him profusely as I made us both cups of tea.

"Made a bit of a mess, didn't they, love? Bloody kids."

Another who was quick to write my problem off. "Have you seen this a lot around here?"

"A couple of villages over, they chucked a rubbish bin through the window of the chippy."

Could I be overreacting?

An hour later, I had a shiny new window, and the man waved to me as he climbed into his van.

"Wait—how much do I owe you?"

"Nothing. All been taken care of."

"By Tate?"

"You want to hold on to that one, love."

Wonderful. Although I appreciated Tate's generosity, his gesture would hardly do much to quash my new reputation as a gold-digger. I wished he'd asked me first so I could have declined his offer.

Rather than risk the wrath of the village, I stayed home for the rest of the morning and listed as many new items as I could on eBay. And while rummaging at the back of the dining room, I found treasure under a pile of zebra-print onesies. A shiny red mountain bike had been hidden from view while the burglar did his worst, still with pristine tyres and plastic sleeves over the paintwork.

Why had Aunt Ellie bought a bicycle she'd never ridden?

Good grief, why was I even asking myself that question? The woman had also bought a set of musical garden gnomes, each dressed in a different coloured bikini, for crying out loud. That line-up made the bicycle look relatively normal.

My discovery meant I now had wheels. Slightly labour-intensive ones, granted, but I didn't have to rely on the bus anymore. A bubble of laughter escaped at my unexpected freedom.

Although I wouldn't be trying my new ride out today—the gloomy sky outside threatened a downpour, and the branches of the old tree outside the window scraped on the rain-speckled glass as the wind did its worst. The thought of venturing beyond the front door made me shudder.

Instead, as the heavens opened, I went full hermit and curled up in bed again, watching a film about guinea-pig commandos on the tiny portable television in Aunt Ellie's bedroom. For a minute, I regretted selling the giant TV from the lounge. If I had to live as a recluse for the rest of my time in Upper Foxford, the extra definition would have been a bonus.

The black clouds over Upper Foxford had lifted by the next morning, and after a good night's sleep, a little of the darkness in my mood floated away with them. It was time to try out my new bike. And the new gloves and scarf I'd found in the piles of peril, because it was chilly outside.

I turned left out of the driveway to avoid the centre of the village, only to hear the toot of a horn behind me.

"Need a lift somewhere?" Warren asked through his open window.

"Thanks for the offer, but I'm quite happy cycling."

"Quicker in the car."

"I'm not going anywhere in particular. It's more... exercise. I need exercise."

"Okay, well, have fun. Don't forget I'm always around if you do need to go anywhere."

I smiled, thankful that at least one person other than Tate was still speaking to me. "I've got your number."

His number and a whole lot of guilt, because I'd turned down Warren and then had dinner with Tate. I honestly had intended to enjoy the single life when I came to Upper Foxford, but what if Warren thought I'd lied? Stupid Olivia, always digging myself into holes.

After Warren disappeared off around the bend, I pushed all thoughts of men out of my head and spent a pleasant morning getting lost in the local countryside. The fresh air in my lungs gave me the energy I'd been missing, and before I knew it, I'd cycled through four villages and ended up in a fifth. Where had I heard the name Stonystead recently? I racked my brains and recalled Tate's mention of petty vandalism. If I hadn't been gasping for a drink, I'd have kept cycling.

The pub on the main road wasn't a particularly pretty one, but the barman greeted me warmly, which was a pleasant change after the last few days.

"Just a drink, or would you like to see the lunch menu?"

My stomach chose that moment to let out a grumble. "Maybe I'll just grab a snack."

Most of the food was fried—chips, spring rolls, scampi—but that came as a welcome relief after the snooty food at The Cock and Bull.

"Can I have a chicken-and-mushroom pie with chunky chips, please? Oh, and a lemonade."

"Coming right up. Haven't seen you around here before."

"I live in Upper Foxford."

He raised an eyebrow. "Slumming it over here, aren't you?"

"Why would you think that?"

"Lower Foxford's not so bad, but the folk in Upper and Middleton Foxford look down their noses at us."

"They don't think much of me, either, so I'll fit right in."

He laughed and gave me a gap-toothed smile. "Maybe we'll see a bit more of you, then?"

"You can count on it."

When I got home, pleasantly full, I parked the bike in the rickety old woodshed at the edge of the garden. It still had a small pile of rotting logs stacked in one corner, but now that Lilac Cottage had central heating, the remainder of the space was empty.

The piles of peril had also yielded a padlock and chain, and I secured the bike to a support beam then walked back down the mossy path to the cottage, cursing softly as I passed the remains of the old sofa. Why hadn't I remembered it when Tate brought the horsebox? I wasn't about to impose on him further, so now I'd have to put up with the eyesore until Dave came by with his van again. If I got lucky, the brambles might have a growth spurt and cover it up.

Next door, I heard the *click* of secateurs—Yvonne was out pruning her bushes. I raised my hand in greeting.

"Hello! Lovely afternoon, isn't it?"

She looked right through me before turning on her heel and marching back into her house. Great. She'd succumbed to the rumours too. I'd been having such a good day, but now my eyes prickled with tears as I pined for my old flat. I'd take being ignored by my neighbours over this outright hostility any day.

There was only one solution.

"Maddie, it's Olivia. How are you?"

"They've only put me on bloody nights again. I barely get to see Dave as it is, and I'm sure that bitch planned it deliberately. The administrator actually smirked when she told me the new rota."

Okay, maybe calling Maddie wouldn't provide the positivity I needed. "I'm so sorry. Could you try looking for a different job? People always need nurses, right?"

"I've started keeping my eye out, but what annoys me most is that I enjoyed working there until she came along. It may sound silly, but the stubborn part of me wants to stick it out in the hope it gets better."

I could understand it—that was how I felt about living in Upper Foxford. Although I didn't have the advantage of having loved it in the first place.

"I don't think it's silly at all. It would be a shame to jump out of the frying pan and into the fire."

"Thank you—somebody who gets it. Dave can't understand why I haven't left already. I can only hope that bitch cracks first. Either that, or I'll get sent down for murder."

"Don't say that. I'm sending virtual hugs."

"How about you bring real hugs at the weekend? Do you remember Valerie from school?"

"The one with the really thick glasses?"

"She had her eyes lasered and married a doctor. Anyway, she's having a party on Saturday, and I'm sure she wouldn't mind if you came as my plus one."

What would I do if I stayed in Upper Foxford? Sit at home watching an American crime series on channel five? I had quite enough drama in my life already, thank you, and I didn't even want to think about dead bodies. A trip back to the big smoke was just what I needed.

"Sounds great. I'll be there."

And for once, I was glad I'd be reliant on public transport. I could have a glass of wine and maybe a cocktail or two. I'd need them.

Little did I know that my alcohol requirements were only going to increase the next day. I did my eBaying—a sideline that was turning into more of a job than my actual job—then put on my leggings to take another bike ride. As well as the escape, I needed to burn off a few calories because my clothes were getting tighter. Granted, the pub in Stonystead wasn't the best place to get diet food, but if I ate a bowl of soup and then came straight back, I'd still be able to fit into my jeans.

But I didn't get that far.

"I don't flipping believe this!"

Nobody was around to hear my wail, but when I saw my bike in the woodshed, complete with slashed tyres and red paint daubed on the seat, I couldn't help myself.

It was a testament to how awful my life had become that I didn't burst into tears or run screaming. On a scale of wild rumours to nasty burglary, slashed tyres only rated as a minor irritation.

Instead of crying, I turned around, walked back into the house, retrieved my emergency bottle of wine, and knocked back most of it. In no time at all, I'd slumped over the kitchen table with my eyes closed. There, that felt much better.

A hand on my shoulder made me jerk awake, and I let out a piercing scream before I snapped my eyes open.

"It's okay, Olivia. It's only me."

"Tate? What are you doing here?"

"You weren't answering your phone, and I got worried. Even more so when I found your back door unlocked."

"I wasn't thinking straight."

He eyed up my wine glass. "A glass of wine? Or the whole bottle?"

"Not quite all of it." There was at least a teaspoonful left in the bottom. "But somebody slashed my bike tyres, so I think I was entitled."

"What? As in slashed them with a knife?"

"I guess so."

"You mean there's some maniac running around with a knife, and you left your door open? Anyone could have got in."

He kind of had a point there. I shuddered at the thought and found I had a headache. "I won't do it again, I promise. Please don't be angry."

His expression softened. "Sorry, I didn't mean to raise my voice. I'm just worried about you, that's all."

"No, you're right. It was stupid."

"I didn't even know you had a bike. Where is it?"

"In the shed out the back."

"I'll arrange to have the tyres replaced."

"You don't have to do that."

"Please, I insist. Shall I stay and keep you company this evening? We could get a takeaway, watch a movie..."

"I don't have a sofa or a television, so that could be difficult." At least, I didn't have a television in the lounge. I wasn't ready to invite Tate up to my bedroom. Yet.

"Then why don't you come over to my place? My housekeeper was off sick today, but it's still reasonably presentable." He gave me a cheeky smile. "I can take your mind off things."

Now, that was an offer I couldn't refuse.

Tate did indeed put on a movie, but I couldn't have told you whether it was a horror flick, a romcom, or a thriller. It might even have been a blank screen. But I could have described every contour of Tate's face, from his smooth forehead, to his perfectly straight nose, to his angular cheekbones. His lips, with their rounded Cupid's bow, were pinker than my cheeks went when he started undoing the buttons of my blouse.

He caught my sharp intake of breath. "Do you want me to stop?"

I quickly shook my head no. His touch took me away from everyday life. Well, his touch and the wine, and I relished the trip. Tate might have been clean-shaven, but my lips still stung from overuse by the time he dropped me home again. Despite his previous offer for me to spend the night, he hadn't got past second base, even though I half wished he'd gone for a home run. I'd need to sit in a bucket of iced water to put out the fire between my legs.

I clutched at Tate's arm as we walked down the path to my front door, praying there wouldn't be a repeat of last time. Tate glanced at the window at the same time as I did, and we let out a synchronised sigh of relief when we saw it was intact.

Tonight, I got more than a chaste kiss as he pushed me up against the front door and wrapped his arms around me, leaving me breathless once more. As he made me forget everything, I slipped my hands inside his shirt and ran my fingers over his chest, so warm in spite of the cool night air.

"Goodnight," he whispered as he pulled away. "I'll call you tomorrow. And don't forget to lock your door."

Words almost escaped me, but I managed to utter, "Goodnight, and I won't," in return.

I fanned myself as he climbed back into his car, and it was only once the roar of the Mercedes's powerful engine faded into the night that I came to my senses and unlocked the front door.

Prickles rose on the back of my neck the instant I stepped into the hallway. Why was the house so cold? I'd definitely left the heating on, and I could feel a draft that was never normally there. The curtains next to me wafted gently in the breeze, casting eerie shadows on the wall. I knew I'd closed all the windows, and I'd checked the back door twice as usual before I left. The chill spreading through the house and my veins told me that somebody had opened one of them for me.

I could hardly run to Bob and Yvonne's house this time, not after Yvonne's reaction to me yesterday afternoon, and I couldn't see the point in calling the police. They'd only send Graham, and by the time he arrived, whoever was here would have had time to bury my body and fly to a non-extradition country. I was still waiting for someone to take my statement after the last episode. My fingers trembled as I dialled Tate, and I cursed under my breath when he didn't answer. Of course, he was driving and would be for the next ten minutes.

I picked up a chunky china dog from the nicknack shelf and crept forward, inch by inch, brandishing the ornament in front of myself like a shield. When I cracked the living room door open, what I saw made me retch, leaving a stream of recycled wine decorating the already disgusting carpet.

GET LOST, BITCH

The words had been painted in foot-high bright-red letters, the same shade used on my bicycle seat. Drips of paint had run down the wall, and it looked as if the plaster itself were bleeding.

I dropped the dog and snatched up the heavy metal poker sitting next to the fireplace. Remnants of ash in the grate suggested someone had once used the poker for its intended purpose, but for now, it would have to do its duty as a makeshift weapon.

Fear gave way to anger as adrenaline pumped through my veins. I'd had enough. I almost hoped my tormentor was still in the house, because I'd enjoy sticking that damn poker somewhere painful.

My heart pounded as I threw open one door after another, checking every cupboard, nook, and cranny, no matter how tight a fit they might be. But the only evidence of the intruder apart from the wall art in the lounge was the open back door, its hinges squeaking as it blew back and forth.

I slammed it in a fury, and the house rattled. Thankfully, only one small pane of glass had been broken this time, and at least I was now on first-name terms with the glazier. I taped a piece of cardboard over the hole to keep the draft out and balanced a pile of saucepans on the floor behind it. At least if anybody came back, the pans would topple over, and I'd get some warning.

Cold and fear made me shiver as I climbed into bed fully clothed. If I had any more unwelcome visitors, the last thing I wanted was for the crime scene investigators to stand over my corpse and lament my poor taste in pyjamas. Assisted by the alcohol still swimming through my veins, I fell asleep clutching the poker close to my chest.

Just let anybody try to take it off me.

Just let them.

Chapter 18

I ROLLED OVER into something warm and furry on Saturday morning. Twiglet. He'd taken to sneaking into bed with me, and I didn't have the heart to kick him out. Hang on. What was that cold thing lying across my stomach? A poker? Why did I have a poker in bed with me?

Exactly how much wine had I drunk last night?

Enough, it would seem, because it took a good thirty seconds before the previous evening's events became clear in my mind. When my thoughts finally crystallised, I leapt out of bed.

Someone had been in my house!

And I'd been stupid enough to sleep there. I smacked my own head. That was it—I was never drinking again. Ever.

Shaking with every step, I picked up the poker again and did a sober circuit of the cottage. Nothing. Nothing but those horrible words on my wall, which told me it wasn't just kids messing around, no matter what everybody said. When I got back to the bedroom, all my false bravado subsided, and my legs gave way. Twiglet mewed on the bed next to me, and I scritched his head.

"I'll get you breakfast in a minute, little one."

Breathe, Olivia. Nobody else was in the house, and

I'd even blocked up the broken window. At least drunk me hadn't been completely incompetent, merely incredibly stupid.

Sometimes I didn't understand myself. Why hadn't I just called Tate again? Or better still, 999?

I rectified the situation as best as I could by calling the police to file a report. Graham made vague promises about doing paperwork but gave me no confidence whatsoever.

"We didn't find any fingerprints last time, so I doubt we'll find anything this time. Hardly seems worth sending a forensics team out."

Good to know my taxes were hard at work, wasn't it? "But somebody's been in my house. What if it happens again?"

"You might want to try and stop upsetting the locals. Keep your head down for a bit," he suggested, making me want to throttle him.

I'd hardly gone out of my way to annoy people deliberately, had I?

I sent Tate a text to let him know I'd had another break-in, but when he called back and offered to cancel his weekend golf trip to stay with me, I insisted he go. Having him change his plans would be yet another black mark in my copybook.

In any case, I wouldn't be at home for most of the weekend. I'd be at Valerie's party with Maddie, and Maddie had offered her sofa bed for Saturday night. I agonised over whether to stay in Upper Foxford instead, but if I did, I'd give the person out to ruin my life even more control. They could try to destroy my home, but I'd be dammed if I'd let them take my soul as well. I'd just have to hope Lilac Cottage was still in one piece when I got back.

On Saturday, the party was in full swing by the time Maddie and I arrived with Mickey in tow. They'd bonded on our initial trip to Lilac Cottage, and when Maddie mentioned on Facebook that I'd be in town, Mickey had invited himself around for a drink, and we figured he might as well come to the party.

"Valerie won't mind," Maddie said. "The more people who turn up, the more popular she looks. She even invited the checkout assistant from Tesco to one of her parties when he asked what all the wine was for."

As I wasn't going home tonight, I suspended my teetotal pledge for the weekend. I needed to have fun, and one glass of wine wouldn't hurt. Or punch, even.

"It's white wine mixed with Prosecco," slurred Valerie, who'd clearly been sampling the product. For most of the afternoon, judging by the lack of focus in her eyes. "And I put some fruit in too so we get our vitamins." She gave me a grin, then hiccupped.

I glanced down, checking she still had all her fingers. How she'd managed to keep them while chopping up the strawberries, oranges, and kiwi fruit was a minor miracle. I ladled myself out a small cupful and took a sip. Not bad.

"Is that all you're having?" Maddie asked.

"I'm trying to cut back."

"Why? Life's too short."

"I've done a couple of really stupid things while I was tipsy, and I want to avoid it happening again."

She bumped me with her shoulder. "Oh come on,

the strip club was fun. You must have seen the funny side of that by now."

I stared daggers at her.

"Okaaaay, maybe not. So, what else have you done? You'd have to have gone some to top that." Her eyes widened as her brain went into overdrive. "Did you do something with one of your hot men? Oh, tell me you did."

"Men? You make me sound like a hussy. I've only been out for dinner with Tate."

She rolled her eyes. "Tate? What's wrong with Warren? Tate sounds like Edward all over again."

"You reckon?"

"Rich bloke in a suit, happy to splash the cash when it suits him."

"Tate's not like that."

Maddie topped up my cup with another ladleful of punch. It was good stuff. And the more I drank, the healthier it was, right?

"You can't just give me that and stop," she said.

"There's not much to tell." But I couldn't help blushing.

"So, have you done it?"

She didn't hold back, did she? Mind you, she never had. "No, Miss Nosey, we have *not* done it."

"Why not? You need to have a rebound fling to get Edward out of your system once and for all."

"I'm not like you, Maddie." Although sometimes I wished I were. Especially with Tate. I'd spent more than a few daydreams imagining him wrapped around me.

"Maddie! Olivia!"

I squinted at the girl teetering towards us on

towering heels. "Rachel?" Another old school friend.

"Yes!" She thrust a garishly coloured cocktail into my hand. "Try this. We've been experimenting."

"What's in it?" I sniffed, but apart from a hint of coconut, I was none the wiser.

Her eyes flicked up as she tried to remember. "Uh... I don't know. But there's definitely alcohol."

She collapsed in giggles as I tried a sip. There wasn't anything *but* alcohol, judging by the way my throat burned.

"Just knock it back," Maddie suggested.

Oh, what the hell? I'd stop drinking tomorrow.

Sometime later, I'd lost my shoes and also my inhibitions. Plus, I may have dirty danced with two guys I didn't know then led a conga line around Valerie's flat. Mickey had been right behind me, and now I spotted him on the improvised dance floor with a blonde girl I didn't recognise. They only had eyes for each other. Aw, sweet.

I twisted an ankle staggering towards the punch bowl then gave in to gravity, collapsing onto a sofa between Maddie and Rachel before I'd managed to top my drink up.

"Did you see me?" I asked them. "I did the lift out of *Dirty Dancing.*"

Maddie choked on a laugh. "No, you tried to do the lift, and then three men caught you when the other one lost his balance."

I giggled uncontrollably. "I know, and it was *awesome!*"

"Are you only back for tonight?" Rachel asked. "I've missed you at events like this."

"Yes, just the night. But I'll try to visit more often."

"At least you're not with Edward now. He was the most boring man in the history of the world. You can let your hair down again."

"Boring? Did you really think so?"

"Everyone did, honey. All he ever talked about was golf and stock options. Nobody liked him."

Oh my goodness. They'd all hated him, and I'd had no idea. Of course, I'd known Edward had disliked my old friends because he told me at every possible opportunity, but I didn't realise the feeling was mutual.

"She's got a new man now," Maddie piped up. "Edward mark two."

"He's not more Edward. I swear. Tate's, uh... His hair's different."

"Bring him next time, and we can all check him out. Is he another wa...banker?"

I was still reeling from the fact that everyone disliked Edward. "No, he's a lawyer."

"We'll forgive him for that if he treats you right," Rachel said. "How is life in the country, anyway?"

Apart from Tate, it was awful, wasn't it? I'd drunk too much to try and sugarcoat it.

"It's all right apart from the two break-ins, the brick through my window, and everyone in the village hating me. Oh, and someone slashed my bike tyres."

Their mouths dropped open.

"*What?*" Maddie gasped. "You didn't tell me any of that."

"I didn't want to worry you. You were having problems with that nasty woman at work."

"I can deal with work. Liv, you're being terrorised!"

At Maddie's urging, I explained the problems I'd been having. "But nobody's tried to physically hurt me.

They seem to want me to leave, but what they don't understand is that I've got nowhere else to go."

"What are the police doing?"

I shrugged. "Nothing much. The local policeman doesn't seem too keen on actual police work. I think he probably wishes I'd leave as well; then he could go back to sleeping on shift."

"You should put in a complaint."

"Rock the boat even further? I'm not sure that's a good idea."

"What about Tate? I take it he's not being a prick towards you?"

"He and Warren are the only people still being nice to me."

"Do they know about this campaign against you?"

"Some of it. Tate helped me clear up after the first burglary, and Warren stopped by to check I was okay. Oh, and Tate had the tyres on my bike replaced. I didn't tell him about the latest break-in, though. I'd been drinking when I got home, and it seemed like the best idea to check the house myself, then go to bed." Maddie's mouth dropped open, her eyes wide. "I know, I know, it was stupid. You don't need to tell me."

She grabbed the remainder of my drink out of my hand and slammed the glass down on the coffee table. "You were right earlier. You're not drinking again, ever. Not if it causes you to risk your life like that."

"I think you're exaggerating just a little bit."

"You don't know that. Now, we need to get your problem sorted. I'll research the police complaints procedure in the morning, and if Tate and Warren are on your side, you need to tell them everything that's been happening. They can help keep you safe."

"What about a private detective?" Rachel asked. "I mean, if the police aren't doing their job…"

"I can't afford a private detective. I can barely even afford food." Especially because work kept getting interrupted by clean-up duty. Every time I had to deal with the aftermath of a break-in, it wasted time that I should have been spending on eBay.

Another old friend stopped behind us. Sophie and I used to sit next to each other in biology class and keep each other awake by writing stories. She'd write six words, I'd write another six, and so on until we'd filled the page. Hours of fun, apart from the time the teacher caught us writing a tale about him arriving from outer space on the back of a giant snail and gave us both a detention.

"Did someone mention a private detective?" she asked.

"Liv needs one, but she hasn't got the cash," Rachel told her. "Someone's trying to kill her."

Sophie's eyes turned into dinner plates. "Oh my gosh!"

"Rachel's exaggerating. I've had a couple of break-ins, and one or two other things have happened."

"That still sounds awful."

Maddie took over and told her all the details, sounding as melodramatic as possible. By the end of the story, Sophie looked ready to drive to Upper Foxford and beat people up with her stilettos. She clenched her fists at her sides and stamped one dainty foot on the carpet.

"That's horrific! You poor thing."

"I'm sure it'll stop soon. It's probably just because I'm a newcomer."

Sophie thought for a few seconds, then clicked her fingers. "I've got it—my brother's friend owes me a favour, and I think he's some sort of investigator. At least, the rest of the guys call him Sherlock. You know, like Sherlock Holmes? I'll get my brother to phone him."

"Soph, I can't afford to pay him."

She waved my protest away. "I told you, he owes me a favour. He forgot his girlfriend's birthday, so I dropped everything and spent the day searching for a last-minute gift to get him out of the hole he'd dug himself into."

"But you love shopping," I pointed out. All through school, Sophie had spent more of her time at the mall than at home. She'd been on first-name terms with most of the shop assistants, and I was sure I even spotted several of them at her wedding last year.

"Yes, but he doesn't know that. I gift-wrapped the present and everything. Bows, fancy bag, the works."

Before I could stop her, she had her mobile pressed against her ear, repeating my sob story to her brother. Somehow, she managed to make it sound even more tragic than Maddie had.

When she hung up with a look of triumph, I didn't know whether to be pleased or nervous.

"He's going to call Sherlock. Can I text him your number?"

I nodded weakly. Trying to talk Sophie down was like trying to stop a suicidal chocoholic from diving into a lake of hot cocoa. I'd learned that at the age of thirteen when she insisted on hiding out in the library instead of going to gym class and we got caught by the headmaster.

"Good. I'll arrange everything." She handed me my glass of wine. "And have this back—I think you'll need it."

Chapter 19

IT WAS ALMOST midnight on Sunday when I arrived home with the remnants of my hangover still knocking about inside my skull. I'd planned to leave London earlier, whereas Maddie hadn't wanted me to leave at all.

"You can have the sofa bed for as long as you need it. We don't mind, honestly."

"Lilac Cottage is my home now, Maddie. It's hard to explain, but I need to be there."

In the end, we'd compromised and she and Dave drove me back after dinner. Dave climbed out of his van carrying a tyre iron while Maddie brandished a can of hairspray.

"What are you going to do?" I asked. "Lacquer him into submission?"

She glanced down at her hand. "I could do. This is super-strong hold."

"Over here," Dave called. "The bastard's been at your front door."

The remains of a dozen eggs and a tin of red paint dripped down it. If Jackson Pollock had been involved, he'd have called it "Sunset over Olivia's life" and sold it for seven figures.

"The bastard probably had the red left over after doing my living room wall."

"How can you take this so calmly?" Maddie asked.

I waved an arm at the door. "Pah! This is nothing. It's like he hasn't even tried this time."

"You know I love you, right? Even if you are crazy."

I gave her a hug. "I know, and I love you too. Thanks for everything this weekend. It's helped just to talk about things."

"Don't ever keep a secret like this again, you hear me?"

"I won't, I promise."

Working on the theory that there was safety in numbers, the three of us checked inside for any evidence of unwelcome visitors. When we found nothing, Maddie insisted on waiting until I'd locked myself in before she and Dave set off home. She'd barely been gone five minutes when her first text arrived.

Maddie: Just checking you're okay?

The messages continued throughout the next day, on the hour, every hour. If I took more than two minutes to reply, I got a phone call.

"Are you still alive?"

"I was in the shower. Please tell me you're not going to keep this up all through the night?"

"You get eight hours' sleep."

"I'm rolling my eyes at you."

"Roll away. Eight hours."

Maddie kept her word. I got a message at eleven and another one at seven. I might have feigned irritation, but I did sleep easier knowing I now had four people looking out for me.

Warren had phoned on Sunday afternoon while I was still at Maddie's, and he'd promised to keep an ear out locally in case anyone mentioned the trouble at the cottage. Kids liked to brag, right? And Tate checked in just after nine on Monday morning.

Tate: How was your weekend?

Olivia: Great! Better than I thought it would be.

Mainly because I'd spent a good portion of it unconscious.

Tate: Any more problems at the cottage?

Olivia: Someone threw eggs and paint at the door, but that was it.

Tate: That's horrific! I'll arrange for a new door to be installed.

It was sweet of him to offer, but I didn't want to become his charity case. Nor did I fancy fanning the flames of the Olivia-is-a-gold-digger bonfire.

Olivia: That's very kind of you, but I've already scrubbed the worst of the mess off, and the door still works fine. How was golf?

Tate: Be sure to let me know if you change your mind. We had a couple of good games, but we hit turbulence on the flight to St. Andrews.

St. Andrews? I hadn't realised he was going that far. Edward had always liked to travel to far-flung places at the drop of a hat like that. How many more of his qualities did Tate share? If he enjoyed fine dining and going to the theatre, that would be lovely, just as long as he didn't have Edward's penchant for playing the field. I couldn't go through that again.

Olivia: Was Scotland cold?

Tate: Freezing. I've been looking forward to you warming me up. Are you free tonight?

How could a text message start my heart thumping?

Olivia: I'm around all day.
Tate: Pick you up at seven?
Olivia: I can't wait :)

I'd told a tiny white lie about my door, and I spent the morning cleaning up the mess. The eggs came off, but the paint was stuck fast. Rather than keep scrubbing, I ordered my own paint from the internet to go over the top of it—a lovely shade of dark purple to complement the name of the cottage. While I was at it, I bought a lighter shade for the window frames. They needed replacing really, but I didn't have the cash for that. Hopefully, they'd last another year with a coat of paint.

Then it was time for my post office run. I'd been avoiding the village as much as possible, but I couldn't get out of it today. I even considered cycling to Stonystead to avoid Betty's glower, but there was just too much to carry. Maybe if I had a rucksack or a bicycle basket, but neither had turned up in Aunt Ellie's stash. At least, not yet.

As it was, it took me two trips to take everything, which meant double the disapproving looks, and not only from Betty—the other customers in the queue stared and whispered behind their hands too.

As I cycled back, I reconsidered selling up. How much would Lilac Cottage fetch in its current state? Certainly not enough for me to buy a flat in London, and I didn't have the steady income required to get a mortgage. And even if I did decide to sell, who would want to view a house filled with tat? How about hiring a storage unit? Or...

I was so preoccupied with "get tidy, quick" schemes, I failed to see the man standing in front of Lilac Cottage until it was too late. Black leather jacket, black jeans, black helmet, black visor, and to top it all, he was standing next to a black motorcycle. The harbinger of freaking death had come to visit.

I skidded to a stop near the top of the driveway. Could I make a run for it? Pretend I'd taken a wrong turn?

Dammit—he'd seen me. He took a step in my direction as I pushed backwards. Should I speed off? I discounted that idea almost immediately—his engine versus my feet was hardly a fair contest.

Who was he? Had he been sent to warn me off? Or worse? A glance at my watch showed I still had thirty minutes until Maddie's next message, and my body could be going cold by then.

Oh, hell—now he'd taken his helmet off. I'd seen his face, and I'd watched enough thriller movies to understand what that meant. Was he going to kill me now?

I froze as he stalked towards me, and the bike clattered to the ground as my hands loosened their grip. Closer... Closer... He stopped two feet away and looked down from eight inches above.

"Olivia Porter?" he asked, his voice low and husky.

If I hadn't been so damn terrified, I might have found it sexy. What were the chances of him believing me if I said no?

Probably not good, considering we were both at my house. I gulped and nodded.

He held out a hand. "Nye Holmes."

I surreptitiously wiped my sweaty palm on my trouser leg before I put my hand into his. Hot, much like the rest of him. My skin sizzled, and for a moment,

I forgot my own name.

"Uh, er, Olivia Porter. Oh. You already knew that."

He raised an eyebrow, expectant.

"Should I know you?"

"I thought Sophie told you I was coming?"

Sophie... The party... I sifted through vague memories. Sophie had mentioned a private investigator—Sherlock—but I'd imagined a middle-aged man in a deerstalker hat. Not...this.

"You're the detective?"

"Who else?"

"Sophie didn't confirm anything, just said she'd pass on my number so you could call me."

"Well, she told me your situation was desperate and I needed to get over here ASAP."

"But how did you know where I lived?"

His look of pity had me doubting my own intelligence. "I'm an investigator."

Way to go, Olivia. Make yourself look like a moron in front of the hot guy, twice.

"I think Sophie overreacted a little. It's nothing—just a couple of break-ins."

"And this?" Nye pointed at the front door.

"They didn't get in the house that time."

"What else?"

"A brick through my window. And someone punctured my bike tyres."

"That's not nothing."

The shakes set in, and I willed myself to grow a backbone. It didn't work.

"I don't know what to do," I whispered.

"Let's talk about this inside."

Nye picked up my bike with one hand and took my

arm with the other, then led me to the front door. Guess I didn't get a choice in the matter. He stood close while I fumbled through my pockets for the key, but when I couldn't fit it into the lock, he made no effort to help, just watched as I demonstrated my remarkable lack of coordination. Finally, we got inside.

"Better go to the kitchen. I don't have anywhere else to sit." In all the stuff Aunt Ellie had bought, chairs were sorely lacking. "Would you like a cup of tea?"

"Milk, no sugar."

I fussed about, trying to keep my hands busy so Nye didn't see how much they were trembling. Teabag into cup, add milk, spill the sugar—dammit—wipe the mess up, add two spoonfuls to my own mug, add water, stir.

Nye watched me, silent, his eyes missing nothing. My skin prickled under his scrutiny, but I had nowhere else to go. The kitchen had never felt small until he sat in it. It wasn't just his physical size that filled it, although he was big. Rather, he dwarfed the room with his presence.

So this was how it felt to be stuck in a cage with a lion.

"Want to tell me what's been going on?" he asked.

Not really, but his question wasn't so much a question as an order.

"I'd only been living here for a few weeks when somebody broke in for the first time."

"Did they steal much?"

"I don't think they took anything, but there's so much junk here, I couldn't be sure. They just made a huge mess—broke things, strewed stuff around, emptied every bottle they could find, and smashed all the jars."

"That sounds more like kids than a career criminal."

"Which is what the police said, but there aren't many kids in the village. It's mostly retirees and commuters."

"What else? The message from Soph made it sound like a crazed mob was trying to kill you."

"Someone threw a brick through my living room window. I didn't know why at the time, but the next time they broke in, they left me a message."

"What kind of message?"

"It's probably best if you see for yourself."

I headed to the lounge for the first time since the night those words were written. Out of sight, out of mind, right?

Seeing the hate again brought all the horror back, and tea sloshed out of my mug as I stumbled. At least the stain wouldn't show on Aunt Ellie's ugly carpet.

"Easy, it's okay."

Nye took the mug from me gently and set it down on the coffee table. I was about to remind him to use a coaster when I saw all the other cup rings and decided against it.

He turned back to the wall. "Have you knowingly upset anybody since you've been here?"

"Everyone, it seems. Someone started rumours about me and they spread more quickly than pictures of Kim Kardashian's naked bottom. The village information network could give a bush fire a run for its money."

"What kind of rumours?"

"That I'm a gold-digger. That I only moved here to snag myself a rich man and take all his money."

"And is that true? Be honest with me."

I faced him square on with my hands on my hips. "How dare you even suggest that! No, it bloody is not. Yes, my ex-boyfriend was well off, and yes, my mother gave me endless lectures on marrying well, but that doesn't automatically mean I'm after cash."

"So, why would the locals think you are?"

What little fight I had left leached out of me and I sagged back against the wall, using it to hold myself up. "Because of Tate."

"And who's Tate?"

"I met him in the pub the evening of the first burglary. We got talking, and he suggested we might go out for lunch. I had no idea he was a rich lawyer."

"So did you go out with him?"

"I have been seeing him, yes. He's one of only..." I counted on my fingers. "Three people around here still talking to me."

"Interesting. So, would you say you've become dependent on him?"

"Not dependent, but he's been supportive. He understands that the rumours are just that: rumours. I couldn't have got through this without him. We were out together when the brick got thrown, and straight away, he arranged for the window to be fixed. I wouldn't even have known who to call."

"Well, at least you've had somebody looking out for you. Who are the others?"

"Others?"

"You mentioned three people."

"Warren, the local taxi driver, and the landlord of the pub in Stonystead. That's a village a few—"

"I know where it is."

Of course he did.

"And what's your relationship with Warren?"

"I don't have a relationship. He's given me lifts on occasion, and he asked me out for dinner once, but I declined."

"So you're a customer of his?"

"He's never charged me."

"When was the last time he offered you a ride?"

"He gave me a lift into town, maybe a week and a half ago. He said he was going anyway, but now I think about it, he was driving in the opposite direction when he first saw me."

"Have you seen him since?"

"Uh... Once, I think. I was on my bike, and he asked if I needed a lift instead, but I declined."

"So he knew you had the bike, then."

"You can't think... Not Warren, surely?"

Nye nodded to himself. "Let's go back to the kitchen."

He nudged between my shoulder blades to steer me in the right direction. Even when he took his hand away, the heat from his palm still seared into my skin. His touch was all I could think about when he sat down at the kitchen table and took a slim laptop out of his rucksack.

"I'm going to take some notes. I want you to start right at the beginning with your life in London and talk me through to the present. Don't leave anything out. Something must have triggered all this."

I took a seat next to him and leaned against the wooden back, trying to keep as much space between us as possible. The air seemed thicker than normal, and every breath was a struggle.

Only when I'd managed to get enough oxygen did I begin my story.

CHAPTER 20

FOR THE MOST part, Nye just listened as I spoke, but occasionally he tapped away on his keyboard. I thought I'd got off lightly, but it turned out he'd saved all his questions for the end.

"So, your ex. Edward. Have you seen him since you moved here?"

"No. I haven't seen him since he came around to pick up the last of his things one evening in London. I never gave him my new address."

"Did you part on good terms?"

I'd glossed over that part. "Not exactly."

"I need details, Olivia."

"Does it really matter?"

"Someone's terrorising you, and there's a fine line between love and hate. I need to know if there's any reason why he might be upset at you."

"Fine. I caught him at it with some floozy. Are you happy now?"

His face softened. "I didn't mean to upset you."

I sighed and looked out the window. Nye's steady gaze made me squirm. "It's been over for a while now, and Maddie helped me to get my own back. Can't we just drop it?"

"What do you mean, get your own back?"

Oops. I hadn't meant to tell him about that. I

shifted in my chair, measuring the distance to the door. Six steps, maybe seven. If I ran, would Nye come after me? Failing that, was there any way I could turn back the clock and erase, say, the last thirty seconds?

He tapped his fingers on the table. Guess not.

"We, er, went into his house and did a few things."

"What sort of things, Olivia?"

Why was it that when he called me by my name, I felt like a five-year-old getting told off by the teacher?

I gave Nye a quick précis—eggs, glitter, hair remover, chilli—and his eyes widened in surprise. So he was capable of emotion, then.

"Remind me not to get on your bad side. I think we can add Edward to the list of suspects. That little lot would be enough to get anybody riled up."

Oh, sugar. Could this nightmare be my fault? I'd been so hell bent on revenge, I never stopped to think about the consequences.

"I'm going to need all the details you've got on Edward. Where he lives, where he works, who his friends are," Nye continued.

"I'll write everything down."

"I'll also need a list of everyone you've come across in the village. If someone's got a grudge against you, there's every chance you've interacted with them at some point, even if it didn't seem important at the time."

Nye jotted down the names as I walked through my time in the village, starting with my first visit to The Cock and Bull.

"There's Jean, the barmaid in the pub, and I met Warren there too. Then Floyd in the grocery store, who's always been a bit grumpy, but I think that's just his manner. And Betty from the post office, but she's at least seventy years old."

"Who else?"

"Daisy in the café. She was friendly at first, but then she turned after the rumours started. Same for Bob and Yvonne next door. A whole bunch of people came round to help tidy after the first burglary, but I didn't even get most of their names. Yvonne might know. She was here part of the time."

"I'll ask her."

"I went to the pub again, and that's the night I met Tate. He stepped in when another man made inappropriate comments. Henry. And Graham the policeman was also there. Anyone else I've met, I only made small talk with."

And that was it, my sad life reduced to a series of interactions, many of them insignificant or unpleasant. Hearing myself talk through them out loud made me wonder once again why I hadn't run for the hills.

Nye typed a couple more sentences, then looked up. "That's a good start."

"Is it? Half of those people are pensioners or girls."

"Women can do every bit as much damage as men."

"Really?"

"You'd better believe it." He paused, focusing on the screen in front of him. "Well, this is interesting."

"What? Did you find something?"

"I'm not sure. A load of the residents of the three Foxfords have files on our system, but they're all sealed. I've never seen anything like this before."

"Who sealed them?"

"One of the directors at the company I work for."

A company? I realised I knew next to nothing about

him. "I assumed you worked alone. Or perhaps you had an assistant. Like..."

"Don't even mention Sherlock Holmes. Please. I've heard every joke in the book, and it's worn thin now."

"Okay, er, I just don't know any other private investigators."

"I work for Blackwood Security. It's one of the largest security and investigation firms in the world. I'm not a lone wolf."

Phew. At least he wasn't some cowboy. "What do the sealed files mean?"

His mouth set in a hard line. "It means we've looked at these people before, but I don't know why. I'll try to find out. But in the meantime, can I have a look around?"

"Of course."

I followed him as he poked and prodded his way through the house. He whistled as he saw what was left of the piles of peril.

"Holy shit. That's a lot of...shit."

I had to agree with him, even if he'd put it rather crudely. "My aunt was a bit of a hoarder, it seems. I've been selling it as quickly as I can. I was going to use the money to modernise the place, but I've ended up spending it on repairs instead."

In my bedroom, I blushed as Nye opened the wardrobe and stared at my clothes. Tell me he didn't plan on checking my underwear drawer too? I breathed a sigh of relief when he headed downstairs, through the kitchen, and out into the garden.

Our first stop was the woodshed, where he picked up the chain and padlock still attached to the support.

"You can't keep your bike in here anymore."

"I know that. I've been wheeling it into the hallway for the last few nights."

Nye shoved his way through the undergrowth around the perimeter with me tripping along behind. Then it was back to the house.

"Your security's terrible. I'll get a man in to sort out decent locks for your doors and windows. And you should stay out of the garden until we've got to the bottom of this. It's too secluded."

"I can't afford new locks at the moment." If I could, I'd have bought them already.

"People owe me favours."

"It's not fair to ask you to do that. I owe you already for coming at all."

"You're not asking. I'm telling you—you're getting new locks. And you don't owe me anything. Coming out here was a favour to Soph."

Before I got the chance to protest further, his phone buzzed. He fished it out of his pocket and checked the screen.

"This is the call I've been waiting for. I'll be back in a minute."

Obviously, I wasn't to be privy to whatever he needed to discuss. I paced the kitchen as he did the same outside the window, up and down in front of the old apple tree. How could I repay him for the security improvements he insisted on making? First Tate, now Nye—I hated being a charity case.

Five minutes later, chilled air flooded in as Nye came back. He kept the phone tucked between his ear and shoulder as he sat in front of his laptop.

"Okay, I've got access now. Put you on speaker?"

The answer must have been yes, because he did just

that, placing the phone down on the table.

"Olivia, this is Emmy. She works at Blackwood, and it turns out she lived in Lower Foxford briefly a year or so ago. She's going to try and help us out."

"Hi." I hated speaking to strangers on the phone.

A well-spoken voice filled the room, the accent British with a faint American twang, soft yet exuding authority. "Some of the things I'll say aren't public knowledge, so I'd appreciate if they didn't go any further."

"Of course."

"So, I hear you've been having a few problems with the delightful citizens of Upper Foxford?"

"They don't seem very fond of me."

Her hearty laugh was unexpected. "Don't worry about it. I got declared persona non grata when I lived there too. Let me guess, you're dating an eligible bachelor?"

"How did you know?"

"Happened to me as well. Now, let's go through your questions. I'll tell you what I know."

Nye took over. "Right, for starters, we've got a guy called Henry."

"Ah, the village sleaze. Slimy as you like, thinks he's God's gift?"

"That's him," I said. "He drives a Ferrari."

"He's an arrogant fuck, but he's harmless for the most part. If he gives you any trouble, knee him in the crown jewels. He shuts up then."

I couldn't help giggling. "You didn't?"

"I did. He steered clear of me after that."

I still wasn't sure whether to believe her, but just thinking about Henry getting his comeuppance made me smile.

"Why are there system files on so many people in the three villages?" Nye asked.

"A while back, a friend of mine got kidnapped from Lower Foxford, and I threw a lot of resources at the problem. Part of that involved basic workups on most of the locals."

"Where's the kidnapper now? Could this be connected?"

"Rotting in jail, and he won't be getting out. I've unsealed everything else in case it helps, but I'm not sure you'll find much that's relevant. Most of it was targeted towards that one particular case—alibis, family connections, fingerprints, that sort of thing."

"You never know. Do you have any contacts around here? Police?"

"The neighbourhood cops are fucking useless. But locals? Hmm... They don't like strangers in Upper Foxford. The villagers get very protective of their own. Middleton and Lower Foxford aren't so bad from what I remember. I'd try speaking to Carol. She runs a bed and breakfast in Lower Foxford, she's chairwoman of the Women's Institute, and she's one of the main branches on the gossip tree. If she doesn't know something, it's probably not important. The biggest difficulty will be sorting out the facts from fiction and exaggeration."

"Rumours are already going around about me," I said.

"And believe me, Carol will have been instrumental in spreading them. When you speak to her, don't tell her anything that you don't want broadcast for a ten-mile radius by the next day. And if she offers you cake, my advice is to eat it. She's a fantastic cook."

"Will she be willing to talk us?" Nye asked.

"She'd talk to a shop mannequin if she didn't have her glasses on. Your problem will be getting her to stop. I still know someone who's a native of Lower Foxford, though. I'll get him to give Carol a call and let her know you're coming."

"Thanks, Ems, much appreciated."

"No problem. Give me a shout if you need anything else."

Nye hung up and scrubbed a hand through his mahogany-coloured hair, leaving it gorgeously messy. *Dammit, concentrate on the task at hand, Olivia.*

"Emmy didn't really hurt Henry, did she?"

"Knowing her, it's extremely likely."

"I feel I should bake her a cake or something."

"She'd love that. Emmy's got a sweet tooth and a militant nutritionist, and they're constantly battling over the amount of junk she eats."

"If I ever meet her, I'll be sure to take cookies."

He chuckled. "I need to work this evening, but I'll come back tomorrow morning, and we can speak to Carol."

"You're going to work? At this time?"

He shrugged. "Yeah."

"But it's almost five o'clock."

"Scum doesn't keep office hours."

"Is it safe, going after those kinds of people?"

"I'm careful."

"What about dinner? Aren't you hungry?"

"I'll pick something up."

"I can make you a sandwich if you like? It's the least I can do."

He looked as if he was about to say no, but then he shrugged again and one corner of his lips flickered. "Thanks. That'd be good."

I needed to do a grocery shop, but there was enough in the fridge for cheese-and-ham sandwiches, and I set them out on a plate with crisps and two big slabs of my own-recipe flapjack. Nye devoured the lot in record time.

"Would you like some more flapjacks to take with you?" I asked.

"Do you have spare?"

For Nye? I'd give him every sweet treat I had to see that half-smile again. "I'll bag them up."

Outside the cottage, Nye settled astride his sporty beast of a bike, and the roar when he started it up turned my insides into a tumble drier, all hot and churny.

He hesitated, helmet in hand. "I don't like leaving you alone here. I'll have a car do a drive-by a couple of times overnight, just to keep an eye."

"I'm going to Tate's this evening. I won't be back until late."

A black look flashed across his face, but it was only for a second, and I could have imagined it.

"Just be careful, okay?"

"I will, I promise."

CHAPTER 21

I THOUGHT TATE would be happy when I told him I'd got a private investigator looking into my problem, but it turned out I was wrong. As usual.

"Don't you think bringing in another stranger might antagonise people in the village further?"

I hadn't considered that angle. "I suppose. But I couldn't keep doing nothing, and it would have been difficult to turn down his offer of help."

Like with the locks, I got the impression that Nye would have ignored the request. He certainly seemed headstrong.

"What do you mean, offer of help? You didn't call him initially?"

"Not exactly. He's a friend of a friend, and she sent him round."

"So some strange old man showed up at your door, and you just let him in, no questions asked?"

"That's not how it was." Okay, that's exactly how it was. I'd been too busy looking at his face to even ask for ID. Okay, drooling. Drooling at his face. "He's not even old."

Tate huffed and gritted his teeth, raising his eyes to his living room ceiling. "That makes it worse. What are his credentials? How many cases has he solved? If he's young, I bet it's not many."

"I don't know."

"You need to be more careful, Olivia. If you feel the need to engage a private detective, I strongly suggest you go down the route of getting recommendations and go from there."

Tate was right. Of course he was right. But I didn't have the money to hire anyone else, and even if I did, it would make me look terribly ungrateful after Sophie and Nye stepped in to help. I made a mental note to call Sophie and ask a bit more about him, though. Hopefully, she could reassure me that he wasn't totally incompetent.

Tate still hadn't unclenched his jaw, and I hated being on the receiving end of his disapproval.

"How about I make us both dinner?" I suggested. "I love to cook."

Anything to break the tension.

That earned me a smile. "That would be lovely, darling. I'll show you where things are in the kitchen."

While Tate disappeared to make some phone calls, I whipped up salmon en croute and a crunchy salad. His kitchen had everything a budding chef could possibly desire, and the layout worked beautifully too. I'd got lost in a fantasy of running my own boutique bakery there by the time Tate came back.

"Smells fantastic. Do you need a hand to carry things through to the dining room?"

I gestured at the more convenient table for six at the end of the kitchen. "You don't eat in here?"

"Rarely. The dining room's so much more civilised, don't you think?"

Dining room tables would forever remind me of Edward and his indiscretions, but I forced a smile.

"Certainly. I'll take everything through."

Tate's icy mood thawed over dinner, and he did help me lug all the dishes back to the kitchen afterwards. Once we'd loaded the dishwasher, he wrapped both arms around me and nuzzled my neck.

"Are you sure you don't want to stay here tonight?"

The row of kisses he fluttered across my cheek made me melt inside, and temptation almost got the better of me. But then I remembered Nye and his promise to check on Lilac Cottage overnight. If I arrived home in the early hours, everyone would know exactly what I'd been up to.

"I'll have to take a rain check. I really should get back."

The hurt in his eyes almost made me change my mind, but as well as the possibility of looking like a cheap tart, I knew deep down I wasn't ready to commit to Tate yet. I wanted to go into my next relationship with my eyes open and my heart protected. Tate could be The One, but I needed to make sure before I gave myself to him.

He dropped me home with a promise to call the next day, and I ran to the front door, fearful of the shadows dancing in the garden. The countryside may have looked idyllic during the daytime, but at night, the trees and bushes turned it into the set of a horror movie.

My phone buzzed as I clicked the door closed behind me, and I jumped out of my skin. Tate already?

Nope.

Unknown: Car sorted to check your place tonight. Black Jeep Cherokee. Nye.

He'd kept his word. I quickly added his number to

my phone and resisted the urge to put it on speed dial. Being in the same room as Nye made my pulse race, not just because he was kind of scary, but because I didn't need that complication right now.

The Jeep woke me up three times as it rolled down the driveway, paused for a few minutes, then drove away again. Once, a man climbed out and did a circuit of the cottage. The headlights cast eerie patterns on my bedroom ceiling as they came and went, and each time, I hopped out of bed to check it was the right vehicle.

I should have slept more easily, knowing Blackwood was keeping an eye on me, but when my alarm finally went off, I still felt drained. The roar of Nye's motorbike engine just after eight did nothing to help my tiredness.

I'd made it as far as the kitchen, and I was about to lever myself out of one of the chairs to fetch my dressing gown when he appeared in the doorway.

I did a pretty convincing impression of a goldfish. "How did you get in? I know I locked the door."

I'd checked it three times instead of two before I crawled into bed and once more in the night.

He gave me a grin, the first I'd seen from him. It transformed his face from surly into heart-stopping. Literally. He'd better not do that too often.

"You did. I was just making the point that your lock's shit. A child could get past it."

"Thanks. That makes me feel so much better."

"My guy's coming to upgrade it the day after tomorrow. He couldn't make it any sooner."

That was a small comfort. "I really appreciate it."

Nye grabbed an apple out of the fruit bowl and started munching on it. "Ready to visit Carol?"

He smirked as he said it, and I looked down at my bunny pyjamas. "Do I look ready?"

"I've seen worse. Remember the onesie fad?"

"I couldn't possibly forget—Aunt Ellie's got a bunch of them downstairs. I'll wear the pyjamas if you fancy dressing up as a zebra. I'm sure there's one in your size."

"Reckon I'm more of a lion."

Yes, he was. Majestic, predatory, kind of scary.

"Well then, I'm changing, but I need a shower first. How come you're even awake? I thought you were working last night."

He shrugged. "I got a couple of hours' sleep. It's enough."

People like that made me feel so inadequate. I dashed up the stairs, determined not to keep him waiting for long.

"Wear jeans," he shouted as my foot hit the landing.

"Why?"

"How were you planning on getting to Lower Foxford?"

Uh, I hadn't thought that far ahead. We only had one push bike between us, so that left walking, the bus, or...Nye's motorcycle.

"Your bike? You want me to ride on the back of your bike?"

"Beats walking. Make sure you wear warm clothes."

The thought of getting on that two-wheeled beast terrified me. Maybe I could splash out on a taxi? I had Warren's number handy, and he did say to call him if I needed help. I'd say this qualified. Yes, that was a good plan. I'd just explain to Nye that I'd come up with an alternative solution.

Except when I finished my ablutions, changed, and hurried downstairs, he held out a leather jacket to me.

"Here—I borrowed this for you to wear. It should fit."

He'd gone to all that trouble? If that was the case, I could hardly insult him by refusing to go, could I? Plus the part of me that still wished to maintain a scrap of dignity didn't want to admit I was scared, either.

Nye held out the jacket, and I slipped my arms into it. He was right—it fitted perfectly, probably because it was a ladies' cut. Who did it belong to? His girlfriend? Did she mind that he'd lent it to me?

"Do you take many girls on the back?" I asked, eyeing the bike up with some trepidation.

"Nervous?"

"No, no, not at all. Not me. No way."

He chuckled. "Don't worry. I rarely crash."

Rarely? Oh, that was all right, then. As long as it only happened once in a while.

"Are you sure you wouldn't find a car more comfortable?"

"The bike does it for me."

He helped me put on a helmet, then straddled the seat and motioned for me to hop up behind him. The perch on the back looked awfully small—not even a proper seat. How was I supposed to travel on that? And what on earth should I hold on to?

"Just swing your leg over the back," Nye said. "Then put your feet on the pegs."

I managed it somewhat inelegantly, and I'd never felt so unstable in my life. What if I tumbled off the back?

"Hold on to my waist."

Wrap my arms around a virtual stranger? Talk about awkward. I gingerly placed my hands on his hips, thankful for the thick jacket between us, and the bike engine started with a throaty rumble.

Good grief. This was really happening.

"Ready?" he shouted above the noise.

"Never more so."

He hit the throttle, and gravel spat out behind the back wheel. The bike shot off down the driveway, and I forgot about etiquette as my arms circled Nye's waist of their own accord.

I could hear him laughing above the noise of the engine as we hit the road. That...that asshole! I was tempted to thump him, but I didn't dare let go.

The vibrations from the engine did funny things to my insides as we sped along, as did Nye's proximity. I was hanging on so tight I could feel his muscles rippling under his jacket. Who on earth rode a motorcycle for fun? It was more like torture for me. At least Nye's broad back acted as a windbreak; otherwise, I'd have blown away.

By the time Nye pulled over and unpeeled my arms from around his chest ten minutes later, my legs had turned to jelly.

"Are you getting off?" he asked, twisting in his seat to face me.

"Can you give me a few moments?"

"Sure. Wasn't that fun?"

I flipped up my visor and gave him the dirtiest look I could muster.

Calm down, Olivia. Get your breath back. I needed to retrieve my sanity too, although admittedly, the latter was looking more and more like a lost cause.

When my heartbeat steadied, I swung my leg over the back of the bike and stumbled as my feet hit the ground. Nye hopped off and caught me before I hit the deck, then held me tight against him.

"Are you okay?"

"Uh, I think so." I nodded half-heartedly. "It was just a little scary."

"You want me to go slower on the way back?"

It wasn't just being on the bike that scared me; it was being on the bike with Nye. That engine wasn't the only thing that exuded power. And the slower he went, the longer I'd have to cling on to him.

"I'll get used to it."

He gave me another grin, and his teeth looked even whiter against a day's worth of dark stubble. "That's my girl."

His girl. I wished.

No! I did not just think that. Nye was merely an added complication in my life, and I still hadn't phoned Sophie to enquire about his credentials.

And of course, he had to confuse me further. His hand brushed against mine as we walked up the path to Carol's cottage, and prickling heat burned up my arm at each touch. My legs had gone wobbly by the time we reached the front door, and the twitching curtains at the window beside it told me our arrival hadn't gone unnoticed.

The door opened the second Nye knocked, and a tiny lady with tightly curled white hair looked up at us. She sported one of those painfully perky smiles that would stay in place through anything short of a nuclear explosion.

"You must be Nye. Luke said on the phone you'd be

coming." She gripped Nye's proffered hand with both of hers. "My, aren't you the handsome one?"

"Nye Holmes. You're Carol?"

"That's right. Are you any relation to Sherlock?"

"I'm afraid not."

Disappointment flashed across her face, but only for a second. "Never mind. I'm sure Sherlock Holmes didn't have such big muscles." She reached up and squeezed Nye's bicep, and he turned a snort of laughter into a sneeze. "Bless you, dear."

"I'm pretty sure he was fictional."

"Maybe so, but he also had Dr. Watson." She gave me a disapproving look. "You must be Olivia."

"Yes, Olivia Porter." I held a hand out, but she barely touched my fingertips.

She turned back to Nye. "You'd better come in, dear. I've just made fresh pastries. Or would you prefer a cooked breakfast?"

What did one call a geriatric cougar? Was there a special term for it? She herded Nye into the dining room without taking her eyes off his backside once.

"I'm not all that hungry, thanks."

"Nonsense. A man like you needs to eat. Here, take a seat."

She bustled off, presumably to the kitchen, while I sat down opposite a bemused-looking Nye at a table for two.

"Well, at least she likes one of us."

He rolled his eyes. "Save me."

"Don't be so melodramatic."

"It wasn't your butt she pinched."

A bubble of laughter escaped just as Carol came back into the room, and she glared at me as she put a jug of orange juice down on the table.

"There you go, dear. Freshly squeezed."

I couldn't stop giggling as she hurried off again. "It's not the only thing."

"Is it too early for Scotch? I think I'm gonna need it."

It didn't take long for Carol to return with two fried breakfasts. My portion was half the size of Nye's and had all the burned bits.

"Everything's made from local produce. Award-winning sausages and home-cured bacon from the Baxters' farm, eggs laid next door but one, and I made the bread myself."

She stared at Nye, and he slowly picked up his knife and fork. "You really shouldn't have."

"It was no trouble."

I tried a piece of sausage, and it was actually very good. Nye did the same and swallowed before he focused on Carol again, who'd dragged up an extra chair.

"Tastes perfect. But while we're here, I was hoping you could help us out with some information."

"I certainly will if I can."

"Olivia here's had a couple of break-ins, and I'm looking for the culprit."

"Luke Halston-Cain told me you were a private investigator. Do you get to carry a gun?"

"That's not allowed in the UK."

Carol's eyebrows pinched together. "That isn't much fun, is it?"

The corners of Nye's lips twitched as he tried to suppress a smile.

"No, it's not, but it's probably safer that way.

Anyway, those burglaries—Luke reckoned that if anyone might have heard anything about them, it would be you."

She drew herself up to her full height and preened, obviously proud of her reputation as queen of the gossipmongers.

"I have heard a few things."

Nye gave her an encouraging smile. "Such as? Anything about Olivia?"

"Oh yes, a lot about *her*." She made "her" sound like a curse. "And you'd be wise to watch your step with that one."

Don't mind me, lady. I'm only sitting right next to you.

Nye leaned forward a little, and Carol mirrored him.

"Shall I tell you a secret?" he asked.

Her eyes lit up as she nodded.

"I've heard those rumours about Olivia myself, but none of them are true."

"Really? But so many people are saying the same thing."

"Terrible, isn't it? Somebody's trying to ruin her reputation. I can assure you that Olivia's one of the nicest girls you'll ever meet, and she definitely isn't a gold-digger. She runs her own business."

"What kind of business?"

Carol looked me up and down, no doubt imagining what occupation would befit the black sheep of the village. Home massage? Mail-order sex toys? Or maybe I peddled drugs to small children?

"She designs websites."

"Are you sure?"

"Her company's called Webs By Design. She started it five years ago while she was still at university. Her site for Longacres Garden Centre is well worth a look—they've got a three-for-two deal on packets of seeds at the moment." He gestured out of the window at Carol's immaculate front borders. "You're obviously fond of gardening."

Carol twirled one tight curl on a finger. "I'm treasurer of the horticultural society."

"Well, maybe you could let your members know about the special offer?"

"Absolutely. They all love a bargain."

Thanks, Nye—at least if Carol was going to spread lies about me, she could also drum up business for one of my clients.

"So, now we've established Olivia isn't the girl you thought she was, you wouldn't happen to know where the rumours about her originated, would you?"

"I heard them from at least six different people. In the pub, at the WI, in the shops. I can't quite remember who told me first."

Nye's smile faded.

"But I can ask around," Carol added hastily. "Someone must know, mustn't they?"

He let her have it, full beam. "I'd be very grateful. And about the break-ins—has anything like that happened before?"

"Our low crime rate is one of the wonderful things about living in the Foxfords. We've got an excellent neighbourhood-watch scheme."

"Nobody's *ever* got burgled before?"

She shifted in her seat, and Nye didn't take his gaze off her.

"There may have been a few small incidents, but that was several years ago." Carol lowered her voice to a whisper. "We don't tend to talk about those."

"Why not?"

"The lad's father was the chairman of the parish council. It all got a bit awkward when Graham had to arrest his son."

"What was the son's name?"

"Christopher Johnston. But he went to juvenile detention. You're not planning to rake up the past, are you? People won't like that."

"I'll try not to cause trouble, but I'm not going to stand by while Olivia gets terrorised."

"No, no, of course not."

Nye shoved one last piece of fried bread into his mouth, chewed, and pushed his chair back. "You make a great breakfast."

"You're welcome back any time. Both of you. I do hope I've been helpful."

He bent to kiss her on the cheek, and she turned bright red. I understood exactly how she felt.

"Very much so, Carol."

We left Carol clutching Nye's business card at the front door, still basking in his aura. With the village about to be set straight over the rumours flying around, even getting back on the bike didn't seem like such a hurdle.

"What do you think?" I asked Nye as he steadied the bike. "Could it be Christopher?"

"I'll get the team at head office to find out whether he's still locked up."

"I'm pretty sure I've never met him."

"You might not have realised it at the time." He

squeezed my hand, now fastened securely around his chest with what was left of my fingernails digging into his leather jacket. "Don't worry, I'll find out."

The ride back to Lilac Cottage didn't leave me with the same feeling of terror as the first trip, and I even managed to get off without falling over. Nye followed me inside and checked every room plus all the doors and windows before he left.

"I'll be in touch tomorrow, but if you think of anything in the meantime, call me. Or if you get worried. I'm only at the other end of the phone, okay?"

"Okay."

"And the patrol will check on you again tonight. Same vehicle."

"Got it."

He turned to leave, but I grabbed his sleeve.

"Nye?"

"Yeah?"

"Thanks for doing this."

He smiled, but there was a weariness around the edges. "No problem, Liv."

CHAPTER 22

THE SENSE OF security Nye's presence had given me faded away with the last rumbles of his bike engine, leaving me alone with my worries. And that got me thinking about Tate's words from last night: How well did I really know Nye?

The answer was, not at all. Time to call Sophie.

She answered on the first ring, which was only to be expected from a girl who went into withdrawal if she got more than three feet from her mobile.

"Ooh, Liv, how have things been? Tell me Nye came?"

"He came, but his arrival gave me a bit of a surprise."

"Oh, dang it, I was going to text you, wasn't I? But I went out to a fashion show, and then there was an after-party, and oh my gosh, there was this model, and... Hang on—where were we?"

"You forgot to tell me Nye was coming."

"Oops. Sorry about that. Isn't he dreamy, though? I went to a pool party he was at the year before last, and wow, he must spend hours in the gym. He has an eight-pack for sure. And he most definitely does not need to stuff socks down there, if you know what I mean."

Great. Now that I had that picture in my mind, I'd never get it out. "Too much information, Sophie."

"Gosh, sorry, I keep forgetting you've got more important things going on. Have there been any more problems?"

"Only some paint thrown at my door. And a dozen eggs."

"Well, don't worry. Nye will sort everything out, I'm sure of it."

"That was what I wanted to ask about. I don't know anything about him, and he seems awfully young to have had much experience at this kind of thing."

"He's a year older than my brother, which makes him...uh, twenty-seven. They met at some martial arts class when they were teenagers. Taekwondo I think it was. Nye's a black belt, did you know that? Oh, no, I guess not. What was it you were asking about?"

"His experience as an investigator?"

"Well, he's been doing it since he turned eighteen. I remember him spending a week on my brother's bedroom floor after he first got the job because he had a massive argument with his father when he decided not to go to uni."

"But he seems so clever."

"Exactly. Anyway, Nye moved out of home and went it alone."

At least he'd been doing the job for a few years. That gave me some comfort. "Do you know any more about his work?"

"Not really, but he must be good at it, because I bet that sexy motorbike he rides cost a fortune. I heard him telling my brother he had the pipes customised, whatever that means. Did you see it? Or did he come in his car?"

Car? Nye had a car? Nye had a car, and he'd left it

at home and made me get on that...that death trap?

Oh, he'd be getting a piece of my mind tomorrow, that was for sure.

"He came on his bike."

"Isn't it awesome? I've been badgering him to take me for a ride for ages, but he keeps resisting. One day I'll get that tight ass between my thighs. One day... And I wouldn't mind helping him out of his leathers afterwards, either."

My nether regions heated up at the mere thought of that, but I forced my mind back to the task at hand.

"You're married, Sophie."

"But I still have eyes."

"Do you know anything else about Nye?"

"He's gorgeous, he's not hurting for money, and he has a steady job. What more do you need?"

"I suppose you've got a point."

I'd forgotten how one-track Sophie's mind could be. Well, two-track; men and shopping.

"Of course I do. Anyway, he's Mr. Tall, Dark, and Mysterious. He doesn't talk about himself much."

Just my luck. "Thanks for sending him, anyway."

"No probs. Good luck with the whole stalker thing, and don't forget to call me if you get any dirt on Nye. Or shirtless photos."

We said our goodbyes and hung up. Shirtless photos? I had more chance of riding a unicycle on a tightrope than getting up close and personal with a man like Nye. Sometimes, I thought Sophie lived on another planet.

Having learned little except that Nye could be a conniving git, I turned to my old friend Google. Twenty minutes of fruitless searching later, I gave up. Either

Nye Holmes didn't exist online, or the internet disliked me as much as everyone else.

Nye didn't even have a Facebook account. Or Twitter. How could he have avoided social media entirely? Although on reflection, that wasn't necessarily a bad thing, because at least it meant he hadn't seen me cavorting with a stripper.

For completeness' sake, I searched for Tate as well. He didn't share Nye's reserve, it seemed, because the timeline of his life was laid out for all to see. Photos from a London wine bar, one of him at his desk, a whole collection from St. Andrews last weekend. Tate teeing off, Tate driving the golf buggy, Tate leaning on a golf club. At least I knew he'd been telling the truth about that.

Edward had been on a number of golf trips which I now doubted involved the type of hole-in-one he'd originally claimed. I couldn't go through that heartache again. And as if I'd invoked some kind of weird telepathic connection, my phone rang. Tate calling.

"How are you, darling? Have there been any more incidents?"

"No, thankfully. Everything seems quiet."

"That's wonderful news. I was calling on the off chance you'd be free for lunch on Thursday?"

Ooh, lunch? I was about to accept when I remembered Nye's friend was booked for that day. "I'd love to, but a man's coming round to fit new locks. Nye organised it for me. I could do tomorrow or Friday, though?"

"I do hope you're being careful with that chap. Other than Thursday lunchtime, my diary's jam-packed until Friday evening. How about dinner?"

"That would be lovely. And I *am* being careful. Nye seems genuine, and he's even arranged for a security patrol to check on the cottage at night."

"At least he's doing something constructive. It's high time more people got concerned about your welfare. Have you heard anything from Graham?"

"No, not yet."

Tate tutted down the line. "I've a good mind to have a word with the old fool. I'll call him today. He can't keep sticking his head in the sand over this."

"Thanks. I appreciate it."

His voice softened. "Anything for you, Olivia. I'll pick you up at seven on Friday."

At least I had something to look forward to. I just had to get through the rest of the week first.

When I took my parcels to the post office that afternoon, Betty managed a greeting and a half-smile, which was a marked improvement on recent visits. Looked as though Carol really did have some clout.

But that moment of brightness in the day was marred when Nye called at five.

"Christopher Johnston's a bust. He's out of juvie now, but on the first night you were burgled, he was in hospital having his appendix removed."

Dammit. I'd hoped we were finally getting somewhere. "Thanks for letting me know." Nye stayed on the line, but the silence grew painful. "Is there something else?"

"Have you met a guy called Laurence Hazell? Larry?"

"The name doesn't ring any bells."

"Son of Betty Hazell."

"Betty in the post office?"

"Yeah. Do you talk to her much?"

"We chatted most days when I first arrived, but she gave me the cold shoulder like everybody else after the rumours started. Why?"

"Be careful what you say to her for the moment. Larry's had a few issues with the police up north."

"What kind of issues?"

"He developed a fixation with a girl in his class at uni, and it escalated."

"What do you mean, escalated?"

"The cops found him hiding in her bathroom one night with a pipe wrench."

I sagged back onto one of the kitchen chairs and gripped my phone harder. "What was he doing there?"

"According to his police statement, she'd mentioned her tap was leaking, so he decided to pay her a surprise visit to fix it. Found the door allegedly unlocked, so he let himself in and got on with the job, which is bullshit. He didn't turn any lights on, for starters. But he did have a good lawyer, so he got six weeks of psychiatric treatment and a restraining order, and then they let him go again."

"Where is he now?" I couldn't keep the quake out of my voice.

"We're not sure yet."

I thought back to my conversations with Betty, but try as I might, I couldn't recall her saying anything about her son. Had she mentioned me to him? Had I seen him in passing and not realised? What if he'd been one of the strangers standing in the post office or browsing in Floyd's grocery store?

"How scared should I be?" I asked Nye.

"I didn't call to worry you. The patrol car will be

back tonight, and chances are, Larry isn't even in the area. Just don't open your door to any strangers."

After that piece of news, I baked a fruit cake and made a batch of stew. I kidded myself that it was a cost-saving measure, that by cooking in bulk and freezing portions I'd save money, but really it was just to keep myself busy. If I concentrated on measuring and chopping, my mind couldn't drift to more sinister affairs.

Like the person out there, watching me. Where were they right now? The trees at the back of the garden seemed to close in, dark and foreboding. A stalker could easily hide there, and I'd never notice. They'd know I was alone, and...

Olivia! Stop it.

Twiglet wove through my legs, providing a welcome distraction. When he wouldn't stop miaowing, I gave him a spoonful of stew, and he licked it up then brushed against me, pleading for more.

"Okay, okay. Here you go."

He'd gone off cat food in the last week, probably because I kept giving him leftovers, but he was such a sweet cat, and when he turned those big eyes on me, I couldn't resist.

He repaid that generosity by nearly breaking my neck as I climbed the stairs to bed, but at least when we got there, he climbed under the covers with me like a feline hot-water bottle. The good news was that I had something to keep me warm at night without running up a huge electricity bill, but I couldn't help wishing it were someone.

As I closed my eyes, I found myself thinking of Tate. Handsome, well-bred, wealthy—he was perfect for me, on paper at least. But when I was with him, why didn't my pulse race? Like the way it did with Nye, for example. Now, there was a man unsuitable in every way, but whenever I got within three feet of him, my heart pounded like a jackhammer.

Thoughts of Tate turned into dreams of Nye as sleep claimed me. And thanks to my conversation with Sophie, those fantasies didn't feature him wearing very many clothes, merely a smile, a pair of tight briefs, and that leather jacket I absolutely didn't like. What was wrong with me?

I woke with a start just as he was about to peel the briefs off, and I cursed into the darkness, angry with myself for waking up and also for having had that filthy dream in the first place.

"Twiglet, I've lost my mind."

He barely stirred, just curled himself into a tighter ball as a creak sounded downstairs. That sound made the hairs on the back of my neck stand up, and I froze, listening to the near silence. The odd noise was to be expected, right? Old houses did that.

Hold on—what was that click? That sounded like the kitchen door.

Outside, a sliver of moon glimmered through the window and reflected in the cracked mirror above the dresser. Superstition said breaking a mirror brought seven years of bad luck, and by my calculations, the burglar should be well into double figures now.

I heard another creak, then another, too rhythmical to be the house settling. No, it was more like somebody walking across the downstairs hallway. I sat straight up, pulling the duvet around me as if six togs and a ladybird-print cover could protect me from whoever was there.

Sweat popped out of my pores as panic took over. What the hell should I do?

CHAPTER 23

I SCRAMBLED TO the nightstand and grabbed my phone. Who should I call? The police?

Living in London, I wouldn't have hesitated to punch in 999, but out in the sticks, where was the nearest police station? I had no idea. Last time I needed help, Graham had taken over an hour to arrive, and he'd been next to useless when he did.

That left Tate or Nye. Tate lived twenty minutes away, and Nye... I had no idea.

Proximity won out.

"You're through to the voicemail of Tate Palmer. I'm not available to take your call right now..."

Oh, hell. Why didn't he wake up when the phone rang?

"Tate, it's Olivia. Can you call me urgently?" I whispered as another creak came from downstairs.

One option left, and Nye answered faster than Sophie did.

"I think there's someone in the house."

He was all business. "Whereabouts are you?"

"In my bedroom."

"Is the door locked?"

"It doesn't have a lock."

"Fuck. Okay, I want you to drag the heaviest thing you can manage up against it. That's the bed, right?"

"Hold on. I'll try."

"I'm not going to hang up, but I need to get on the other line and send the nearest team to you ASAP. Just try and breathe, okay?"

All very well for him to say—he wasn't the one about to get attacked and murdered in their own home. I shooed Twiglet off the bed and tried to push it over to the door, recalling belatedly how it had taken three of us to get it into the bedroom in the first place. A *thunk* came from downstairs as I found superhuman strength and slowly slid the thing across the worn carpet. Breathe? I was panting by the time it nudged against the door.

"Have you done it?" Nye's faint voice came from the phone I'd dropped on the chest of drawers.

"Yes, I've moved the bed."

"Now, do you have any kind of weapon up there?"

I thought longingly of the poker snugly back in its rightful place next to the fire. For the first time ever, I cursed my obsession with tidiness.

"I don't think so."

"Nothing heavy? Or a can of hairspray? Deodorant?"

Hairspray! Maddie had left her can of super-hold here after she and Dave dropped me off the other day. I snatched it off the dressing table under the window and clutched it to my chest.

"I have hairspray."

"Well done, babe. The patrol's five minutes out. You just need to hold on until then."

Five minutes. Just one song. A cup of filter coffee. Sex with Edward. It didn't seem like long on a normal day, but when I was a sitting duck with a madman after me, every second stretched into infinity.

Footfalls sounded on the stairs, soft and steady, and I heard a muffled expletive as the intruder hit the noisy ninth step and the creak echoed through the house.

"He's upstairs!" I whispered to Nye.

"Just breathe, babe. My guys are on their way, I promise."

Steps tracked across the landing, and slowly, so slowly, the handle on the bedroom door began to turn. The visitor had come straight to my room, no hesitation. He'd been in the house before, and he knew exactly where he was going tonight.

"Nye, he's here."

A dark gap opened up around the edge of the door, and a black-gloved hand reached inside. The crack was wide enough for Twiglet to dash through when I screamed, but the solid wood jammed against the bed before a human could fit through. The man didn't bother to muffle his swearing this time.

"Open up, bitch."

I couldn't even open my mouth to reply, let alone the door.

Then I heard the most glorious sounds in the world —the roar of an engine followed by the crunch of gravel as the patrol car sped down the drive outside.

"You're going to regret this," the man outside my door shouted, then ran down the stairs. The back door bounced hard against the frame as he left in a hurry.

Car doors slammed outside, and the yelling that followed grew quieter as the chase went through my garden and into the woods beyond. I finally managed to heed Nye's instruction to take in air, huge gulping breaths that turned into helpless tears.

"I think he's gone," I told Nye, speaking between sobs.

"I'm on my way, babe. I'm in the car, and I'll be there as soon as I can. You don't open the door for anyone but me."

"Okay."

The phone slid from my grasp and hit the floor, and Twiglet slunk back in and licked my face with his sandpaper-like tongue. I petted him, needing something to do with my hands other than biting my nails.

It seemed like forever before Nye arrived, and I didn't move from my position wedged against the wall until I heard his voice outside the door.

"Liv, it's Nye. Can you open up?"

I struggled to my feet, but the bed wouldn't move no matter what I did. How on earth did I manage to shift it earlier?

"I-I-I can't move the bed."

"Not even a little?"

I tried again. Nothing. My adrenaline had subsided, leaving me drained. "It just won't."

Visions of starving to death in Aunt Ellie's bedroom flashed through my mind, with nothing but a crackly television for company. Perhaps Nye could send Twiglet in with food, or better still, brandy, like one of those St. Bernard dogs in the Alps.

"Can you open the window?" Nye asked.

"Now?"

"Yes, now."

Thankfully, nobody had painted over the catch, and a minute after I pushed the window wide, Nye climbed into my bedroom. At the sight of him, my trembles became uncontrollable shudders, and then the tears started again, much to my embarrassment.

He pulled me to him and wrapped me up in his arms. "Shh, it's okay."

In my cocoon of safety, I wept against his chest, leaving a nice damp patch.

"I'm sorry about your shirt."

"I don't give a shit about the shirt. I'm more worried about you."

"I'll be okay," I lied.

Rather than letting me go, he held me tighter and stroked my hair as I began shivering again.

"I should have put a car out there full-time," he muttered. "Babe, I'm so sorry. I should have foreseen this."

"How could you?" I leaned back enough to see his face, and his eyes swam with torment. "Nobody's ever come while I'm here before."

"I shouldn't have taken that chance."

"You've already done more to help me than anybody else." A shout came from downstairs, and I looked towards the door. "Did they catch him?"

"I don't know. I came straight for you, so I haven't spoken to the others yet."

"C-c-can you find out?"

He dropped a kiss on my hair, then let me go. A part of me tore away and went with him as he strode across the room and shoved the bed out of the way as if it weighed nothing.

"Coming?"

He held out his hand, and I hurried over to take it. My lifeline.

Downstairs, the living room was packed with

people, all talking amongst themselves. Nine men plus a dog. Twiglet took one look at our four-legged guest and leapt on top of the shelves, hissing.

"Well?" Nye asked.

Everyone turned to face him, and one man stepped forward. They all wore matching uniforms—black with a shield logo on the breast pocket.

"The upshot is, we lost him," the spokesman for the group said.

"We tracked him through the woods, but he got in a vehicle on the far side," the guy with the dog added.

"We've got photos of the tyre tracks, and we'll fingerprint the house."

I shook my head. "There's no point—he was wearing gloves."

Nye's grip tightened, cutting off my circulation. "You saw him?"

"Only his hand. He was right outside the bedroom door when the first car arrived."

Nye's mouth set in a hard line, and I was glad someone else was on the receiving end of his fury.

"Did he say anything?"

"Not much. 'Open up, bitch,' and when the men arrived, he shouted that I was going to regret this as he ran off."

"That's it. You're not staying here any longer."

I snatched my hand out of his. "Yes, I am. This is my home."

Nye's tone softened. "Babe, there's a lunatic out there with a grudge against you."

"And if I move out, he'll have won. That's what he wants. So I'm staying."

"I've never met anyone as stubborn as you."

Nye stomped off, and the front door slammed shut behind him. Marvellous. Now I'd managed to upset the man who'd dropped everything to help me.

"Am I crazy?" I asked the nearest black-clad ninja.

He shrugged, which pretty much gave me my answer.

Should I bow to Nye's wishes and stay with Maddie? I couldn't deny the thought of a proper night's sleep was appealing. I was on the verge of going after him to grovel when he came back carrying a duffle bag.

"What's that for?"

"I'm staying with you." He turned to ninja number one. "I need a car out there twenty-four seven. Two men. The locks are getting changed on Thursday, and I want CCTV installed as well."

The guy saluted. "Consider it done."

As the men filed out, I was still stuck on the "staying with you" part. "You can't stay here."

"Watch me." He unzipped the hold-all and shook out a sleeping bag.

"But what about work?"

"Babe, the people at work tend to be fairly understanding about this type of thing, seeing as it's a security company."

I looked down at the floor. "But I can't afford to pay."

He tilted my chin up, forcing me to look at him. "Then it's a good thing your mate Soph likes shopping, isn't it?"

"What about your girlfriend? Won't she get upset if you don't go home?"

"Girlfriend?"

"Sophie said she went shopping for your girlfriend's

birthday present."

"Turned out I got her birthday confused with the previous girlfriend's. We split up over her not-so-birthday dinner."

I couldn't help the burst of laughter that escaped. "I'm sorry, I know that shouldn't be funny, but..." I giggled again.

"I'm just happy you're smiling."

His gaze burned into me with the heat of a distant sun, and I looked away, suddenly unable to withstand the intensity.

"I should try to get some sleep," I muttered.

"Yeah, you should." He herded me upstairs and made sure my bedroom windows were secure before turning to leave.

"Will you be okay?" I asked. "On the floor, I mean? I'm sorry I don't have a spare bed, or even a sofa."

"I've slept in worse places, believe me." He leaned down and kissed me on the cheek, brushing my jaw with his thumb as he did so. The roughness of his stubble contrasted with his soft lips. "I'll see you in the morning."

My cheek burned as I went to use the bathroom. I touched where he'd caressed me, expecting to see flames coming from my fingers, but they looked no different from normal. How could that be? My insides had gone nuclear.

Then I caught sight of myself in a shard of mirror as I climbed back into bed, and I groaned. I'd faced my stalker and a crowd of Blackwood's finest while wearing a pair of Hello Kitty pyjamas. No wonder even the dog had stared at me funny.

If there was an afterlife, my mother would be up

there crossing herself, asking what she could have done to make her only daughter just a little bit more normal. I imagined her frown as I lay there on my once-luxurious king-sized mattress. I'd bought it to share with Edward, but now I had a very different man on my mind.

My last thought, as I drifted through the dreamlike limbo between me and oblivion, was that I wished he were lying beside me.

CHAPTER 24

I PULLED HALF of my clothes onto the bed the next morning before finally settling on a pair of jeans and a soft V-neck jumper. Anything smarter would have looked out of place. Dammit, Nye had seen me in my pyjamas! And not even one of the classy silk pairs Edward had bought me with their lace trim and fancy buttons. Why hadn't I been wearing those? Because they were uncomfortable, that was why. For years, I'd sacrificed comfort for style to please him.

Nye looked depressingly awake as I tripped over the cat and fell into the kitchen. My gawky entrance made him glance up from his computer and smile faintly as he gave his head a barely perceptible shake.

Yes, I was an idiot. I already knew that, okay?

"I made coffee," he said.

"My hero."

"Don't get too excited. I can't make anything else."

"I'll cook." Making him breakfast was the least I could do. And lunch. And dinner. "What do you fancy?"

He looked at me for a full ten seconds before answering, and his scrutiny reduced me to the size of a Barbie doll, minus the tiny waist and long legs.

"I'm not fussy. Not when it comes to food, anyway."

Good to know. "And what about the men outside?"

I'd seen the Jeep parked outside next to a new

BMW I assumed was Nye's.

"I've already taken them coffee, and they'll eat anything you care to make."

If I'd known I'd have extra mouths to feed, I'd have stocked up on food. The cupboards were almost bare, but I found a packet of part-baked baguettes, a few rashers of bacon, and a box of eggs—enough to make breakfast rolls all around.

"Where are you going?" Nye stopped me halfway to the door with a tray in my hand.

"Taking breakfast to the men in the car."

"I'll take it."

"But—"

He'd already gone, leaving me empty-handed in the middle of the kitchen, so I set his plate on the table with a napkin and orange juice instead, smiling as I did so. Edward would have thrown a fit at a breakfast roll. He only ate organic muesli in the mornings.

But Nye tucked in the moment he got back without a murmur of complaint.

"Babe, a man could get used to this."

A blush spread across my cheeks. "It's nothing."

"To you, maybe."

Surely plenty of women must have cooked for him in the past? He probably had them queueing around the block, aprons on and recipe books in hand. He gave me a strange look as I giggled, and I hastily banished that vision.

"What are your plans for today?" he asked once we'd finished eating.

"I need to package up anything I've sold on eBay and take it to the post office, do some work on the computer, and buy groceries."

He glanced at his watch. "I've got a video conference at eleven, but I'm yours after that. Call me when you want to go out, and I'll come with you."

"I'm sure I'll be fine on my own. I mean, it's daylight now."

"Liv, until we catch this guy, you don't set foot outside by yourself. I'm your shadow, got it?"

A big sexy shadow wearing a T-shirt that stretched across his pecs and a pair of jeans made to hug the curves of his ass. I could think of worse things.

Stop it, Olivia!

I shouldn't be thinking like that at all, but it was so hard with temptation sitting right in front of me.

"Yes, got it."

When I opened the laptop to distract myself, I found I'd sold six items on eBay. Another eighty pounds, and the pesky foot spa with seventeen attachments was finally on its way to a new home. It didn't take long to pack everything, and Nye insisted on carrying the parcels as we walked into the village. He'd wanted to drive, but I begged to walk in the sunshine. I'd got fitter since moving to Upper Foxford—one of the few advantages of living there.

In the post office, Nye dumped everything on the counter, and Betty looked up at him with undisguised awe.

"Recorded delivery for the two big parcels, please, and second class for the rest," I said.

Nothing. Today, I didn't exist.

Nye tried instead. "Olivia would like to send the two big parcels recorded delivery, and the rest can go second class."

"Right away, Mr... I didn't catch your name?"

"Nye Holmes."

"Are you new in the village?"

She knew damn well he was.

"I'm helping to keep Olivia safe from the man who keeps breaking into her house."

"You're a bodyguard?"

"More of an investigator."

"Now I come to think about it, I've been hearing strange noises in the night myself."

"Probably her bones creaking," I muttered as Betty turned to weigh the foot spa. Or that strange son of hers. I wondered whether Nye would ask about Larry, but he didn't.

Instead, he choked back a laugh. "I could ask a colleague to look into the matter, if you like. Shall I get someone to call with details of our rates?"

Betty hastily shook her head. "No, no, dear. I'm sure it's just my imagination."

She barely took her eyes off Nye the whole time we were in there, and when he asked if she sold chewing gum, I thought she was about to vault the counter and show him where it was herself. At least I wasn't the only woman he caused to act crazy around him.

"Do many old ladies flirt with you?" I asked when we got outside.

He shifted from foot to foot. "A few," he admitted, clearly uncomfortable. "Do you want to get groceries before we go back?"

Not really. I couldn't deal with Floyd's sullenness at the moment, or his prices. "Could we head into town later? There's more choice."

"Whatever you want."

Tate phoned just as we walked in the door, and I

glanced at my watch. Eleven thirty.

"Good morning, darling. You left a message?"

"I did."

"You said it was urgent, so I slotted you in right after my third meeting. What's wrong?"

Well, at least I'd found out where I lay in Tate's list of priorities. "The urgency's gone out of it now. I got broken into again last night."

"That's awful. Did they take much?"

And his first question was about my belongings rather than me. "Nothing that I could see. He got disturbed by a patrol car."

"At least the police made a bit more effort this time. Good to know my chat with Graham had the desired effect."

"It wasn't the police. Nye sent someone."

"That cowboy? What did he do, round up a gang of vigilantes?"

"Not at all. They seemed very professional."

"And the Mafia wear suits. Olivia, your cottage clearly isn't safe. Why don't you come and stay at the manor until the police get to the bottom of this? My housekeeper can cater to your every need."

A month ago, I'd have leapt at that invitation. The chance to be taken care of rather than fending for myself. I'd grown used to being on a rich man's arm when I was with Edward. But had I truly enjoyed it? Now that I had the chance to fall back into that lifestyle again, I found I didn't want to.

Despite the difficulties at Lilac Cottage, I'd achieved something for myself and experienced a freedom I'd never had living under Edward's thumb in a rented flat.

And then there was Nye. An added complication.

He made me feel things I shouldn't, and it wouldn't be fair to stay with Tate with another man at the forefront of my mind.

"I appreciate the offer, Tate, really I do. But I'll have to decline."

"But you're in danger. Who knows what that man will do next? And there's your burglar on the loose too."

And so jealousy reared its ugly head. Tate was more worried about Nye's presence than my damn stalker.

"I'm not going to be scared out of my own house."

"For the record, I think you're making a terrible decision." And there was the lawyer in Tate making an appearance.

"Noted. But it's still my decision to make."

"Well, call me when you come to your senses."

And with those words, it hit me. Maddie had been absolutely right—Tate was Edward all over again. My whole life, I'd gravitated towards men my mother would have rated A+. She'd ingrained a mental checklist in me.

- Does he have a pretentious job? Check.

- Is he reasonably handsome? Check.

- Does he have enough money to look after me? Check.

- Is he well-connected socially? Check.

Tate met every one of those criteria, and so had Edward, and I didn't want to waste another two years of my life on a man who'd hurt me without a second thought when he moved on to a new model. Quite literally, in Edward's case.

No, I needed to start a new list, my own this time. One that would most likely leave my mother's ghost tutting in the background every time I added an item.

What should I start with?

- *Does he make my heart pound?*

- *Does every nerve ending burn at his merest touch?*

- *Does the timbre of his voice send shivers through me?*

- *Do I want to push him onto the nearest flat surface and ride him until I'm screaming?*

Freaking hell, Olivia! My own thoughts shocked me.

They scared me too. Because right now, there was one man in my life who ticked all of those boxes, and he wasn't Tate.

Those thoughts weighed on my mind all afternoon as I tried to get some work done. "Tried" being the operative word. With Nye sitting opposite me, I couldn't even remember the password for my own website.

"Can we go out for groceries now?" I asked. "My concentration's shot to pieces."

"Something to do with that phone call earlier?"

Damn him for being so perceptive. "Why do you say that?"

"Because you bit your bottom lip so hard while you were listening that you still had tooth dents in it five minutes later."

My finger came up to feel automatically, and Nye tracked it with eyes that missed nothing. I'd never known a man to make me feel quite so nervous—fear and lust and intimidation made my insides feel like a termite nest, full of tiny insects crawling around and nibbling away at my sanity.

"Fine. It was Tate, and I finally realised he's not as

special as everyone around here seems to think he is. Maddie's right, one hundred percent right. If I decide to date again, I'll be looking for a nice, normal man. One without a posh car and a wine cellar and room for a pony." Words vomited out of me, and I blamed the termites. My brain didn't function with Nye in close proximity. "Sorry. You probably didn't need to hear all that."

Nye's lip twitched, but I didn't know whether it was the beginning of a smile or a hint of a scowl. I played safe and returned to my first question.

"Can we go out and buy food? Please?"

"Sure."

He picked up his keys from where he'd flung them onto the counter. I'd noticed he had a habit of doing that—dropping things where they didn't belong—and I'd already removed a pair of gloves and a sweater and put them in more appropriate places.

Outside, he opened the car door for me, showing he did have some manners hidden away under that tough exterior. By the time I'd moved my seat into the right position, he was fiddling with the SatNav.

"Sainsbury's do you?"

Once upon a time, I'd have insisted on Waitrose, but now I'd realised there were more important things to worry about in life.

"Sainsbury's is fine."

On the bus, the trip into town took almost an hour, and when Warren drove me, we did it in twenty minutes. Nye drove the car like he rode the bike and took fifteen. At least I had a seat belt and airbags in the 5 Series.

"Thank you for driving. And in a car, this time."

"You didn't like the bike?"

"It was terrifying. And I'll admit I'm still a little peeved that you brought it when you had access to a perfectly good BMW."

"The BMW was at my flat, and I didn't go home that night. I slept in the office and came straight back to yours the next morning."

He did? Now I felt terrible. He'd made it his priority to help me, and I'd just chewed him out for it. I turned to apologise, but he'd already got out of the car and was on his way around to open my door.

I was trying to think of the right words when he bent his head to whisper in my ear.

"Even if I had gone home, I'd still have brought the bike."

My mouth dropped as he sauntered off to fetch a trolley. I couldn't believe him! He'd deliberately manipulated me into wrapping myself around him.

And now my libido laughed. *Who are you kidding? Nye would have only had to ask.*

I sighed as I followed him into the supermarket. Judging by the ache between my thighs, my libido was right on the money.

I'd tried to write a shopping list before I left, but when I caught myself adding chocolate four times, I gave up. I'd just wander the shelves for inspiration. Fresh vegetables, fruit, chicken, and minced beef. Maybe I'd make a lasagne this evening. Pasta. Flour, eggs, sugar, and cocoa powder because I needed a cake. Nye wandered along, tossing his own items into the trolley.

"Pre-made microwaveable hot dogs?" I asked when I caught sight of one of the boxes.

What else had he chosen? Pop-Tarts, a ready-cooked omelette, individual trifles. I picked up a packet of burger "cheese."

"You realise there isn't actually any cheese in this?"

He shrugged. "It comes pre-sliced."

"Have you ever cooked anything? Or do you just reheat?"

"I tried boiling an egg once, but it didn't work out." At least he had the good grace to look sheepish.

"Look, put that stuff back. I'll cook for you."

He brightened. "You will?"

"Of course, and for the teams outside. You're all doing me such a big favour."

"In that case..." Nye scooped his shopping out and dumped it on a shelf.

"You can't just leave it there."

"Why not?"

"Because it's not in the right places."

He put an arm around my shoulder and steered me away. "Look at it this way, babe—I'm keeping someone in a job."

It still made me twitch, but I liked the feel of his arm too much to go back. Instead, we traipsed through the healthier sections of the store again and bought enough food for everyone.

Then we had our second disagreement when Nye got his credit card out.

"I'll pay."

"Liv, hardly any of that food's for you."

"But—"

"You can do magic things and transform it into something edible. That's your contribution, okay?"

What could I do but nod? The lady behind us in the

queue was already tapping her foot.

Back at Lilac Cottage, Nye checked in with the security team while I unlocked the front door.

"Nothing to report," he said, picking up all the shopping in one go. I grabbed my handbag and scurried in after him. The dark gave me the creeps.

Now I had to find somewhere to put everything. Aunt Ellie's kitchen was perfectly adequate for two, but three shifts of two guards who'd each eat one meal a day with us meant we'd bought a week's worth of food for four plus enough snacks to feed an army battalion. According to Nye, his colleagues hoovered up food like stray dogs. Careful packing of the fridge would be required.

I took out the washing-up liquid and the packet of dishcloths and put them by the sink, but as I turned back to the bags, something outside the window caught my eye.

What was it?

I leaned forward to take a closer look, then wished more than anything that I hadn't.

Chapter 25

NYE HEARD MY scream and caught me just before I hit the floor.

"Liv, what happened?"

I pointed with a trembling finger at the drooping cat duct-taped to the outside of the window, blood dripping down its fur from the gash across its throat. Narrow rivulets trickled down the glass, lit by the harsh light overhead, Twiglet's life reduced to a few sorry streaks.

"It's my cat," I sobbed.

Nye hugged me against him, his heart steady as mine pounded. My ears made a strange whooshing noise, and I put my hands over them to make it stop.

"I'm so sorry, Liv."

"Twiglet was just a cat. What did he ever do to anybody?"

"Nothing. The guy's sick. Fucking sick."

With his free hand, Nye fumbled in his pocket for his phone. "When did you last check around the back?"

A pause.

"Because in the last half hour, someone's managed to kill Liv's cat and tape it to the damn window." He tossed the phone onto the draining board. "They're going to check the grounds."

"What if the man's still out there?"

Nye narrowed his eyes. "Then he'd better watch his back."

My ears worked overtime as they strained to hear what was happening outside, but all I got was the crack of twigs and an occasional shout. Nye's muscles grew more rigid with each passing minute until the men came back empty-handed half an hour later. Talk about an anticlimax.

Nye stayed with me in the lounge while one of his team got poor Twiglet down and another found a set of gardening tools in the dining room. I chose a spot under the boughs of the old apple tree where I'd seen Twiglet sitting to watch birds on occasion, and Nye dug a grave by torchlight. An insignificant resting place for a cat who'd left tiny paw prints on my heart.

"I can't believe he's gone," I said, choking on the words as Nye cleaned Twiglet up as best he could with paper towels.

"I'll get the guy, Liv. I promise."

We buried his tiny body in the box from a rice steamer that I'd liberated from the piles of peril. One of the other men made a grave marker with a Sharpie and a rock he found in the garden, and we held a makeshift funeral under the light of the not-quite-full moon.

I gave up trying to hold back my tears. Twiglet had survived months on his own after Aunt Ellie died, and just as he'd got his home back again, someone took everything away from him. I was shaking as we walked back inside, not just from fear, but from fury.

"How dare he? How dare some psycho come into my home and scare me? If I ever get my hands on him, I'm going to rip his testicles off and put them in my blender."

The three men all winced.

"Why would he do this? I mean, why would someone want me out of Lilac Cottage that much? I tried so hard to fit in. Even though the pub only serves weird food, I still ate there, and I used the local shops."

I didn't realise Nye had stopped walking until I heard his voice from a few feet behind.

"Fuck me."

Gladly, but that wasn't the sentiment his tone expressed. We all turned to look at him as he ran forward, pausing only to scoop me up on his way into the house.

"Uh, boss? Is there anything we can do?" one of the men asked.

He waved them off. "No, go back to your patrol. I need to think."

"What is it? What's wrong?" I asked, too nervous to move from the chair he deposited me in.

"We've been all wrong on this," Nye said as he paced up and down between the half-empty grocery bags, running one hand through his hair.

"Wrong in what way?"

"What this bastard wants. It's not you that he's after at all."

"I don't get it."

"He wants the house."

CHAPTER 26

I TWISTED IN my seat to look at Nye. "What do you mean, it's the house?"

He paused in his pacing for a second. "It has to be. Whoever's doing this wants the house, not you. Think about it—apart from the initial burglary, everything that's been done wasn't only designed to scare you, but to scare you away from here."

The brick through my window, the message on the lounge wall, the eggs, my bike tyres, and now Twiglet. Nye's idea definitely had some merit. "But I wouldn't leave."

Was that a smile or a grimace? Hard to tell, but he still looked sexy. Oh boy, was I in trouble.

"I bet he didn't expect you to be so damned stubborn. What's the value of this place?"

"I don't know. I inherited it, remember?"

"And it never went on the market?"

"No."

"So, somebody could want it for themselves, and they just never had the opportunity to buy it?"

It was possible, but I couldn't really see it. "I guess, but it's not in great condition, or even in the best part of the village."

"Has anyone made you an offer for it?"

"I had one of those 'we sell any house' cards

through the door from an estate agent, but apart from that, no."

"So, that leaves us with option two."

"Which is?"

"There's something in here that somebody wants."

I looked around the dilapidated kitchen. I'd done my best with it, but the whole place was still...tired.

"What could possibly be in here? It's full of junk."

"The first burglary, nobody took anything, right?"

"Not that I could tell."

"They just made a whole lot of mess. I reckon they were looking for something, and they clearly didn't find it, because everything since then has been done to terrify you into leaving."

Which could be the case if not for one massive flaw in his logic.

"Why now? The place was empty for months. If somebody wanted to search it, why didn't they turn the whole place over then? Nobody would even have noticed."

Nye stopped and leaned against the sink. "I can't answer that. Yet. Maybe they didn't know the thing was here? There must have been a trigger for all this. Who else knew your aunt left you this place in her will?"

"Nobody. She didn't have one. I was her only surviving relative, and one of those heir-hunting companies tracked me down from the Bona Vacantia list."

"I'll need their details."

"Mickey wouldn't have done anything. He's harmless."

"No such thing. And even if it wasn't him, he might have tipped someone off when he started digging into your aunt's life. Eleanor Rigby. Like the old Beatles song?"

"That's right."

"This started with her—I'm sure of it. You need to tell me everything you know about her."

"But I don't know anything. I only met her a couple of times when I was a child. She and my mother fell out, and I never saw her in later years."

"Well, we'll need to come at this from a different angle. Someone must have known her." Nye talked at a hundred miles an hour, no doubt mirroring his thoughts. I'd never seen him so animated. "What was the argument with your mother about? Do you have any other family who might be able to help us?"

"Only my father."

"Can you call him?"

Could I call him? Nye made it sound so easy. Like I could just pick up the phone and dial the man who'd shattered my childhood.

"Liv, what's up? You've gone white."

"I haven't spoken to my father in a decade," I whispered.

Nye crouched beside me and took my hands in his, making me feel dainty yet insignificant at the same time. Pluto to his sun.

"What happened, babe?"

"He ran off with his secretary when I was twelve, and I haven't seen him since. I don't even know where he is."

"What about other relatives?"

I shook my head, fighting back tears. "There's no one."

He enveloped me in his arms, and that hug took

some of the pain away.

"Shit always happens to the sweetest people. Sometimes, I think karma's playing a joke on us."

Sometimes, yes. I nestled into Nye and breathed in his scent—a woodsy cologne over musk that was all man. His warmth seeped into me, and I never wanted to move again. Sometimes, karma came through.

"We can ask in the village about Eleanor," Nye said into my hair. "Are you up to paying Carol another visit?"

"I survived the first one, so why not?"

He pulled back and gave me a lopsided smile. "Yeah, you're right. I'm the one who's gonna be in trouble. I'll have a flak jacket sent over."

Nye found Carol's number and tried calling her, but there was no answer.

"She's probably gone out to a gossip session," I said. "WI meeting, knitting society, that sort of thing."

"Let's go tomorrow morning. She'll be around at breakfast if she's got guests in."

"What do we do now?"

"I'll get the geeks in the office to search in the meantime, but for you, I'd suggest dinner and an early night. Want me to order takeout?"

"No, I'm fine to make dinner." After all, that was what I'd promised.

Even though I felt jittery inside, I knocked out a quick spaghetti bolognese with a chocolate fondant for dessert. Nye cleaned his plate and had seconds.

"You weren't kidding when you said you could cook, were you?"

"Baking's more my thing, really, but I'm glad you liked it."

"There's only one thing more delicious in this room, and I'm looking at her."

Was it possible for feet to blush? Because I'm pretty sure mine did. I flushed from head to toe. Nye got up and walked towards me, and I waited in anticipation, every nerve ending aflame.

He carried on walking.

When he got to the sink, he put his hands on the edge and stared through the window at the darkness.

"Shit, I shouldn't have said that. Not to you."

I stood up. "What do you mean? Why not?"

Desperation tinged my voice, and I hated myself for that.

"I shouldn't be leading you on."

Words fell out of my mouth before I could stop them. "But I-I-I really like you."

I'd never bared my feelings to a man like that before, but when Nye turned, his stony mask told me my effort had been in vain.

"Liv, if I thought you were the type for a fling, I'd have you moaning underneath me upstairs by now. But you're not. You need a white knight."

"But what if I've fallen for black?" I whispered.

Because I had. The timing couldn't have been more wrong, but the man was right. Nye might have made my insides churn and my legs tremble, but it was more than that. He also made me feel secure. Nye was no Edward, and no Tate either.

He backed me up against the counter and leaned forward, one hand either side of my hips. Stormy eyes looked down into mine.

"I'm not the man you're looking for."

"Why don't you let me be the judge of that?"

"Stress does funny things to people."

"I didn't say that because I was stressed!"

Nye stared at me, and I pushed his hand away and sidestepped. Okay, I did sound just a little stressed.

He closed the gap between us again and cupped my cheek in his hand. "I'm going to save us both from future heartache and walk away. One day, you'll thank me."

"You arrogant—" I started, but he'd already left the room.

How dare he assume he knew what was best for me? A few seconds later, the living room door closed behind him. Not closed. Slammed. I eyed up the bottle of red on the table and got halfway through pouring myself a glass before I gritted my teeth and threw it down the sink.

No, I wouldn't resort to alcohol this time. If nothing else, I had to thank Edward for preparing me for this. Although my heart hurt worse for a man I'd never even kissed than it did after the demise of a two-year relationship.

I washed the dirty dishes on autopilot, then climbed the stairs alone. How did I misread things so badly? I'd dreamed of having Nye beside me in bed, and now I didn't even have a cat.

The cool expanse of cotton seemed to taunt me as I closed my eyes. Sleep wouldn't come easily tonight. Life would have been so much more straightforward if I'd liked Tate or Warren in the same way as I did Nye.

Why did my heart crave the one man I couldn't have?

CHAPTER 27

ANOTHER NIGHT PASSED with little sleep. I kept thinking of Nye on the floor in the lounge and wishing I could turn the clock back. Why hadn't I just laughed off the "delicious" comment? I should've known he wouldn't have wanted to get involved, but no, I just had to lay my cards on the table and make a complete fool out of myself.

My only consolation was that when I got downstairs, bleary eyed and dopey from lack of rest, Nye looked the same.

"Sleep well?" he asked.

"Nope." I couldn't be bothered to put a brave face on things anymore. "You?"

He shook his head. "Coffee?"

"Make it strong."

After two cups of liquid caffeine, Nye pulled a sports jacket on over the top of his customary black jeans and T-shirt instead of his usual leather one.

"What?" he asked when he caught me looking. "I can do smart."

I wrinkled my nose. "Sort of."

"I'm not wearing a tuxedo to visit Carol."

"Do you even own a tuxedo?"

He flashed a smile. "Of course. Every man should own a tuxedo. I tie my own bow ties too."

It surprised me, finding out those little things. Nye didn't seem the type to go out to posh functions, although that hardly mattered to me now. Not after last night.

We rode to Carol's in silence, but not the comfortable silence we'd shared on the trip back from the supermarket yesterday. No, this was a yawning chasm of awkwardness that stretched between the two front seats.

At least Carol didn't seem to notice. As with last time, she only had eyes for Nye as she served up coffee and Danishes. Plural for Nye, singular for me.

"I ground the beans myself," she told him as she put his cup down.

He managed to muster up a "terrific."

"So, what can I do for you today? I still haven't managed to get to the bottom of those awful rumours, but I've started a few of my own." She gave me my first smile. "All complimentary, of course."

"We're very grateful," Nye said. "But today we're trying to find out more about Olivia's Aunt Eleanor."

Carol sucked air in through her teeth. "Not a very nice woman, was Eleanor Rigby. That's probably why the tales about Olivia were swallowed so easily."

"Why? What did she do?" I asked.

"It wasn't so much what *she* did. She mostly kept herself to herself. It was more about who she married and who she gave birth to."

"What do you mean by that?"

"Eleanor married Harold Rigby." Carol spat the words as if they were poisonous. "A petty criminal through and through, and the apple didn't fall far from the tree with their son. Eleanor turned a blind eye to all their misdemeanours. Worshipped the very ground they walked on."

Could that be why my mother fell out with her? Something to do with her husband? I'd never know for sure, but my mother wouldn't have been one to tolerate a criminal in the family.

"What sort of misdemeanours, Carol?" Nye asked.

"You name it, and Harry Rigby probably had a finger in it. Shoplifting, burglary, running illegal poker games. A con artist, too. That's what he got sent to jail for. He swindled a lady in Sandlebury out of her life savings."

I could almost see Nye's mind working. There was money involved. Did someone think Harold Rigby's ill-gotten gains were hidden in Lilac Cottage?

"How long ago was that?" Nye asked.

"Must be fifteen years ago now. Harry was only inside for a couple of years, but it must have taken its toll, because he died two months after he got out. A stroke, if I recall correctly. The landlord of The Coach and Horses gave everyone a drink on the house in celebration."

Fifteen years. That was a long time for someone to have hung on to a significant amount of money, especially with the amount of junk Aunt Ellie seemed so fond of buying.

And Nye appeared to be thinking along the same lines. "What about Eleanor's son?"

"Ronnie. That was his name. Ronald Rigby. He followed in his father's footsteps, all right. I caught him stealing one of my chickens when he was barely ten years old. He went to jail too, for breaking Horrible Henry's nose. With the two Rigbys out of the way, the crime rate dropped to almost zero."

"Horrible Henry?" I asked.

"It's what all the girls call Henry Forster. That one can't keep his hands to himself. I still remember Luke Halston-Cain's ex-girlfriend giving him what for in his you-know-whats at the Hunt Ball. At least, that's what Henry claimed."

Was that Emmy? Surely it must have been.

"I should have thought Ronnie deserved a medal for that, not jail."

"And every woman in the Foxfords agreed with you. But it went to the Crown Court. Henry's father played golf with the judge, and Ronnie got five years."

"When did he get released?" Nye asked.

"He didn't. Upset a few too many people, did Ronnie, and came out feet first after barely a year inside. He's buried in the same row as his mother."

That much I knew. Aunt Ellie's son was long gone, and we'd hit a dead end, quite literally. A shame, because Ronnie would have made such a promising suspect.

"What about Betty Hazell's son? Do you know him?" Nye asked.

Carol's mouth set in a hard line. "Larry always was a strange one. When he was a teenager, he used to go around borrowing from washing lines. Ladies' smalls were his favourite. I always thought Betty must have dropped him on his head as a baby, but she won't hear a bad word said against him."

A bit like Aunt Ellie and Ronnie, then.

"Have you seen Larry around lately?"

Carol leaned back in her chair and took a sip of tea as she thought. "He picked Betty up after a WI meeting, let's see, two months ago? No, three. We'd just begun discussing the Christmas food drive, and that was at the beginning of November."

"She told one of my men she hadn't seen him for at least twice that long."

"I'm sure it was him. He got out to open the door for her, and I remember thinking he needed a good haircut."

"Can you remember what he was driving?"

"I'm not very good with cars, dear. It was maroon, that's as much as I can tell you."

"Don't worry—I'll check whether there's a car registered to him." Nye paused to take a gulp of milky tea. "How about Warren Hannigan?"

Warren? Why was Nye asking questions about him?

"Young Warren? I don't know him personally. Why? Is he a suspect?"

"Should he be?"

"Well, I'm not one to gossip..."

I glanced at Nye, and he couldn't keep a straight face either.

"But there was an incident not so long ago that made everyone see him in a different light."

"What kind of incident?"

"Warren's an artist in his spare time."

"What kind of artist?" Nye asked.

"Landscapes, mainly, but that's not what he used to paint. Women..." She leaned closer. "Women with no clothes on!"

Nye smiled faintly. "I'm not sure that's a crime."

"No, but he hired one of the girls from the village to pose for him, and she said he touched her. Inappropriately."

I choked on a mouthful of coffee and coughed until Nye thumped me on the back. Warren did what?

"I understand Warren doesn't have a criminal record," Nye said.

"Young Claire never did press charges. Too scared, if you ask me. What kind of man takes advantage of an innocent girl like that?"

"How do you know he took advantage of her?"

"Well, it's obvious, isn't it? All the arty-farty stuff was just a ruse to prey on the fairer sex. If I were you, I'd pay close attention to that one."

"I'll look into it."

The thought that Warren could be a predator left me cold inside, but I stopped myself from jumping to conclusions. After all, the whole village had swallowed any number of lies about me. Perhaps that was why Warren hadn't judged me when almost everybody else had?

Carol shuddered despite the fact that her dining room was heated to a balmy temperature. "What are the Foxfords coming to? First Ronnie, then Warren and Larry, and now this man fixated on Olivia. Back in my youth, parents disciplined their children properly, and we didn't have any of this trouble."

Nye pushed his chair back a couple of inches and glanced at his watch. "You've been very helpful, and thanks so much for breakfast."

Carol's face fell. "You're leaving already?"

"Like you said, I should look into the matters you raised."

"Yes, yes, of course. Let me pack you up a bag of pastries to take with you."

I trailed Nye out to the car, and once again, he held

the door open for me. Manners. It seemed every man around here had them, even the perverts like Larry.

Where did Nye learn his? He knew my entire life story, but I didn't even know where he lived. Did he have a family? What was his upbringing like?

Then again, what did it matter? Nye wasn't interested in me, and after this mess got sorted out, I'd probably never see him again. It wasn't as if we ran in the same circles.

That thought left me more depressed than ever as Nye started the engine.

"What's next?" I asked.

"I'll ask my team to take another look at Larry and Warren, and while they're doing that, I want to speak to Betty."

I had a horrible feeling that little chat would put me firmly back in her bad books.

In the post office, Betty was holding court behind the counter with a group of her acquaintances huddled around. Their eyes lit up when they turned and saw Nye. I'd always imagined they discussed recipes for apple pie and the latest knitting patterns at WI meetings, but maybe I was wrong. Maybe they ogled calendars and compared the models' assets.

As we got closer, I realised Betty didn't share their glee. If anything, she looked a little nervous.

"Can you spare a few minutes?" Nye asked.

Her smile disappeared. "Now?"

"We can come back later if it's more convenient."

She motioned at a door on the far side of the shop. "Better to get it over with. We'll have to continue our chat tomorrow, girls."

Betty flipped the sign from Open to Closed as they

left, then led the way upstairs to her tiny flat.

"It's about my Larry, isn't it?"

At least Nye's questions wouldn't come as a complete surprise.

He nodded, and she waved at a two-seater sofa. "You'd better sit down. Would you like a cup of tea?"

"White with one sugar for Olivia, no sugar for me."

The sofa felt entirely too small as I perched next to Nye, and it sagged in the middle so our thighs touched. I should have stayed at home.

"I've had a difficult time with Larry," Betty admitted once she got comfortable in the chair opposite.

"In what way?" Nye asked.

"He's a flighty soul. I wish he'd find a good girl and settle down, but he keeps flitting from one lady to another. I can't keep up. And it's like he's embarrassed for them to meet his old mum. He's never brought a single one home to visit me."

Probably because it wasn't the done thing to meet your stalker's parents. That would be more like kidnapping.

Nye went for diplomatic. "Perhaps he just hasn't met the right woman yet?"

Betty nodded.

"He did show a liking for Olivia here, which gave me hope, but once I heard she was chasing Tate, I told Larry she wasn't suitable for him."

"What kind of liking did he show for Olivia?"

"You know, an interest—he said she was pretty and asked me what her name was."

"And you told him?"

"Well, yes. New blood in the village, I thought I

might finally get my grandbabies. Oh, and he had some pictures of her."

"What kind of pictures?"

"Just a few photographs. Nothing special."

"Can you remember what Olivia was doing in the photos?"

Betty stared past us as she thought, her eyes focused on an ugly painting of a dog on the far wall. "She was riding a bicycle. You should smile when someone takes your picture, dear. Nobody likes a sad sack."

Maybe I would have freaking smiled if I'd posed willingly. How on earth had he got so close without me noticing? I gave a shudder and squashed against Nye without thinking, but before I could move away again, he slipped an arm around my waist and pulled me closer.

His voice hardened a little. "Olivia's still having problems with a burglar. If Larry's been nearby, he might have seen someone. He could prove to be a valuable witness. Do you think we could talk to him?"

Good going, Nye. Flattery will get you everywhere.

Betty's chest puffed out with pride. "My Larry's always been observant. He only pops by from time to time, though, and I haven't seen him in over a week."

Which was a hell of a lot more recently than she admitted before. It was amazing where a handful of well-directed questions from Nye got us.

"We really do need to talk with him."

"I'll ask him to call round at your cottage next time he's here." She turned to me. "I'm sure now we know those nasty stories aren't true, he'd love to get to spend more time with you."

Oh, wonderful. Did Aunt Ellie have a flamethrower hidden away anywhere? Because I'd be tempted to use it if Larry ever turned up within spitting distance.

"Do you have his address?" Nye asked. "We could swing by and save him the trouble."

"He moves around, does my Larry. Never did stick in one place for long. Would his phone number help?"

"More than you could know, Betty."

CHAPTER 28

"WHO'S THAT?" I hissed as we pulled up outside Lilac Cottage.

A blond-haired man stood in the front garden, eyeing up my windows. I say blond—his close-cropped hair was so light it was almost white.

"It's okay," Nye muttered, forgetting to open my door as he got out to greet our mysterious visitor. From the way the guards were sitting in their car, relaxed but alert, I assumed he wasn't my burglar. Could this be the locksmith?

"Aren't you going to introduce me to the lovely lady?" he asked when I got near.

Nye didn't look as if he wanted to, but his manners came to the fore. "Liv, this is Spike. Spike, meet Olivia."

Spike took my hand and kissed it, and Nye glared at him with murder in his eyes.

But Spike only laughed. "Easy, mate. Treading on your toes, am I?"

"No." Nye sounded like a sulky toddler.

"Whatever you say, buddy."

"Can we just talk about the house? Where are the weak spots?"

"Where *aren't* they?"

"If you were going in, how would you do it?"

"With the Blackwood car out front, it would have to

be around the back. That door's practically cardboard. I'll fit a deadbolt, but it could do with being replaced."

"Then replace it. What else?"

"The old tree next to the house is an invitation to any burglar. You might as well hang out a red carpet. It'd take me thirty seconds to climb into the bedroom at the back."

And I'd thought it had so much character. "Really?"

"Yeah. Except I didn't need to today because it only took me fifteen to get in through the kitchen. The place is a nightmare—full of hiding places. What's with all the junk? A thief wouldn't know where to start in that lot. Reckon that's your only saving grace."

"Which is our first problem," Nye said. "My theory is that our culprit's looking for something Olivia's aunt hid before she died."

"Good luck with that. What is it?"

"That's the second problem—we've got no idea. Her husband and son were both known thieves, so possibly cash or an item one of them stole."

"Where are they? Can't you persuade them to tell you?"

The way Spike said that sent shivers down my spine. I looked at Nye, but he wouldn't meet my eyes.

"They're both dead."

"Natural causes?"

"One yes, the other in prison, so not likely."

"Prison? Have you tried finding his cellmate? Mine used to tell me all sorts of shit. Your man might've been the type to talk."

Cellmate? Spike had been in prison? I took a step backwards and eyed up the screwdriver in his hand.

Nye seemed disturbingly unbothered by Spike's

revelation.

"Good point. I'll look into it. Any other ideas?"

"Nope, but you'll be the first to hear if I get a brainwave. You really lucked out with this case, didn't you?"

Nye looked at me. "Yeah, I did." There was no hint of sarcasm.

I didn't understand him. Why look at me like that? Why say those words when he'd turned me down?

"So what's your plan?" Spike asked him, waving a hand at my windows and turning the conversation back to Lilac Cottage.

"What do you recommend?"

"Apart from new doors, I'd suggest locks on the windows, motion-activated floodlights outside, and CCTV cameras to cover each side of the building."

"Isn't that a bit excessive?" I asked.

"No, it's not," Nye said. "Do it all."

"I'll get started right now."

Spike had helpfully left the door unlocked, and I followed Nye into the hallway, anger simmering inside me.

"How dare you invite a criminal into my home?"

"Do you mean Spike?"

"He said he'd been in prison."

"He did three months for beating up the drunk driver who killed his wife."

"Oh." My indignation leaked away. Who wouldn't want revenge in those circumstances? "I'm sorry. I shouldn't have spoken like that."

"And I should have explained. In the interests of transparency, Spike was a burglar—one of the best—but the police never got near him." Nye must have seen the steam coming out of my ears, because he hastily added, "He's gone straight now."

"How do you know that? He could just be, what do they say, casing the joint?"

Nye chuckled. "Trust me, babe, he's not. When he was inside, he spent three months away from his baby daughter, and he won't take the chance of that happening again. As soon as he got out, he started his own company. Now he advises householders how to stop people like him."

"You're absolutely sure he's safe?"

Nye walked over to me and took both of my hands in his. "Liv, believe me when I say that if there was the slightest doubt in my mind, he wouldn't be here."

Just like that, I went weak at the knees again. How could Nye do that to me with one look? One long, smouldering look.

A beeping noise sounded from outside, and I rushed to the front window in time to see a truck reversing up the driveway.

"What's going on?" I asked.

I wasn't expecting any deliveries. With the cottage still stuffed to the gunwales, I hadn't been remotely tempted to follow in Aunt Ellie's footsteps.

"I'm redecorating my apartment, and I had a spare sofa going, so I got someone to deliver it here. I figured you could do with somewhere to sit."

I reached the truck as two men carried the first piece of a luxurious pale grey leather sectional onto the tail lift.

"Nye, that looks brand new."

He shrugged. "I'm not home much."

"It's very kind of you, but I can't possibly accept it."

"I knew you'd say that, which was why I didn't tell you it was coming."

I opened my mouth to argue, but he cut me off before I could speak.

"You're doing me a favour, taking it off my hands. I need the space."

"Are you sure?"

"Positive. And it'll save me from spending another night on the floor."

I understood he was trying to be kind, but those words stabbed me in the heart. I'd offered him my bed, and he'd made his position quite clear.

But I had to be gracious. "I'm very grateful."

"Anything for you, Liv."

Nye parked himself in front of his laptop while I started lunch. Nothing fancy, just a few sandwiches seeing as we'd already eaten pastries at Carol's. But I'd only got the fillings out of the fridge when Tate phoned.

I saw his name flash up on the display and stifled a groan. It was a conversation I didn't want to have. Yesterday, once it finally clicked that Tate was basically Edward with more tweed, I'd vowed I wouldn't go running back to him, especially after the way he'd dismissed me so rudely. Even though Nye didn't want me either, I'd rather be single than mould myself into a man's accessory once more.

I sighed as the phone kept ringing, and I slipped out of the kitchen to take the call. No point in putting off the inevitable.

"Olivia, I need to apologise for what I said yesterday."

"It's okay. Apology accepted."

He couldn't help it. I realised that now. Tate was

one of those men who always had to know best.

"Thank you, darling. I really shouldn't have flown off the handle. I'm just worried about you, that's all."

His reasonableness made me feel even worse. "You don't need to worry, I promise. Nye knows what he's doing."

"Let me take you out for dinner to make it up to you."

Yes, Edward all over again. Everything could be fixed by three courses, as long as the restaurant served pretentious food at ridiculous prices.

"It's a kind offer, Tate, but I'm not in the right frame of mind for any of this right now."

Gah! Why couldn't I just come out and say what I really felt? That someone else had replaced him in my affections, unrequited or not?

"I guess I can understand that. A rain check, then?"

"Okay."

"I'll call you in a day or two; we can slot something in then."

Why did he make me sound like a business meeting?

"Uh..."

His voice softened. "I'll be thinking of you, darling. No other woman has affected me in quite the way you do. Until we meet again, I'll treasure the softness of your lips against mine."

Those words didn't have the effect they once might have done. Old Olivia would have swooned at his feet, but in the past few weeks, I'd learned more about myself and the future I wanted.

However, I still struggled to put that into words. "I'll be thinking of you too."

Grrr. *Olivia, you're a coward.*

Angry with myself for being so weak, I headed back to the kitchen, where Nye had inhaled a bag of crisps in my absence. I picked up the empty packet and put it in the bin, then carried on with the sandwiches.

"I've got people out looking for Ronnie's cellmate," Nye said. "Plus, I've got Ronnie's police files. His name came up in connection with a fair few burglaries, and only the local bobby's incompetence meant he didn't get banged up for those too. Fucked up the chain of evidence, according to my source."

"You mean Graham?"

He glanced at his screen. "Yep. Know him?"

"He came round after the first break-in. Someone had to remind him to fingerprint."

"Asshole. Hardly surprising Ronnie and his father got away with what they did for so long."

"So, what now?"

"We wait."

"That's it?"

"My team are out doing the legwork. I get the best job."

"What's that?"

He grinned at me. "Looking after you."

How could he be so flippant? Didn't he understand how much he hurt me last night? I couldn't stay near him, but when I stomped off into the living room, he came right after me.

"Shit. I said something else wrong, didn't I?"

A tear rolled down my cheek, and he wiped it away with his thumb then rested his forehead against mine.

"I've never felt like this before," I confessed.

"Babe, you don't know me. I'm not the man you

think."

"Then why don't you show me who you are?"

"Fuck. I shouldn't be doing this."

He leaned down and kissed me, softly at first, but within seconds his tongue tangled with mine as we grabbed at each other with a fervour that bordered on desperation. Fire burned through my veins, and only one thing could extinguish the heat.

Okay, make that two things. The piercing wolf whistle that came from outside had the same effect as a bucket of cold water.

I looked up like a guilty teenager, only to see Spike grinning at us through the window. Nye scowled as his friend gave us a round of applause.

"Steel toecaps, mate, that's what you need," he shouted through the glass, no doubt referring to his earlier comment about treading on toes.

"Shit, Liv, I lose my mind around you."

Guilt clouded Nye's eyes, and my heart sank. He was going to tell me the kiss was a mistake, wasn't he? That it shouldn't have happened. I hastily attempted to build a wall around my fragile heart, but every time I picked up a brick, it crumbled.

"But I like it when you lose your mind."

"Really? If Spike had turned up five minutes later, I'd have had you stripped naked and bent over the couch. I wasn't thinking."

Holy cannoli!

I cupped his cheek with my hand, and he clutched my wrist, holding me to him.

"Don't be angry. Neither of us was thinking."

"You're too good to be on display like some cheap trash." His face softened. "Liv, your pulse has gone crazy."

"I'm waiting for the bit where you tell me you don't want me again," I whispered.

He pressed his lips against my forehead. "It was hard enough the first time. Saying it again would kill me."

The fear faded away, and as I melted against him, I felt his heart beating every bit as wildly as mine.

"So what do we do now?"

"I have no idea. This is uncharted territory for me," he said.

"I've always told myself I should explore new things."

Nye's cock twitched against my hip, and he groaned. "Babe, you can't say that right now."

Another twitch. Actually, more of a vibration. "I think your phone's ringing."

"I know. I'm ignoring it."

"But it could be important."

"Yes, it could." Still, he didn't move.

The caller hung up but tried again a few seconds later, and from the way we were positioned, I'd have been a very happy girl if the buzzing didn't stop.

"You need to answer it."

"In a minute."

"Uh, if you don't, those vibrations are going to give me a problem." I could only imagine how red my face must be.

Nye laughed as he shifted enough to get his phone out of his pocket, but he still didn't let me go.

"Nye Holmes," he barked once he'd answered.

I could only hear his end of the conversation.

"You have? That was quick. Where is he?" A pause.

"Make sure he stays there... I'm on my way."

Had his team found a lead?

"We've got to go," he said, already shrugging into his leather jacket.

"We?"

"I'm not leaving you here without me."

I barely had time to grab my coat and bag before he shepherded me out into the BMW.

"Where are we heading?"

"I'm going to talk to Ronnie's ex-cellmate. You're going to a safe house while I do it."

A safe house? Were things really that bad?

"Will it be dangerous? Your meeting?"

"I don't know."

"That's not very comforting."

He cut his gaze to me, then flicked it back to the road. "I care about you too much to lie."

CHAPTER 29

NYE MADE A couple of calls on the way, speaking mostly in code, it seemed, and when we got into London, he drove straight to Belgravia. I'd barely ventured into that part of the world. Even Edward's income didn't have enough zeroes at the end of it.

The underground car park Nye pulled into was filled with expensive cars—a Mercedes SUV, a Porsche, and an Aston Martin to name but a few.

"This is the safe house?"

"Like Fort Knox."

The owner probably had as much money too.

We took a lift to the ground floor, where a huge multicoloured chandelier dominated a luxuriously appointed atrium. Nye headed down a hallway to the left, led me past two closed doors, and knocked on a third. A man whose casual attire clashed with the opulent surroundings opened it, and I recognised the Blackwood Security crest on his jacket. A second man looked out the window at the street below.

"These guys will take care of you till I get back. Behave yourself, yeah?"

Nye gave my hand a little squeeze and then he was gone.

Gone for two movies, an episode of *EastEnders*, and a pizza delivery. Three large pepperonis, but I only ate one slice, and even that felt as if it was going to come up again. Luckily, the taller of the two men seemed to have a metabolism that allowed him to eat for three, because he got through two of the pizzas on his own.

Where was Nye? What was he doing? And, more importantly, was he okay?

"Do you know how Nye's getting on?" I asked Pizza Guy.

He dragged his eyes away from the television and shrugged. "Don't worry about him—he knows how to look after himself."

All very well for him to say.

By the time Nye walked through the door, totally unscathed, my mind had cycled through him getting in a fight, to landing up in hospital, to lying dead in a gutter somewhere.

I ran over and threw my arms around him. "You're all right! Thank goodness."

Nye blushed while the other two men chuckled.

"That's quite a welcome, mate," Pizza Guy said. "Wish my missus gave me that kind of greeting every time I got back from a job."

I mumbled an apology. "Sorry. I was just a bit worried."

"I think I got that." Luckily, Nye was smiling.

"Did you find what you needed?" Pizza Guy asked.

"Partly. But it raised more questions than I've got answers for."

"Always the way, ain't it? Do you need us for anything else?"

"No, I've got it from here. Thanks."

The men filed out, leaving us alone, and Nye

reached straight for one of the leftover slices of pizza.

"What happened?"

I was dying of curiosity. Quite literally, if my mystery assailant had anything to do with it.

"I had an interesting chat with Ronnie's ex-cellmate."

"He talked to you? Like, voluntarily?"

Nye burst out laughing. "Don't look so worried, babe. What did you think I was going to do? Beat it out of him?"

Well, yes, but I couldn't exactly admit that. "Er..."

"We went out for a beer, and I bunged him a few quid. That's how it normally works."

Oh. That sounded almost civilised. Except it meant that Nye had shelled out yet more money on my behalf, which left me feeling guilty once again. I'd pay him back somehow, even if it took me years to earn enough.

"What did he say?"

"That Ronnie was a prick. No surprises there. But he did recall a conversation they had soon after they met about the families they'd left behind. The cellmate worried his wife wouldn't be able to pay the mortgage."

"Perhaps he should have considered that before turning to a life of crime?"

"Probably wouldn't have stopped him. They all think they'll never get caught. Anyway, Ronnie didn't seem bothered by money. He said he only had his mother left, and he'd made sure she had a good retirement plan. My contact got the impression Ronnie wasn't talking about a pension."

"That does make sense. Aunt Ellie bought all manner of things off the internet, and I never did work out where she got the money to do it."

"Eleanor only had forty pounds in her bank account when she died. I spoke to your mate, Mickey, and he swears there wasn't any other cash with the estate."

"I don't think Mickey would lie. So, how did she afford that stuff?"

"That, babe, is what we're going to find out. She could have kept funds in an online eWallet. PayPal or similar. I've got someone looking into that."

"Do we just wait again now?"

"No, we've got another visit to make."

"We?"

"Reckon this one'll be safe enough for you to come with me. Your presence might even help."

"Who are we going to see?"

"Ronnie's ex-partner."

"Like his girlfriend?"

"No, his partner in crime. Are you up for a road trip?"

With Nye? Always, and I trusted he wouldn't take me anywhere dangerous. "Where does he live?"

"About an hour north. Straight up the M1."

Edward had always insisted that conversation in the car distracted him from driving, but Nye was happy to chat away. Not only that, he held my hand the entire trip, and I snuck surreptitious glances at him while he concentrated on the road. My imagination began to run away with me. Maybe we could take a proper road trip together, driving across France, or even farther into Europe. Beautiful scenery, gourmet food, boutique hotels...

Olivia, stop it!

"Uh, was Ronnie's partner in prison too?"

"He never got caught. I don't even know for sure

they were partners, but I've seen his name pop up a few too many times. Call it a hunch."

"But surely he won't admit to being a criminal if we just turn up and ask?"

Nye shrugged. "I'll play it by ear. I'm hoping he'll decide it's the right time to confess."

Confess? Who in their right mind... Nye pulled up outside a small cottage next to a church in a village that reminded me of Upper Foxford, all twee and a bit of a time warp. I got the chance to ogle his muscles when he swapped his leather jacket for a sports one in the boot.

"Ready to go?" he asked.

I took his hand and read the name on the gate as he held it open for me.

"The *vicarage*? Are you kidding? Ronnie's ex-partner's a priest?"

"Seems he saw the error of his ways. Either that or he's pilfering from the collection plate."

A man wearing a white collar answered our knock. Clean-shaven, wholesome-looking, in his late thirties at a guess. Not at all how I'd imagined Ronnie's accomplice would look. Could Nye have got this wrong?

"Have you come to request a hymn for the service on Sunday?" the vicar asked.

"Not exactly. Can we come in? It shouldn't take long."

"What's this about?"

"Ronnie Rigby."

I'd heard the expression "white as a sheet" many times, but this was the first time I'd seen it. The man matched his own collar. Score one for Nye's intuition. The vicar swung the door open and shuffled along in front of us to his kitchen, a condemned man on his trip to the gallows. He'd aged a decade by the time he took a seat opposite us.

"I knew this would come back to haunt me one day. I've begged God for forgiveness every day since I became a believer. If I had the money, I'd repay everyone, but I live simply now. And I do good work in the community—the church, the youth group, the local scouts."

"Relax, would you? We're not here to cart you off to jail. You answer our questions, we'll leave, and you'll never hear from us again," Nye said.

The man's shoulders rose a notch. "Really? That's it? Just a few questions?"

"I don't care what you did in the past. You're the one who has to live with yourself."

"I understand now that my actions were wrong, but back then... Every day, I pray for the Lord's forgiveness, but inside, the dirt still clings." He leaned back and sighed. "What do you want to know?"

"Olivia here lives in Eleanor Rigby's old house, and somebody's looking for something hidden inside it. They keep breaking in and threatening her."

"I'm sorry to hear that."

He did sound genuinely sorry, and his sympathetic eyes confirmed it.

"We need to find out what Eleanor hid so Olivia can get some peace."

"Eleanor died?"

"Popped her clogs in the middle of an online poker game, apparently," I told him.

"I shouldn't speak ill of the dead, but..." He shook his head. "And poker? The old bag was working to the last, then. There's dedication for you."

"What do you mean, working? She played poker for a living?"

"Not exactly—the poker was a means to an end. Eleanor and Ronnie were every bit as dirty as each other."

"Define dirty," Nye said.

"We...we stole the goods, and Eleanor fenced them then laundered the proceeds. There was nobody better."

Nye seemed to be following, but I was lost.

"She used the poker games to clean the money?" he asked.

"Always did. That and the fixed-odds betting terminals inside the bookies'. She'd catch the bus with a handbag full of dirty money, stick it through those games machines, and come back with ninety-five percent of what she started with. Spotless."

"Son of a bitch."

"No, that was Ronnie. Eleanor was a cantankerous old biddy. She moaned like hell about having to trek into town to do his dirty work. Said it played havoc with her bunions."

"Did you only steal cash?"

"No, Ronnie wasn't fussy."

"What else did you take?"

"Anything Eleanor could flog. She auctioned it all off online, but Ronnie had a terrible job to stop her from buying as much as she sold. Still, it made a good cover. I don't think anyone ever suspected her."

"No, they didn't. So, any ideas what Eleanor might have tucked away in the house?"

"Sometimes Ronnie pinched expensive jewellery, even though it could be hard to sell. He made off with an engagement ring once, two names and the date engraved inside the band." The vicar shook his head, and a forelock of grey-brown hair flopped over one eye. "Stupid."

It felt wrong hearing a man of the cloth talking so casually about his criminal activities. It just went to show—never judge a person by what's on the outside.

"All the jewellery I found looked cheap. I didn't see any engraving," I said, although my chest seized. Had I accidentally sold someone's prized possessions for a fiver?

Nye squeezed my hand under the table. "Where in the cottage might Eleanor have hidden her stash?"

The vicar shook his head again, more emphatically this time, hands spread in a helpless gesture. "That place was a mess. I avoided it if at all possible. But it might not have been jewellery. Last time I saw Ronnie, he asked me to give an envelope to his mother. Said it was her retirement plan, so whatever it was, it had to be worth something."

"Did he elaborate on the contents?"

"No, and I didn't ask questions. I just assumed it was documents. It was only one of those small padded envelopes, so he couldn't have fitted much inside."

An envelope? I'd sorted through Aunt Ellie's piles of old mail, and most of it had gone in the rubbish. What if I'd thrown something important out?

"Any other insights?" Nye asked.

The vicar walked over to one of the cupboards and found a bottle of Scotch. His hands shook as he poured himself a generous measure and slugged back half.

"You know about the incident with Henry?"

Nye nodded.

"Well, a few weeks before that, Ronnie had one too many beers and let slip that he'd hit the jackpot. Easy money, he said, but he was nervous. Very nervous. He even cried off a couple of jobs, which wasn't like him at all."

"Any idea why?"

"No, but Ronnie used to do work on the side as well as with me. I figured he'd had a close call. Look, are we done here yet? I'm not the same man I used to be. Now it's my mission in life to stop young boys from going down the same path I did."

"Very admirable." The hint of sarcasm in Nye's voice went unnoticed by the vicar. "Here's my card. Do me a favour and call if you think of anything else?"

"Sure, I most certainly will."

He wouldn't. He couldn't show us out fast enough.

Back in the car, I tried to process what had just happened. A burglar turned vicar. I'd seen it all now.

"So, what did you think?" Nye asked as he slid behind the wheel and started the journey home.

"I can't believe it—the man's an ex-burglar, and now he's holding a position of such responsibility. Surely he should be in jail?"

"What good would that do?"

"Well, it would be a punishment for his crimes."

"Prison's supposed to help people see the error of their ways and stop them from reoffending. It seems to me like he's already done that."

"I suppose. I've never thought of it that way."

"And not only that, he's helping to keep kids out of jail too."

"I guess that makes sense. Do you always see the good in people? Spike? The vicar?"

"I've learned a lot working at Blackwood. If I hadn't had their support, I'd have ended up alongside Ronnie."

I half gasped, and then swallowed it into a cough. "You were a thief?"

"No, but I'd have landed in an early grave. I wasn't a good guy as a teenager, Liv."

"I don't believe that." Nye might have had a tough exterior, but that hid a heart of gold.

"It's true. I hated living at home, and I used to act out. But I met one of Blackwood's founders in a bar when I was eighteen, and he helped me to see the world differently. He gave me the chance to be myself."

I reached over and squeezed his hand, an automatic gesture. "I'm glad you got that chance. I like the man you've become."

Nye pulled the car over into a lay-by and killed the engine.

"What are you doing?" I asked.

"Kissing you."

And then he did.

CHAPTER 30

A FEW MINUTES later, Nye started the engine again. "When I asked what you thought, I meant about Ronnie and Eleanor rather than the rights and wrongs of the prison system."

"What? Ronnie?" I couldn't think straight. Nye had magic lips.

"Babe, you're so sweet when you get like that."

Nye thought ditzy was cute? That was good news. If he kept kissing me with all that heat and darkness and knee-trembling wizardry, ditzy promised to be a permanent state of affairs.

He squeezed my hand. "Ronnie and Eleanor?" he prompted.

"Oh, yes, of course. Eleanor wasn't a very nice lady, was she? I'm not surprised my mother stopped talking to her."

"You said she was playing poker online when she died. How do you know that?"

"Someone told me. In the pub, I think." I snapped my fingers. "Yes! It was Graham, and he'd been drinking. It was soon after I arrived in Upper Foxford, and I'd just heard Eleanor had died on the couch. That's why I threw it out."

"He said that in the pub? In front of everyone?"

"Yes, on curry night, so the place was packed."

"And right after that, the trouble started?"

I saw where Nye was going with this. "You don't think the two are connected, do you?"

"I don't believe in coincidences. Something set this dude off, and poker can be a dirty game. I need you to give me a list of everyone you can remember being there that night."

"I can try, but there were so many people. Floyd in the grocery store might be able to help. He was the person who introduced me to Graham in the first place."

"I'll get somebody to speak to him, although I bet he'll be even less help than last time if he was pissed."

"He did seem a little tipsy."

"So it'll probably be a waste of time. If Eleanor was playing online poker, what happened to her computer? Did it get stolen?"

"No, both of them are at my friend's house. I couldn't guess the passwords, and she knows a computer guy."

"Both?"

"A laptop and a MacBook. I did wonder why Aunt Ellie had two."

"Money laundering. Did she have two internet connections as well?"

"How did you know?"

"Do you know anything about money laundering?"

"I assume you don't mean accidentally putting a ten-pound note through the washing machine?"

He laughed. "It's the process of taking the proceeds of criminal activity and making it appear as if it was earned legitimately."

"I don't really get it."

"There are three stages. First comes the placement, when the dirty money's introduced into the financial system. Then layering, when it's moved around to disguise the origins. Lastly is integration, where the money's reintroduced to the economy, and it appears to be clean."

"But how can poker do that? And what was the vicar saying about bookies? What if she lost her bets? Wouldn't she just lose all the money?"

"It's easy enough to cycle money through the betting system and lose very little of it. At a betting shop, you can play on the game machines, and over time, the bookie's always going to keep a couple of percent, no more. It's written into their own rules. So if you keep the stakes small and just keep feeding the money in, you'll get most of it back. And better than that, you'll get a receipt saying you won that big wedge of cash in your pocket in a game of chance. It looks legitimate, and it's even tax-free."

"Wow. I'd never even have thought of that."

"Or you can back all the possible outcomes in, say, a football match. Win, lose or draw, one at each bookie. By calculating the amount you bet on each option, you'll only lose a tiny amount, no matter what happens in the game."

"That all sounds very complicated. What about the poker?"

"Easy. She'll have set up an online poker game where she was both of the players. One on each computer, using the two connections so it wasn't obvious. I bet she had variable IP addresses as well. Then she just lost the money from one player to the other and withdrew it to an eWallet."

It was hard to reconcile business-savvy Aunt Ellie with the woman obsessed with buying musical Christmas ornaments. Like the vicar said—nobody ever suspected.

But there was one part of the puzzle missing. "How did the money get into the poker account in the first place? The dirty money, I mean."

"That, babe, is the fifty-thousand-dollar question. We need to get hold of those computers."

Which meant we needed to go back to London. "Let me call Maddie."

It took two tries to get through to her, and when she answered, the piercing din of the smoke alarm nearly deafened me.

"Hang on," she shouted. "The bloody alarm's malfunctioned again."

I held the phone away from my ear until the noise subsided.

"Liv! How are things going with the cottage? Any more problems?"

"A few. You know that guy Sophie was talking about? The investigator?"

"Huh?"

"At the party? Fruit punch, burglary, investigator?"

"Oh, yeah, I remember. Sherlock. He turned up? Did he bring his magnifying glass?"

"He came all right." Well, not yet, but I hoped to rectify that as soon as possible. "But no magnifying glass."

And I certainly wouldn't be needing one judging by the bulge in his trousers.

"Is he any good?"

Hell, yes. "Er, he seems to know what he's doing.

Anyway, we need to swing by and pick up those laptops. There might be something useful on them."

"Perfect timing—I'm just making dinner, and I miscalculated the portions a tiny bit. There's plenty enough for four."

Those words struck fear into my heart. Maddie had many strong suits, but cooking wasn't one of them.

"We're a bit short on time."

"Nonsense. It's almost ready, and you've got to eat. I'll keep it hot until you get here."

I hung up with a feeling of dread in the pit of my stomach, soon to be replaced by indigestion or food poisoning, no doubt.

"Seems to know what he's doing? Seems?" Nye asked. "I know *exactly* what I'm doing, babe."

He ran a finger up the inside of my thigh, stopping just short of ringing the bell. "I'll prove it to you very soon."

Please say the dampness in my knickers wouldn't soak through to the seat, because he'd be needing a valet if it did.

"Maddie's making us dinner," I blurted.

"That's good, right? I'm hungry."

"No, it's not good. If you don't have any weird food allergies, I suggest you invent some now. Just say you can't eat solids or something."

"That bad?"

I nodded, already feeling a little nauseated. "Usually I insist on doing the cooking, but she's already prepared it."

I clutched Nye's hand on the way up to Maddie's flat. The smells drifting along the hallway were horrific enough to make even the most dedicated foodie turn to anorexia.

"We could get a takeaway on the way back," Nye suggested.

"I don't want to hurt her feelings."

"Too sweet," he muttered as he knocked on the door.

Maddie yanked it open almost immediately and wafted smoke out with a tea towel just as the alarm blared again. Nye rushed past and dismantled it to save our eardrums from further damage.

"Who are you?" Dave asked Nye, walking into the kitchen.

I rushed to do the introductions. "Maddie, Dave, this is Nye. He's been helping me get to the bottom of the break-ins."

"Tell me that's not the only thing he's been helping you get to the bottom of?" Maddie whispered as Nye shook hands with Dave.

"Maddie, stop it."

At least she turned as pink as I did when Nye bent to kiss her on the cheek.

"Want a beer?" Dave asked as Maddie waved us over to sit at the table.

Nye shook his head. "I don't drink when I'm working."

"You're going to regret that."

I clutched my hastily poured glass of white like it could ward off salmonella as Nye squeezed my leg under the table. I did note he looked slightly nervous.

"I've made liver mousse to start," Maddie said, carrying in a plate of brown jelly.

Liver? I closed my eyes and wished I could close my nostrils too. Yeuch. This was even worse than the salmon mousse she'd attempted last year.

"I might have burned it a bit," she confessed.

At least the charring improved the flavour. I pushed my portion around the plate as Nye tried a forkful and then grimaced. Opposite us, Dave tucked in with the look of a man who just wanted to get things over and done with.

"Aren't you hungry?" Maddie asked me.

"I haven't had much of an appetite lately. You know, with everything that's been going on."

Maddie leaned over and patted my hand. "That's quite understandable, sweetheart."

Nye didn't have the same excuse, and he turned a delicate shade of green as he forced most of the plateful down. I caught him glancing towards the door a few times, no doubt trying to think up an excuse to dash out of it.

As Maddie took the plates out to the kitchen, Nye downed half of my wine.

"How did you eat that?" he asked Dave. "What's the secret?"

"I've been with her a couple of years now, mate. She's destroyed all my taste buds."

But the worst was yet to come. Maddie soon bustled back out with the main course. "I used your recipe for beef Wellington," she told me, looking thrilled.

It wasn't difficult to make, but somehow the meat had ended up dry while the pastry was soggy. And what was that crunchy bit? I loved Maddie dearly, but she was a terrible, terrible cook.

"I'm turning vegan," Nye whispered.

"I'll join you in that."

Even Maddie couldn't mess up dessert, surely?

Over the years, I'd encouraged her to buy frozen and simply defrost, but today she'd pushed the boat out.

"I've made baked Alaska. My first try. What do you think?"

Now, the idea of baked Alaska was to keep the ice cream underneath cold while the meringue top went hot and crispy. Maddie had managed to reverse that, then decorated the concoction with gummy bears.

"It's a good first try, but maybe you need a tiny bit more practice."

She wrinkled her nose. "You're right. Next time you come round, I'll have another go."

Nye leaned in close enough for his lips to brush my ear. "I'm busy that day."

With dinner over, Dave fetched the two computers for Nye while I helped Maddie clean up in the kitchen. Once again, she'd ruined the non-stick surface on a perfectly good saucepan.

"That man is super hot. You know that, right?" she said.

It hadn't escaped me. "He's not my usual type, though."

"And who's that? Edward? Edward only cared about himself."

"At least I knew where I stood with him. Most of the time, at least."

"He treated you like a doormat, and you lived with it. That wasn't good for you, Liv."

"But I'm not sure Nye is either." I couldn't deny the chemistry, but long term? He'd already damaged my heart once. "I don't understand him. He scares me a little."

"What do you mean? Has he hurt you?" Her

defensive streak came out—she'd always take my side.

"No, no, nothing like that. It's more my feelings for him that scare me."

Because he *could* hurt me. No, more. Nye could destroy me.

Maddie gave me a hug. "That's how you're supposed to feel. Any man who makes you crazy that way is worth fighting for." She met my eyes. "You never felt that way about Edward, did you? Or Tate?"

I shook my head.

"There's your answer. And Liv?"

"Yes?"

"I saw the way he looked at you. Like you were a chocolate fudge brownie with sticky toffee pudding on the side."

My stomach groaned as I climbed back into Nye's car. Bulimia had never looked like such an attractive option.

"Are we going back to Upper Foxford now?"

"Not yet. I need to drop these laptops at the office, and I need to find some edible food."

"I'm hungry too."

He raised one eyebrow and looked at his crotch. "Good to hear."

"You've got a dirty mind."

"Would you want me any other way?"

I wanted him any way I could get him. After my talk with Maddie, I realised I had to take a chance, even if I risked heartache.

This time, we weren't in the car for long before we

drove into another underground car park, this one beneath a fancy office building in King's Cross. Nye punched the button for the second floor, and our first stop was the kitchen.

"Do you want a sandwich? Or fruit?" He rummaged deeper in the fridge. "There might be some chocolate at the back."

"Are you allowed to help yourself like that? What if that's somebody's dinner?"

"Nah, it's all communal. People spend a lot of time here, and the bosses like to keep us happy. That means fully stocked kitchens, a gym, and decent rest areas. If people burn out, productivity goes down. Why don't you stay here and eat something while I shoot over to the tech team with these?" He held up the bag with the computers.

An egg-and-mayonnaise sandwich had never looked so appealing—at least it helped to take the lingering taste of the liver mousse away. I kept to myself in one corner, and while I attracted curious glances, nobody spoke until a petite black girl took the seat opposite me.

"Are you new?" she asked.

"Oh, I don't work here. I'm just visiting with Nye Holmes."

"Nye? He's here?" She looked around.

"I think he headed over to the tech department."

"I need to catch up with him before he leaves." She pulled out her phone and fired off a message. "Forgive my manners. I'm Janelle, his PA."

She leaned over and shook my hand. Nye had a PA? That seemed so...civilised.

"Olivia Porter."

Her eyes went big, and she let out a squeal. "Ooh! I thought your face looked familiar. I've only seen it on video, and it was a bit blurry. We've all been dying to meet you."

"Video? What video?"

"On Facebook? With the stripper? You're something else, girl!"

Oh, hell. She saw that video? How high up were we? If I jumped out the window, would I be sure of dying?

"You've gone all white," Janelle said. "Should I call Nye?"

"No! I mean, please don't." I had a worse thought. "Did Nye see the film?"

"Of course. He was the one who showed it to us, up on the big screen. What a hoot! The whole room was in stitches."

He'd been laughing at me? Was that all I was to him? A joke? And maybe a quick shag while he was stuck out in the countryside?

I felt sick again, and not from Maddie's cooking this time. How could he have done that? Showed everyone my most embarrassing moment?

My vision went fuzzy as tears gathered, and I abandoned my half-eaten sandwich and ran out of the room. I managed to find a lift before the first sobs came, and I stabbed at the button until the doors opened.

"Is everything okay?" the girl on reception called as I ran through the expensively decorated lobby.

No, nothing was okay. Perhaps it never would be again.

Once my feet hit the pavement, I carried on going, away from Nye, away from everything.

CHAPTER 31

EVEN IF I hadn't been crying, I'd have had no idea where I was going. I just kept sprinting until I ran out of steam, which was quicker than I'd have liked seeing as I'd cancelled my gym membership, then settled for walking quickly.

I'd known Nye had the power to hurt me, but I'd had no idea it would happen so soon.

How could I have been stupid enough to think he genuinely cared? Sophie and Maddie were both right—Nye had the handsome face, the hot body, and the decent job, all of which put him way out of my league. Mother might have wanted me to aim high, but right now, I couldn't even raise the gun.

What did I have to offer? A tumbledown cottage and a stalker. No wonder he thought I was worth laughing about.

Too late, I realised I'd left my bag in the kitchen at Blackwood. Not only was I hopelessly lost, I couldn't call a cab, and even if I managed to wave one down, I wouldn't be able to pay the driver.

Another block, and my tears of embarrassment and devastation turned to fear. Half of the street lights didn't work, and judging by the boarded-up house next to me, it wasn't such a good area. I passed by the entrance to a narrow alley and jumped as a plastic bag blew across in front of me. A straggly bush rustled in the breeze, stretching my nerves to breaking point.

Where was I? I looked for a street sign, but somebody had attacked it with graffiti. A dog barked in the house opposite just as a shadow flitted across the street. Was somebody there? I squinted into the gloom, but ominous shapes blurred together. The Big Bad Wolf. The Wicked Witch of the West. Bloody Edward and bloody Becki Harris.

I kept walking, my ballet pumps squeaking on the cracked paving slabs. A crowd of youths passed on the other side of the street, laughing and joking, and a couple stared across at me. *Look away, Olivia.* I kept my head down to avoid eye contact. As their shouts receded, the loudest sound was my own breathing, a rasp of desperation in the near darkness.

How could I get back? Even if I turned around, I doubted I'd remember the way, and I didn't want to see Nye in any case. A cat shot out of the shadows a foot away, and an involuntary squeal escaped my lips. Okay, facing Nye might have been the better option.

Footsteps sounded behind me, and I walked faster, on the verge of running now. But to where? The quiet slap of rubber soles on the pavement kept coming, and I glanced behind as a man with a dog walked under a street light. Out for an evening stroll? Or something else?

I was about to say "to hell with it" and break into a sprint when a car sped past and braked sharply in front of me. Nye leapt out of the back, and before I could instruct my feet to sprint, he'd grabbed my arm.

"Liv, what the fuck happened? Jannie said you shot out of the building like the fires of hell were after you."

Oh, thank goodness! Nye was here.

Actually no, this was terrible.

"You think I'm a joke," I blubbed, tears flowing again. Not that they'd ever really stopped.

"What? Why would I think that?"

"You saw that horrible video. The one of me at the cabaret."

He started laughing. "Babe, that video was hilarious."

"See, you're laughing."

He took both my hands in his. "When I saw that clip, I realised I'd finally found a woman who knew how to let her hair down and have a good time. The girls I dated in the past would have a single dry martini then switch to water to avoid extra calories, and they wanted to be in bed by ten so they could make their early morning spa appointments. I watched you, uh... sliding...and saw someone I wanted to get to know."

"But you showed everyone."

"Not exactly. I was running standard searches on the big screen, and the video came up. I tried to switch it off, but there'd have been a mutiny if I'd deprived the girls of, what was his name, Taurus? At least six of them have asked me if you can get his number."

"So they don't all think I'm an embarrassment?"

"They've been badgering me to invite you on their next night out. You're a legend in the office."

"Oh."

"'Oh' is right. Next time you decide to run off, would you mind taking your phone? It's easier to track that than send out a sniffer dog. Or better still, you could talk to me first?"

"I'm sorry."

"Come on, let's go back, eh?"

Nye helped me into the car, and I cuddled up against him, thankful for his arm around my shoulders. The driver had us back to the office in no time.

"How am I supposed to face people?" I asked Nye.

"Nobody judges here. Just be yourself."

I clung to Nye's hand while we went to collect my bag. Janelle was still there, and she handed it to me.

"Night, chicky. Don't do anything I wouldn't do." She gave me a wink.

"I hope you're going to be doing something Jannie wouldn't do," Nye whispered to me in the lift. "Or rather, someone."

Good grief, I'd need to wring my knickers out when we got back.

Except when Nye parked the car outside Lilac Cottage, the events of the day had caught up with me. I was vaguely aware of him lifting me out of the passenger seat and carrying me upstairs to bed.

Then nothing.

Nye's phone woke me in the morning, ringing on the nightstand. I'd fallen asleep in his arms, my back to his front, and something long and deliciously hard pressed into my bottom as he reached over to answer.

The conversation didn't make any sense as I only heard Nye's end—"Yeah... Yeah... Right... Yeah... Got it..."—but it was soon forgotten when he flipped me over to face him.

"I have morning breath."

I covered my mouth with my hand, but Nye nipped

at my fingers until I moved it, then kissed me.

"Do I look bothered?" he asked when we came up for air. "I wanted to do that last night, but you were out of it."

The memory brought on another yawn, and I clapped a hand over my mouth again.

"That's the spirit, babe, open wide."

I closed it so fast my jaw cracked, and he laughed.

"So sweet."

I was still dressed, but Nye had taken off his shirt, and I ran a finger over his hard chest. Hey, I'd have challenged any girl to be greeted by that sight and keep her hands off. Or her tongue. On second thoughts, I wouldn't—they were mine.

I was just going in for a taste when I heard laughter. Where was it coming from? Not the TV—the screen was dark.

Movement over Nye's shoulder caught my eye, and I screamed before I realised it was only Spike hanging from a ladder outside. Nye leapt out of bed and yanked the curtains closed, shouting a few choice words at the locksmith-slash-burglar as he did so.

"Shit, Liv, I didn't know he was coming so early. That asshole's turning into a regular cock-blocker."

A month ago, I'd have been mortified, but after our talk last night, I saw the funny side. I started giggling, then that turned into full-blown laughter, and Nye joined in as he climbed back into bed beside me.

"At least we hadn't started anything," I spluttered.

He arched his hips into me. "Speak for yourself."

"Oh, hell. What should we, er, I mean, should we…"

He gave me a soft kiss. "Our first time will be special. Not some fumble with Spike six feet away. I'll take a cold shower."

He got up to do just that while I threw some fresh clothes on and made breakfast. After Maddie's concoctions and last night's aborted attempt at eating a sandwich, I was ravenous.

"I hope you like pancakes," I said to Nye when he got downstairs.

"I like anything you want to cook."

"Was the phone call earlier important?"

"The London office transferred the contents of the two laptops to the US, and they analysed them overnight. There was an interesting pattern."

He paused to drizzle maple syrup on his pancakes, and when he added lemon juice as well, my impatience got the better of me.

"And?"

"As I suspected, Eleanor had a whole host of poker accounts, but one of them kept cropping up. Every month, exactly two thousand pounds was deposited into it, and then that money was 'lost' to one of her other aliases and withdrawn via an eWallet."

"What does that mean? That she was still laundering money for someone?"

"It's possible, or she may have been fencing. The two thousand could have been her payment for services rendered."

"But you don't think it was?"

He shook his head. "The amount never changed, and there wasn't the pattern of large deposits you'd usually see with money laundering."

"Then what?"

"Regular payments like that? Month in, month out? My bet's on blackmail."

My jaw dropped. "Aunt Ellie was blackmailing someone?"

"Or Ronnie was. The payments started a couple of months before he went to prison. Eleanor could have just carried on with the collection process."

Burglary was one thing, but blackmail? That was a whole lot worse in my eyes. At least with burglary, the victim suffered one short, sharp shock. Blackmail could drag on for years and make a person's life unbearable.

"Who were they blackmailing?"

"I don't know yet. But when we track that person down, we might well find your mystery attacker."

"What if we can't work out who it is?"

"We will." Nye furrowed his brow as he pondered. "I don't think we can discount Larry, and I still want to look into Warren further. But this angle's promising. Blackmail brings out the worst in people, and Ronnie, assuming it was him, chose a smart amount. Your average person could live on two grand a month, but not so lavishly the transactions would arouse suspicion. And it's also low enough that even someone on a moderate income might scrabble around to cover the payments rather than have their secret get out."

"I still don't understand why the blackmailer didn't search the cottage years ago, or even threaten Eleanor to make her reveal where she'd hidden the...the *thing*. They don't seem averse to a bit of heavy-handedness."

"Because he didn't know it was her until recently." Nye ate another mouthful of pancake and chewed slowly. "That night in the pub where Graham was shooting his mouth about Eleanor and her online poker habit—I bet it was news to the culprit. When he goes to deposit more money in the account, he'll see the balance, and he'll know it hasn't been touched since the day she died. If I were a gambling man, I'd put a few quid on him realising that night who'd been conning him."

"But she's dead now. She's hardly going to ask for any more money, is she? So why does it matter? Why didn't the burglar just stop paying the money in and disappear?"

"This is about more than two grand a month. He's worried that whatever she had on him is still in this house, and you might find it."

That did make a certain amount of sense. "But how would I know if I found it when I haven't got a clue what it is?"

"Thanks to his persistence, we've got an idea now. It's something small that fitted in that padded envelope the vicar gave Eleanor. And whatever it is, it's also the key to something bigger."

"So now what?"

"Now, we look for it."

CHAPTER 32

NYE MADE IT sound so simple.

"Just like that? We look for it?"

"You have a better idea?" he asked.

"Well, no, but..."

"Why don't we get started, then?"

While I'd managed to duct-tape my subconscious, which still wanted to scream every time I set eyes on the piles of peril, the mess was still there. And now Nye wanted to dig through everything and make it worse? The thought alone made me want to move into a convent. Nuns didn't have possessions, right?

A simple, uncluttered life. That was my new dream. Forget opening a bakery, just the ability to open a door all the way without it jamming against a mound of junk would do.

But Nye was serious, and he was also waiting. I procrastinated for five minutes longer by making coffee. I was tempted to add a slug of brandy to mine, but I didn't want Nye to think I was a lush.

"Which room do you want to start with?" I asked, desperately hoping he'd change his mind and suggest a nice ride on his motorcycle instead.

No such luck.

"Statistically, women tend to hide most things in the kitchen. So I vote we search in here first."

Over the next six hours, we pulled the room apart. Every cupboard got emptied, and we checked the bottoms and backs for hidden compartments. I inspected every can and bottle left from the days of Aunt Ellie in case it contained something other than food, and Nye even sifted the old bags of sugar. Apart from a brand-new hand mixer stuffed at the back of one cupboard, which I got tragically excited about, and a rather disgusting desiccated mouse, we found nothing.

"Lunch break?" I suggested, even though I still felt slightly queasy from the dead rodent. Perhaps I could suggest we head out for a bite to eat in, say, Scotland?

Nye nodded and sat back in a chair. "This is harder than I thought. How could one woman own so much shit?"

"I don't know. I'll admit, the untidiness offends me."

He laughed. "Babe, you sounded so prim when you said that."

"What's the problem with liking things neat?"

"There isn't a problem. You're adorable when you get all indignant."

I tried to look peeved, but it proved impossible when Nye leaned forward and captured my lips with his. He wound his hand around my ponytail and tilted my head back to give himself better access, and for a few blissful minutes, the worries of my life disappeared. Kissing Nye consumed me.

I longed to stay there for the rest of the day, but storm clouds hovered on the fringes of my mind, threatening to burst if we didn't get on with the task at hand.

Nye groaned as I pulled back. "Do we have to keep looking through this crap?"

"I don't want to either."

"I could take you upstairs and make you forget it existed."

My nether regions heated at the mere thought. If only I could give in to temptation. "We have to carry on searching. And isn't Spike still outside?"

"Yeah. Fuck it, you're right. Let's get this mystery solved. Then I can lock you in my bedroom for a week."

"Are you serious?"

He waggled his eyebrows and glanced at his lap. "Don't worry—I'll feed you."

"Stop it, or we'll never get this done." One of us had to act like the grown-up. "Which room's next?"

"Your bedroom. It's Eleanor's old room, right?"

I nodded.

"I had more ideas while we were looking this morning, and I want to bring in help tomorrow when we tackle the other rooms."

"What kind of help?"

"Extra manpower and a truck to put some of the crap in. Otherwise, it'll be like one of those plastic puzzles where you've got one free space and you have to keep slotting other pieces into the gap."

He wasn't wrong. Even in the kitchen, which was arguably the tidiest room in the house, we'd struggled for places to put things while we emptied out the cupboards. I had visions of getting stuck in the middle of a pile of junk with no escape if we tried the same tactic in the other rooms.

Although if Nye was with me, I could see the advantages.

"What other ideas did you have?" I asked.

"I want to look into any burglaries that were reported just before the payments started, and I'm also going to give Carol a call. Even if nothing went on record with the police, she might remember if there were rumours."

He tried the office first and soon had a colleague hunting through crime reports. Then he dialled Carol and put his phone on speaker.

"Mr. Holmes! How wonderful to hear from you."

She mooned over him for ages before he managed to get a word in and ask whether she recalled anything that fitted in with our timescale.

"Five years ago, you say? Well, that would be around the time Moira Fleming's niece got married. Quite the scandal, it was, because her ex turned up at the church and objected on the grounds that she'd been in his bed the night before. The wedding went ahead, but the divorce six months later got a bit nasty."

I could only imagine.

"Then young Tate Palmer went off to university. Oxford or Cambridge, one of the two. He was only seventeen, and his father crowed to everyone about it for weeks. All the girls in the village were heartbroken. He had quite the little fan club." There was a long pause. "Goodness me, I got mixed up. That was the year before. Five years ago, Tate's mother ran off with the gardener. Fenton didn't have quite so much to say about that."

Really? Poor Tate. What a terrible thing to happen to anybody. Perhaps I should have tried harder to be understanding with him over our relationship, or rather, our lack of one.

"Then there was Megan Shaughnessy. She decided she wanted to be an actress and moved to Hollywood. Following her dreams, she told everyone."

"Did she make it?" I asked. I loved a fairy-tale ending.

"She starred in a number of movies, but they weren't quite what her parents had envisaged. Not so many clothes involved, if you know what I mean. Mr. and Mrs. Shaughnessy couldn't hold their heads up at the horticultural society any longer, so they moved to Benidorm."

"And Megan?"

"Nobody's seen her since. Oh, and around that time, Maggie Bottomly had her nervous breakdown. A truck driver found her wandering along the road at midnight in her pyjamas, and—"

Nye rolled his eyes and interrupted. "I was thinking more about unexplained thefts than anything else, Carol."

"Oh. Let me have a think. As it happens, there were a few burglaries. A couple of months, that spate lasted, in all three of the Foxfords and half a dozen more villages besides. The culprit seemed to like the expensive things. Jewellery, mainly, but some art went missing as well."

"Did they ever catch anyone?"

"No, dear. Except for Mr. Benson. It turned out he'd faked his own burglary to claim the insurance money. He'd been drinking away his fortune, you see, and he ended up owing money to some loan shark."

"What happened to him?"

"Do you know, I've got no idea? I must be slipping. I'll try to find out for you."

"Thanks, Carol."

After he'd hung up, Nye sat back with the faraway look of someone deep in thought. "The fake insurance claim is an interesting angle. What if someone else tried the same trick and didn't get caught?"

I saw where he was going with that thought. "And Ronnie could have guessed, because he knew he didn't do the burglary."

This detective thing was getting exciting!

"Exactly. When we get the list of crime reports, we'll go through it for high-value thefts and see which of those had big insurance payouts."

"How would that fit with something being hidden in the house?"

"I'm not sure," Nye admitted. "The vicar thought the envelope he gave Eleanor had papers in it. Maybe Ronnie managed to get copies of the insurance documents?"

"So we have to keep searching?"

"Afraid so."

I started with the wardrobe while Nye took Aunt Ellie's dressing table. I'd only cleared out a tiny corner for my things, seeing as I didn't have much left, and most of the space was still taken up by her clothes. Shapeless old dresses and worn cardigans.

Her shopping habits clearly hadn't extended to her own attire, or she'd have been outfitted in colourful kaftans and sparkly tops you could wear in three different ways. I hunted through all the pockets to no avail, then emptied everything onto the bed.

"Nothing?" Nye asked.

"Not yet. I'll start checking the wardrobe itself."

I tapped the panels and checked the joints, but

there was no Narnia-like realm hidden away at the back, or even space for Ronnie's envelope. I was about to ask Nye to double-check when I heard a low whistle from behind.

"Tell me these aren't Eleanor's."

I looked around and saw him holding up a pair of the lacy knickers I'd bought in a vain attempt to keep Edward happy. A barely there pale-pink thong with tiny bows at the top.

I gasped, conflicted over whether to grab them off him or die of embarrassment as a blush rose up my cheeks.

"I wish you'd warned me," he said, dropping the offending item back into a drawer. "How can I concentrate on the job now?"

"Maybe you could take a break?"

And stop rooting through my flipping underwear drawer.

"Good plan."

He shoved Aunt Ellie's clothes off the bed, and before I realised what was happening, I was lying on top of it. Nye knelt astride me, giving me an eye-level view of the bulge in his jeans. Not quite what I had in mind, but that didn't matter anymore.

"Liv, you're so fucking sweet. A proper English rose."

Mr. Tall, Dark, and Dangerous was always calling me sweet, but he could be quite sugary himself.

I was just about to have a taste when my phone rang. Why now? Why couldn't I have a teensy bit of fun in my life?

"Ignore it," Nye said.

"I can't. I hardly ever get calls. It might be

important."

It was.

A whispered voice sent shivers through me. "I know what you're doing. Call off the search, or you'll regret it."

"Who is this?" My voice came out as a squeak.

"You know who this is—your worst nightmare."

Nye snatched the phone from me. "Leave her alone, or you'll fucking regret it." He threw the phone down in disgust. "Asshole hung up."

"You heard what he said?"

Nye nodded as he pulled out his own phone and began muttering into it about monitoring and traces. Now this was getting more personal, and I couldn't stop shaking as I stared through the window at the drizzle outside. Would this game ever end? Every move we made, the mystery man seemed to be a step ahead.

"Are you okay?" Nye asked, dropping his phone onto the bed.

No, but I didn't want to look weak, so I shrugged. "At least he didn't come into the house this time."

It seemed I wasn't the only one affected by Nye's presence.

"We'll find him, Liv. I won't let anything happen to you."

"How did he even get my number?"

"It's on your website."

Oh. Yeah. "What do we do now? Should we stop searching?"

"No, we bloody shouldn't. We've hit a nerve, and that means we're getting closer."

"But isn't that dangerous? I mean, he must have been near the cottage to know we're pulling the place apart."

Nye shook his head. "He'd need to have looked in the windows, and Spike's set up motion sensors. The control room would have called me if anyone got that close."

Or perhaps he was just psychic. I'd got to the stage I'd believe anything.

"Are you sure?"

"Yeah, I'm sure. My guess is that Carol's been asking more questions and one of them's touched a nerve."

"The insurance thing?"

"Could be. The smell of money brings out the monster in people. But I do have a small piece of good news."

Oh boy, did I need that. "What is it?"

"My team have found Larry in a homeless shelter a couple of towns away. He lost his sales job a few months back after he made inappropriate advances towards a colleague. My guess is he hasn't told Betty."

"So he'll be feeling the pinch as well?"

"Exactly. With the amount he earned, he'd have been under pressure paying Eleanor two grand a month. If a new demand came, he'd be sunk."

"But I wouldn't blackmail him!"

"He doesn't know that."

"What happens now? Do we talk to him?"

"'We' don't do anything. You're not going anywhere near that man. He's under surveillance, and when he goes out, Spike'll take a closer look at where he's living."

"Is that legal?"

Nye gave me a look.

Right, I forgot. This was the new Olivia. New Olivia lived daringly on the dark side. At least, she did as long as she could manage the "lived" part.

CHAPTER 33

A COMBINATION OF turning my entire bedroom upside down and the nasty phone call a few hours earlier left me drained. And worse—our efforts were in vain. I groaned as I surveyed the mess. It looked as if a poltergeist had thrown a tantrum in there.

"How about we sleep on the couch tonight?" Nye suggested.

"I can't." Damn my OCD. "I'm so sorry, but I just can't leave it like that."

Nye rubbed a hand over his eyes. "It's okay, Liv. We'll put it back."

It was nearly two in the morning by the time we got some semblance of order, and the moment we could see the bed again, we both collapsed into it.

"I never thought I'd say I was too tired, babe, but I'm too..."

I didn't hear the last bit, because I fell asleep.

Beeping from outside woke me the next morning, and I rolled out of bed to see a truck trundling down the driveway. A second one soon followed, along with half a dozen cars.

There were definite advantages to sleeping fully

clothed. My feet stayed warm, Spike didn't see me naked, and it saved ten minutes in the morning. My mother was probably having afterlife palpitations, but I took a deep breath and blocked her out. Nye went to open the front door while I brushed my teeth, and by the time I got downstairs, he was holding a briefing in the kitchen.

"Every box, bag, and basket gets examined. We're looking for something small, possibly documents, and they might be in an old padded envelope. Anything you're not sure of, call me, and if I'm busy, put it aside for checking later. Any questions?"

"What do we do with things once they've been checked?" a blond-haired boy asked.

"Items Olivia isn't using for day-to-day living get stacked out in the trucks until this is over. Anything else?"

Everyone shook their heads.

"Great. Let's get started with the dining room."

Except we didn't make it out of the door before a man with his black hair plaited into intricate cornrows sidled up to speak to Nye.

"Got a minute?"

"Tell me it's not that woman with the lost King Charles spaniel again? I've already told her we're not consulting a psychic."

"It's about the surveillance detail."

"Which one?"

There was more than one? I knew about Larry, but what hadn't Nye told me?

"The first one. He's taken off for a dirty weekend in France with Pneumatic Barbie, so we've handed over to a team from the Paris office to keep an eye. Don't suppose we'll see much of him—they've ordered the 'pleasure pack' and a magnum of champagne."

"Too much detail," Nye snapped.

His colleague backed off, hands up. "Sorry, boss."

"What's he talking about?" I asked.

"Sorry you had to hear that, babe."

"Why? Who is it?"

Nye sighed. "Your ex. I didn't trust him, so I had him followed, but he hasn't been near here."

That bastard! The only time Edward took me to Paris was on a business trip, and he left me on my own for most of it. I'd spent more time with the housekeeping staff than I did with my boyfriend.

Anger welled up inside me, but I forced it down. You know what? It didn't matter. My heart beat for Nye now. He was twice the man Edward would ever be, even if Edward got assistance from a cosmetic surgeon and packets of Viagra.

I stood on tiptoe to kiss Nye on the cheek. "I don't care about him anymore."

He pulled me tight against him, and I felt every inch of what Edward had been missing.

"Good. Because I'm planning to make you forget he ever existed."

Dammit, why did he have to say that when we had a house full of people? We had no choice but to assist as Aunt Ellie's cottage was systematically dismantled and the contents stowed in the trucks. Even once they were half-full, we'd barely made a dent in downstairs.

I tugged at a piece of tinsel, which unravelled to reveal a huge bag of Christmas decorations, and... What was that?

"Woohoo! I found a dining table."

A nice one too, with expanding leaves to seat six. I could hold a dinner party if the house was ever tidy enough for me to invite guests over. Were there any chairs hidden away? I kept my fingers crossed as I carried out yet another box.

By late morning, the mood was still positive even though we'd found nothing, and I took a break to make lunch.

"Don't worry," Janelle said. She'd been roped into helping as well. "If there's anything here, we'll find it."

"I hope so. Even with Nye staying, there's not much more I can take."

"These cases have a habit of breaking suddenly. I've seen it loads of times. Last year, there was this..." She trailed off and looked up at Nye, who'd walked in looking grim. "Did something happen?"

He perched on the edge of the table. "Spike had a poke around Larry's room this morning."

"And?"

Nye's face darkened even more. "Larry had photos of Olivia and three other women in his nightstand."

A tremor ran through me, and Nye squeezed my hand.

"A lot of photos?"

"Enough. The ones Betty mentioned of you on your bike and more of you walking down the high street..."

"What else? Tell me."

"There were some of you sitting on the floor in the living room, packing up parcels."

So Larry *had* been at the cottage. I felt sick. "How could I have missed him?"

"It was evening when he took the pictures. It's hard to see out into the dark when you're in a lit room."

"I should have drawn the curtains."

"You weren't to know."

"Well, I won't be making that mistake again."

"I know, and I'm beyond furious that you've had to learn this way. We'll keep watching Larry, and if he comes near you again, we'll have more evidence against him."

"But the photos..."

"We can't admit we've seen those, not to the police." He pressed a soft yet heated kiss to the corner of my mouth, full of promise. "I'll stay with you the whole time, Liv. But in the meantime, we need to find whatever's hidden in this house."

By the end of the day, the optimistic mood had diminished somewhat, and I'd heard murmured suggestions of tearing down walls. I sincerely hoped it wouldn't come to that.

"We've still got most of upstairs left to do," Nye said once everyone else had left for the night. "Maybe our missing piece is up there?"

"It just feels hopeless."

He gave my shoulders a squeeze. "At least we'll know, one way or the other."

"But if we don't find anything, how will the man after me know that? What if he keeps coming?"

"Maybe we could take out an advert in the local newspaper." Nye was only half joking.

"Or hire one of those planes to fly a banner?"

"How about a leaflet drop? Or one of those town crier dudes with the bell?"

I couldn't help smiling at the thought of that.

Better to laugh than cry, right?

Nye traced my dimples. "That's better. If we don't

find anything, I'll tell Carol. Job done. Shall I order a pizza?"

The last thing I felt like doing that evening was cooking. "Please."

"You want everything on it?"

"Except anchovies."

"Got it."

Our food arrived forty minutes later from the Italian place in Middleton Foxford, evoking memories of my trip there with Tate. He hadn't contacted me since that last phone call, and the relief I felt told me I'd made the right decision by not pursuing things further.

"Heaven on a plate," Nye said, flipping the lid open.

"Well, a cardboard box."

He shrugged. "Saves washing up."

Edward would have had a fit if I'd suggested eating without cutlery, but snuggling up on the sofa with Nye while he wrapped one arm around my shoulders and held a slice of pizza in the other hand felt like the most natural thing in the world. Every so often, his fingers strayed downwards, and soon there was a very different kind of hunger coursing through me.

"I should clear up," I mumbled when he finished the last slice.

"Leave it."

"But—"

His kiss caught me by surprise, and I ran the back of my hand down his cheek, feeling the bite of his stubble against my skin as his embrace tightened. His lips might have been soft, but other parts of him hardened rapidly as he pulled me into his lap.

"You want to head upstairs?" he asked.

I locked my gaze on his, and no other answer was necessary.

A shriek escaped my throat as he lifted me, one arm around my back and the other under my knees as if I weighed nothing. Effortless. Although he did trip over a stray footstool on the way to the stairs, mainly because I blocked his vision by kissing him again.

In the bedroom, he paused only to rip off his jumper before following me onto the bed, and I got my first look at him shirtless.

What had I done to deserve this man? I traced his abs with a finger in the dim glow from the bedside lamp, then moved my attention downwards. Flipping heck. It promised to be a tight fit—I could see that much.

But before I could explore further, he pinned my arms above my head with one hand while he used the other to undo the buttons on my blouse.

"Not so fast, Livvie. I want to have fun too."

That seemed fair. Frustrating, but fair.

He raked his gaze down my chest before he dipped his head and trailed his tongue along the same route. When he blew across the cool trail it left behind, I broke out in goosebumps.

"Are you sure about this?" Nye whispered.

"I've never been so sure about anything in my life."

I wanted to tear my own trousers off as he reached for my zipper. For goodness' sake, hurry up!

And then his bloody phone rang.

Not with its usual ringtone, either, and he snatched it up.

"Nye."

A pause.

"Okay, understood."

He was already off the bed as he stuffed the phone into his trouser pocket.

"Get dressed, Liv. The team just spotted somebody out there."

As we got downstairs, my newly installed security lights blazed on, and dark shadows dashed across the front garden. I tried to look out the window, but Nye pulled me away, into the gloom at the back of the room.

"Stay back, babe. Don't make yourself into a target."

I cowered in his arms as shouts came from outside, praying nobody would get hurt. Well, apart from my stalker, obviously. If he fell and broke his neck, it could only be a good thing.

It seemed like forever before Nye's phone rang again, and when he listened to whatever the person on the other end had to say, his mouth hardened into a thin line.

"Search him, cuff him, and bring him inside."

They'd got him?

"Who is it?" I asked the instant Nye hung up. "Who did they catch?"

"Your friend Warren."

Warren? No. He'd always been so nice to me. Even when Nye found out about those awful accusations against him, I'd taken his side. But why on earth was he skulking around my home in the dark?

The front door slammed. Looked as if I'd soon find out.

"It's better if you wait in here, babe."

"Are you kidding? I want to be there when you question him." I could already hear cross words coming from the hallway.

Nye pushed a few stray hairs out of my eyes. "It might not be pretty. I'm so fucking angry right now."

I uncurled his fist and squeezed his hand. "I know. But please don't hurt him. I don't want you to get in trouble."

He laughed. "I won't. Don't worry about that."

Warren narrowed his eyes as Nye walked into the hallway, but when he realised I was there too, his expression softened.

"Olivia, I was trying to help. Honestly, I was only trying to help."

Nye shielded me with his body as he faced up to Warren.

"Go on—I'm dying to hear it. Why were you outside at eleven in the evening?"

"I heard someone had been bothering Olivia, and I wanted to check everything was okay."

"You didn't think a phone call would suffice?"

"I figured if I came in person, I might catch whoever it was in the act."

"And let me guess, that's why you parked your car up on the main road and came in on foot."

"Kind of. I also didn't want to wake Olivia if she was asleep."

"We found a Swiss army knife in his pocket," one of the Blackwood men said.

"That means nothing," Warren protested. "I carry it because it's got tweezers and a toothpick."

Even I did an eye-roll at that one.

"And I suppose you're also fond of the nail file and the compass?"

"I use them sometimes."

"Bullshit."

Warren gave a sullen shrug, difficult with his hands cuffed behind him. "I'm telling the truth."

"Like you told the truth about Claire Downing two years ago?"

Warren lost a little more of his colour. "That was all lies. Nothing happened like she said it did."

"You didn't sleep with her?"

"I did, but I sure as hell didn't rape her. She was fine when she left my place."

"Really? Because if a woman leaves your bed and even contemplates reporting an assault, I'd suggest she was anything but fine."

"I swear, that's what happened. I painted her portrait, we had a couple of drinks, and things just happened. Next thing I knew, Graham hauled me in for questioning."

Nye shook his head, his expression one of disbelief. "So, is this the first night you've decided to pay Olivia a visit?"

"I came once last week after I'd finished my shift, but all the windows were dark, so I had a quick check around then left."

"And you didn't see anyone else?"

"I'd have told the police if I did."

"Why Olivia? I take it you don't offer your amateur surveillance services to every girl in the village."

Warren looked down at his feet. "Because I like her, okay?" His gaze landed on my hand, firmly clasped in Nye's. "I can see you understand that feeling."

"Yeah, I do. And you'd better back the fuck off."

"Okay, okay. I get the message. Now, will you uncuff me? You're not allowed to keep me here like this."

"You'd rather spend the night in the police station?"

"No."

Nye let go of me and stepped right up to Warren, never breaking eye contact with him.

"I'll uncuff you, but I'll be watching. And if I see you anywhere near this place again, I'll make your life hell. Got it?"

Warren nodded, although he looked furious about the situation. "Got it."

CHAPTER 34

WARREN. I STILL didn't know what to believe. Nye had spent most of the night on the phone, asking questions and organising another surveillance team, and I'd barely slept a wink.

The tiredness showed as we ate breakfast. Nye's stubble had gone well past a five o'clock shadow, and I'd been wearing the same pair of leggings for two days.

"Do you think it was Warren who broke in?" I asked.

Nye stared into his coffee—already on his second cup before we'd started work. "Circumstantial evidence suggests it could well be, but until we get something concrete or he admits it, we can't be sure. I've got a team working around the clock on it. We're checking his alibi for each of the incidents, but seeing as he's self-employed, it's hard to pin down his whereabouts at each particular time."

My earlier feelings of guilt came creeping back. "Nye, how much is this costing?"

"Don't worry about that. At Blackwood, we all help each other out, and at some point, I'll have to return a few favours, but it's worth it to see you safe."

"I'd like to do something to thank everyone too. Perhaps I could bake some cakes?"

"I'm sure they'd love that, babe."

The front door slammed, signalling the arrival of today's team of reinforcements. "Did you give everybody keys?"

"Nah, I took the deadbolt off when I came downstairs, so they just pick the lock."

This new life I'd fallen into certainly was different. None of Edward's friends knew how to pick a lock. The one time Edward managed to lock himself out of his house, on a Sunday evening, no less, he'd had to call the emergency locksmith and spent the next week moaning about the cost.

"Hey! We've come to help."

A girl's voice I didn't recognise echoed through the flat, and seconds later, a young brunette bounced into the kitchen. Nye groaned, and she pressed the corners of his mouth into a smile with her fingertips.

"Don't be such a misery guts. Where do we start?"

"We start by leaving me in peace to finish my coffee. I've been up half the night."

"Max said you caught the asshole?" She jerked her head at the man who'd appeared behind her in the doorway, a Chinese guy who would have been handsome if he'd smiled.

"We caught someone. Not sure if it's the right man. Olivia, this is Tia. She's a friend of Emmy's, and she likes to stop by and annoy everyone from time to time."

Tia stepped forward and surprised me with a hug. "I also live in Lower Foxford, so I thought I'd come and give you a hand. Well, I sort of live there. I've mostly moved to the US now." She turned back to Nye. "So, who'd you catch? Do I know them?"

Nye shrugged. "Warren Hannigan."

"The taxi driver?"

"Yeah."

"Seriously? Warren?"

"The surveillance team found him in Olivia's garden last night, plus he's been in trouble over a woman before."

"The Claire Downing thing?"

"You've heard about that?"

"Everybody at my old school knew." She shook her head and tutted. "Claire's such a bitch."

Nye raised an eyebrow. "Really? She made some very serious allegations."

"And it backfired when she realised the police needed, like, you know, evidence."

"You think she made the story up?"

"Claire's sister Marianne told my friend Arabella that Claire's boyfriend flipped out when he found a used pregnancy test in her bathroom bin when they hadn't even slept together yet. So, rather than admit she'd cheated, she told him Warren took advantage of her while she modelled for one of his paintings."

"Shit."

"Yes, it was. We felt sorry for Warren, and Arabella's brother, Mark, is a cop in London, so she told him what Marianne said. He had a word with Claire, and she dropped the charges."

"The local policeman doesn't have a record of any of that."

"Graham? He's an idiot. But Warren's nice. Once, Arabella and I bought too many drinks in town and didn't have enough money for the cab fare home, so he drove us for free." She clapped a hand over her mouth. "Don't tell my brother that, okay? He doesn't know."

"Your secret's safe. Dammit, I was ninety percent

sure Warren was our man, but that throws more doubt in. Have you got Mark's number?"

"I can get it. Is that coffee? I could do with a cup before we start on this tidying, searching, whatever."

With the news from Tia, I felt both anxious and relieved. Relieved that my instincts about Warren hadn't been totally wrong, and anxious because if Warren wasn't the culprit, the man was still out there somewhere, watching us and plotting.

And Nye still had his doubts.

"Who checks on a woman in the dark without calling to warn her first?" he muttered in the evening. "We're running out of surveillance teams."

"Someone might be a teensy bit jealous," Tia whispered to me as Nye took a phone call.

"You think? But I never even went out for dinner with Warren when he asked." Although that was mainly because of Tate, admittedly. If Warren had invited me again and Nye hadn't been on the scene, I'd have been buying another new frock.

She shrugged. "Nye can see that you still like him, which I get. He was always kind, but..."

"But?"

"The garden thing *is* a bit weird." She shuddered. "And I found out first-hand the consequences of men skulking around the Foxfords in the dark."

Before I could ask her to elaborate on what she meant, Nye hung up and wrapped an arm around my waist.

"We need to call it a day. Most of us have got an early meeting in the office tomorrow, but we'll finish off the rest tomorrow afternoon."

At least that would give me the morning to catch up

on work. "What about all the stuff out in the trucks? We need to put that back."

"I asked around, and the farmer down the road's diversified and converted one of his barns into storage units. I've rented you one for six months so we can put all the crap there instead." He pressed a soft kiss to my cheek. "Then you can make this place into a proper home."

Nye got me. He just got me, and that was the moment I realised my heart was in big trouble. The "L" word fluttered around in my throat. *Too soon. Much too soon.*

"Thank you. You have no idea how much that means."

His eyes hooded, and I wasn't imagining the fire smouldering beneath the half-closed lids.

"You can show me later," he whispered, too quietly for anyone else to hear.

"How quickly can we get these people to leave?"

He chuckled and gifted me one of those smiles that made me melt. "I'd better make them coffee for the drive back."

"I can do that, and dinner too. If you could just hurry up the rest..."

"Okay, babe, I get the hint." He pulled me close and kissed me, ignoring the whistles from the doorway. "You're mine tonight. Nothing's gonna stop us this time."

I hadn't been jittery last night, when things had just happened, but tonight, I grew ever more apprehensive as I picked at the pasta I'd made us for dinner. What if I didn't measure up to the girls in Nye's past? With his looks and that damn motorbike, he must have had a few. Didn't he say they were socialites? How long before the novelty of being with a girl who didn't even need alcohol to make bad decisions wore off? And if...

"More wine?"

"Huh?"

Nye gestured at my glass. "You've just drunk it all."

Oh. Oops. "I guess."

"What's wrong?"

"Nothing."

He kept staring at me, and I realised seeing a detective had its disadvantages. "I'm nervous, okay?"

"About the stalker? I'll keep you safe."

"Not him... Tonight... I, uh..."

Nye pushed his chair back, and two seconds later, I was in his arms. When he kissed me, my insecurities faded away, and all I felt was him. Every last inch.

"Want to forget the rest of dinner?" he asked.

"Who needs dessert anyway?"

"I'm not planning to skip dessert. She's standing in front of me."

He carried me up the stairs again, and this time I was the one who pulled his shirt off as we got into the bedroom. I'd worn a T-shirt with no fiddly buttons this time, and it only took him a second to return the favour.

"Fuck me, Liv."

Nye's eyes widened as he hooked his thumbs in my waistband and peeled my trousers down. Okay, I might have worn that fancy underwear with the little bows too.

And I'd got used to his crude words, enjoyed his dirty talk, even.

"Make it hard," I whispered.

He guided my hand downwards. "Not a problem."

Then his *damned* phone rang.

"Can't you leave it?"

"Not this time, babe. It's the control room."

It only took a second before he was reaching for his shirt again, and I lay back on the bed and groaned. Would I ever get a proper taste of Nye?

"One of Spike's sensors just went off. I need to check it."

"You're going out there?"

"Don't worry—it's probably just a fox."

Chills replaced the heat I'd felt only moments ago, and my heart didn't just race, it pounded in a series of wild palpitations as Nye did his jeans up.

He grabbed my phone from the nightstand and pressed it into my hands. "Stay here, and if you hear anything you don't like, I've programmed Blackwood's control room as speed dial one. Call them, then the police."

"Please don't go."

"I'll be right back."

He hadn't even got to the stairs when I heard a window break downstairs, followed by a soft *whump*. Then another window, and another. Nye came running back in and slammed the door.

"What's happened? Is somebody down there?"

"Worse. Molotov cocktails, three of them. Lounge, dining room, and kitchen by the sounds of it. We'll have to go out the window."

I tore the curtains open and saw flames leaping into

the darkness—both trucks were on fire too.

Nye leaned past and threw the window open. Acrid smoke drifted inside, burning the back of my throat and making me cough.

"I'll climb down first," he told me. "Then I need you to wriggle out backwards and hang from the windowsill. When I tell you, let go, and I'll catch you."

I should have been terrified, but there was no time to think. Nye shinned down the old wisteria tree like a monkey, then landed safely next to the overgrown flower bed. Then it was my turn.

I used the dressing table to boost myself up onto the windowsill, but as I looked down, the fear hit. The ground looked an awfully long way away.

"Turn around, Liv," Nye shouted.

"I-I-I can't."

"Babe, you can. I'll catch you, I promise."

I shuffled around onto my knees, clinging to the scarred wooden frame as if my life depended on it. Which it did. Tendrils of smoke curled under the bedroom door, creeping towards me, and I knew there was no other way out. Knuckles white, I lowered myself off the edge.

"Let go, Liv." Nye's voice sounded above the crackling fire, and I released my grip.

I couldn't have been falling for more than a second or two, but it felt a lot longer before his arms flew around my waist and stopped me inches from the ground.

"We need to move. Quickly!"

He half carried me, and we ran for the edge of the garden as the fuel tank on the closest truck exploded, sending a ball of flame skywards. Fire had consumed the entire cottage in Upper Foxford's version of Armageddon. It seemed Aunt Ellie hadn't heard of flame-retardant furniture.

"Are you hurt?" Nye asked, patting me down to check for injuries.

"I'm fine," I lied, right before my knees gave out.

Nye kept me upright as sirens pierced the night, the emergency services rushing to save something I knew was already a lost cause.

CHAPTER 35

THE SIRENS DREW closer, and before long, firemen were running everywhere. Hoses criss-crossed the ground like sleeping snakes, all over the garden, to the hydrant on the road, and even into the swimming pool next-door-but-one. And I was right—Lilac Cottage couldn't be saved.

"This is going to be damage control, I'm afraid," one of the firemen told Nye. "At least you got out safely."

"That's all that matters."

Easy for him to say. He hadn't been left homeless.

The police arrived soon after, followed by a couple of ambulances, and Nye insisted I get checked out even though he refused to be poked and prodded himself.

"I'm fine, Liv. I only dropped one floor out of a building. It happens."

How he could be so blasé about it? Me, I couldn't stop trembling.

While I sat in the back of the ambulance, Nye headed to the side of the garden where his group of black-clad ninjas had congregated. Every couple of minutes, another shadow appeared and joined them. As soon as the paramedics let me go, I hurried towards them, their silhouettes lit up by the dying flames.

"Looks like things have escalated," Max said in the understatement of the decade.

"He might not have been trying to kill Olivia before, but he definitely is now," said another.

"The fucker won't get away with it." Nye's voice came out of the darkness, and I stumbled towards it on shaky legs.

"The problem is that whatever he wanted to keep hidden's gone up in flames," Max said.

I made it to Nye and gripped his hand before collapsing onto the remains of Aunt Ellie's old sofa next to him, bodily fluids be damned. Trivialities didn't matter so much anymore, not when my home had just become its own funeral pyre.

Nye bent to give me a soft kiss and tuck a jacket around my shoulders. "You're okay. That's all that matters."

"We could have died."

"But we didn't." He straightened again. "How the hell did anybody get close enough to do this?"

A man from the outside security detail shifted from foot to foot. "We saw movement at the end of the drive, and he must have snuck behind us when we went to investigate."

Nye muttered a string of curses. "Where are Hazell and Hannigan?"

"Hannigan's in town, waiting at the taxi rank. Still checking on Hazell."

So, it wasn't Warren. That cheered me up a little bit.

Nye, not so much. "If this was Larry, the next time he gets close to a fire, he'll be warming himself in front of Satan."

"The surveillance team followed him back to the shelter and parked up outside. He didn't come out the front, but he's not in his bed either."

Nye gave the corner of the sofa a vicious kick with one of his steel-toed boots, and the judder ran through me.

"Find the bastard. I don't care how many men it takes. If the guys upstairs have a problem with it, tell them to call me."

Nye's stress transferred to me, and I began chewing a nail. Dammit—I'd been so good about that for the last few weeks. I forced myself to grip the edge of the cushion instead, but my fingers couldn't keep still, and before I knew it, I'd pulled out a pile of stuffing. It floated around my feet in the breeze like a pile of fluffy snow. I should have stopped, but the motion was soothing, like popping bubble wrap or the rocking of a patient with no hope of escape from the asylum.

I went back for another handful, only this time my fingers hit...

Hang on. What was that?

I gripped the damp edge and pulled. A padded envelope popped out, the ends sealed with sticky tape.

"Nye! Look at this!" I leapt up, waving my prize in his face. "It was in the sofa cushion."

Eight faces stared down at me, the whites of their eyeballs reflecting the dying embers of the fire.

Then Nye started laughing. "Fuck me, it was out here all along."

"Can we open it? I want to know what it says."

He gently uncurled my fingers and took my treasure, holding it by the corner. "Not here. It's already soggy. We need to take this into the lab."

"Your car's not looking too healthy," Max said. "Some of the roof tiles popped off in the heat and landed on it."

"Can you give us a lift into London?"

"No problem."

Max had parked his SUV by the road, and as we walked past the remains of Nye's BMW, I realised what a close call we'd had. Most of the panels were dented, and fragments of the smashed windscreen twinkled orange in the light.

"I'm so sorry," I said. "This all happened because of me."

"The car doesn't matter. It's insured. Was the cottage?"

I sent a silent thank you to my ex-landlord, who'd told me only idiots didn't have building insurance. "Yes. I bought a policy as soon as I moved here."

"Smart cookie."

Insurance was only part of the problem, though. Where was I going to live in the meantime? Maddie's sofa, most likely. She wouldn't mind, but the thought of sleeping there for the months it would take to rebuild the cottage filled me with misery. I wished I could take the insurance money and run, but when I'd skimmed the small print, I was pretty sure it precluded that option.

With the envelope safely stowed in the centre console, Max reversed into the lane, and we sped out of the village. Nye held me as tightly as the seat belt would allow.

"I want you close, babe. What could have happened back there…" He shook his head. "I don't even want to think about it."

The feeling was mutual. I snuggled against his chest until we pulled into the now-familiar parking garage of the Blackwood building.

"Test-tube's waiting upstairs," Max said. "He came in specially."

"Test-tube?" I asked.

"Tudor Testino, our head of forensics. But everyone calls him Test-tube."

"That's some name."

"His father's Italian, and his mother's Welsh. His father wanted to call him Angelino, so he reckons he got off lightly."

I put Test-tube in his early fifties, with neat grey hair and a ready smile. He took the envelope from Nye and hurried off with it, followed by three other men in lab coats. Nye took my hand, and we trailed along behind.

"We'll try the scanner first," Test-tube said. "It won't cause any more damage."

He ran the envelope through a machine similar to those in airports, and a dark shadow showed up in one corner.

"That's a key!" I said, leaning forward for a closer look. "But what to? I didn't find anything that was locked."

Test-tube donned a fresh pair of latex gloves and carefully sliced open one end. "I'm hoping the letter with it will tell us."

The bubble-wrap lining had kept the paper reasonably dry, and when Test-tube gently removed the sheet and unfolded it, the flowing script was still legible.

Thank goodness.

Once an assistant had taken photographs with a fancy camera, we all gathered around to read.

Mam,

If you're reading this letter, it means I've gone to prison. I didn't give it to you before the trial because I knew you'd worry. Tempting fate, you'd say.

I'm sorry I messed up. I shouldn't have walloped Henry, but if you asked whether I'd do it again, the answer would have to be yes. The bastard deserved it. Anyway, I'll be away for a bit, so I made sure you'd be set up financially before I went.

A couple of months ago, I did a job, and I saw something I wasn't supposed to see. That night you gave me the alibi for, remember? A man did something he shouldn't have, and I found him disposing of the evidence.

I thought about going to the police, but they haven't been too kind to me lately. Me and Graham hadn't seen eye to eye since he clipped me around the ear in Mr. Bright's garden. How old was I then? Nine? Ten? The old git's never got any friendlier.

So, I gave the man a choice.

I sent him an anonymous letter, telling him what I'd seen and how I'd kept a key piece of evidence, one that could send him to jail in a heartbeat. Either he paid two grand a month, or I'd go to the police with the details.

He chose the first option. I knew he would.

The payments have been coming in steady for a few months now, into an account on your favourite poker site. Easy to clean. The username is "WilyFox" and the password is Grandma's middle name.

Mam, as long as the money keeps rolling in, take it and keep your mouth shut. We'll be set up for life, as long as he doesn't find out who's behind this.

I've written out a statement of what I saw that night and left it with the evidence in a safe deposit box in Metro Bank. The branch opposite the supermarket. Box twenty-two, your lucky number.

If the payments stop, send the contents to the police. He deserves it.

Ronnie.

So near, yet so far. At least we knew what we were looking for and where it was, but we couldn't get at it until Monday morning.

"Do you think it was Larry who Ronnie saw?" I asked Nye.

"Maybe. He's been acting like a pervert since his teenage years, and when Ronnie got banged up he'd have been, what, thirty-five? His behaviour would have been well-established by that point."

"Perhaps Ronnie caught him hiding in someone's house? Like that time he got caught in the girl's bathroom?"

"Whatever he did, it won't be long before we find out. We'll be first in line when the bank opens."

"But it's Sunday tomorrow. That means we've got a whole day to wait."

Nye made a face. "Yeah, and it'd be difficult to get the bank to open up early without a warrant."

"Could you get one?"

"At the speed the cops move? Sure, for about next Thursday. Don't worry, I'll keep you well away from Upper Foxford until Monday." A mischievous smile replaced his black look. "I'm sure we can find something to keep ourselves occupied."

Wonderful, but where? I'd been left homeless and everything else-less. I didn't even have a change of clothes to replace my torn outfit.

"Can we stay here tonight? You said you slept overnight once."

"My office has glass walls. Unless that sort of thing floats your boat, you might find my apartment more comfortable."

With the focus on Lilac Cottage, I'd never stopped to think about Nye's home, but no, I didn't want to put on a show.

"Do you live near here?"

"Not too far. We can borrow a pool car for this evening."

I had an awful thought. "What about the keys to your flat? Did you have them with you when we jumped out the window?"

He just looked at me.

Oh. Right. "You don't need a key, do you?"

"I'll get the door open for tonight. One of my colleagues lives in the same building, and I can pick up the spare from him tomorrow."

Soon we were driving through the streets of London, deserted save for the occasional black cab.

"Where are we going?"

Nye glanced across, a little sheepish. "Chelsea."

Chelsea? I figured his job at Blackwood paid well, but I couldn't picture him living in millionaire's row.

But he did, in a huge apartment building right next to the Thames. I bet the views must be spectacular from the roof terrace I spied in the early morning light. Who on earth could afford to live on that floor?

Nye, it turned out.

He led me into the lift in the underground car park, and I watched the numbers on the panel count up until they reached fifteen.

"The penthouse? You live in the penthouse?"

He shrugged. "I like to watch the boats on the river."

It only took him a minute to let us inside, and he punched a code into a scary-looking alarm panel then clicked on the lights.

"Well, this is me. Make yourself at home."

Wow. I followed him into the lounge, tastefully furnished in creams and greys. A fluffy sheepskin rug lay in front of a designer fireplace in brushed steel, and the coffee table looked too expensive to risk putting a drink on. But there was something missing.

"Where's the sofa? You weren't redecorating at all, were you?"

"I just wanted you to have something nice to sit on. Please don't be mad."

How could I be mad? That was the sweetest thing anyone had ever done for me. I flung my arms around him.

"You're the most amazing man I've ever met, Nye Holmes."

He gripped my bottom and hoisted me up so I could wrap my legs around his waist. "How tired are you?" he asked.

"Not so tired that I don't want to rip your clothes off you and kiss every inch of your naked body."

He looked shocked. I felt shocked.

"Sorry, I don't know what came over me." I tried to backpedal in a hurry. "Stress, I think. It must have been stress."

His answer was to carry me through to the master bedroom and lay me on his luxurious quilt.

"I'll have to get you stressed more often. Rip away."

Chapter 36

"RIP AWAY," NYE had said. Where should I start?

I might have been a little forward in my words, and my hands were twitching, but I wasn't used to this. Edward had been a strictly missionary man, and from the way Nye gazed down at me, I guessed his tastes ran more to the *Kama Sutra*.

My mouth went dry as all the moisture pooled between my legs. Nye lay down beside me, propped up on one elbow, the contours of his face lit by the first rays of sun shining in through the floor-to-ceiling windows that led to the terrace.

He'd changed out of his smoky T-shirt and into a checked button-down in the office, and I slid both hands underneath it. His breath hitched as I ran my hands across his stomach, his abs tensing at my touch. A smattering of hair led downwards under his belt, and I fumbled to open the buckle.

"What happened to the ripping, Liv?"

"Uh..."

"This is how you do it." He reached up and tore my top in two, then flicked my bra across the room with an ease I didn't want to think about.

Sod it. I grabbed his shirt and yanked, wincing as buttons flew across the room. A couple plinked as they hit the window, and I grimaced. Who would pick those up? If someone trod on one barefoot, it was going to hurt.

Good grief, Olivia. Forget tidying for five seconds, would you?

Nye rolled us over, trapping me underneath him as his hardness dug into my stomach. A groan escaped my lips as he ran his tongue across my breasts, paying particular attention to each nipple, and my core throbbed in time with his strokes. Freaking hell, why wouldn't these leggings come off?

Luckily, he helped me out, or perhaps unluckily, seeing as they were the only item of clothing I had left. My knickers soon followed, flung across the room where they hooked themselves over a lamp by the door to the en-suite bathroom. Good thing the bulb wasn't lit —it would have been a fire hazard, and I'd had enough flames for one day. Not one of the dozen firemen had been a patch on Nye, either.

I found his zipper and slid it down slowly, eager and nervous at the same time. Nye raised his hips to give me better access, and I slipped a hand into his boxers and felt him for the first time, skin on skin. A pulse beat through him, perfectly in time with my own, and I ran a thumb over the tip.

"Easy, Liv. If you keep that up, I won't last long."

But I didn't stop, and suddenly my hand was empty. Nye had shifted down the bed with a speed that belied his size, and when he looked up with a cheeky grin, I realised what he was about to do.

"You're a bad girl, babe, and you need to be taught a lesson."

Before I could protest, he swiped his tongue along my centre and sucked gently on the magic spot. I hadn't been far from the edge, and that tipped me over it. The throb turned into fireworks as I let out a squeal like a cat in pain. Ouch. I slammed my mouth shut and bit my tongue, and the squeal turned into a yelp. *Way to go, Olivia.* Girls never sounded like that in the movies.

Nye must have had a problem with his hearing because he didn't even cringe. Instead, he grabbed a condom from the nightstand and covered up. Wow, this was really happening. And let's just say that Nye had nothing to be ashamed of in the showers. Suddenly, I felt more nervous than I'd been all night, and considering I'd nearly died, that was saying something.

He didn't speak, just positioned himself at my entrance and flexed his hips. Oh holy shit, I'd never felt this full. He slid out a tiny bit, then pushed back in, testing.

"You okay?"

I couldn't speak. My entire vocabulary had deserted me. I managed a nod, and he brought his mouth down on mine, his tongue moving in time with his cock as he taught me what a real man could do in bed. Beside Nye, Edward was a mere amateur.

My toes curled as I came for the second time, and I clutched at the thousand-thread-count sheets as I thanked the asshole who'd tried to ruin my life for delivering Nye to me. The man who went against everything I'd ever wished for, yet managed to fulfil fantasies I hadn't even had.

Nye gave a quiet grunt as he came, and a glow spread through me. Not just the heat of lust, but the warmth of a new relationship built on friendship and respect rather than fancy clothes and a shared love of fine wines. This man meant everything.

And he didn't speak, just kissed me softly on the lips before trailing his tongue down my jawline. When he blew on me gently, I shivered.

"You okay?"

"I'm... I don't even have words."

Nye twitched inside me, softer now, and as our breath mingled, I got the urge to do something I'd always hated doing with Edward.

"Can I taste you?" I whispered.

"Fuck me, is it Christmas again already?"

Christmas, my birthday, Easter, Valentine's, Hanukkah, Thanksgiving, but definitely not Independence Day. I didn't want to be alone anymore.

Nye peeled off the condom and dropped it onto the floor—something else to clean up later.

Dammit, Olivia, stop with the OCD.

The only thing I should be cleaning was Nye, with my tongue. So I did, and I discovered my new favourite thing to eat.

Better even than chocolate. I gave it one last lick. Maybe next time I could mix the two: Nye and chocolate. Who needed three Michelin stars when you had that combination?

"What are you thinking, babe?"

I felt heat rise in my cheeks, and he laughed.

"That bad?" he asked.

"I'm beginning to see the merits in a little naughtiness."

"With you on that."

Chocolate sauce was definitely going on the shopping list for tomorrow, and maybe some whipped cream. I could get a piping bag and...

Nye went at me again with his tongue, and this time

I managed to gasp his name. Before I could blink, all other thoughts flew from my mind.

What did I need them for, anyway?

All that mattered tonight was us.

Chapter 37

DESPITE A BURNING curiosity about my new surroundings, and even more interest in the contents of the safe deposit box, I was almost grateful the next day was Sunday because I needed a rest. By the time morning rolled around, I could barely walk.

Nye had no such problems. "You up for another round?" he asked as the early afternoon sun glinted through the gap in the curtains.

I couldn't move, and I mumbled as much into the pillow.

"How about I just roll you over and make you happy?"

That did it. I was in love with this man.

As he started work, I went beyond happy, further even than delirious. Nye had invested in gold-standard equipment and was clearly familiar with the operating manual. He certainly knew how to push my buttons.

"Hungry, babe?" he asked as I collapsed back onto the mattress.

I slid my jaw from side to side, testing it. "Muscles I didn't know I had are aching."

He laughed. "I meant for food."

"Oh. Yes, some food would be lovely."

Except there was a slight flaw in that plan, because when we staggered through to Nye's kitchen, he didn't have any.

"I've got Kit Kats, Rice Krispies, and a microwaveable cheese toastie," he called out, rummaging through his cupboards. "Actually, the Rice Krispies aren't so crispy anymore."

"What about proper food?"

With that many preservatives in his system, an archaeologist could dig Nye up in a few hundred years' time and find a perfectly lifelike corpse.

I opened the fridge and found five cans of beer, a bottle of ketchup, and a jar of pickles that had expired two years previously. A foil container lurked in one corner, and I didn't even want to think about what horrors it might harbour. It went straight into the bin.

"What do you eat?" I asked.

He wandered over to me and shrugged. "Mostly takeaways. Or I eat out. Or I get something at work."

"Can we buy some proper food?"

"You'll cook?" He grinned like a kid on Christmas Day.

His kitchen was a chef's dream. Stainless steel and granite with every appliance you could imagine. Everything except the microwave was spotless. Had the rest of the kitchen ever been used?

"I'd love to. Why did you buy such a fancy kitchen if you don't like cooking?"

"I hired a decorator, and she told me all of this stuff was essential, but I think she got carried away."

"Then I'll christen it for you."

He nuzzled my neck. "Fancy christening the rug in the lounge later too?"

I turned and kissed him.

"Is that a yes?" he asked when we broke apart.

"That's a yes."

He looked towards the lounge, then sighed. "We'd better go to the supermarket first."

"There might be a small problem with that. I don't have any clothes left. You shredded my last outfit."

"Shit, I'm sorry. Actually, I'm not." He loosened the belt on the bathrobe I'd borrowed and slid his arms around my naked waist. "I'll get you more clothes."

It turned out Janelle did more than just Nye's paperwork. She turned up an hour later with her hands full of expensive-looking paper carrier bags and held them out to me.

"Nice one, girl. I had this week in the pool."

"Sorry, the what?"

"The betting pool for when you and Nye did the deed. Luther nearly always wins these things, but he went for next month."

"Excuse me? You were gambling on my love life?"

"Not gambling, honey. Nye was a sure thing. I saw the way he looked at you."

"I don't believe this."

Nye walked into the hallway, shirtless, and I put my hands on my hips.

"Your colleagues have been wagering on us," I told him.

"Did you win?" he asked Janelle.

"Thirty quid."

He held his hand up for a high five. "Donuts tomorrow?"

"Krispy Kreme. Don't worry, Olivia. Nye'll save you one."

Oh, that was all right, then.

Once Janelle had departed, Nye took my hand as

we walked to Waitrose. Going shopping together seemed like such a normal thing to do, though my life was anything but. How many other people on that London street had narrowly escaped death the night before?

I tried not to shudder as I pressed closer to Nye, and he dropped my hand to wrap an arm around my shoulders instead.

"You okay?"

"Things are just getting to me, that's all."

"Nobody followed us to London, babe. You're safe here."

His words made my stomach unclench a little, and in Waitrose, Nye once again fetched a trolley and rolled it next to me.

"How much are you planning to buy?" Surely for one day's worth of food for two people, a basket would be sufficient?

"Enough for a week, I guess. I hate grocery shopping. Unless you want to go every day; then I'll join you."

"You will?"

"I thought you said you liked cooking? I don't expect you to. We can eat out otherwise, or I'll get something delivered."

"It's the 'we' part I'm not sure about. You're planning for us to be together all week?"

"You're not?"

"I didn't think that far ahead. I guess I figured I'd move in with Maddie for a while."

"You don't want to stay with me?"

I'd never seen him look crestfallen like that, and I stood on tiptoes to press a kiss to his cheek. We may not have been together for long, but now I'd spent the night in his bed, I never wanted to leave it. Yes, he could be mercurial, but he looked after me, and more than anything, he treated me as if I mattered. To Edward and Tate, I'd just been an accessory.

"I do want to stay. I just wasn't sure you were ready for that kind of commitment."

"I want you in my life and in my home and in my bed. Clear enough?"

"Crystal."

"So, a week's worth of food?"

"Yes, we'll stock up."

I walked the aisles in a daze. In the space of twenty-four hours, I'd gone from living in a cottage I'd tried my best to like without much success to staying in my dream apartment with a man way out of my league. I pinched myself as I walked down the bakery aisle, but the loaves of bread didn't disappear.

"Got everything?" Nye asked as we neared the checkout.

"Yes. I mean no." I'd forgotten the squirty cream. "I'll be right back."

Nye turned the can over in his hands before he put it on the conveyor. "Is this for both of us to play with?"

He hadn't kept his voice down, and the checkout lady raised an eyebrow.

"Shh!" I leaned in closer, blushing. "I get first dibs."

"Not gonna say no to that, babe."

Back in Nye's kitchen, I set to work. The place even had a state-of-the-art sound system built in. Nye walked in just as I was bopping around to Robert Palmer's "Addicted to Love," and when I turned and saw him, I went the same colour as the raspberry coulis I'd just whipped up to go with the lemon cheesecake.

Instead of laughing, he just whirled me around the kitchen island until the song ended, then leaned in for a kiss.

"My kind of cooking," he said.

"I think I could be a convert."

He surveyed the counters, which I hadn't quite cleared up yet. "Did you invite the local football team for dinner and forget to mention it?"

"No, why?"

"You know there are only two of us? Even *my* appetite isn't that big."

Hmm, as well as dessert, I'd made a main course, fresh bread, a small starter, and a couple of batches of cupcakes, just to test out the oven, you understand. "I might have got a bit carried away."

"We'll be shopping again tomorrow, won't we? Right after I go to the gym for five or six hours." He tried to put on a stern face, but he was still laughing as he said it.

"Maybe?"

He smiled. "What's for lunch?"

"Salmon mousse followed by beef Wellington."

He helped me to carry it over to the table, and we both tucked in. Delicious, if I said so myself.

"This is that thing Maddie tried to make, right?"

"It is."

"If she offers to cook again, I'll get work to fake an emergency. Have you ever thought of becoming a professional chef?"

"I always had this dream of opening a cupcake shop. I love to bake more than anything." Soul exposed, I kept my eyes fixed on the table. "Stupid, I know."

"It's not stupid, Liv. Everyone needs a dream."

"What's yours?"

"I'm living it. I wanted to make my own way in life, doing a job I love. And I wanted to meet a girl who made me happy. I've just achieved the last part."

My fork clattered onto the plate, food forgotten. "What were you saying about that rug?"

Nye threw me over his shoulder and carried me into the lounge, pausing to grope my ass before he lowered me onto the soft sheepskin. Dirty, and I loved it.

"You want the fire on, babe? Or..."

I knew what he was thinking, but his fancy hearth was a world away from Lilac Cottage. I nodded, and flames danced as we undressed each other, more slowly than last night, although Nye still got frustrated and ripped my knickers off at the last second. After the rug, we tried out the kitchen island, and I didn't even feel a burning need to sanitise it afterwards, much to my shame. Nye had mellowed me.

Lunch had gone cold by the time we finished, so Nye grabbed a few cupcakes and the can of cream to bring through to the bedroom with us. At this rate, I wouldn't need to think about renewing my gym membership. Nye was giving me all the exercise I needed.

"Hurry up!" I checked my watch for the hundredth time in the last hour.

Nye reached for his jacket, a smart one this time. "Easy, babe. The bank's not going anywhere."

"But I wanted to be there when it opened."

And we would have been too, except when I woke up, I couldn't stop fidgeting and Nye had resorted to drastic measures to take my mind off things. Now, I couldn't wipe my smile away. I'd have to get stressed more often.

Test-tube met us outside the bank, dressed in jeans rather than a lab coat, carrying a small box I assumed contained his forensics kit. Would we need it?

Yes. The answer was most definitely yes.

Once the bank manager left us alone in the viewing room, Nye flipped back the lid on the slim metal box, and we all peered in. I'd half expected to see the sparkling loot from one of Ronnie's burglaries, but the space was almost empty. Just an envelope on the bottom and...

"Is that... Is it a knife?"

Test-tube leaned closer, peering at the sealed plastic bag. "Indeed it is, with dried blood on the blade by the looks of it."

I sat down on a plastic chair with a bump. Despite the escalating nastiness, it hadn't crossed my mind that we'd be dealing with murder, but I'd bet my last penny that kitchen knife had been used for more than preparing Sunday dinner.

Nye held a video camera with one hand and my hand with the other as he filmed Test-tube gathering the evidence. The knife, the envelope, and he fingerprinted the box for good measure. As soon as he'd finished, he cleaned up the mess, and we slotted the box back into its rightful position.

"What now?" I asked.

"Back to the lab," Nye said.

Of course, we hit Monday morning traffic, and I bit my tongue to keep from cursing all the incompetent drivers we came across.

"I could walk faster," I muttered.

"Want me to distract you?" Nye asked.

Test-tube might have been sitting up front with the driver, but even so...

"You're not serious?"

Except he was. He draped his jacket over my lap, and I barely noticed as we pulled into the underground car park at Blackwood's offices. Nye helped me from the car and half carried me to the lift in the corner.

"I can't believe you did that!"

"You were a willing participant, babe."

Yes. Yes, I was.

Down in the lab, Test-tube went through the envelope-opening procedure again, with this sheet of paper in much better condition. Surely this would be the end of the line? I just wanted answers.

A small crowd had gathered by the time Test-tube projected Ronnie's words onto a big screen, no doubt as intrigued by the mystery as I was. My heart raced as I began reading his heavy scrawl for the second time in two days.

I, Ronald Rigby, do testify that this is the whole truth and nothing but the truth.

Last night, I travelled alone to the village of Middleton Foxford with the intention of committing a burglary. I'd selected my target in advance, and over the past few weeks, I'd visited the property a number of times to check it out.

My intention was to wait until the occupants of the house were sleeping, then steal Helena Palmer's jewellery box, which I'd heard she kept on a chest of drawers in the bedroom. I arrived at Prestwold Manor at thirty minutes past midnight and gained access through a downstairs window which I'd previously identified as having a faulty catch.

As I walked through the dining room, I saw a light on in the lounge. Wanting to check the whereabouts of Fenton and Helena Palmer, I looked through a gap between the door and frame.

On the far side of the room, Fenton Palmer was crouching over the body of Helena Palmer. There was a large quantity of blood visible—on Fenton, on Helena's chest, and all over the rug she was lying on. The knife found with this statement was visible on the coffee table.

Helena Palmer did not appear to be moving, and Fenton Palmer made no effort to call for help. I hid in the hall closet while he rolled his wife's body up in a piece of plastic sheeting he fetched from the garage.

He carried her to his car (a Range Rover) and drove approximately four hundred yards to St. James's church, where he parked outside. I followed on foot and got there as he carried Helena's body into the churchyard and placed her next to a freshly dug grave.

Over the next hour, Fenton used a shovel which was already there to deepen the hole and bury his wife at the bottom of it. He then filled the hole up to its original depth. That grave was intended for Eunice Briggs, who died earlier in the week.

While Fenton was filling in the final shovelfuls of dirt, I made my way back to Prestwold Manor and removed the knife from the scene to stop him from disposing of this key piece of evidence.

I hope that with my statement and the knife, Fenton Palmer can be brought to justice.

Ronald Rigby

I was shaking by the time I read the last sentence. Tate's father was a murderer? He'd killed his wife, and the evidence was right there in front of us, in all its blood-streaked glory. Poor Tate. Our relationship might have fizzled out before it properly started, but I still ached for him.

Test-tube gave a low whistle. "A bit rough and ready, but Ronnie's got all the good stuff in here."

Nye nodded. "Timeline fits. The village busybody told us Fenton's wife ran off around the same time as the blackmail payments started. Looks like she didn't leave voluntarily."

"What do you want to do with this stuff?"

"Prepare a document detailing the chain of evidence and linking everything we have. We need to pass it over to the police, and they'll have to dig up that grave as the final piece of proof."

"Will do. The local police?"

"Hell no. The village bobby couldn't detect his asshole with both hands and a map. I'll give Jason from the Met a call and see if he can suggest someone."

"This is gonna upset a few people, I bet."

He wasn't wrong there.

Chapter 38

"OLIVIA, ONCE AGAIN, I'm sorry for being so rude," Daisy said as she topped up my coffee. "I'll know better than to listen to rumours in future."

She'd apologised at least seventeen times in the last half hour, but I pasted on another smile.

"Daisy, it's fine, honestly. I'm not one to bear a grudge."

Luckily, neither was Warren, and he'd joined Maddie, Mickey, and me for drinks and cakes in the café. Carol had tracked the origin of the gold-digger rumours down to an evening canapé party thrown by the Palmers. It seemed every guest got given a version of the story with their glass of champagne, and once they left the manor, the tales spread like wildfire.

"This is all on the house, of course. I still can't believe Fenton Palmer murdered his own wife. Do you know why?"

"Nobody does yet."

"They used to fight," Warren said. "She called me a couple of times, drunk, wanting me to drive her to stay with a friend in London."

"Do you know what the arguments were about?" I asked, my nosiness coming to the fore.

Warren stared at the wall, thinking. "One time, it was the amount of time Fenton spent on the golf course. Another night, a disagreement about Tate's upbringing, and then she reckoned Fenton was having an affair." He wrinkled his nose. "She was wasted that time. Puked in the footwell, but at least she forked out for the valet."

"I suppose that's something."

"Yeah. I got the impression she was high maintenance, but killing her?" He shook his head. "That poor woman."

"At least he can't hurt anyone else."

Fenton had been taken to jail two days earlier. Nye made sure I was safely tucked up in front of the television when it happened, but he'd driven to Upper Foxford to make sure the locals didn't balls things up, in his words.

A task force from the neighbouring town had done the honours, advised by Nye's friend from the Met, and they'd woken Fenton at dawn and arrested him in his pyjamas. The local reporter had been more switched on than Graham, because he'd hotfooted it down there with his camera and snapped Fenton being led out of Prestwold Manor in handcuffs, looking furious. The pictures were plastered all over the front of the *Foxford Express* the next day.

Mickey had a copy spread out on the table in front of him.

"A crime of passion, it says here. Fenton told everybody she ran off with the gardener so they'd think she was still alive."

"Cold," Maddie said. "You had a lucky escape, Liv. Just think, he could have been your father-in-law."

Just think. No, I didn't want to. "It's Tate I feel sorry for. I mean, all that time, he thought his mother had abandoned him, when really she was lying six feet under just a few hundred yards away. Nye said he broke down when the police interviewed him."

Mickey's eyes dipped to the paper again. "It says here that Fenton even sent postcards to Tate, pretending to be his mother."

I nodded. Nye had told me that much was true. Apparently, Tate had been distraught over what his father did to me as well, especially as it was he who'd told Fenton which evenings we were going out together.

I'd considered calling him to offer my...sympathy? Condolences? But I wasn't sure what to say. Maybe I'd leave it a week or two and then try? When my own mother passed, the pain had eased with time.

"At least Tate can bury his mother properly now," Maddie said.

"I guess that might help."

Nye had been there yesterday afternoon when they found Helena, right where Ronnie said she would be. Her body had still been wrapped in the plastic sheeting described in the letter.

"These cakes are good." Maddie shoved another slice of Bakewell tart into her mouth. "But not as good as yours, obviously. What time is the loss adjuster coming?"

With Nye's time taken up with the aftermath of the Fenton Palmer case, Maddie and Mickey had offered to keep me company while I travelled to Upper Foxford to meet the man from the insurance company.

"Midday. How many more calories are you planning to burn this afternoon? We won't have any heavy lifting to do—the building surveyor said it's not safe to go inside."

"Maybe I'll go to the gym when we get back to the city. Or Dave can give me a workout. How are things going with Nye, by the way?"

I glanced at Warren, who looked away. Dammit, I felt awful for the way he'd been treated in this whole debacle, and I still wanted him as a friend. Thankfully, he'd accepted when I invited him to join us, and the last thing I wanted to do was rub my new relationship in his face.

"Okay. They're going okay."

"I never put on weight," Mickey said, munching his way through a giant cookie. "It's the family curse."

We both glared at him, and Maddie huffed.

"People like you make me sick."

He just grinned at her and took another bite.

Another cake or two later—okay, three—I couldn't put off my return to Lilac Cottage any longer. Thank goodness I didn't have to go alone. Not only had Fenton terrorised me there, but Larry Hazell's nocturnal visits creeped me out. He was still on the loose, and that bothered me. How many other women's privacy had he violated? They wouldn't all have a Nye to stick up for them.

"You okay?" Warren asked. "You've gone pale."

"I'm just dreading going back to the cottage, that's all."

Mickey gave my hand a squeeze. "I still feel bad about what happened. If I hadn't tracked you down..."

"She'd have been sleeping on my couch, baking constantly and tidying everything," Maddie said. "Actually yes, you should be sorry for tracking her down."

I laughed. "Mads, you'd be the size of a house by now if you ate that many cakes. A gym membership wouldn't cut it. You'd have to hire that boot camp guy off the telly. Besides, Mickey, if you hadn't found me, I wouldn't have met Nye."

"Good grief, your eyes have glazed over," Maddie said. "Where is Mr. Dreamboat today, anyway?"

"In a meeting. He's taking me out for dinner later, though. It'll be our first proper date."

"Is he splashing out on somewhere nice?"

Warren and Mickey had gone on ahead to Maddie's car, but I still lowered my voice. "I don't know. It's a surprise. But I can hardly wait—all his other surprises have been amazing."

"Ooh, I want details."

"You're not getting any."

"But you clearly are."

A few minutes later, Maddie drew up outside Lilac Cottage and parked at the top of the driveway. Further up, it was still impassable. This was the first time I'd been back since the night of the fire, and the place looked even worse in daylight. Soot-blackened water had formed into icy stalactites holding on to any part of the building still standing.

Not that there were many of those.

The dining room end had collapsed completely, leaving a pile of broken bricks and charred roof timbers. A single chimney breast and part of the front wall rose jaggedly from the debris.

An involuntary sob escaped. I may not have loved Lilac Cottage, but it had been my home.

"It's okay, Liv," Maddie said, giving me a hug.

Thank goodness Nye had been with me that night.

If I'd been alone, or if Spike hadn't installed his sensors, I wouldn't be standing here now. Graham would be puzzling over my murder rather than watching Spike's video of a black-hooded figure stealing out of the woods to throw firebombs through my windows, and Maddie would be planning my funeral. According to Nye, the police had added attempted murder to Fenton's list of charges.

Looking at the devastation in front of me, I hoped he got a good long stay in jail.

The insurance man turned up five minutes late, then spent twenty minutes poking around, pulling faces and tapping his clipboard.

"Total loss, this," he said as he snapped away with his camera.

One didn't need to be a genius to work that out.

"So, what happens now?"

"We'll get the place rebuilt. Have you got somewhere to stay in the meantime, or do you need us to find you alternative accommodation?"

"I've got somewhere."

He scribbled more notes. "That makes things easier. I'll get a partial payment issued in the interim so you can start replacing your clothes and whatnot."

"Thank you."

At least I could offer to pay Nye back for the clothes he'd bought me, although I had a feeling he wouldn't accept my money. He'd already given me his credit card and told me to buy anything I wanted. His only request was that I bought plenty of fancy knickers so he could tear them off me. I'd been only too happy to oblige.

Tonight's were pale pink with black lace, complete with a matching bra and stockings. I planned to cook us a nice dinner, but I wasn't sure we'd make it through to dessert.

After the loss adjuster left, we took a last look around ourselves, but there was nothing to salvage. Anything that didn't succumb to the fire had been covered in water or trodden on. Nye's dented, windowless BMW was still sitting beside the twisted remains of the two trucks. It had suffered even more damage after we'd left when Graham accidentally reversed his squad car into it.

"Do you want to head back to London?" Maddie asked. "I'll buy you a drink before you go to Nye's. You look like you need it."

Coming from anyone else, the comment might have insulted me, but Maddie had a heart of gold. "Make it a double."

We'd almost reached her Fiesta when a shiny Mercedes pulled up in front of us.

"Is that…" she started.

Warren finished for me. "Tate Palmer? Yes."

He looked every bit as awful as I'd feared when he climbed out of the driver's side. His rumpled clothes and stubble were a far cry from his usual dapper appearance. On Nye, that look worked, but Tate just came across as untidy.

Even worse were his eyes, swimming with torment as they met mine.

"Olivia."

"Hi, Tate."

"I was driving past, and I saw you here… I… I…" He gave his head a little shake, as if he was trying to get rid of unwanted thoughts, and glanced at my support team. "I don't know where to start."

"I'm so sorry about your mother."

"I just can't... My father... How could he..."

I took both of his hands in mine. "It must have been such a shock."

A tear rolled down his cheek, and he looked behind me again. "Have you got a few minutes to talk? I need to apologise."

I glanced behind and sighed. Maddie had fixed him with a hawk-like stare, and he was withering under it. "Do you want to go somewhere more private?"

"Would you mind? This is...well, it's not easy with an audience."

Tate was as much a victim in all this as I was. The least I could do was listen to what he had to say, especially as I'd had a hand in his life falling apart, however unwittingly.

"I won't be long," I told Maddie. "Maybe half an hour?"

I raised an eyebrow at Tate, and he nodded his confirmation.

"Can you drop me back here?"

He held the passenger door open for me. "Of course."

"We'll be waiting," Warren said.

Maddie took a step towards her own car. "Not here. The café. We'll be waiting in the café."

CHAPTER 39

NYE LEANED BACK in his chair and glared at his laptop screen. This was the part of the job he hated. The admin. Jannie did her best, but there were always things left over that he had to deal with, especially when he took a couple of weeks off at the last minute.

For years, he'd resisted promotion to a managerial post, preferring the challenges of being in the field, but the directors had kept asking him, and in the end they'd come to a compromise—he'd take the job, but he'd have an assistant and a big enough team that he didn't spend his whole time stuck behind a desk.

He had to admit the role had grown on him, and being Head of Investigations for Blackwood's London office was a good career move. Even his mother had been grudgingly impressed by the title.

The screen full of emails in front of him was a worthy trade-off for what he'd gained in the last fortnight. Sure, he'd missed out on a hell of a lot of sleep and had to flee a burning building, but that was nothing compared to his past escapades.

And now he had Olivia.

He took out his phone and snuck a glance at the last photo he'd taken of her, blonde hair spread out over his pillow as she'd slept beside him. That was exactly where he wanted her to stay. She wouldn't be moving back to Upper Foxford, not if he could help it, but there was still so much she didn't know about him. How would she react when she found out?

No, he didn't want to think about that, not at the moment.

Instead, he shoved his chair back and headed to the kitchen. The coffee machine was burbling away as Max wandered in, whistling a remarkably tuneful version of "Love is in the Air."

"Knock it off, would you?"

Max shrugged. "Tell me it's not true."

Nye couldn't, not when Liv had taken over his heart and mind. "You wait. It'll happen to you one day."

"Not likely. I've got enough on my plate with work and house renovations."

"Fifty quid says I'm right."

Max held out his hand, and they shook.

"Easy money," he said as he disappeared with an apple.

One meeting left until Nye could escape for the rest of the day. If it had been anything but the monthly conference for all the heads of department, he'd have sent his apologies and gone to find Liv already, but one of the directors was in the UK, and an excuse wouldn't work with her.

Back at his desk with an espresso, he wondered how the hell to tell Liv how he felt. He'd never declared his love for anything more than a prime beef burger with bacon and extra cheese, and that only happened after a few beers.

Should he buy her flowers? Chocolates? Jewellery? His previous girlfriends had liked those things, but Liv was different. The vacuous socialites had been pretty on his arm but not so pretty inside, while Liv was real and beautiful to her core.

He pressed the intercom on his desk. "Did you confirm the reservations for tonight?"

"For the third time, yes." Jannie's voice came through loud and clear and just a little bit peeved. She hated it when he questioned her efficiency. "Quiet table for two, candles, music, the works."

For his first proper date with Liv, Nye had chosen a mid-range Italian place that served excellent food without being overly pretentious. Unlike most of the women he'd dated, Liv actually liked to eat. His hand strayed to his lap. Yeah, she definitely liked to eat. He'd hit the fucking jackpot with that woman.

Twelve thirty. Finally! He could get the meeting over with and finish up the rest at home. Blackwood allowed staff to work flexibly, and he'd done enough overtime during the past nine years to justify a couple of easy days.

In the conference room, the table was stacked with snacks. Apple slices, pita bread with houmous, celery sticks—where was the proper food? He picked up a chicken satay and bit into it. Yuck. What the hell was this?

"Sorry. It's tofu," Emmy said from behind him. "Toby flew over with me."

That explained it. As Special Projects Director, Emmy had to stay in tip-top shape and often brought her nutritionist when she came to the UK. So now they all had to eat weird shit.

The man himself bustled in carrying a plate of pineapple pieces. "And if you even think of bringing biscuits into this meeting, I'll put decaf in all the coffee machines."

Emmy clenched her teeth. "You wouldn't."

"Watch me."

"For fuck's sake... Guys, we need to hurry this up so I can go and find cake."

Despite Emmy rattling through the agenda, Nye was still fidgeting by the end of the meeting. Had Liv finished up at Lilac Cottage yet? He'd seen the charges from Agent Provocateur on his credit card statement, and he kept his fingers crossed she'd be trying out one of those skimpy outfits tonight.

Finally, Emmy finished up. "Anything else?"

Everyone shook their heads, thank goodness. Nye would have cracked a tooth if he'd clamped his jaws any harder.

"What's up with you?" Emmy asked as she followed him out. "Didn't you get enough last night?"

Oh, if only she knew. Liv may have been inexperienced, but she was an excellent pupil and made up for it with enthusiasm. The fact that Nye had been late for work was a testament to that.

"I got plenty."

"Are you coming out for pizza?" one of their colleagues asked.

Emmy shook her head. "I've got mayhem to plan. But if you can sneak me a deep-pan pepperoni past Toby, I'd be eternally grateful."

"Nye?"

"Not today, sorry."

Three o'clock. Liv should be on her way back by now, which would give them time for a quick trip to the bedroom before dinner. He just needed to pick up the gift he'd ordered for her on the way back. A pair of oven mitts, go figure. She'd mentioned wanting them.

He'd got one arm in his jacket sleeve when the phone on his desk rang. Sod it—Jannie could answer.

"Nye, wait a second," she called.

He paused, halfway through the door. Dammit. "What is it?"

"Inspector Carling from Hertfordshire Constabulary is on the phone. You know, the guy dealing with the mess in Upper Foxford? He says it's important."

Nye huffed, but he couldn't ditch work in favour of visiting a bakeware shop. "Transfer it through, will you?"

He stomped back into his office and perched on the edge of his desk. A second later, the phone beeped.

"Nye Holmes."

"Rory Carling. We met briefly the other night."

"Yes, I remember." Nye wished he'd get to the point.

"We've got a problem here, and I wanted to bounce it off you, if you've got a few minutes?"

Nye didn't want problems. He wanted sex, a chilled Peroni, and pizza. In that order. "What kind of problem?"

"Well, we've got Fenton Palmer in custody, and we've got a statement, a body, and a murder weapon. But forensics just called, and the fingerprints on the knife don't match the suspect."

"You're kidding me? No way the lab could have screwed up?"

"They've checked it twice. There's one set of prints, in blood, and they don't belong to Fenton Palmer."

"Have you run them through the database?"

"We did that right away, but we didn't get any hits."

Shit. What the fuck was Ronnie playing at?

"Can you send a copy of the prints over? And a set of Fenton's? I'll get our tech guys to take a look too."

"On their way. I'm going down to talk to Palmer next, but he's been hiding behind his lawyer so far."

"Has he said anything at all?"

"Not a dicky bird."

Nye thumped his fist down on the desk then yanked his chair out. It looked as if he wouldn't be going home yet after all. And what was he supposed to tell Liv?

Nothing. He'd tell her nothing for the moment. She'd only get worried.

He fired off a quick message.

Nye: Something's come up at work. Do you want to go home with Maddie and I'll meet you there when I'm done?

"Everything okay?" Jannie asked.

"Not really. I'll be in the lab if anyone needs me."

An hour later, Test-tube confirmed what Carling had already told them—the fingerprints weren't Fenton's.

"Then who the hell left them on that knife?" Nye growled.

"If the police database hasn't found anything, it's not someone with a criminal record, at least in the UK. I'll run them through Interpol just in case."

The call-waiting light flashed, and Nye jabbed at the button to switch to the other line. Today was turning into a nightmare. He'd need to move the restaurant booking and call Liv to apologise.

"Carling here again. I've spoken with Fenton Palmer."

"And?"

"He's giving us some bull about walking in and finding his wife dead on the floor. Now he's claiming a mystery man broke in and killed her."

"You believe him?"

"Not in the slightest. He's shifty as hell. But his lawyer's got wind of the letter from Ronnie, and he's trying to pin everything on him."

Bloody lawyers. Always trying to twist the facts to suit them and their guilty-as-hell clients.

"I take it you've compared the prints on the knife to Ronnie's? He's in the system already."

"That was the second thing we did. No match."

Nye kicked at his desk leg. "This is crazy. Why'd Fenton bury the body if he just walked in and found her like that? That alone says he's guilty."

"It just doesn't make sense."

"Any chance the prints could belong to the wife?"

"It's possible, I suppose, but checking will be difficult. She's been dead for years, and you saw the condition the body was in."

Yeah, Nye did, and he could still smell it. Time hadn't been kind.

"Try anyway."

"We will. I'll keep in touch."

Nye began pacing. It helped him to think, except when the rubbish bin got in his way. He gave it a kick. What he needed was a bigger office.

Fenton Palmer had to be responsible. *Had* to be. The man radiated guilt, and the police had found leather gloves in his hall closet next to a pair of muddy boots with rosemary sprigs stuck in the treads. His gardener confirmed a can of petrol had gone missing from the shed, and his internet history showed a search for Molotov cocktails. Plus, he had no alibi for any of Olivia's night-time visits.

There was only one explanation, and not a palatable one: Fenton Palmer wasn't working alone.

The phone rang again, the display flashing with Test-tube's name. Nye snatched it up.

"What?"

"Good afternoon to you too."

"Sorry. No time for pleasantries."

"Well, the good news is we've identified the prints."

Thank goodness. Nye sagged with relief. Maybe now they could put this nightmare to rest once and for all. "Interpol?"

"Our own database, actually."

"Ours?" Blackwood had a tendency to skirt the rules that bound the police on occasion. They kept prints that might be useful on file, even if a person hadn't been convicted. "Who the fuck do they belong to?"

"One Tate Palmer. He was part of the sweep we did for the Lower Foxford kidnapping case a couple of years ago."

The details clicked into place. Fuck. Carol had said Tate was at university when his mother disappeared, but he must have come back for a visit. If Fenton Palmer was going to cover for anyone, it would be his son. A son who'd been involved with Olivia before Nye came onto the scene. Was that why he'd been sniffing around? So he could get into Lilac Cottage and find the missing evidence?

He needed to let her know what was going on, and that would be better done in the privacy of his apartment. They could go out another night. Nye wanted their first date to be perfect, not overshadowed by the asshole who'd tried to ruin her life.

Was she back in town yet? He checked his phone, but she hadn't replied to his earlier message. Busy gabbing with Maddie, no doubt. He dialled her number, but it went straight to voicemail.

"Babe, there've been a few developments here. Can you call me? I want to know you're safe."

Nye's next call went to Inspector Carling to give him the good news.

"We'll pick the Palmer boy up as soon as we can, but we'll have to be careful with the paperwork seeing as you're not supposed to have those prints."

Damn the law and its finicky rules. "Whatever you do, don't let him walk on a technicality."

"We won't. Don't you worry about that."

"And try not to leave it too long. Tate must be feeling the heat by now, and we don't want him to do anything stupid."

"Understood. Can you send Blackwood's report over?"

Nye did so right away then tried Liv again, but she still didn't answer. Where was she? He called his apartment just in case she'd gone back there already. Nothing. Now what? He needed to get hold of Maddie, but he didn't know her surname, only where she lived. Time for the research department to earn their money.

Jannie buzzed through. "Madonna's on the line for you."

"Is that a joke?"

"No joke. She says she's a friend of Olivia's."

Madonna... Maddie? Suddenly, Nye felt sick. His gut ached worse than after he'd eaten her liver mousse.

"Put her through."

"Nye?" came Maddie's voice.

"It's me. Is Liv okay?"

"I don't know. I can't get hold of her. Tate stopped by and said he needed to talk, so they went for a drive. She said she'd only be thirty minutes, but that was over an hour ago, and she's not answering her phone."

Fuck! That bastard had the only woman he'd ever truly wanted.

"Where are you?"

"At Daisy's café in Upper Foxford."

"Stay there. I'm on my way."

CHAPTER 40

"WHERE ARE YOU going?"

Emmy's voice came from Nye's left. He looked over his shoulder and saw her squashed down the side of her Aston Martin, sitting on the concrete floor of the parking garage with a pizza box balanced on her knees. She put a finger to her lips.

"Olivia's in danger."

"Olivia? That's the girl you've been shagging?"

"No, that's the woman I'm in love with." He'd thought those words so many times, but he'd never spoken them aloud before.

"Wow. Never thought I'd see the day. What kind of danger?"

"I don't have time for this."

He carried on jogging towards his motorbike, parked near the exit, but Emmy abandoned her contraband meal and followed.

"I know that look," she said. "You're about to do something crazy."

"Don't try to stop me."

She caught up as he fished the key out of his pocket.

"Hell no, I want in. It's been a boring week so far. Meetings, meetings, more meetings. But I will postpone your fun if you don't tell me what's going on."

And she would, he knew that much. She might look

like a pin-up girl, but she fought like a demon with the devil in her corner. Nye stopped to give her a sixty-second rundown, cursing every wasted second in his head.

"So, let me get this straight—you're going to ride to Upper Foxford and strangle Tate Palmer."

"That's pretty much it, yeah. You have a better idea?"

"As it happens, I do."

A smile crossed her devious face as she explained, and Nye couldn't help returning it. Emmy may be a world-class bitch, but when she was on his team, he loved that side of her.

"Good plan. Ready to go?"

She grinned. "Four miles, and whatever you do, don't get caught."

Nye knew there was a reason he'd bought this bike.

Emmy clung to his waist, blonde hair streaming out behind her as he blasted the Ducati 1098S out of the garage. He hit the first red signal ten seconds later and dodged a van coming across the junction as he ignored the light. Emmy had ripped off his registration plate before they left, but he'd still be lucky if he had a licence after this.

"Left," she yelled.

"That's a one-way street."

"Left!"

Oh, what the hell. If anything happened to Olivia, life wouldn't be worth living, anyway. Drivers laid on their horns as he swerved around them, focused only on covering the distance to Belgravia as fast as possible. Brake lights glowed ahead, and he bumped the bike up onto the pavement to avoid the traffic jam. Pedestrians scattered as he twisted the throttle. Shit. He was either going to hell or jail.

The first sirens sounded as they shot down the street Emmy lived on, and she reached past him with the gate opener in her hand. The huge iron gates opened slowly, oh so slowly. He revved the engine and squeezed through the gap, hurtling past the corner of Albany House just as a police car flew past with its blue lights flashing. The gates closed silently, hiding them, and Emmy's underground garage filled with the smell of burned rubber as he parked up next to the stairs in the far corner.

"Well, that was fun," she said, hopping off the back. "We'll have to do it again sometime."

"Are you insane?"

"Certifiably." She patted him on the ass as he climbed up to the ground floor next to her, two steps at a time. "Get what we need from the weapons locker, and I'll meet you upstairs."

CHAPTER 41

TATE LOOKED LIKE a broken man, just as anyone would if they'd found out their father killed their mother. Had Tate ever suspected she hadn't run off with another man? Surely not—nobody would have kept quiet about something so serious, even a teenager. How old was he when it happened? Seventeen? Eighteen?

Beside me, he gripped the wheel, his gaze fixed on the tarmac as he sped along the winding lanes of Middleton Foxford.

"Where are we going?"

No answer.

"Tate, where are we going?"

He glanced over at me, and his eyes had an odd glint. Grief did funny things to people, I knew that, but he didn't look as if he was all there.

"The house. We're going to the house."

"The house? Do you mean your cottage?"

Again, silence. I started to get a bad feeling about the whole plan.

"On second thoughts, it might be best if we met up another day. Maddie and Mickey are waiting to go back to London."

"You said we could talk."

"Yes, but I didn't realise how late it's got. Can you

drop me back at the café? Please?"

"We're going to talk."

His mouth set in a thin line, and he gripped the wheel harder. We were travelling at almost seventy along narrow lanes. Did he have a death wish? A branch whacked the wing mirror, and I jumped, but Tate didn't seem to notice.

"Please stop. I'll get out here and make my own way back. It's no problem."

But he didn't even slow. I considered making a grab for the wheel, but at the speed we were going, that would end in disaster. Whatever Tate had planned, I had no choice but to go along for the ride.

Ten minutes later, the car skidded sideways in a hail of gravel as we arrived at Prestwold Manor. Almost before we stopped, Tate leapt out. He pulled my door open, and not in his usual gentlemanly manner.

"Get out."

"I think I'd rather stay here."

I clung on to the sides of the seat, but he grabbed my arm and hauled me out. Blood blossomed on the knee of my jeans as I tripped over the doorsill and landed heavily on the ground.

Tate's fingers bit into my wrist as he pulled me to my feet and across the drive, and I stumbled again. Thoughts jumbled together in my head as if I'd drunk one too many glasses of wine. Why was he being like this?

The stone facade of the old manor loomed in front of us. "Why are we here? This isn't your home."

"No, it's my father's. And it would have been mine one day if you'd managed to do what you were told."

"What are you talking about?"

"Such a simple request. All you had to do was get out of Eleanor's house." He gave his head a little shake. "I even offered you somewhere else to stay. Why did you find it so difficult?"

Realisation hit me like a blow to the stomach, and I regretted eating all those cupcakes earlier. "You *knew*? You knew your father was trying to scare me away from Lilac Cottage?"

"Knew? It was my idea. The problem was that I only had an incompetent fool to help me. He managed to screw things up, just like he screwed up disposing of my mother's body all those years ago."

Tate had been in on it? What sort of man could live with that secret?

He unlocked the door, shoved me inside, and slammed it behind us, looking more unhinged by the second. When I didn't move fast enough, he pushed me, and I tripped over the edge of a rug. Pain shot through my wrist as I caught it on the edge of a table, but he didn't care, just twisted it behind my back and propelled me forwards.

"Come on, Olivia. Pick your feet up."

I could barely walk at all, I was shaking so much. How could I have been so stupid? I'd considered dating this man, for crying out loud. Was my judgement really that bad?

We arrived in a lounge, a huge, high-ceilinged room filled with stuffy-looking furniture, and he flung me onto a leather couch. As I rolled against the back, he yanked my wrists in front of me. Rope dug into my skin as he knotted it tight.

"Sit up."

I didn't get the chance to comply before he dragged

me into the position he wanted and went to tie my feet as well. I tried to kick him, but he trapped my legs with his and slapped me.

"Save the fight for later, my darling. It'll make what I have planned for us more fun."

My vision went fuzzy as it hit me what he meant. Once, I'd found Tate attractive, but now? He repulsed me. The thought of him forcing himself on me made lunch rise up my throat. How could I get out of this? My phone was in my pocket, but I couldn't reach it, not with Tate watching me like freaking Larry. Tate began muttering while he paced, but he still didn't take his eyes off me.

He'd gone insane. That was the only explanation.

"How could you live with your father, knowing that he killed your mother? Why didn't you go to the police?"

"Olivia." He crouched in front of me, hands on his knees. "Poor, stupid little Olivia. So naïve. My father didn't kill my mother. I did."

That was it. Spots floated before my eyes as I heaved up Daisy's offerings onto Tate's shoes. Pastel icing and rainbow sprinkles covered the handmade Italian leather, and there was even a bit of glitter in there. The measure of satisfaction I felt was tempered by the punch to the gut he gave me.

"Oof!"

"Shut up!"

He'd lost it. He'd totally lost it. He strode up and down the hideous rug, talking to himself again as the last of his sanity leached out from between his ears. I needed to stall him, and I needed to find a way to contact Nye.

"W-w-why? Why did you k-k-kill her?"

He paused in front of me, staring down. "My mother had this ridiculous idea in her head that I should learn to live as a pauper. She wanted my father to cut off my allowance until I turned thirty so I'd have to get a proper job."

What, like a normal person?

"Thirty years old! Can you believe that?"

"No, Tate. It's absurd."

He didn't pick up on my sarcasm as he continued his tirade.

"Why would I want to do that? Rent a house and save up for a shitty car? We had money coming out of our ears, and Father had promised me the cottage. My godfather was only too happy to give me a position in his firm where I could take as much time off to play golf as I wanted. The bitch tried to ruin that." He stepped closer, eyes wide and unfocused. "Someone needed to put her in her place."

His hot breath washed over my face as he stroked my cheek with his fingertips. I jerked away, but he yanked me back again.

"That's no way to be polite, Olivia. I'll need to teach you some manners as well."

He pinched my cheeks between the thumb and fingers of one hand, making it difficult to nod, but I managed it.

"I-I-I'm sorry."

Tate sighed. "This is a difficult time for all of us. I wish things could have been different, really I do."

When he headed for the drinks cabinet on the far side of the room, I leaned to one side, trying to wiggle my phone out of my pocket, but it snagged on the lining. Try as I might, I couldn't get it free. Tate poured himself a generous measure of Scotch, and it sloshed over the sides of the glass as he resumed pacing.

A tear trickled down my cheek, followed by another and another. Right now, I should have been on my way to a restaurant with Nye. What would he think when I didn't arrive home? Would he think I'd stood him up? That I didn't love him? Because I did, and I'd never got the chance to say it. This should have been the best day of my life, and instead, it had turned into the worst.

Tate stalked back to me, red-faced. The glass only had a few dregs and an ice cube left in it.

"Why, Olivia? Why? Why did you have to be like that? We could have been so happy together. Once I show you what you've been missing, you'll understand that."

He grabbed my legs and pulled me flat on the sofa. I writhed like a demented caterpillar and tried to throw myself onto the floor, but he caught me and flipped my legs back onto the seat.

"Get off me!" I screamed.

"Shut up, Olivia, or I'll have to gag you. And I have plans for your pretty mouth."

So did I. I was going to bite the fucking thing off if it got that far.

"I hate you."

He pressed a hand over my mouth, and in the moment of silence, I heard the sweetest sound in the world—a knock at the front door.

CHAPTER 42

TATE NARROWED HIS eyes at me. "Who's at the door?"

"How should I know? It's not my house."

He bit his lip as he glanced towards the door. *Go on, answer it.* I just needed one more minute to get to my phone and call for help.

Another knock, louder this time, startled both of us, and Tate came to a decision.

"Don't you move."

"I'm tied up, Tate. I can't go anywhere."

He got halfway to the door before he stopped in his tracks, reaching out to tug a tasselled tie-back off one of the curtains.

"No, I just can't trust you."

He knotted one end of it around my ankle and tied the other to the leg of the couch, but that wasn't the worst part. As he straightened, he spotted the bulge in my pocket.

"What's this?" He pushed me sideways and delved in. "A phone? Tsk tsk tsk, Olivia. You weren't thinking of calling the police, were you?"

"No. I honestly wasn't."

Tate threw my smartphone against the wall by the fireplace, and it smashed into smithereens. Dammit. I should have stuck with my old Nokia. That would have survived Armageddon.

Low voices came from the hallway, Tate's and another man's, but I couldn't afford to waste time listening. Instead, I heaved the couch with all my might and managed to slide the tie-back off the leg. I wasn't free, exactly, but at least I could hop. Somebody shouted my name, and I'd stumbled six feet when the sound of breaking glass stopped me in my tracks. A few groans, and then everything went quiet again. What had happened?

A scraping sound came from the passage outside, and Tate backed through the door dragging a body. Black leather boots, denim-clad legs. My heart leapt into my throat. *Please, don't let it be Nye.* The rest of the visitor came into view, and I retched again, bringing up the last of a chocolate cookie.

Oh, hell. *Oh hell, oh hell, oh hell.*

"Is he dead? Tate, is he dead?"

Tate shrugged as he dropped Warren's legs, and they hit the carpet with a hollow *thud.*

"I hope so."

"How could you?"

"It was easier than last time. I just hit him over the head with a vase. But I'm not sure what to do with the body. Digging is such a menial task."

He'd gone out of his upper-class mind. "What did Warren ever do to you?"

"Nothing, but he came looking for you, and that could have made things tricky."

Maddie and Mickey knew who I was with too, but with Tate unravelling fast, I avoided mentioning that in case he went on a rampage.

"You didn't have to kill him."

"Sometimes it's just easier." Tate nudged Warren with one stinky shoe before heading back to the drinks cabinet. "Why does some common oaf always have to ruin things? First Ronnie, now this waste of space. I had so many plans for us this afternoon, and now I have to dispose of an extra corpse."

My heart bled. But devastated though I felt over Warren, I had to use the situation to my advantage.

"You should probably do that right away, before he stiffens up."

"Do you think?"

"He'll be more difficult to handle if you wait."

I needed more time. Just enough for Maddie to realise something was wrong and call the police. I only hoped she'd insist on speaking to someone other than Graham.

Hold on, did Warren just twitch? Or was it my imagination clawing onto any hope, no matter how faint?

Tate topped up his glass and turned back. Quick—I needed to distract him. If Warren was still alive, who knew what Tate would do if he realised?

"On second thought, we shouldn't let Warren ruin our afternoon. Why don't we have a drink together and deal with him afterwards?"

"I suppose that would be acceptable. Red or white? Or would you prefer something stronger?"

I choked back a laugh. *Now* his manners came back? "Red would be wonderful."

If I broke the glass, that would give me a weapon. Then I could aim a jagged shard for his eye, and...

A strange noise took my attention. Distant at first, but it quickly came closer. *Whomp-whomp-whomp.*

Tate heard it too and ran to the window on unsteady legs.

"Those bastards!" he screamed. "You told them, didn't you? You told them!"

What was out there?

"Told who? You're not making any sense. How could I have told anybody what you did when I didn't know myself?"

Tate ignored me and dashed to a walk-in cupboard in the farthest corner of the room. When he emerged, I nearly wet myself in fear. He'd gone from a vase to a gun, and from the way he loaded a cartridge, he knew how to use it. Tate swung the barrel in my direction, and I looked into a black hole that led straight to hell.

A crash came from the far side of the house, and a door slammed. Whoever was running through the corridors didn't worry about staying quiet. The footsteps came closer and closer, and I knew what would happen if they came through the door of the lounge.

"He's got a gun," I shouted as the person paused outside.

"You little bitch!" Tate screamed, and I stared in horror as he tightened his finger on the trigger.

Behind him, the door burst open, and relief became fear as Tate turned his sights on the man I loved. Nye leapt for him, arms outstretched, and my eyes screwed shut of their own accord. My boyfriend versus a shotgun. I couldn't bear to watch.

Time slowed, until the moment of silence was broken by an almighty *bang*.

CHAPTER 43

SCREAMS FILLED THE air as Tate and Nye both fell to the floor.

Mine.

The screams were mine.

Blood leaked onto the carpet as I tried to get to Nye, but my feet were too tightly bound to walk. I ended up jumping, desperately trying to keep my balance. *Please, don't let Tate have claimed another victim.*

Nye didn't move, but as I got closer, Tate groaned. Oh shit, he was trying to get up.

I grabbed an ugly statue of a dog from a side table and hefted it in both hands. It looked antique and, to my untrained eye, solid bronze.

And that meant it was heavy. Good.

I raised my hands as high as I could and brought the ugly ornament down on Tate's head.

He lay still.

Carol's voice popped into my head, telling her tale about Emmy and Horrible Henry, swiftly followed by a replay of Tate's words from earlier. He had plans for my pretty mouth, did he? Well, let's see how those plans went with a third testicle. I raised the dog once more and walloped him between the legs. If he was unconscious, there were no witnesses, right?

The bronze slipped out of my hands and thudded to

the carpet as I fell to my knees next to Nye. I pressed my bound hands to his chest. An age passed before I felt the flutter of his heart under my palms, and I sagged in relief. But the wetness seeping into the knees of my trousers told me this wasn't over. Nye's blood had formed an abstract pattern on the floor, more Kazuo Shiraga than Jackson Pollock.

But at least he was alive.

A phone. I needed a phone, but before I could find one, a stranger walked through the door. Blonde, beautiful, and even with bodies lying all over the floor, she had a composure I could only dream of.

"Please help him," I sobbed as the nightmare overcame me. "Please."

She dropped to her knees beside Nye and tore open his leather jacket. His white T-shirt had turned red.

"That bloody idiot," she said. "He jumped out the helicopter while it was still five feet off the ground."

"Is he going to die?"

"Only if I kill him myself. He should have waited."

"We need to call an ambulance."

She tapped her ear. "I'm miked up, and it's already on its way. I'm Emmy Black, by the way. I'd shake hands, but..."

"It's a problem for me too."

Before I could blink, she'd whipped out a knife and sliced through the rope. A second later, my ankles were free too.

"Are the others alive?" she asked.

"I'm not sure."

I stumbled over to Warren and felt for a pulse. As my fingers pressed against his wrist, he stirred and opened his eyes.

"Olivia, are you okay?"

Oh, thank goodness. "Shouldn't that be my question?"

He smiled up at me and raised a hand to his head, wincing as he touched the lump on his temple. "Palmer said you'd fainted and gone for a lie-down, and when I insisted on coming to find you, he must have whacked me with something."

"A vase."

"So much for storming to your rescue."

"You tried, and I'll always be grateful for that. Now, lie still until the ambulance gets here."

Warren lay back again, but a groan from Tate on the other side of the sofa sent me reeling onto my backside, and I scrambled in the opposite direction. Emmy didn't even flinch.

"He's alive! What do we do?" I squeaked.

"How about you pop out to the helicopter and get my first-aid kit? The big green bag in the back."

"But what about Tate?"

"Don't worry about Tate. Nye needs fluids."

I paused, torn between helping Nye and making sure Tate didn't hurt anybody else, but Emmy flicked her wrist at the door and I went through it. I got the distinct impression it wasn't a good idea to argue with her. The helicopter was parked on the back lawn between the swimming pool and the tennis court, and I yanked the door open. Green bag... Green bag... There it was. From the size, it was more of a portable hospital than a first-aid kit, and I lugged it back inside as fast as I could.

"I've got it."

"Thanks. Left-hand compartment, I need a bag of

Ringer-lactate, an IV administration set, and a packet of QuikClot EMS dressing—the little squares."

"Do you know how to use all of this stuff?"

"I watched a couple of episodes of *Grey's Anatomy* a while back."

"Uh, I'm not sure..."

Nye cracked an eye open. "Ignore her bullshit. She knows exactly what she's doing."

Oh, thank goodness. "Then what about Tate? Should I tie him up or something?"

"No need," Emmy said.

"I really think we should. What if he wakes up properly?"

"No, what I mean is Tate died. While you went to get the first-aid kit."

What? "But he was waking up."

"Head injuries can be funny things." She shrugged. "Unfortunate."

Her demeanour said it was anything but. "They can?"

"Do you have a problem with that?"

Did I? After all the pain Tate had caused to not only me, Nye, and Warren, but to his own family? Hell no. "Not at all. Sometimes it's just easier."

She smiled, more to herself than me, it seemed. "It is indeed."

"But I feel fine," Nye told the doctor six hours later.

"Mr. Holmes, you lost several pints of blood and took a nasty crack to the head. You need to stay in overnight for observation."

"Can't someone observe me at home?"

"I can do that," I offered.

"You've already tested me for everything. How the hell is a stool sample relevant to getting shot in the shoulder?"

Apparently, Blackwood had a great insurance package, and the hospital had taken full advantage of that. I swear I heard the technician working the MRI machine mention something about today's patient paying for a great Christmas party.

"You never know," the doctor said. "And head injuries can be unpredictable. Look at Mr. Palmer. Miss Porter here clonked him with an ornament, and now he's in the morgue."

I wasn't entirely convinced my efforts were to blame, but when I glanced over at Emmy sitting in the corner, her expression didn't change.

"How about me?" Warren asked from the bed next to Nye's.

A shortage of space meant they'd ended up sharing a room, but Nye had been surprisingly accommodating about the situation once he found out what Warren's timely interruption at Prestwold Manor had saved me from.

"Same goes for you, Mr. Hannigan."

"Nye, if the doctor thinks it best that you stay here, you really should." I squeezed his hand. "I'll worry otherwise."

He pulled me down for a kiss, and he would have moved on to tongues if the doctor hadn't cleared his throat.

"So, that's settled," he said. "I'll get the nurse to bring you the dinner menu. I believe it's beef

Wellington tonight."

Nye caught my eye and snickered. "Look on the bright side; it can't be as bad as Maddie's."

"You haven't tried her Moroccan tagine yet."

"I'm busy that year."

"Speaking of Maddie, she's offered to come round tonight and keep me company."

I said she offered, but I didn't exactly get a say in the matter. Still, at least I could say sorry in person for being so stupid with Tate earlier, in addition to the thousand apologies I'd given her on the phone. And if she hadn't called Nye when she did... I shuddered. The consequences didn't bear thinking about.

"That's good of her, babe."

"Mickey's coming too. He reckons he's been researching my family tree, and I was related to Queen Elizabeth the first about seven hundred generations ago."

"Doesn't surprise me."

"Maybe we could ask him to do yours?"

Emmy had a coughing fit, and I passed her a glass of water as Nye shook his head.

"Doubt Mickey would find anything interesting there."

A knock at the door made us look up, and everyone groaned in unison as Graham poked his head into the room.

"Evening, all. I think I need to take a statement."

He *thought*? Good heavens, didn't he know anything about his own job?

Nye waved him inside. "How about we make it quick? I need to get some sleep."

"Of course, of course. Oh dear. I seem to have

forgotten my pen."

Emmy rummaged in her bag and passed over a sleek-looking black ballpoint. "Here, borrow this."

"Thanks. And you are?"

"Nobody important. Hospital quality control."

"Ah, in that case, let's start with you, Miss Parker."

"Porter."

"Sorry?"

"Miss Porter. My name's Olivia Porter."

Graham questioned us for an hour, although we could have finished in half the time if he hadn't kept asking the same things twice. By the end, Nye had feigned sleep and Warren pretended he had a headache and called for the nurse to save us. Then Emmy told Graham she needed her pen back, and he gave up.

"Do you think he wrote it all down?" I asked Emmy as we walked out to get a taxi back to London. Apparently, somebody else had already retrieved her helicopter from Tate's garden.

"Doesn't matter. That pen had special ink in it. Everything'll be gone by tomorrow morning."

I giggled. "Funny joke."

"He deserves a disciplinary."

"Wait—you weren't serious, were you?"

She just smiled and kept walking.

CHAPTER 44

MADDIE AND MICKEY were waiting on a swanky leather sofa in the lobby of Nye's apartment building when I climbed out of the cab.

"Thought we'd got the wrong building for a minute," she said. "You really live here?"

"I can't quite believe it either."

She pulled me into a hug. "I was so worried about you earlier. We all were. And then Warren insisted on going to look for you at Tate's while I checked Lilac Cottage and Mickey waited at the café, and I knew something bad had happened."

"We're okay, that's all that matters."

"Apart from Tate. He got everything he deserved."

He did, although I couldn't help wishing I'd kicked him in the ribs for good measure. "Can we just not talk about it?"

"Of course. What was I thinking? Why don't we go upstairs and I'll cook you a nice dinner?"

"I feel quite bad enough as it is," I said, before clapping my hand over my mouth when I realised what had come out it.

Thankfully, Maddie saw the funny side. "I suppose trying to cook without my recipe book isn't the best idea. Shall I order a pizza?"

Janelle ran out of the lift just as the delivery guy left

half an hour later, and she was clutching a bottle of champagne in one hand and a bag from Hotel Chocolat in the other.

"So you can celebrate when Nye comes back," she said, holding them out to me. "I was going to get party poppers as well, but I guessed you'd had enough bangs for one week."

Yes, I had, at least of the noisy variety.

"Do you want to join us for pizza? We've got plenty."

Mickey wanted spicy hot, I'd gone for vegetable, and Maddie had retained her crown as the queen of bad taste and chosen a Hawaiian. Pineapple on pizza made me shudder.

"Why not? Saves making dinner."

Dinner turned into drinks, and I woke up next to Maddie in the early hours, both of us squashed onto one of Nye's luxurious armchairs. Different location, but just like the old days. I tucked blankets over her before heading for the bedroom, looking forward to sharing it with Nye tomorrow.

One advantage to having Janelle with us was her connection to the Blackwood control room. She checked her phone every few minutes, and as I cooked us all breakfast the next morning, she let out a whoop.

"Fenton Palmer's confessed all."

With a good night's sleep under my belt, curiosity got the better of me.

"What did he say?"

"Tate came back from uni for a few days and spent

most of the time arguing with his mother. Helena didn't grow up rich, and she hated the sense of entitlement Tate had developed. Fenton claimed to love his wife, but he'd secretly been considering a divorce according to the files we absolutely didn't find on his solicitor's computer."

"You hacked into it?"

"Of course not. That would have been illegal. Anyway, Fenton got back from the pub one night and found Helena dead on the floor and Tate sitting on the sofa, watching an episode of *Antiques Roadshow*."

"That's...that's..."

"Sick? Warped? Freaky? All of the above?"

"Yes, all of them. I can't believe I went out with that man. Why didn't I see he was a psychopath?"

Janelle patted my hand. "Sociopath. It's different. Half of the people I work with have psychopathic tendencies and they're not all bad. You met Emmy?"

"I did."

"There you go. Her husband's a Grade A candidate too."

"Did you do a degree in psychology or something?"

"A masters. Helps with working at Blackwood, let me tell you. Plenty of quirky personalities there. But to answer your question, Tate was good at hiding his true character. Money and looks blind a lot of people, and it can be difficult to see through that veneer. You had a lucky escape, girl."

It sickened me to think just how close I'd come to getting sucked into Tate's insane world. Instead of making crêpes, I could have been wrapped in plastic and buried in a shallow grave. Those damn prickles made my eyes itch again.

"Hey, hey." Janelle wrapped an arm around my shoulders. "Don't cry. In fact, don't even give that fruitcake another thought. Is there any maple syrup to go with these pancakes?"

More news came after Nye arrived home. Janelle had arranged a car for us to go to the hospital at ten, but he walked through the door at nine with a tired smile and a bag of pills.

"They let you out early?"

"Not exactly."

"Oh, Nye. You discharged yourself?"

"I left a note. Are those pancakes?"

Good grief. I was dating a twenty-seven-year-old child. "For goodness' sakes, sit down. You should be resting."

Before I could form another thought, he'd pinned me against the wall, my arms trapped over my head as he kissed me thoroughly. It seemed several parts of his anatomy didn't agree with my suggestion, but as his fingers walked over my bare stomach, Janelle appeared, phone in hand.

"Oh, you're back. I'll cancel the car. Did you hear the latest?"

"Define latest."

"Zander found Larry Hazell."

"News to me."

Janelle grinned. "I love it when I know more than the boss."

"Just spill it, Jannie."

"Fine. Well, Zander tracked down a couple of the girls in Larry's photo album and put them under surveillance. One of the teams spotted him last night rifling through the bins behind Susie Marsden's house.

When they got to him, he was sniffing a sanitary towel."

A little bit of sick came into my mouth, and I was glad I hadn't gone for that fourth crêpe.

"Bloody freak," Nye muttered.

"Right. Susie said the bins had been tampered with a few times before, but she thought it was foxes."

"What have we done with him?"

"Zander had a nice chat, and Larry said he just liked to watch the girls. It was difficult to prove otherwise, but you never know how things are going to escalate, so Emmy had a word with a guy she knows. The only girls Larry's going to be watching for a while are the nurses in the secure hospital we've parked him in."

Nye gave a low groan. "So I owe Emmy another favour now?"

Janelle shrugged. "Larry won't be getting out until she gives the okay."

"How is it possible to lock somebody up like that?" I asked. "Aren't there rules?"

Nye bent to kiss me on the forehead. "Best not to ask. Does it bother you?"

That Larry couldn't prey on more women, "just watching" or not? "Honestly?" I blew out a breath, thinking over how much I'd changed in the last few weeks. "No, it doesn't. I'm glad he's out of the way."

"Good." Nye sniffed the air, bloodhound-like. "Is that food? They tried to make me eat cold toast with jelly this morning." He made a face. "I couldn't stomach it."

"This coming from the man who used to live on Pop-Tarts?"

As he swung me into the air, I shrieked and wrapped my legs around his waist.

"What can I say, babe? My tastes have changed." He leaned in closer and nuzzled my ear. "Do we have any of that cream left?"

"Yes, but Maddie and Mickey are still here."

"Not for long. Jannie, can you take Liv's friends out somewhere?"

She stood up straighter and her eyes took on a devious glint. "Lunch at Le Coeur Noir?"

Well, Janelle sure knew her restaurants, because she'd just picked out the most expensive one in West London.

"You're killing me."

"Three courses and cocktails."

"Two courses and wine, and only if you're out of here in ten minutes."

"We'll be gone in five."

Maddie blew me a kiss as the three of them ran for the lift. "Be bad, Liv."

Alone at last, and despite Nye's brave face, I'd seen him wince when he lifted me up.

"How's your shoulder?" I asked.

"I've got painkillers."

"That's not what I asked."

"The doctors picked out all the pellets. I might end up with a few scars, and it stings like hell, but there shouldn't be any lasting damage." He closed his eyes and leaned his forehead against mine. "Fuck, Liv. I've never been so scared as when I saw him pointing that gun at you."

"That's my line."

"Let's agree to share, okay?"

I blew out a long breath, letting the last of Tate's poison leach out of my body. "It's over now. Tate's dead, Fenton's going to jail, Larry's out of the way, and we've got a whole future to look forward to."

A slow smile crept over Nye's face. Slow and devious. "At the moment, I'm only looking ahead to the next couple of hours. You're wearing far too many clothes."

"What about the crêpes?"

"Later."

"Are you up to this?"

"Oh, I'm up all right."

A quick glance downwards showed the truth in that statement, and I slipped my hand around Nye's waist and squeezed my favourite part of him. There was nothing sexier than a pair of firm buttocks in well-worn jeans. Except possibly those same buttocks out of the jeans. And maybe, just maybe, I'd worn another set of that fancy underwear in anticipation of him tearing it off me.

"Then do your worst, Sherlock."

"Don't call me that, or I'll be forced to spank you."

"Sorry, Sherlock." I cupped a hand behind my ear. "I missed that."

My squeals echoed down the hallway as he chased me to the bedroom. New Olivia wasn't such a good girl anymore.

EPILOGUE 1

A MONTH LATER, I was still waiting for Nye to come to his senses, but last week, he'd cleared out half of his wardrobe for me and bought a new food mixer. That said he wanted me in his life, right?

So why did he keep sending mixed messages? He asked about my friends, but if I touched on his family, he shut me down. Although he didn't mind me going to the office with him, last week, he'd disappeared for the whole of Saturday and changed the subject when I asked where he'd been. And his daily questions about the progress at Lilac Cottage seemed more than just a friendly interest. Did he want me to go back there?

Today was no different.

"How's the work going?" he asked, looking up from his plate of toast.

"The men have finished clearing the site now, and they said the materials for the rebuild should start arriving today. It's going faster than I thought."

"I got a friend of a friend to have a word with the insurance company, so there shouldn't be any hold-ups."

He did? Was he that desperate to get rid of me? Suddenly, I'd lost my appetite. I got up and threw the rest of my scrambled eggs into the bin, then shoved the dirty plate into the dishwasher.

"Babe, what's up?"

"Nothing. I'm fine."

"Oh shit. What did I say?"

"It doesn't matter."

I'd forgotten how fast he could move, and he closed the door before I managed to escape to the lounge. "Liv, I can't make things right until you tell me."

I turned to him, hands on hips as tears tickled my eyelids. "I'm upset because you want me to leave, okay?"

"Huh?"

"Every day, you ask if the cottage is ready for me to move into yet, and now you're trying to hurry things along."

"Oh, Liv." He pulled my hands free and clasped them in his. "I want the cottage finished because I'm a selfish bastard. It's taking up half your time at the moment, and I want it all."

"You don't want me to leave?"

"No, I want you to stay." He swallowed and closed his eyes for a second, and when he opened them again, he sucked my soul into his clear blue eyes. "I want you to stay permanently. Don't go back to Upper Foxford."

"Really? You want me to move in here?"

He nodded, looking a little worried until I squealed and leapt into his arms.

"Is that a yes?"

"It's a yes. I love being back in London."

And more than anything, I loved being with Nye. Breakfast was forgotten as he carried me to the bedroom and reminded me of all the reasons why I never wanted to leave the apartment. Or, in fact, his deluxe king-size. I'll give you a hint—it didn't have anything to do with the glorious view from the terrace.

"If I don't need to move back to Lilac Cottage, what should I do with it?" I mused afterwards.

Nye had given up on the idea of going to the office and brought his laptop into bed, where he was answering emails in between twirling my hair around his fingers and feeding me chocolates. As long as he didn't hit the video conference button, we were all good.

"Sell it, rent it out, use it as a holiday home?" he suggested.

"I'm not sure a trip to Upper Foxford would be much of a holiday." But me as a landlord? If someone had suggested the idea a year ago, I'd have laughed, but with the state of my finances, I couldn't deny the extra money would come in handy. "The rental income could tide me over until I get my business built back up again."

No way was I going to fall into the trap I'd been stuck in with Edward again.

"Website design?"

"What else?"

"I thought you wanted to open a bakery?"

"That's just a pipe dream."

"Why? You could sell the cottage and use the cash to start one."

I'd never seriously considered the idea, but Nye had planted a little seed and I couldn't flick it away. "Do you really think that's possible?"

He reached over and tucked a strand of hair behind my ear. "You can do anything you put your mind to, and I'd help you to set it up. You only have to ask, babe."

I knew then that all the trouble and heartache over Lilac Cottage had been worth it. Apart from Nye and Warren getting hurt, obviously. I'd rather have avoided that. But if I hadn't inherited that place and Tate and Fenton hadn't played their sick games, I'd never have met the man who completed me.

"Tate did me a favour when he led me to you."

"Forget him."

"I will, I promise." I gave my head a quick shake, wishing I could get rid of those damned memories. "I still can't believe he pulled the wool over my eyes like that." My mother's indoctrination, that's what it was. "He would have been Lord of the Manor one day, and I couldn't see past the title or his trust fund. Well, never again. I want to make my own way in life and earn my own money. And I'm going for a plain old Mr. this time."

Nye's smile faded, and he turned a shade paler.

"What? What did I say?"

He laughed, but it sounded forced. "You think I'm plain?"

Me and my stupid big mouth. "A sexy, gorgeous, hot, delicious Mr."

"Better."

Nye always seemed so confident, but after my thoughtless comment, he was on edge for the rest of the day. *Well done, Olivia.* I needed to think before I spoke in future.

My new man came with a new set of friends. Janelle had badgered Maddie and me into going on a night out with her and some of the Blackwood girls, although I put my foot down when they suggested a visit to Taurus. Even though Nye had seen the funny side, one of us per month being hospitalised was quite enough.

"We're celebrating tonight," Maddie said as I let her into Nye's apartment.

"Dare I ask why?"

With Maddie, it could be anything from finding a forgotten bottle of wine at the back of a cupboard to winning ten pounds on the lottery.

"You remember that woman at work I was having all the trouble with?"

I nodded.

"Well, she quit."

"Quit? Just like that?"

"Apparently, she left the area in a hurry. Something about being caught cheating with her tax credits. I heard a whisper that somebody reported her to HMRC."

"Any idea who?"

"Nope. But if I ever meet them, I'll buy them a drink. Heck, I'll even fork out for the good stuff."

Nye was sitting across the room with Warren, and he glanced up at her words. What was that look on his face? Satisfaction?

And yes, you did hear that right: Warren. Despite their rocky start, he and Nye had cleared the air and bonded over a shared hatred of hospital food, needles, and MRI scans. Which meant Warren was going to watch rugby with Nye while us girls headed for something slightly less muddy.

At least, I hoped so. Janelle had offered to organise, and she'd been a little hazy on the details.

"Where are we going?" Maddie asked when Janelle arrived with her posse in tow.

She made a sad face. "The river cruise-slash-strip show idea fell through because the dancers complained it was too cold, so we're going to Black's."

Maddie let out a whoop. "Really? As in *Black's*, the best nightclub in the city? I thought you had to have at least six zeroes on your bank balance to get on the guest list?"

"I've got six zeroes."

"Jannie, they're supposed to be at the end, not the beginning," one of the other Blackwood girls said.

"Not my fault the sales are on."

Janelle headed straight to the kitchen to find the chocolate supply. Nye had bought me so many boxes I'd begun to suspect he had shares in Cadbury. And he'd need to invest in a vineyard next if Maddie didn't stop raiding his wine rack.

An hour later, I clutched at Maddie, trying not to fall out of my stilettos as we followed Janelle past the queue for Black's. When I'd suggested joining it, she'd just laughed.

"We don't need to wait."

"But—"

"Trust me."

So I did, but before we got to the front, Maddie dug her nails into my arm.

"Do you see who I see?"

"What? Who? Where?" I followed her gaze, and the truffles I ate before I left nearly came back up. "Oh, hell."

Edward and Becki were waiting halfway along the block. Edward was bald, and unless my eyes deceived me, Becki's blonde tresses were a wig.

"Quick—keep walking," I whispered, but Maddie slowed down and veered in their direction.

"Edward, I haven't seen you for ages. Not since Liv came to her senses and decided you were pond life."

"Madonna, you're as charming as ever."

"What's this? A new look?" She waved a hand at his head. "You decided to go for something younger? Or did you just want to look a little less dull?"

"If you must know, I've been suffering from alopecia. My trichologist blames stress. We've already had to move because of the smell from the drains without you adding to the problem."

"I'm so sorry to hear that."

I bet she was. Now Edward had moved out before summer, it meant he wouldn't see the hail of glitter when he switched on his ceiling fan.

He turned his sights on me. "How are you, Olivia? Enjoying the single life?"

"I was until I met my new boyfriend." Edward looked surprised, the bastard, and I decided to take a leaf out of Maddie's book. "Now I've moved to Chelsea, I'm farther away from my old haunts, but the view of the river from the penthouse is worth it."

Becki shifted uncomfortably, and I couldn't resist sticking the knife in.

"Oh, and Becki, I happened to see an excellent anti-cellulite cream advertised in *Cosmo* last month. It might be worth you giving it a go?"

I choked back my giggles as we hurried to catch up with Janelle. She greeted the doorman by name, and the velvet rope magically moved aside to let us through.

Oh yes, revenge was sweet.

In the club, the music pounded as the cocktails kept coming. We may not have had Taurus, but our waiter certainly gave him a run for his money, and when Janelle slid a twenty-pound note into his waistband, he even took his shirt off.

"Should have brought that baby oil," Maddie whispered.

All I could do was blush—I'd already used it playing with Nye the week before.

"My head hurts," I complained the next day.

"Probably something to do with the naked dude serving you cocktails."

"He wasn't entirely naked."

Okay, Janelle had convinced him to lose the trousers too by the end of the night, but we had a private room and she let him keep his boxers. And Nye wouldn't have found out anything if she hadn't drunk-dialled him at two in the morning begging for a cheeseburger.

Saint that he was, he'd turned up with Happy Meals for all of us and carried me to bed.

Now we were cuddled up on his new sofa, and he passed me a packet of paracetamol. "I warned you Jannie was a bad influence."

"Yes, I know that now."

I was just about to pinch a mouthful of his tea when his phone rang with a ringtone I hadn't heard before: Meredith Brooks singing "Bitch." Nye groaned, and when I glanced down at the screen, it said *Mother calling*.

We still hadn't talked about his family, and I'd assumed they weren't close. After all, Nye said he'd hated living at home, and whenever I hinted about his past, he swiftly moved on to a new topic.

"Why don't you let it go to voicemail?" I suggested.

"Because I'll never hear the end of it."

He picked the phone up, holding it like a poisonous snake. "Hello, Mother."

I only heard his end of the conversation, but he seemed far from happy. The worry lines that had started to fade turned back into deep furrows.

"No, I haven't forgotten Grandma's birthday dinner... No! I certainly don't want you to invite Cressida Haworth as my date... I'm perfectly capable of meeting a nice girl by myself."

He clearly hadn't told his mother about me, and that stung. Was he ashamed? Did my background not meet with his family's expectations? He may have been happy to have me in his home and his bed, but now I realised there were parts of his life I wasn't compatible with.

"I'll be there, Mother. Just promise you won't invite any more women."

He hung up and looked at me sheepishly. "I'm sorry you had to hear that."

"I'm sorry I had to hear it too. Why didn't you just tell me you had a problem with me meeting your family?"

"I didn't know where to start."

"It's simple, Nye. I know I can be a disaster in public. I'd rather you'd simply said up front that you didn't want me embarrassing you at family functions."

"Babe, that's not how it is at all. You know which

fork to use better than I do."

"Then why the secrecy?"

He sighed. "It's my family that's the problem, not you. I don't want them subjecting you to the third degree and scaring you off."

"It would take more than petty questions to scare me off."

"That's only the half of it."

"I mean it. I'm yours. Hook, line, and sinker."

He stared past me for a few seconds, thinking. "In that case, do you want to come to my grandma's birthday party? Dinner and a trip to the opera. I'll understand if you don't want to, because I'd rather not go either."

Mother had spent years trying to educate me in the delights of opera, but I'd never learned to appreciate it as much as I should have. Probably because most of the time they sang in Italian and I didn't understand the storyline. But I'd pushed for the invite, so I could hardly back out now.

"I'd love to go, and I promise I won't let you down. My mother used to read me DeBrett's etiquette guide every night before I went to bed."

That earned me a tight smile. "You couldn't let me down if you tried."

He picked up the phone from where he'd dropped it and grimaced as he dialled. "About Grandma's dinner— I'll be bringing someone. Her name's Olivia, and I'd appreciate if you could send an extra ticket."

A pause.

"Porter. Olivia Porter... No, she's not one of the Old Windsor Porters. She lived in Clerkenwell before I met her... No, she's not living there now. We moved in together... Stop putting words in my mouth, Mother. I'll do that in my own time."

He hung up with the demeanour of a condemned man. "The deed is done. We're going, for better or worse."

"Aren't you being a teensy bit melodramatic?"

"You haven't met them yet."

EPILOGUE 2

DON'T BE NERVOUS, Olivia. It's just dinner and the opera.

Oh, who was I kidding? Just an hour or two, and I'd meet Nye's family. I still didn't know much about them, not even their names. If he'd given me a few hints, I could have looked them up on the internet, Facebook perhaps, but he was being really cagey over the whole thing. Surely they couldn't be that bad?

I'd splashed out on a new dress, maroon with an appropriately demure neckline, feeling a pang of regret for the designer outfits I'd sold after my split with Edward. But the Karen Millen sale was within my budget, and I'd even got a sparkly new necklace, albeit a cubic zirconia one.

I twisted my handbag strap in my hands as we purred along the M40 motorway in Nye's new BMW. Anything to stop myself from biting my nails. I'd already had a go this morning and chipped the pale pink polish before I realised what I was doing.

"Where are we going again?"

"Kendall Grange. It's some fancy hotel near my parents' home."

"That's in Northbury village, right?" I'd got that much out of him. Upper Foxford on steroids, he said.

"Yes."

"And you grew up there?"

"Yes."

See? He hated to elaborate. "Why the opera? Is your grandma a fan?"

He shrugged. "We go every year. A birthday treat."

I sighed and gave up. I'd meet his family soon enough, and maybe then I'd get some answers.

"Have we got everything?" I asked for the tenth time since we left.

"We don't need a lot, babe. I've got my wallet. You've got your bag full of woman crap, and we've got the tickets."

"Which opera is it?"

"Does it matter? I never understand them anyway." He passed me the envelope with the tickets from his door pocket. "It'll probably say on there."

I unpeeled the flap, and my heart sank as I pulled out the single ticket inside. Just when I thought we'd covered everything, another hiccup revealed itself.

"Nye, they've sent us the wrong one. Do you think they'll still let us in?"

"What do you mean, the wrong one? It's not for the opera?"

"Oh, it's for *Tristan und Isolde* all right, but it's not ours."

"Then whose is it?"

"The Viscount Northbury, plus one."

Nye went white and skidded to a halt on the hard shoulder, breathing hard.

"What's wrong? Nye, what is it? Should I call an ambulance?"

"I'm going to kill my mother. I swear, I'm going to kill her."

"It's just a wrong ticket. Isn't that a bit drastic?"

He grabbed both of my hands in his and shifted so he was facing me. "Babe, I wanted to tell you, really I did. I just didn't know how. And when you said you hated the idea of dating a posh bloke again..."

"What are you talking about? You're scaring me."

"Shit." He took a deep breath. "It's not the wrong ticket. I'm Viscount Northbury. I've told Mother over and over not to use that bloody title."

"I don't understand."

He gave me a nervous smile. "My full name is Aneurin Kendrick Holmes. My father's the Earl of Northbury, and as his eldest son, I get to use his secondary title, which is Viscount. I never wanted it, honestly. People treat me differently if they think I'm nobility, and I'm just Nye."

All the little bits of the puzzle fell into place—Nye's automatic manners, his expensive home, and his reaction when I'd told him I didn't want to date a man with a title again.

I squeezed his hands back. "You dope. I might have said I wanted a plain old Mr., but what I meant was that I want you. I'll love you whatever bits you stick in front of your name."

"You love me?"

"How could I not?"

He collapsed forward and threw his arms around me. Looked as if it was his turn to do drama today.

"I love you, Olivia. Don't ever forget that."

"I won't, I promise. Is there anything else I should know?"

I was joking, but he took me seriously.

"Someday I'll be expected to move back home and

manage the family estate. My father's still sprightly at the moment, but that time will come."

"Then we'll do it together."

"Thank fuck for that. I've been stewing over it for weeks. I know how much you hated living in a small village."

"My home is wherever you are. Is that really it now?"

"Not quite. On my twenty-eighth birthday next month, I'll get access to the rest of my trust fund. How do you fancy a bloody nice holiday?"

I burst out laughing. "A holiday sounds wonderful. Anything else?"

"Just one thing. If you could keep quiet about the gunshot wound, I'd appreciate it. My mother would flip if she found out, and Grandma would want to see the evidence."

"I won't say anything, I promise." I gave him a mock salute.

Nye put the car in gear and pulled back onto the carriageway, looking more relaxed than I'd seen him all week. He reached over the centre console and rested one hand on my thigh, and I twined my fingers through his.

"Thank goodness that part's over," he said. "Now we just need to deal with my relatives. I should probably give you the low-down."

"Forewarned is forearmed?"

"Something like that. You remember how you said your mother used to make you read DeBrett's?"

"Every evening."

"*My* mother could recite it word for word. And there's my grandmother..."

"Is she the same?"

"Not exactly. My great-grandmother could have written DeBrett's. Mother idolised her, but Great-Grandma died a couple of years ago. The funeral's still talked about today—a horse-drawn hearse, morning dress for the men, and she insisted the Bishop of Oxford came and did the service. Mother wore black for a month straight, while Grandma drank half a bottle of sherry at the wake and asked the bishop what he wore under his dress."

"Are you serious?"

"Unfortunately, yes."

"Should I be worried?"

"About Grandma? No. She'll love you and you'll love her. It's my mother you need to watch."

I wanted to grip Nye's hand as we walked into the venue, but I looped my arm through his instead. He held the door open, then led me over to a table near the stage. I glanced at the ladies' outfits as we passed. Marc Jacobs, Versace, Gucci, Vera Wang, and enough fancy shoes to pay off the debt of a third-world country. Dammit, I should have got my credit card out.

Nye shared his mother's straight nose, high cheekbones, and strong jaw, and I recognised her immediately. He got his eyes from his father—piercing, they missed nothing, and now they regarded me with suspicion.

"Olivia, this is my mother, Lucinda, and my father, George. Mother, Father, this is Olivia."

"Hello. Good to meet you," I said.

George nodded, while Lucinda managed a stiff smile that didn't reach her eyes.

"And this is my grandma, Ivy. Grandma, this is—"

"Olivia, I know. Can I offer you both a glass of sherry?"

"Perhaps later, Grandma."

Ivy was about half Nye's height, but her hot-pink cocktail dress spoke of a big personality. She'd stuck a lily behind one ear and wore enough diamonds to give a hip-hop star a run for his money.

She pulled me down and kissed me on both cheeks before a waiter handed me a glass of champagne. "Welcome to the family, sweetie. It's nice to have another girl, isn't it, Cindy."

"It's Lucinda," Nye's mother said through gritted teeth. "I suppose I should look on the bright side. At least you didn't bring that awful Daniela girl again."

"I rather liked Daniela," Ivy said. "What was that dance she taught me?"

"Twerking, Grandma," Nye told her.

I tried to avoid spitting my champagne across the table and ended up choking on it instead. That earned me a couple of dirty looks.

"Dan's a colleague from work," Nye whispered. "She helped me out when I was in a bind. Mother threatened to set me up with a girl who laughs like a horse."

I managed a sound that wasn't too dissimilar from a horse myself. "Dan sounds like fun."

"She lives in the States, but I'll introduce you next time she's over."

We were saved from further conversation by the orchestra, who struck up with the first bars of *Tristan und Isolde*. The lights dimmed, and I took my seat next to Nye to get lost in the music.

Literally lost. I had no clue what was going on. Was this opera supposed to be happy or sad? I raised an eyebrow at Nye, and he shrugged.

Great. An hour and a half of my life wasted, and now I needed to pee. I'd got halfway out of my seat when Ivy clutched at my arm.

"Wait a minute, sweetie. I'll come with you."

Super, a family outing.

"I always have to dash off at the end," Ivy said as we hurried towards the restroom. "Cindy asks me questions about the story, and I never have a clue what's gone on, so I hide in the loo and Google it on my iPad."

Nye was right. I loved his grandmother.

"But I thought you enjoyed the opera. Nye said it was your birthday treat every year."

"It's Cindy's idea of my birthday treat. I just come for the gin."

By the time I'd used the facilities, Ivy was waiting with a briefing. "It was a German tragedy, sweetie. Everybody died. If Cindy asks you a direct question, just pretend you're overcome with emotion."

"Emotion. Got it. Thank you."

"Don't mention it. And let me tell you, I'm glad Nye's found himself a normal girl and not one of those plastic-faced debutantes Cindy keeps trying to set him up with."

"Er, thanks?"

She patted me on the arm. "I want some great-grandchildren while I'm still young enough to eat solid food, and none of those women would put up with the stretch marks."

My heart started thumping so loudly I worried Ivy might be able to hear it. Until today, Nye had never even discussed his own family, let alone the possibility of having one with me in the future.

"I'm not sure about that."

"Nonsense. You'll make a beautiful bride. Will you have a summer wedding? August is always the best month. A marquee in the grounds, a live band, Dom Perignon flowing, and if Cindy tries to pressure you over the colour scheme, just ignore her."

"I don't know that Nye will ever propose."

"Of course he will. He already asked me for my old rings when we went out for lunch the Saturday before last." She peered at my left hand, turning it over in both of hers. "He'll need to get them resized, though. My fingers are thinner than yours."

Back at the table, I sat down in a daze.

"Everything okay?" Nye whispered.

"Great, never better." I fixed on a perky smile.

"What did you think of the opera, Olivia?" Lucinda asked.

"German tragedies always make me feel so emotional." I sniffed for effect, and Nye looked impressed.

"Oh. Good." Lucinda turned her attention to a new victim, and I breathed a sigh of relief.

Then Ivy passed me a gin and tonic—at least, that was what she called it, but I couldn't taste the tonic—and Nye may have had to help me to the car afterwards.

"You were quiet," Nye said once we'd got on the motorway.

"I was overcome with emotion."

"Bullshit. My grandma told you to say that. I know how she works. Now, what's really up?"

"Ivy mentioned grandchildren." Dammit! The alcohol had loosened my tongue.

Nye reached over for my hand. "Does that scare you?"

Did it? Truthfully? No, what scared me was the fear that Nye might not want that kind of relationship.

"I didn't know what to say to her. I don't know what you want for the future."

He pulled over onto the hard shoulder in a repeat of his earlier move, tyres smoking, and flipped on the interior light.

"I'd like kids. One day."

"Me too. One day."

Nye let out the breath he'd been holding. "Thank goodness."

He leaned over to kiss me, but my heart was still pounding from Ivy's revelation, and I felt light-headed. Or maybe that was the gin.

Nye pulled back and watched me. "Oh, hell. What else did she say?"

"Nothing else. Nothing at all."

"You're a terrible liar, Liv."

My gaze dropped to my fingers of its own accord, and he groaned.

"Oh, shit. She told you about the rings, didn't she?"

Oops. "She might have mentioned them."

"Fuck." He smacked the steering wheel. "Driving down the M40 wasn't how I'd imagined asking you, but Olivia Porter, will you marry me? One day?"

"Any day. Tomorrow if you like."

He unclipped my seat belt and dragged me into his lap, then kissed me with more passion than I'd ever experienced before. Nye's entire soul flowed through his lips and twined with mine.

"You've just made me the happiest man alive."

"And I'm the happiest woman. I love you, Nye."

"Love you too, Liv." In the absence of champagne, he held up the bottle of cola that was in the cupholder. "Here's to the future."

"Here's to us."

WHAT'S NEXT?

The Blackwood UK series continues in a new novella, *Cherry on Top*.

"Let's keep this civil. We should treat each other with respect."

When Cherry Sanders gets unceremoniously dumped by Craig, those are his parting words. And she tries, really she does. But when Craig accidentally lets slip how he really feels, Cherry and Olivia, her boss at the Red Velvet bakery, decide a little revenge is the only option.

Enter copious amounts of frosting, one shiny BMW, and Lachlan, a handsome astro...astro... Does it really matter after what they do? Just pass the damn wine...

Find out more here: www.elise-noble.com/cherry

The next full-length novel in the series is *Roses are Dead*.

Roses are dead, Lily is blue,
The killer's escaped without leaving a clue.
Will he come back with flowers and more?
To end what he only started before...

Find out more here: www.elise-noble.com/roses

If you want to see more of Nye and Emmy, they also appears in *Pitch Black*, the first book in my Blackwood Security series.

Even a Diamond can be shattered...

After the owner of a security company is murdered, his sharp-edged wife goes on the run. Forced to abandon everything she holds dear - her home, her friends, her job in special ops - she builds a new life for herself in England. As Ashlyn Hale, she meets Luke, a handsome local who makes her realise just how lonely she is.

Yet, even in the sleepy village of Lower Foxford, the dark side of life dogs Diamond's trail when the unthinkable strikes. Forced out of hiding, she races against time to save those she cares about. But is it too little, too late?

WARNING
If you want sweetness and light and all things bright,
Diamond's not the girl for you.
She's got sass, she's got snark, and she's moody and dark,
As she does what a girl's got to do.

Find out more here: www.elise-noble.com/pitch-black

If you enjoyed *Joker in the Pack*, please consider leaving a review.

For an author, every review is incredibly important. Not only do they make us feel warm and fuzzy inside, readers consider them when making their decision whether or not to buy a book. Even a line saying you enjoyed the book or what your favourite part was helps a lot.

Want to Stalk Me?

For updates on my new releases, giveaways, and other random stuff, you can sign up for my newsletter on my website:
www.elise-noble.com

Facebook:
www.facebook.com/EliseNobleAuthor

Twitter: @EliseANoble

Instagram: @elise_noble

If you're on Facebook, you may also like to join Team Blackwood for exclusive giveaways, sneak previews, and book-related chat. Be the first to find out about new stories, and you might even see your name or one of your ideas make it into print!

And if you'd like to read my books for FREE, you can also find details of how to join my advance review team.

Would you like to join Team Blackwood?

www.elise-noble.com/team-blackwood

END OF BOOK STUFF

What do you get when you cross an old Beatles song, a few glasses of wine, and a strong desire to avoid work for a day?

For any normal person, a few laughs and a hangover. But I've never pretended to be normal.

Joker started one sunny day at Blenheim Palace in Oxfordshire, not too far from Olivia's imaginary home. The High Sheriff of Oxfordshire (yes, that really is a thing—he was a nice old dude in a frilly outfit) decided to run a series of charity fundraisers, and the company I work for was looking for volunteers to embarrass themselves. I'd already run, swum, and died of exhaustion at a sports day a few weeks previously, so I figured I might as well sign up for the singing and die of mortification too. Hey, it was another day off work and a free dinner.

Anyhow, we all turned up at the palace where our pianist was the amazing Derek Paravicini—you can't say his name without using a superlative first because he's a freaking genius. Blind from birth and autistic too, he can play any song in any key in any style after hearing it only once. Such an awesome guy.

One of the songs chosen for our wonky rendition was Eleanor Rigby by the The Beatles. Somehow, I'd never heard it before, but I loved it from the first run-through. And as I sang, I wondered what would happen if there really was an old woman who nobody knew. Would she be sweet and kind, just a bit lonely? Or would she be a bitch who kept to herself by choice because she preferred her own company to anyone else's? Well, guess which one was more fun to write about?

I slung the first version of Joker (or House of Cards as it was then called) up on Wattpad, and ended up gobsmacked a few months later when it won a Watty Award. That old book makes me cringe a bit now, but it's good to see how much my writing's changed over the past few years. Joker 2.0 got completely rewritten with extra chapters, new characters, and a different ending.

And Nye has friends now. Hot friends, snarky friends, sometimes grumpy friends. You'll be able to meet them soon, starting with Lachlan in Cherry on Top. The Blackwood Brits are ready to give the Yanks a run for their money :)

I hope you enjoyed Joker, and if you're reading this in release month, there's a giveaway on my website to win a signed copy. If you're not and you want to hear about my new books so you can get in on the free stuff, the links to stalk me are in the previous chapter.

Right, I'm heading back to the writing cave. I've got a little secret project with the first three Blackwood books going on, plus Tia and Dan's books to edit. Oh, and a whole new series to write...

Laters,
Elise

Other Books by Elise Noble

The Blackwood Security Series

For the Love of Animals (Nate & Carmen - prequel)
Black is My Heart (Diamond & Snow - prequel)
Pitch Black
Into the Black
Forever Black
Gold Rush
Gray is My Heart
Neon (novella)
Out of the Blue
Ultraviolet
Glitter (novella)
Red Alert
White Hot
Sphere (novella)
The Scarlet Affair
Spirit (novella)
Quicksilver
The Girl with the Emerald Ring
Red After Dark
When the Shadows Fall
Pretties in Pink (TBA)

The Blackwood Elements Series

Oxygen

Lithium
Carbon
Rhodium
Platinum
Lead
Copper
Bronze
Nickel
Hydrogen (TBA)

The Blackwood UK Series
Joker in the Pack
Cherry on Top (novella)
Roses are Dead
Shallow Graves
Indigo Rain
Pass the Parcel (TBA)

Baldwin's Shore
Dirty Little Secrets (2021)

Blackwood Casefiles
Stolen Hearts
Burning Love (TBA)

Blackstone House
Hard Lines (2021)
Hard Tide (TBA)

The Electi Series
Cursed
Spooked
Possessed

Demented
Judged (2021)

The Planes Series
A Vampire in Vegas
A Devil in the Dark (TBA)

The Trouble Series
Trouble in Paradise
Nothing but Trouble
24 Hours of Trouble

Standalone
Life
Coco du Ciel (2021)
Twisted (short stories)
A Very Happy Christmas (novella)

Books with clean versions available (no swearing and no on-the-page sex)
Pitch Black
Into the Black
Forever Black
Gold Rush
Gray is My Heart

Audiobooks
Black is My Heart (Diamond & Snow - prequel)
Pitch Black
Into the Black
Forever Black
Gold Rush
Gray is My Heart

Neon (novella)

Printed in Great Britain
by Amazon